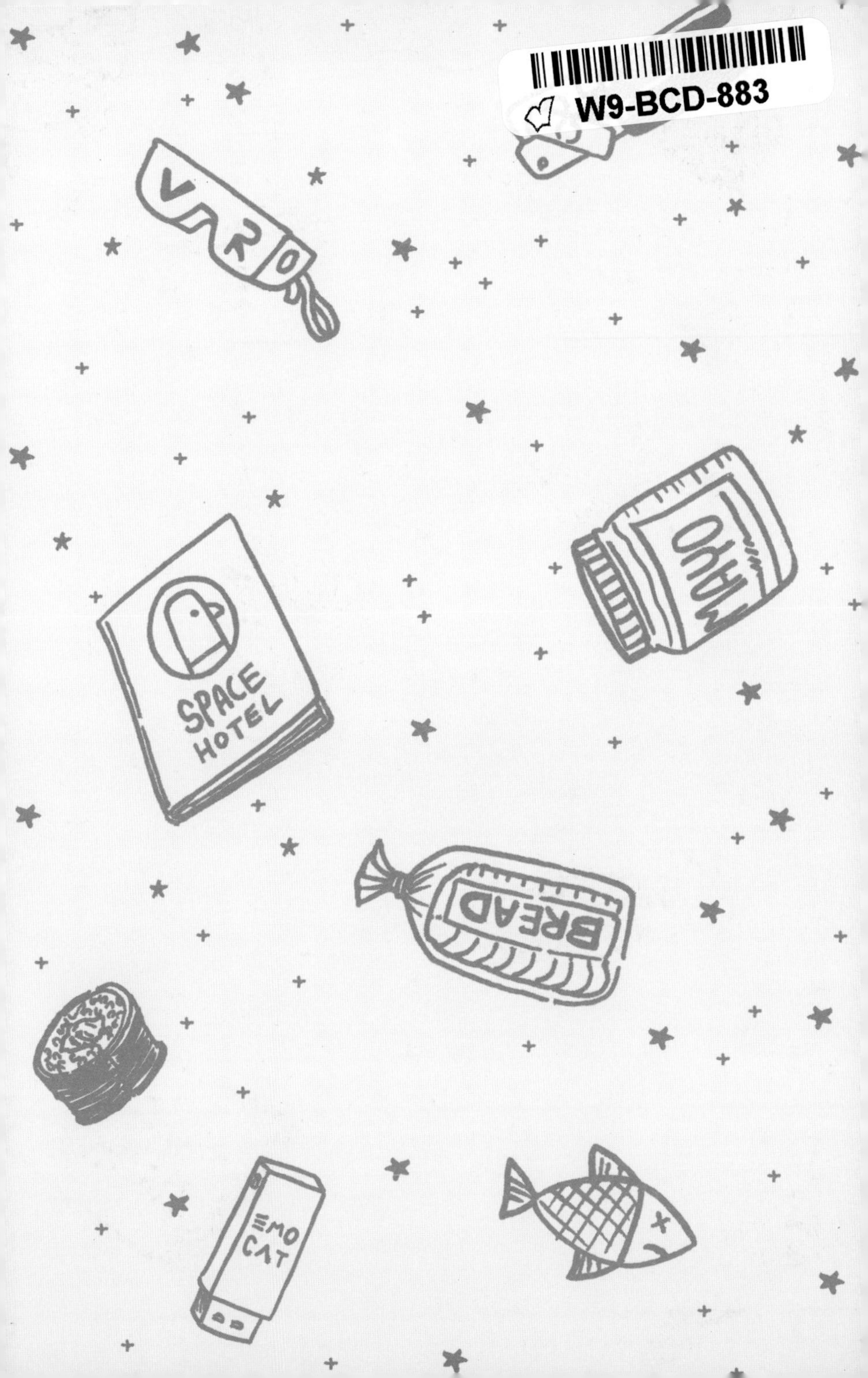
VR
SPACE HOTEL
MAYO
BREAD
EMO CAT

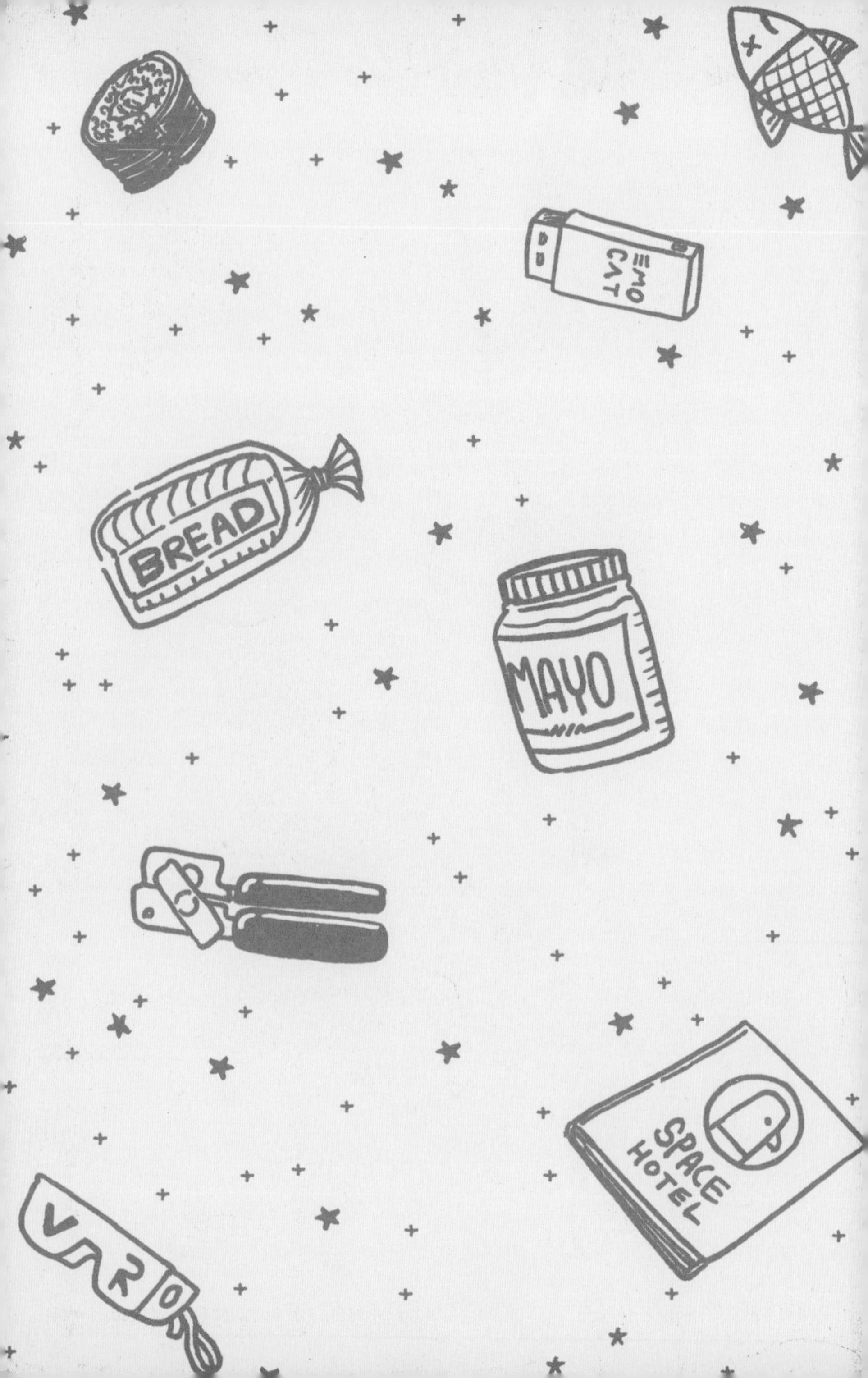
EMO CAT
BREAD
MAYO
SPACE HOTEL

CatStronauts

DIGITAL DISASTER

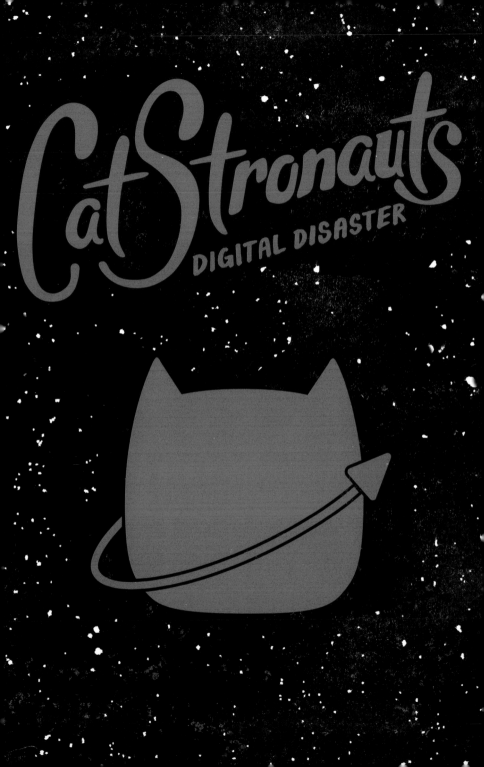

CatStronauts

DIGITAL DISASTER

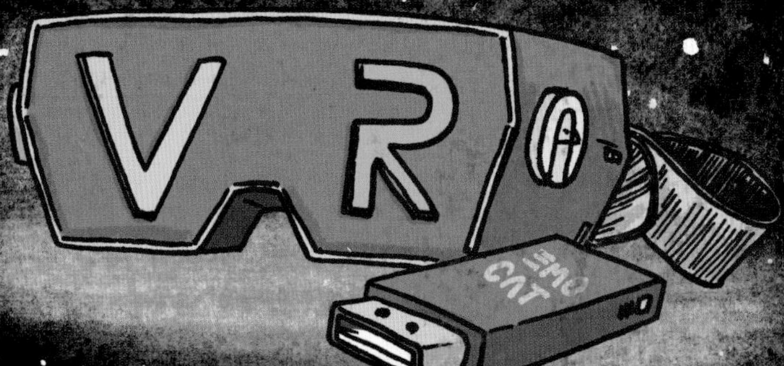
VR

BY DREW BROCKINGTON

LB

Little, Brown and Company
New York Boston

About This Book

This book was edited by Russ Busse and designed by Ching Chan. The production was supervised by Erika Schwartz, and the production editor was Lindsay Walter-Greaney. The text was set in Brockington, and the display type is Brockington.

This book is a work of fiction. Names, characters, places, and incidents are the product of the author's imagination or are used fictitiously. Any resemblance to actual events, locales, or persons, living or dead, is coincidental.

Copyright © 2020 by Drew Brockington

Cover illustration copyright © 2020 by Drew Brockington. Cover design by Ching Chan. Cover copyright © 2020 by Hachette Book Group, Inc.

Hachette Book Group supports the right to free expression and the value of copyright. The purpose of copyright is to encourage writers and artists to produce the creative works that enrich our culture.

The scanning, uploading, and distribution of this book without permission is a theft of the author's intellectual property. If you would like permission to use material from the book (other than for review purposes), please contact permissions@hbgusa.com. Thank you for your support of the author's rights.

Little, Brown and Company
Hachette Book Group
1290 Avenue of the Americas, New York, NY 10104
Visit us at LBYR.com

First Edition: August 2020

Little, Brown and Company is a division of Hachette Book Group, Inc. The Little, Brown name and logo are trademarks of Hachette Book Group, Inc.

The publisher is not responsible for websites (or their content) that are not owned by the publisher.

Library of Congress information available.

ISBNs: 978-0-316-45132-1 (hardcover), 978-0-316-45127-7 (pbk.), 978-0-316-45130-7 (ebook), 978-0-316-45129-1 (ebook), 978-0-316-45128-4 (ebook)

Printed in China

1010

Hardcover: 10 9 8 7 6 5 4 3 2 1
Paperback: 10 9 8 7 6 5 4 3 2 1

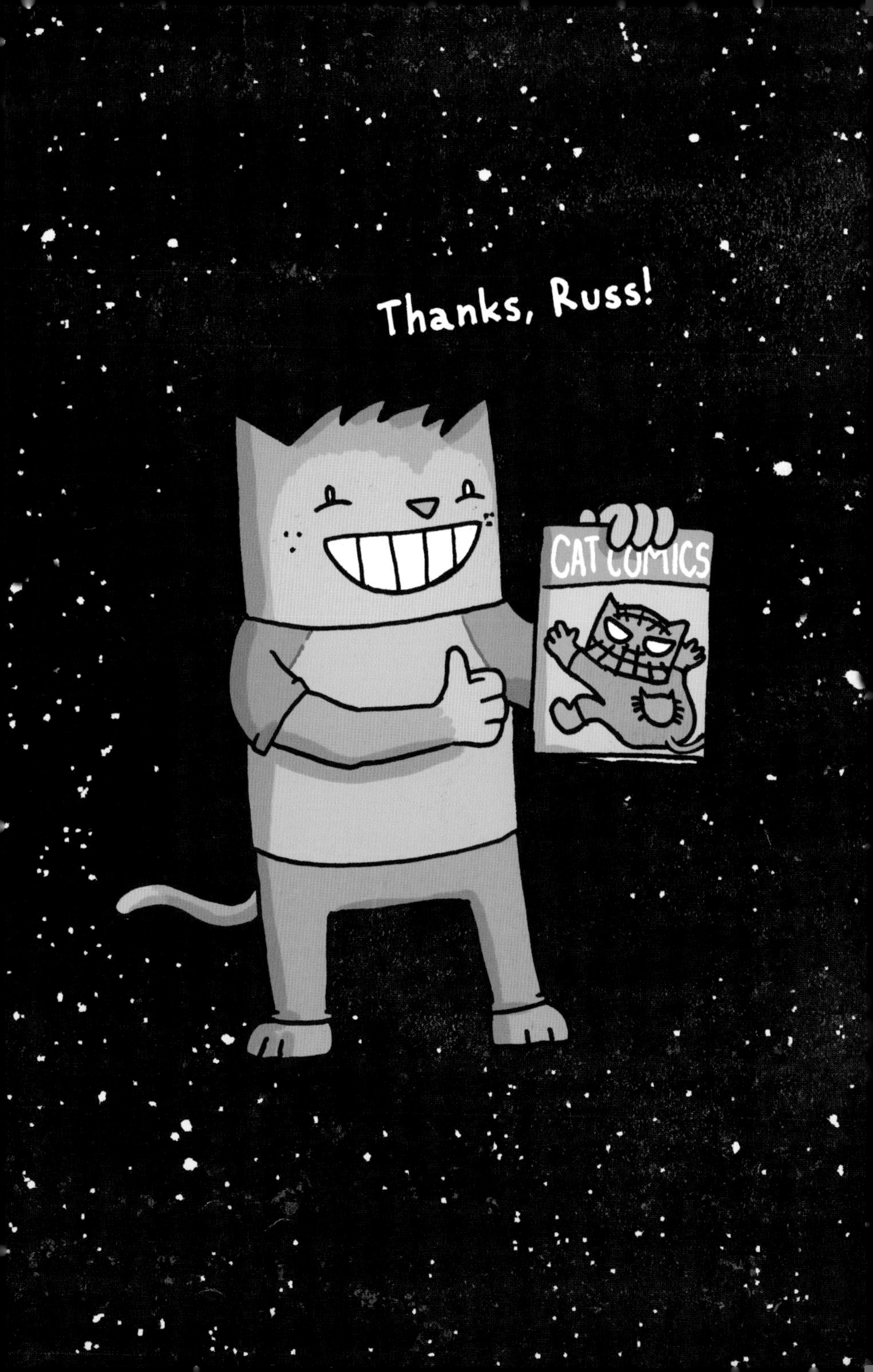
Thanks, Russ!
CAT COMICS

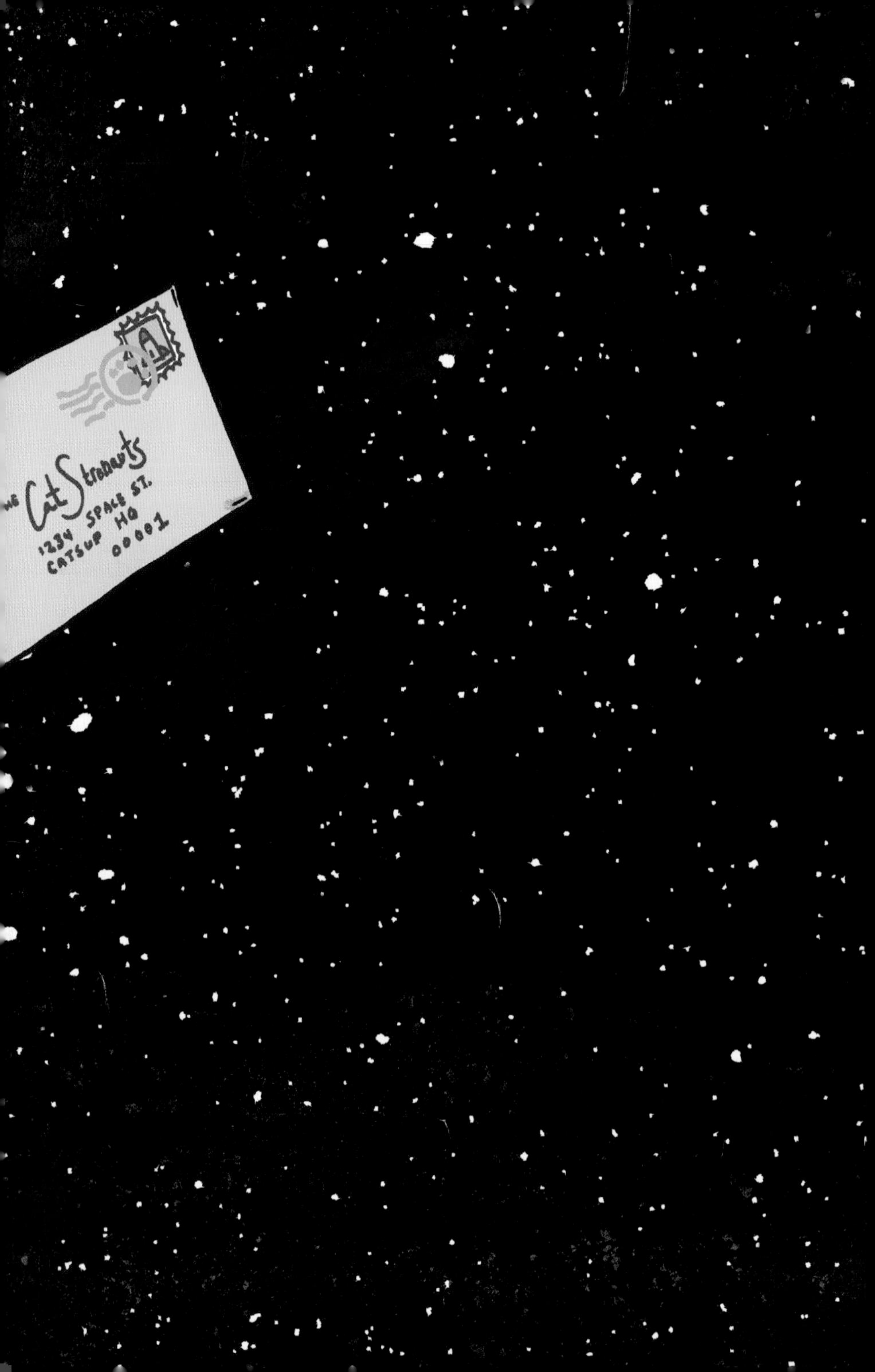

The Cat Stronauts
1234 SPACE ST.
CATSUP HQ
00001

CHAPTER 1

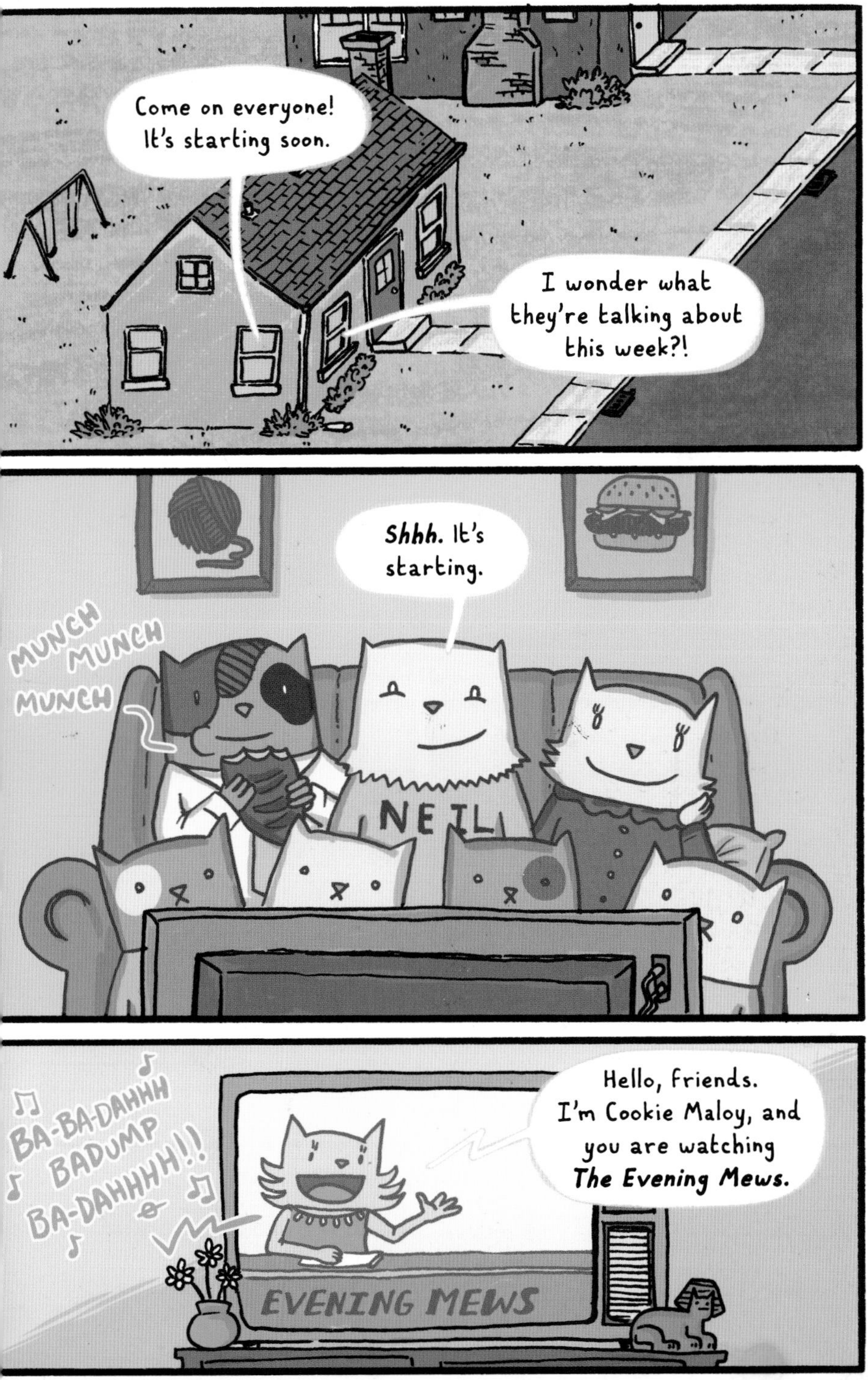
Come on everyone! It's starting soon.
I wonder what they're talking about this week?!
Shhh. It's starting.
MUNCH MUNCH MUNCH
NEIL
BA-BA-DAHHH BADUMP BA-DAHHHH!!
Hello, friends. I'm Cookie Maloy, and you are watching The Evening Mews.
EVENING MEWS

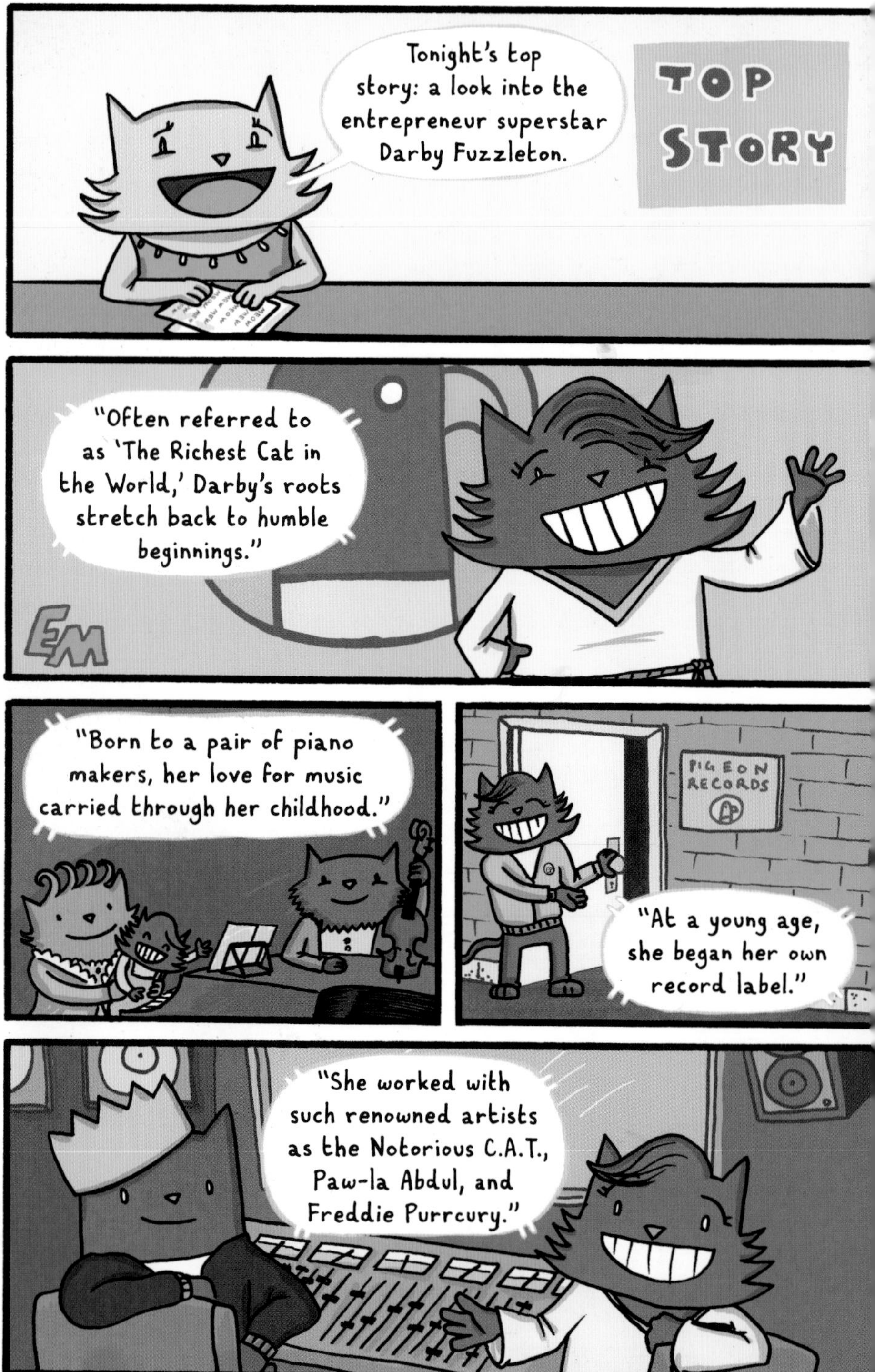
Tonight's top story: a look into the entrepreneur superstar Darby Fuzzleton.
TOP STORY
"Often referred to as 'The Richest Cat in the World,' Darby's roots stretch back to humble beginnings."
EM
"Born to a pair of piano makers, her love for music carried through her childhood."
PIGEON RECORDS
"At a young age, she began her own record label."
"She worked with such renowned artists as the Notorious C.A.T., Paw-la Abdul, and Freddie Purrcury."

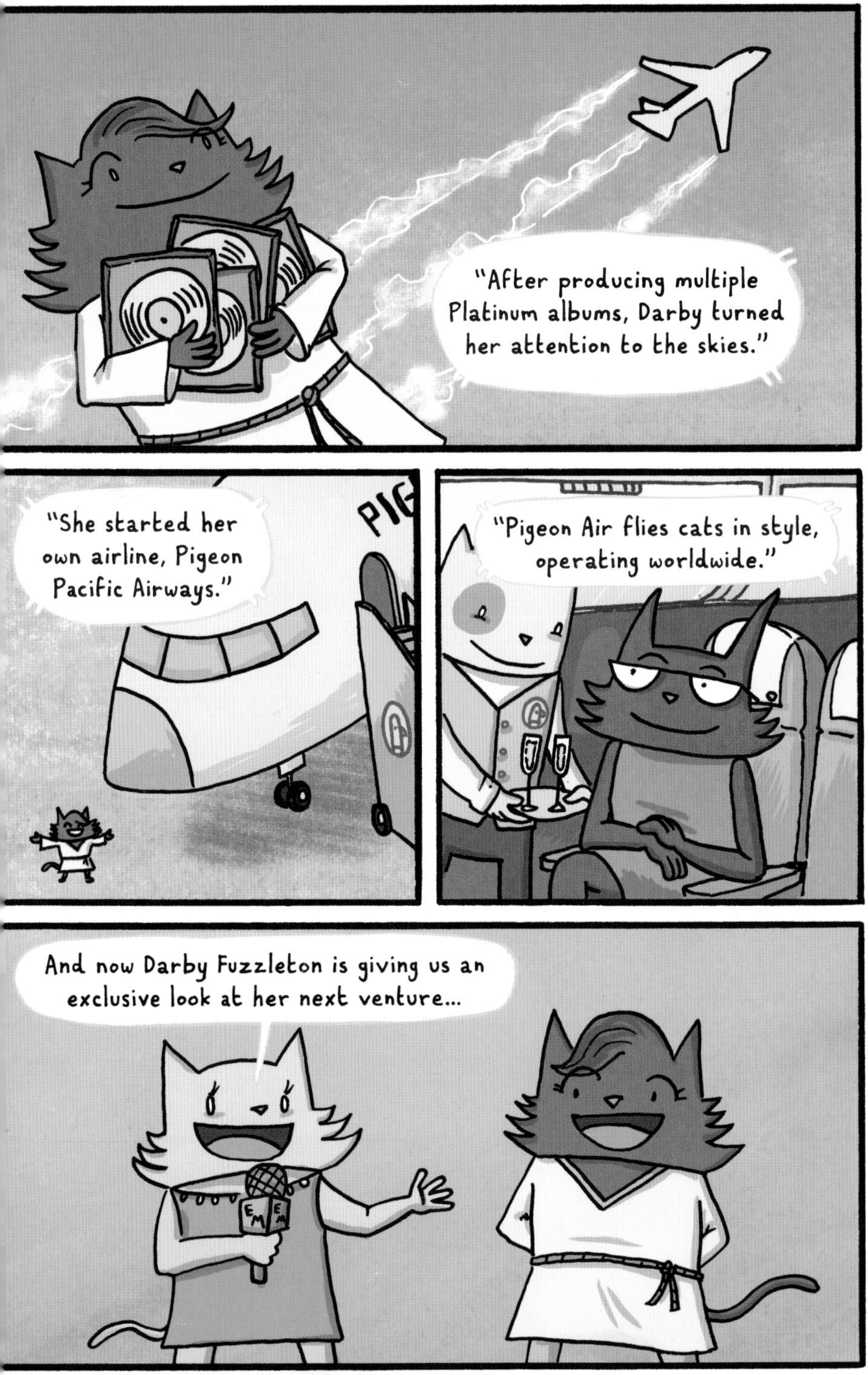
"After producing multiple Platinum albums, Darby turned her attention to the skies."
PIG
"She started her own airline, Pigeon Pacific Airways."
"Pigeon Air flies cats in style, operating worldwide."
And now Darby Fuzzleton is giving us an exclusive look at her next venture...

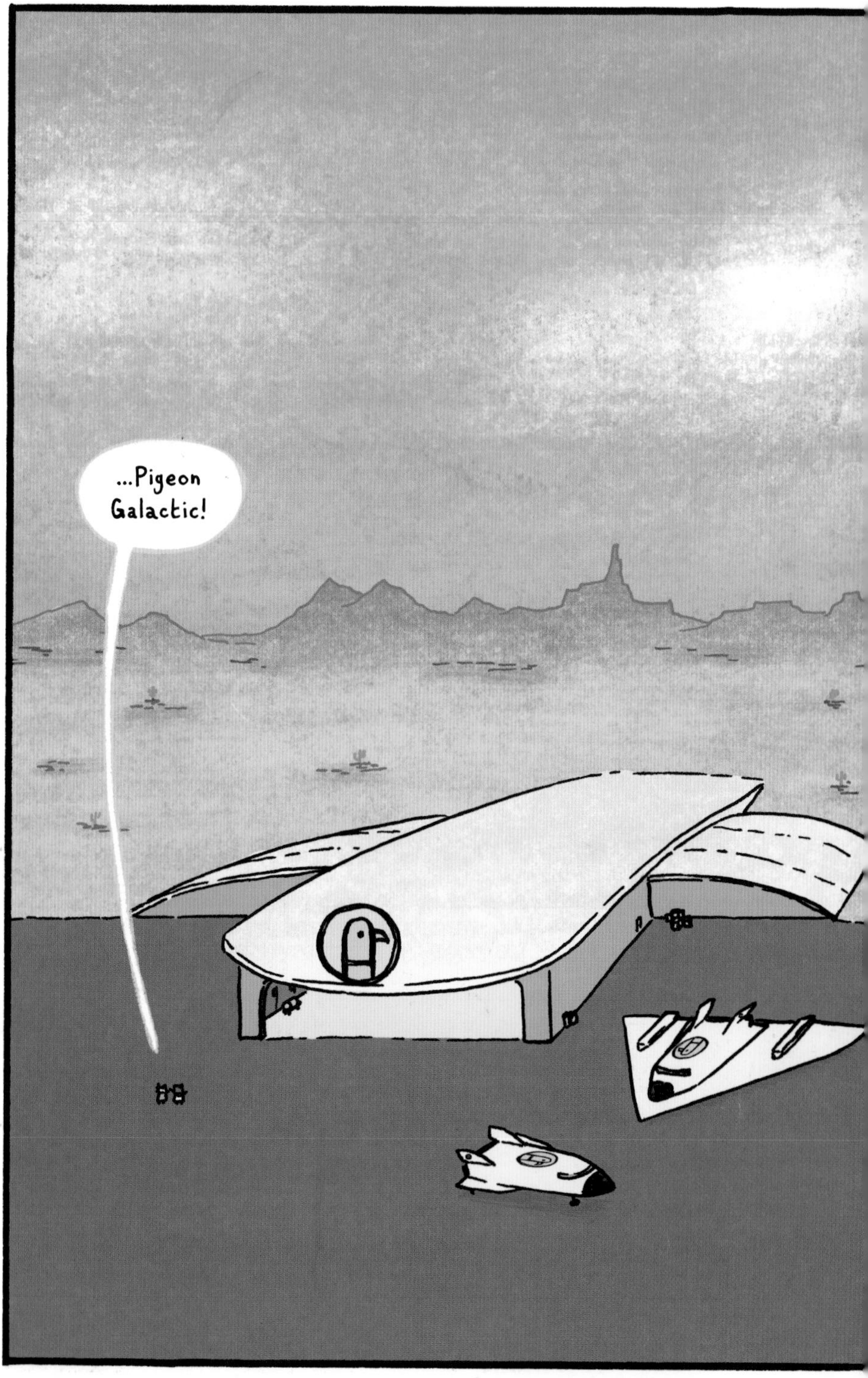
...Pigeon Galactic!

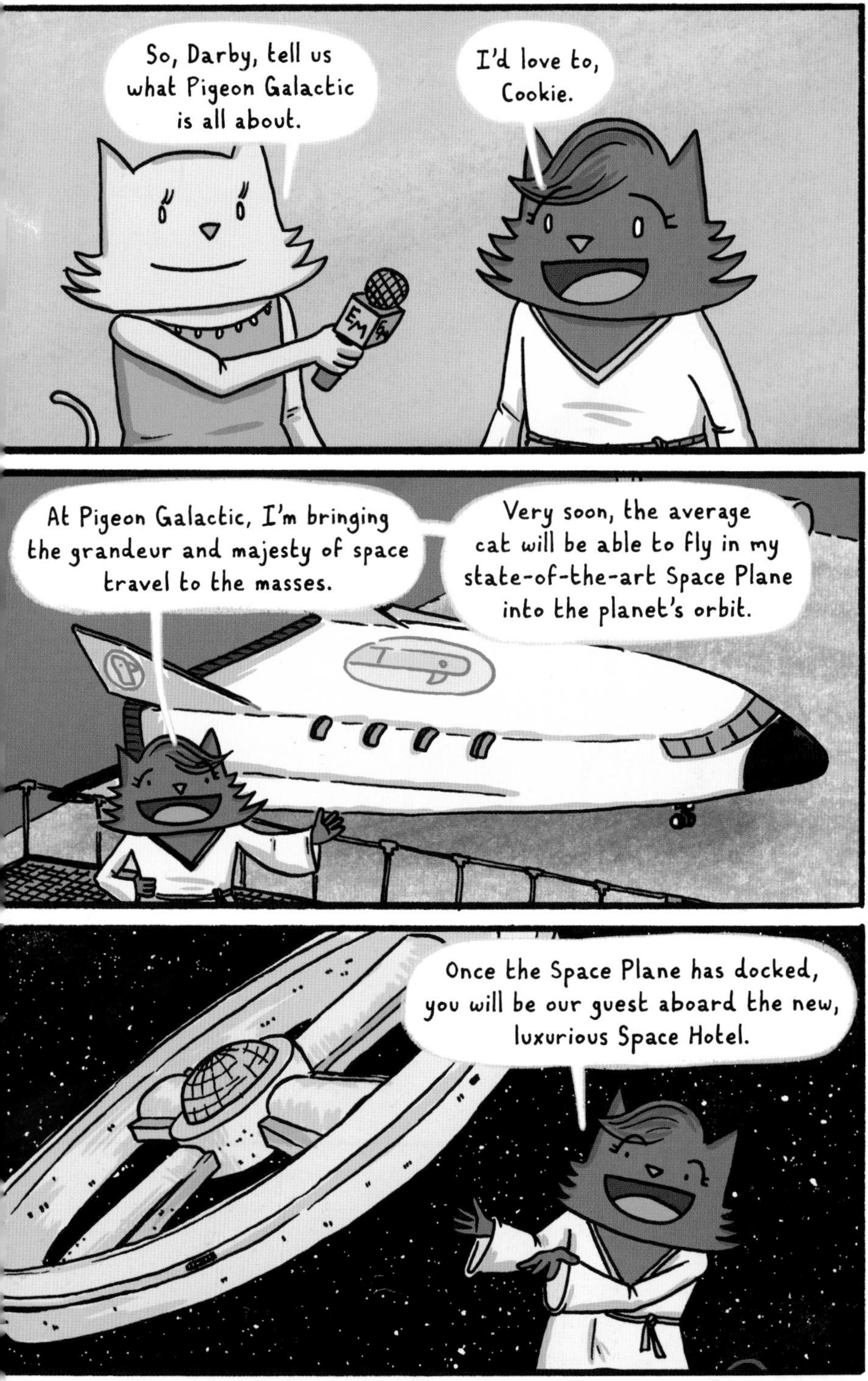
So, Darby, tell us what Pigeon Galactic is all about.
I'd love to, Cookie.
EM
At Pigeon Galactic, I'm bringing the grandeur and majesty of space travel to the masses.
Very soon, the average cat will be able to fly in my state-of-the-art Space Plane into the planet's orbit.
Once the Space Plane has docked, you will be our guest aboard the new, luxurious Space Hotel.

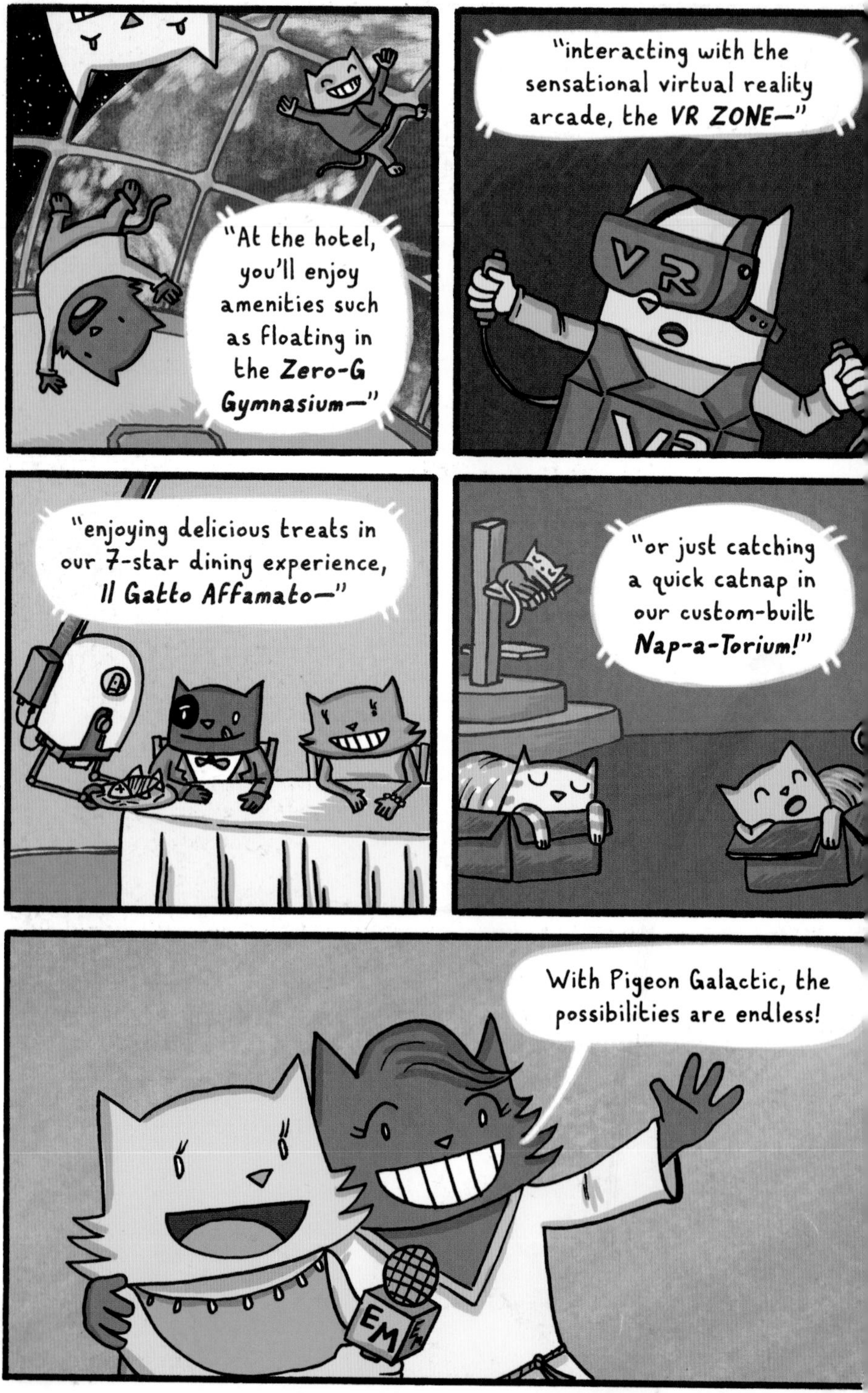
"At the hotel, you'll enjoy amenities such as floating in the Zero-G Gymnasium—"
"interacting with the sensational virtual reality arcade, the VR ZONE—"
VR
"enjoying delicious treats in our 7-star dining experience, Il Gatto Affamato—"
"or just catching a quick catnap in our custom-built Nap-a-Torium!"
With Pigeon Galactic, the possibilities are endless!
EM

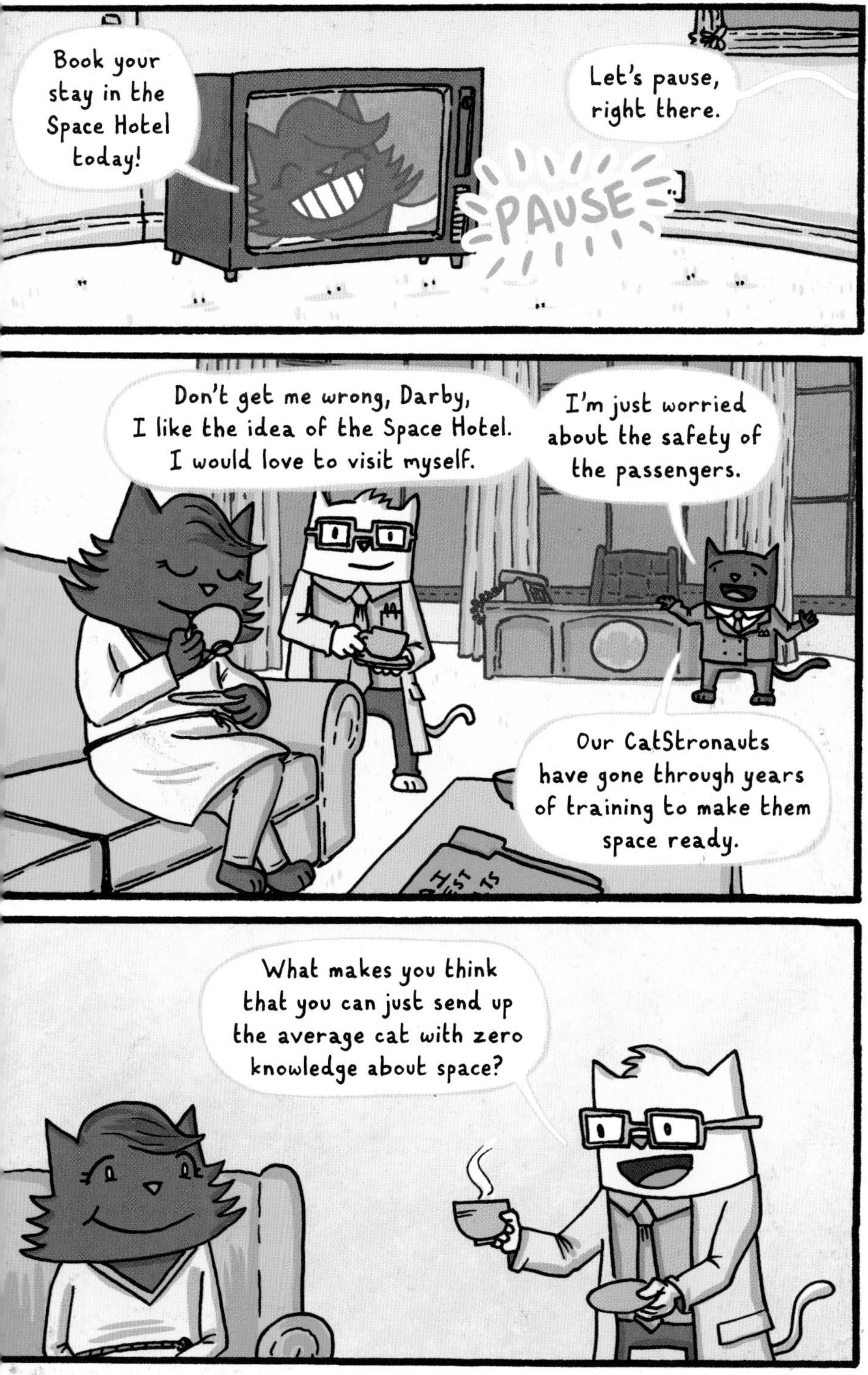
Book your stay in the Space Hotel today!
Let's pause, right there.
PAUSE
Don't get me wrong, Darby, I like the idea of the Space Hotel. I would love to visit myself.
I'm just worried about the safety of the passengers.
Our CatStronauts have gone through years of training to make them space ready.
What makes you think that you can just send up the average cat with zero knowledge about space?

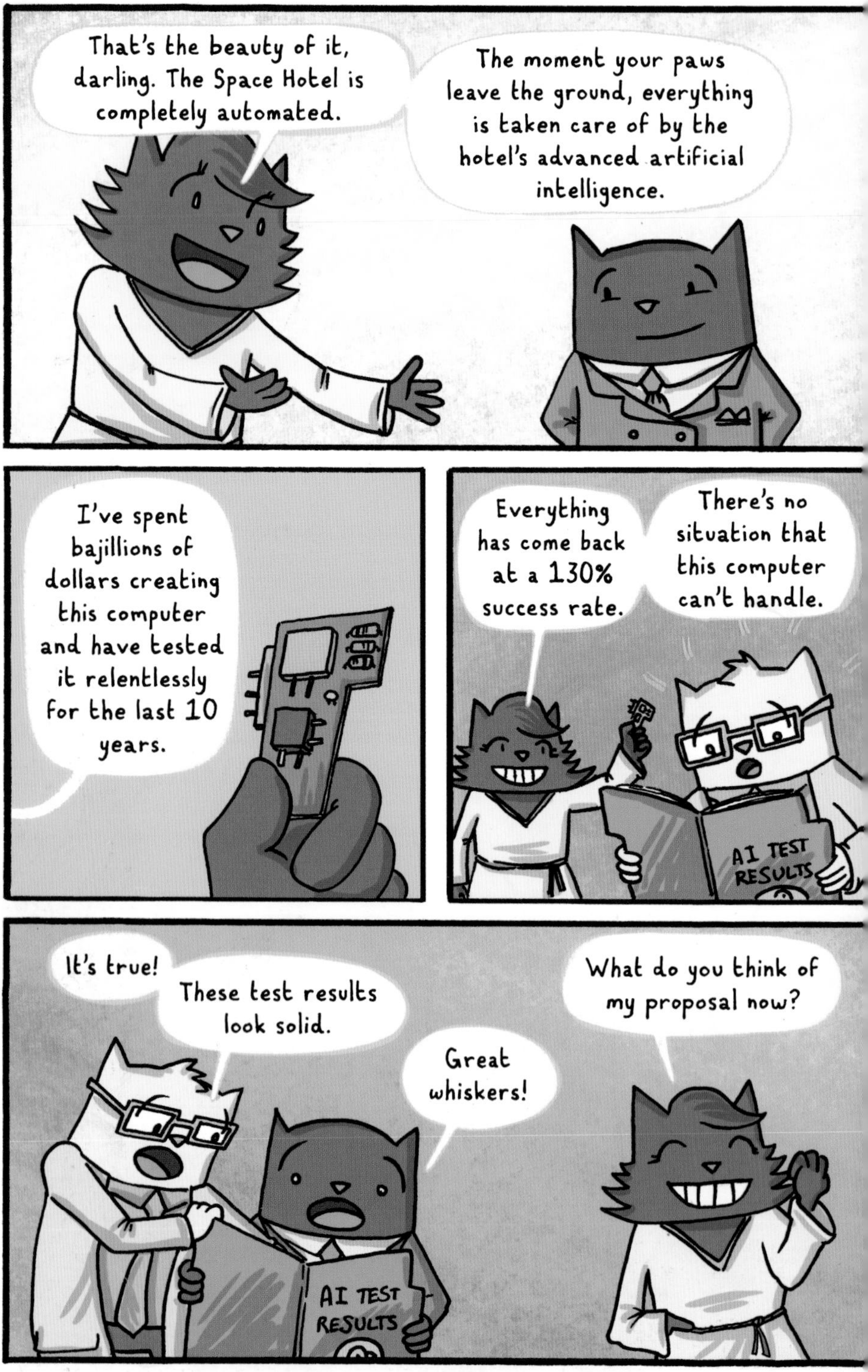
That's the beauty of it, darling. The Space Hotel is completely automated.
The moment your paws leave the ground, everything is taken care of by the hotel's advanced artificial intelligence.
I've spent bajillions of dollars creating this computer and have tested it relentlessly for the last 10 years.
Everything has come back at a 130% success rate.
There's no situation that this computer can't handle.
AI TEST RESULTS
It's true!
These test results look solid.
Great whiskers!
What do you think of my proposal now?
AI TEST RESULTS

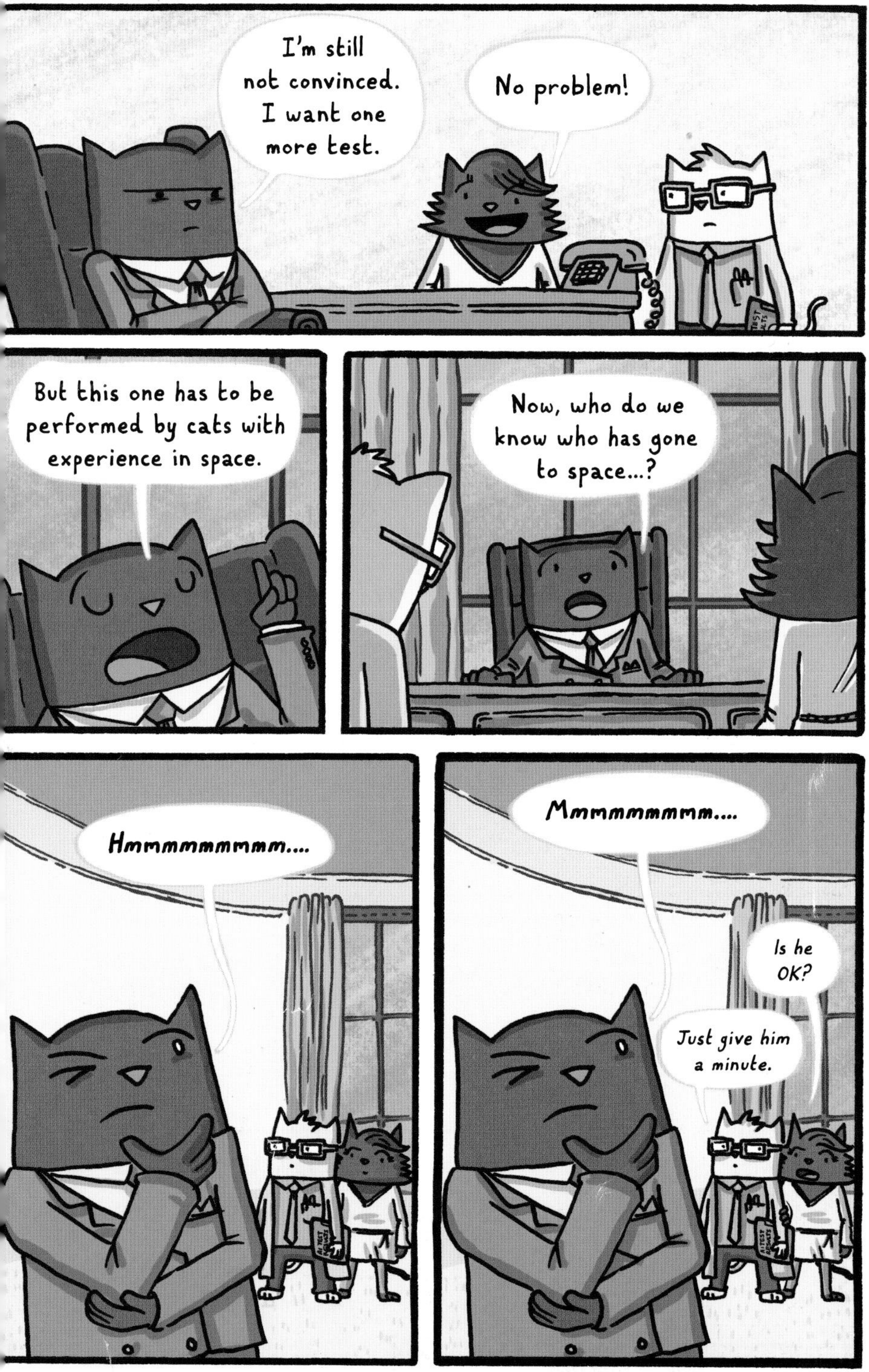
I'm still not convinced. I want one more test.
No problem!
But this one has to be performed by cats with experience in space.
Now, who do we know who has gone to space...?
Hmmmmmmmmm....
Mmmmmmmmm....
Is he OK?
Just give him a minute.

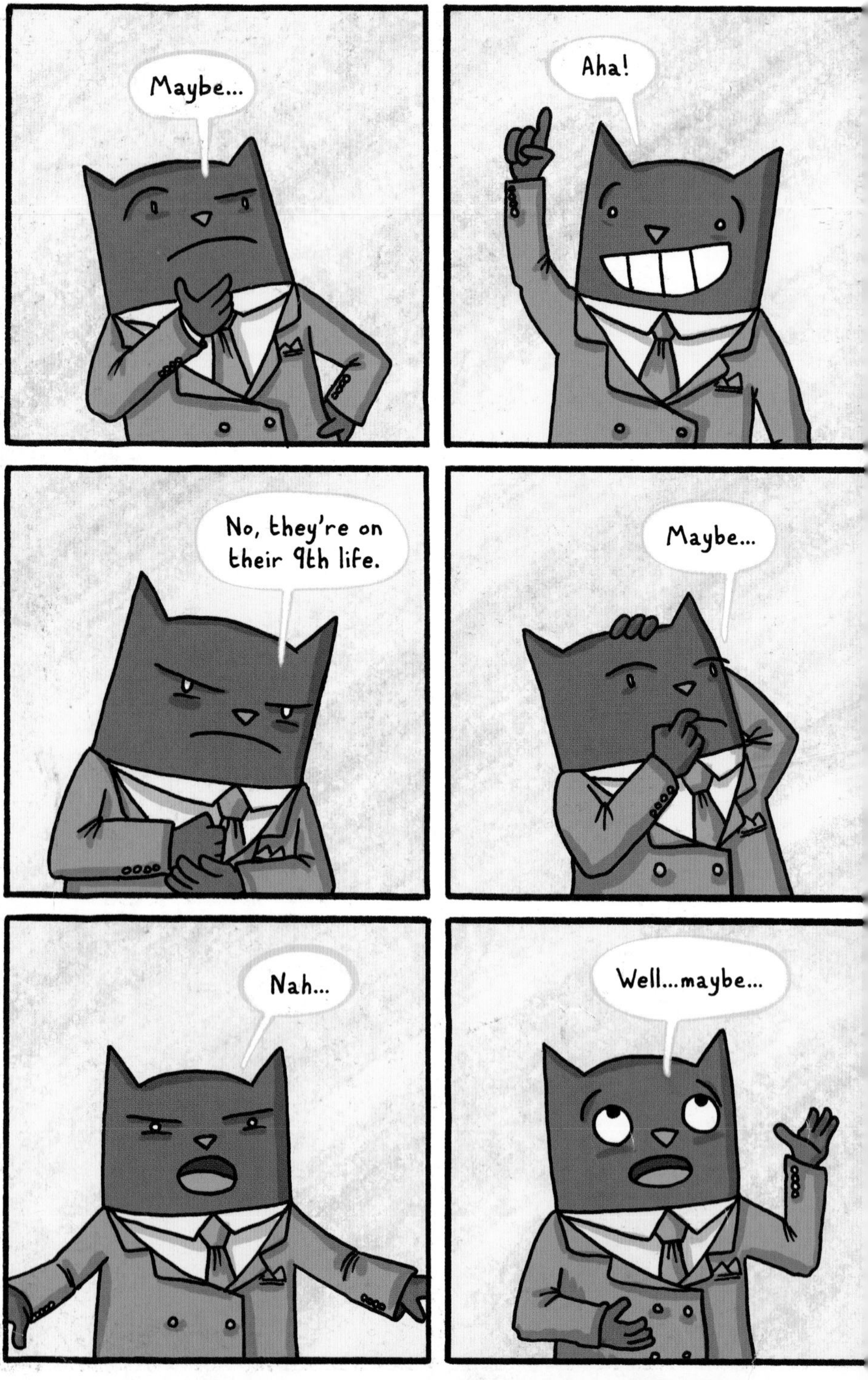
Maybe...
Aha!
No, they're on their 9th life.
Maybe...
Nah...
Well...maybe...

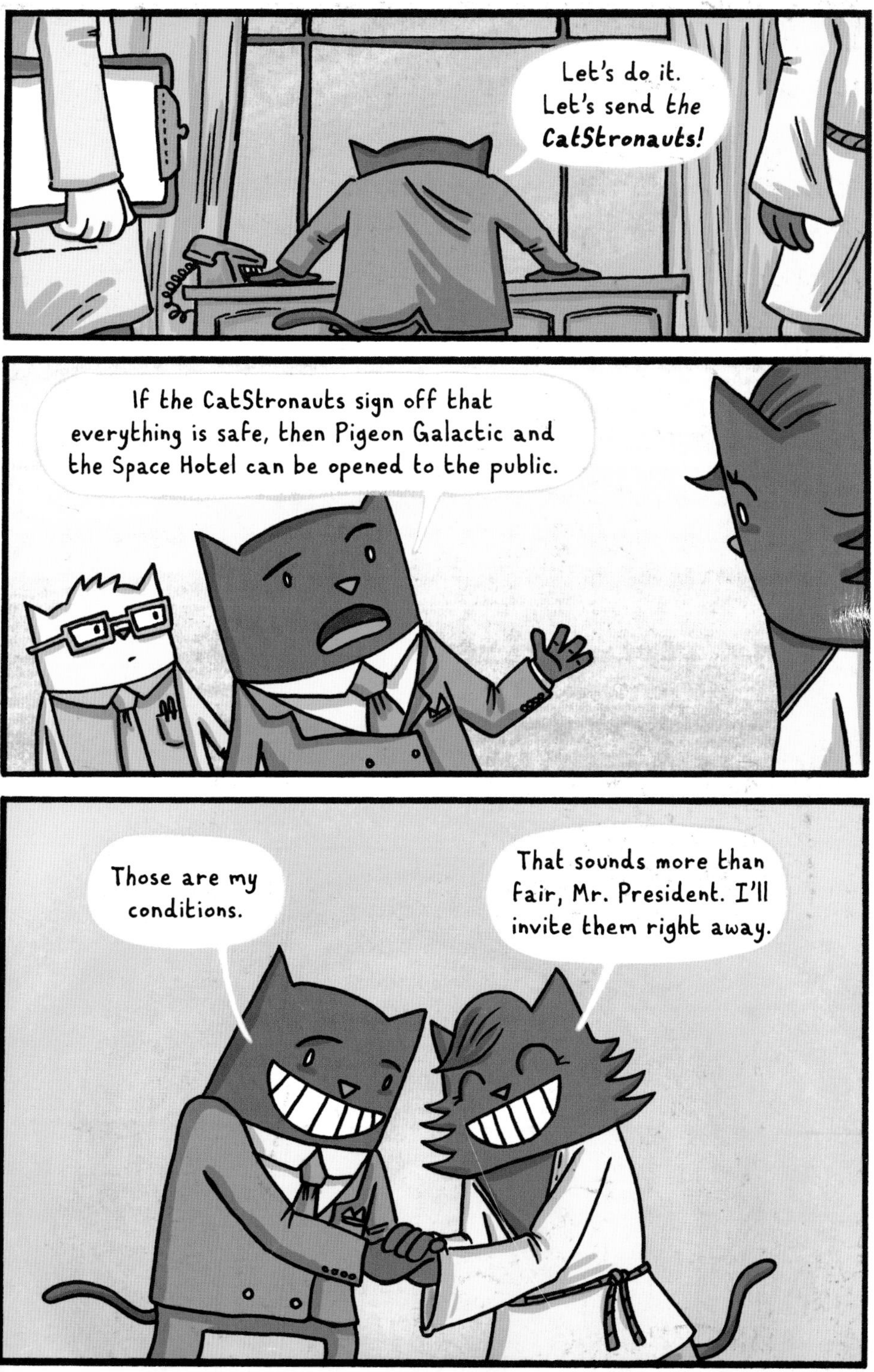
Let's do it. Let's send the CatStronauts!
If the CatStronauts sign off that everything is safe, then Pigeon Galactic and the Space Hotel can be opened to the public.
Those are my conditions.
That sounds more than fair, Mr. President. I'll invite them right away.

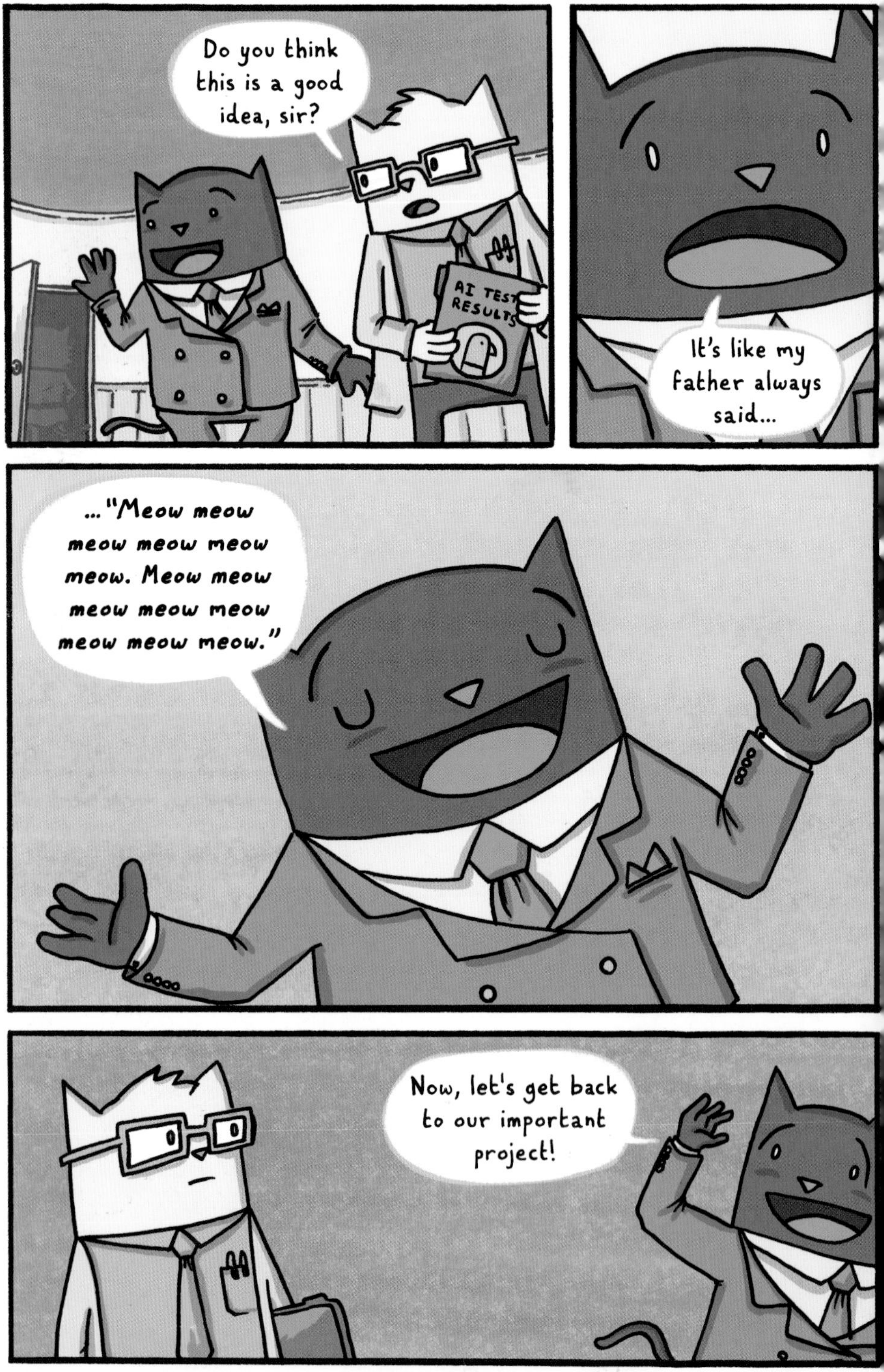
Do you think this is a good idea, sir?
AI TEST RESULTS
It's like my father always said...
..."Meow meow meow meow meow meow. Meow meow meow meow meow meow meow meow."
Now, let's get back to our important project!

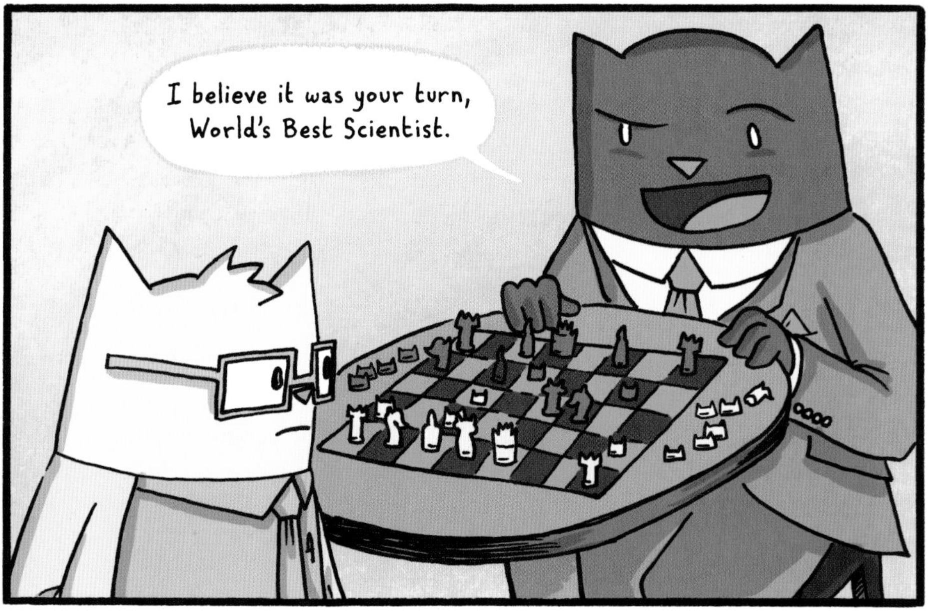
I believe it was your turn,
World's Best Scientist.

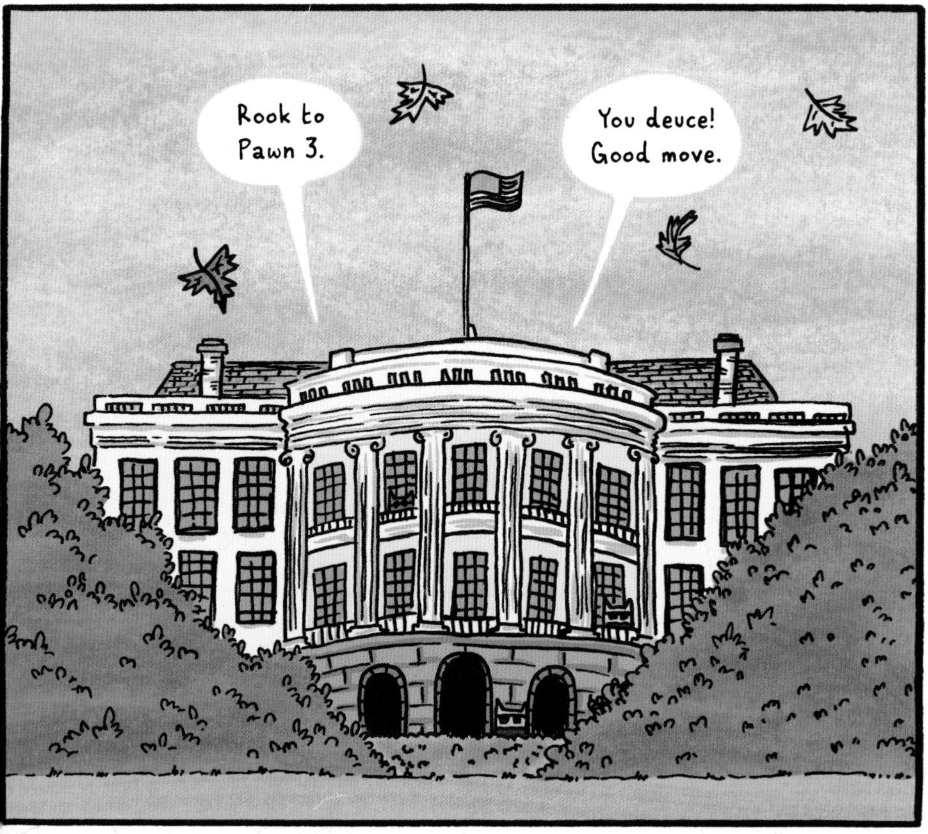
Rook to
Pawn 3.
You deuce!
Good move.

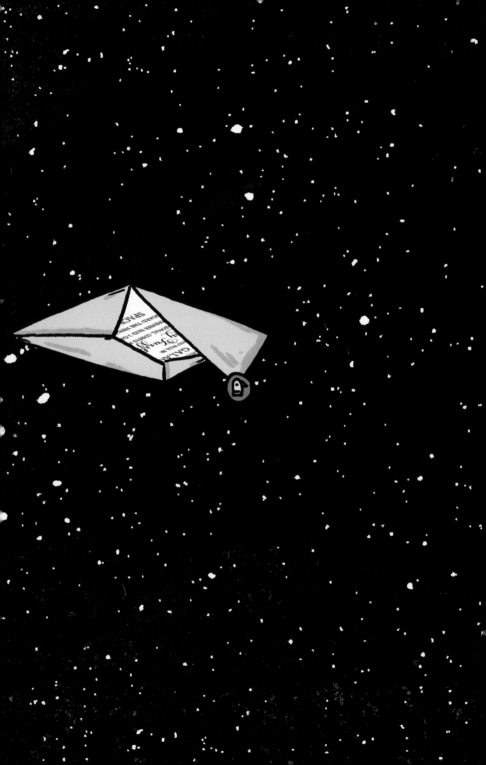

CHAPTER 2

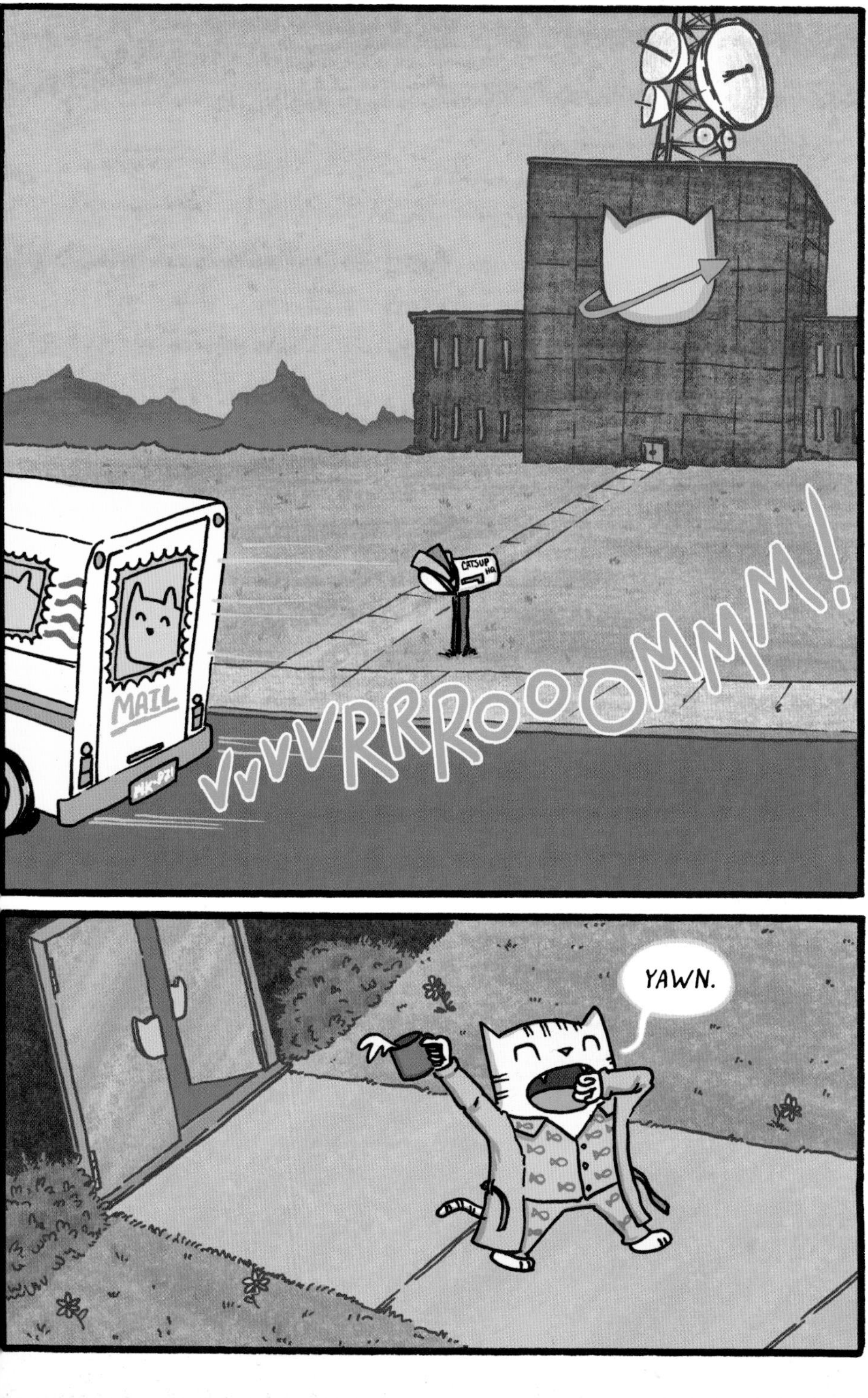
MAIL
CATSUP HQ
VVVVRRROOOMMMM!
YAWN.

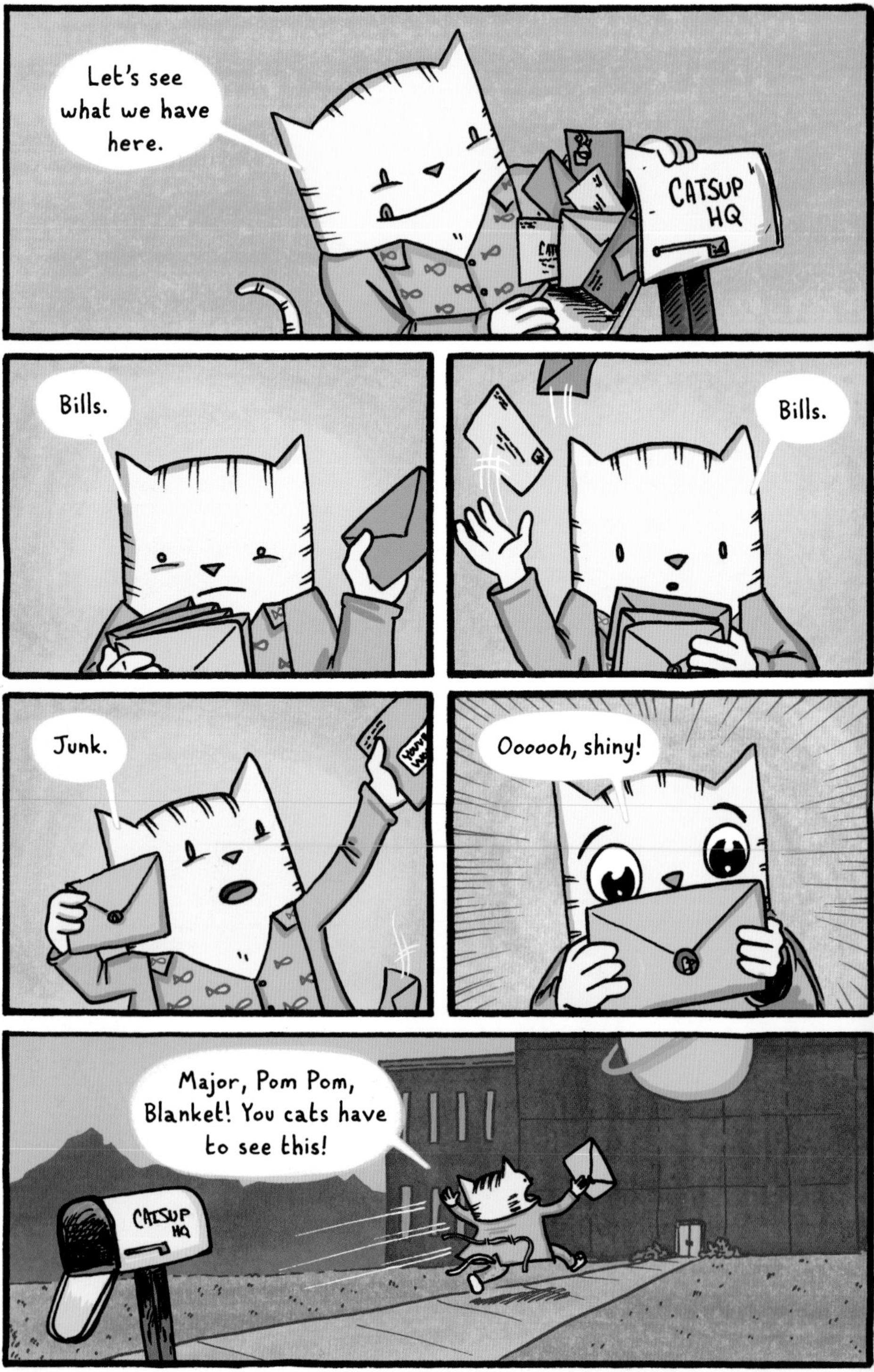
Let's see what we have here.
CATSUP HQ
Bills.
Bills.
Junk.
Ooooh, shiny!
Major, Pom Pom, Blanket! You cats have to see this!
CATSUP HQ

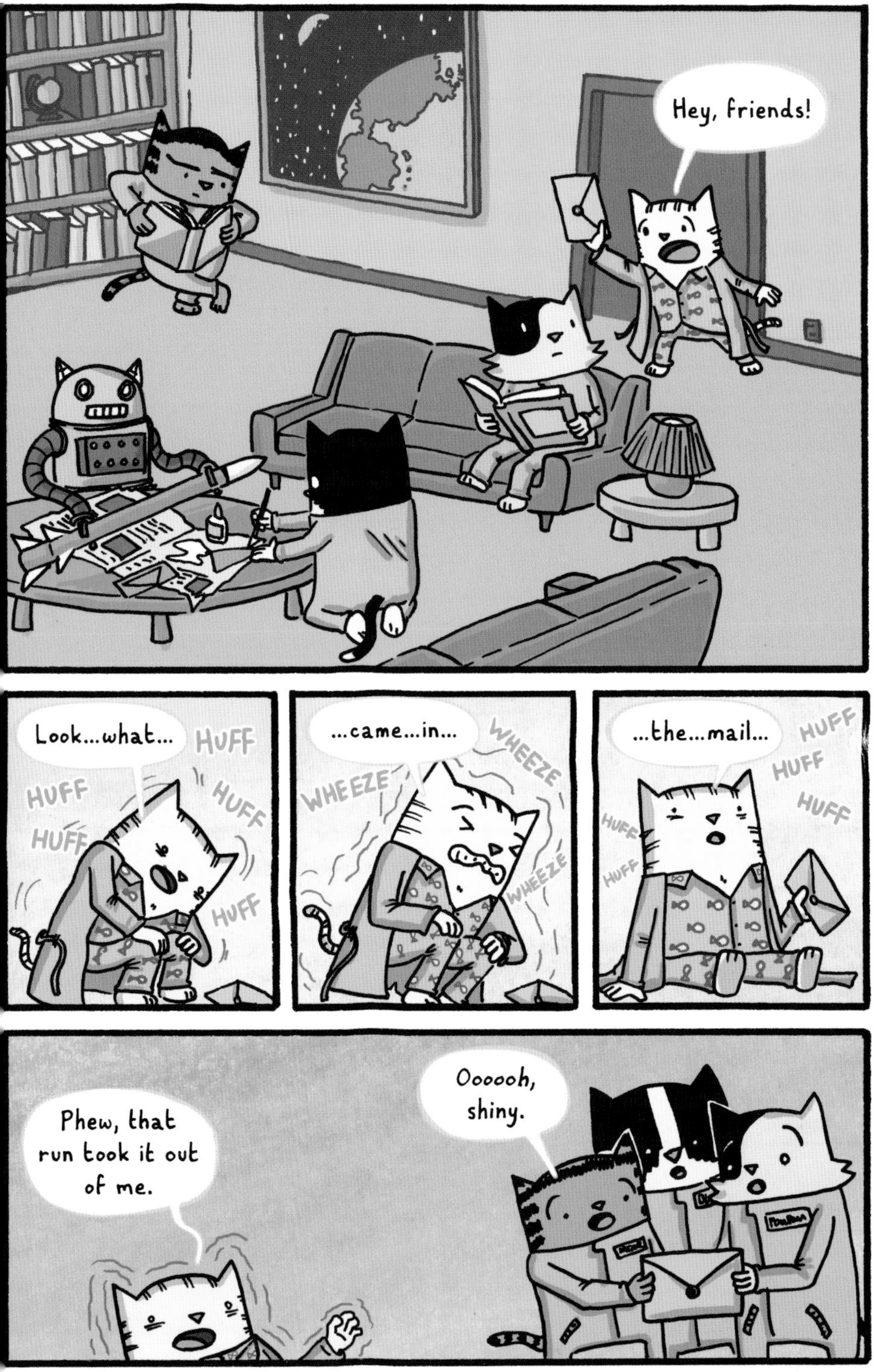
Hey, friends!
Look...what...
HUFF
HUFF
HUFF
HUFF
HUFF
...came...in...
WHEEZE
WHEEZE
WHEEZE
...the...mail...
HUFF
HUFF
HUFF
HUFF
HUFF
Phew, that run took it out of me.
Oooooh, shiny.

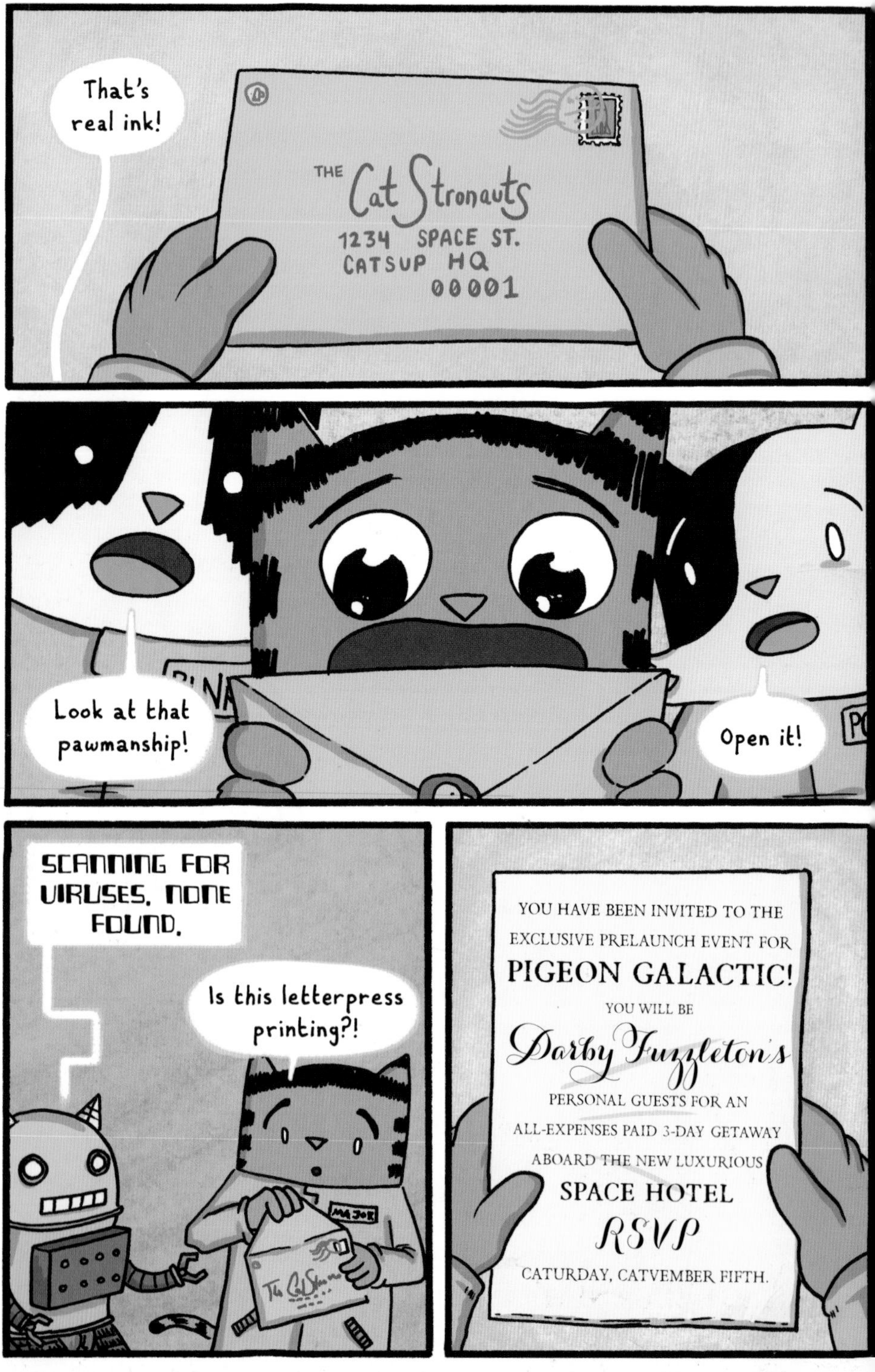
That's real ink!
THE Cat Stronauts
1234 SPACE ST.
CATSUP HQ
00001
Look at that pawmanship!
Open it!
SCANNING FOR VIRUSES. NONE FOUND.
Is this letterpress printing?!
MAJOR
YOU HAVE BEEN INVITED TO THE
EXCLUSIVE PRELAUNCH EVENT FOR
PIGEON GALACTIC!
YOU WILL BE
Darby Fuzzleton's
PERSONAL GUESTS FOR AN
ALL-EXPENSES PAID 3-DAY GETAWAY
ABOARD THE NEW LUXURIOUS
SPACE HOTEL
RSVP
CATURDAY, CATVEMBER FIFTH.

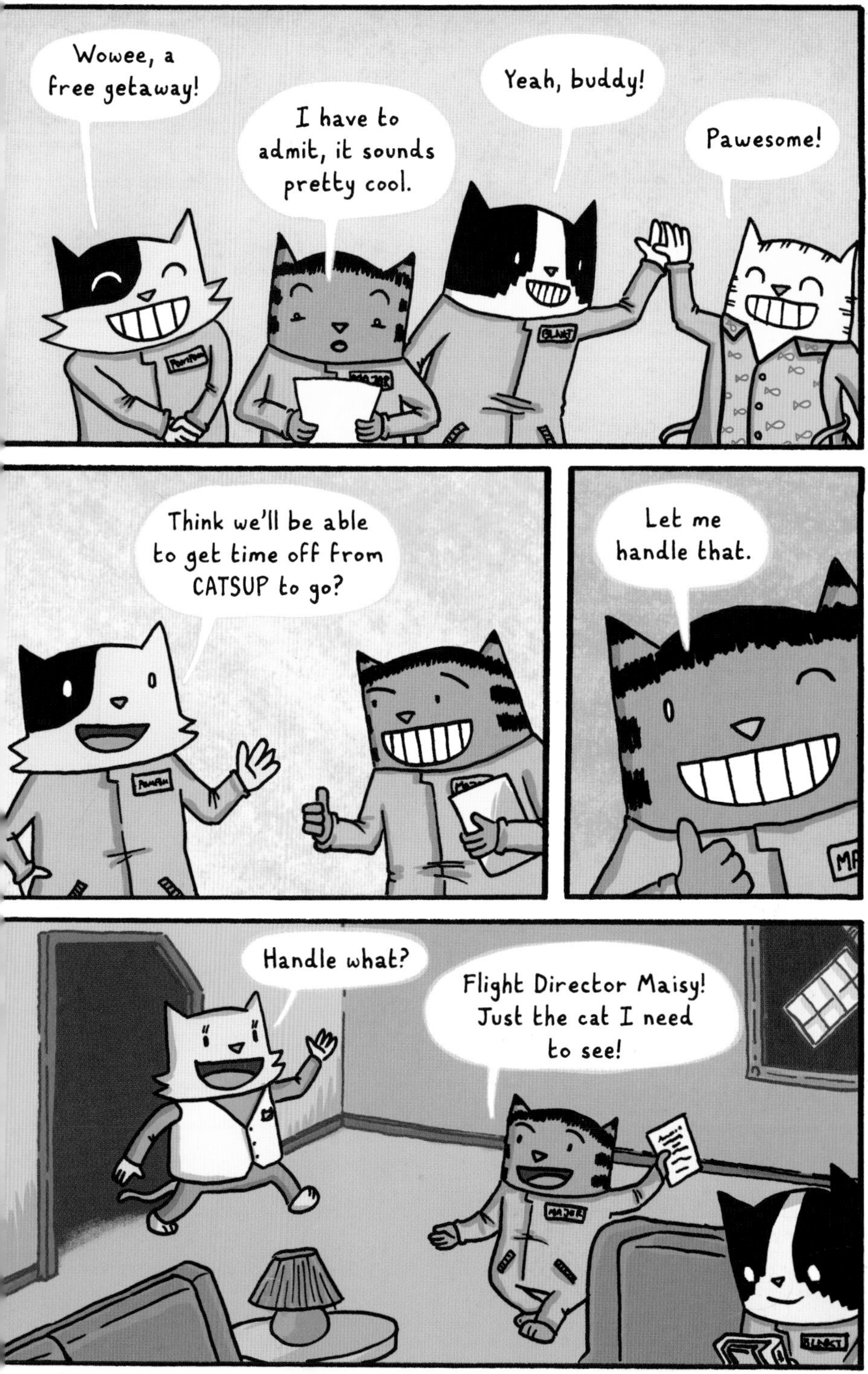
Wowee, a free getaway!
I have to admit, it sounds pretty cool.
Yeah, buddy!
Pawesome!
Think we'll be able to get time off from CATSUP to go?
Let me handle that.
Handle what?
Flight Director Maisy! Just the cat I need to see!

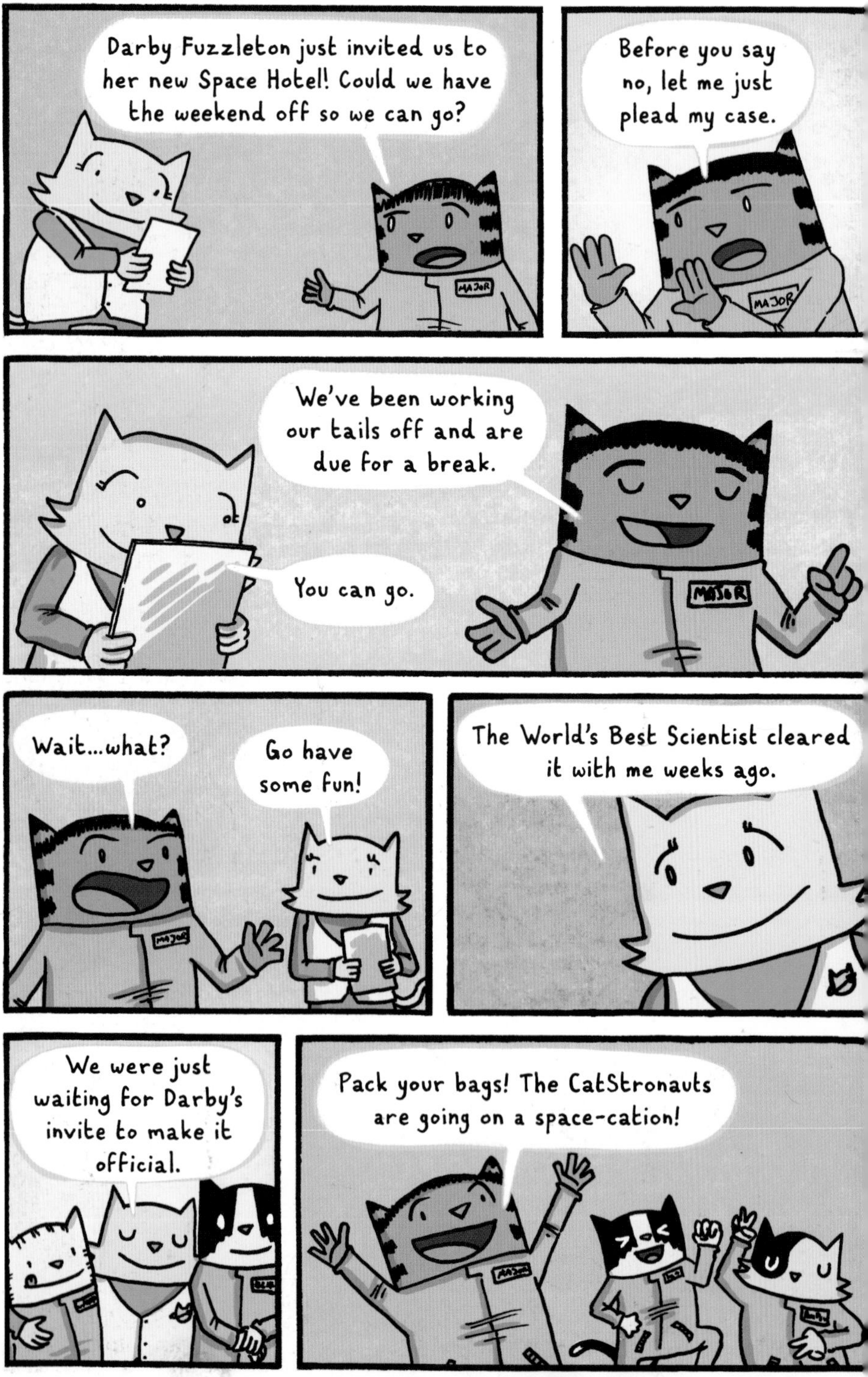
Darby Fuzzleton just invited us to her new Space Hotel! Could we have the weekend off so we can go?
MAJOR
Before you say no, let me just plead my case.
MAJOR
We've been working our tails off and are due for a break.
You can go.
MAJOR
Wait...what?
Go have some fun!
The World's Best Scientist cleared it with me weeks ago.
We were just waiting for Darby's invite to make it official.
Pack your bags! The CatStronauts are going on a space-cation!

THREE DAYS LATER.

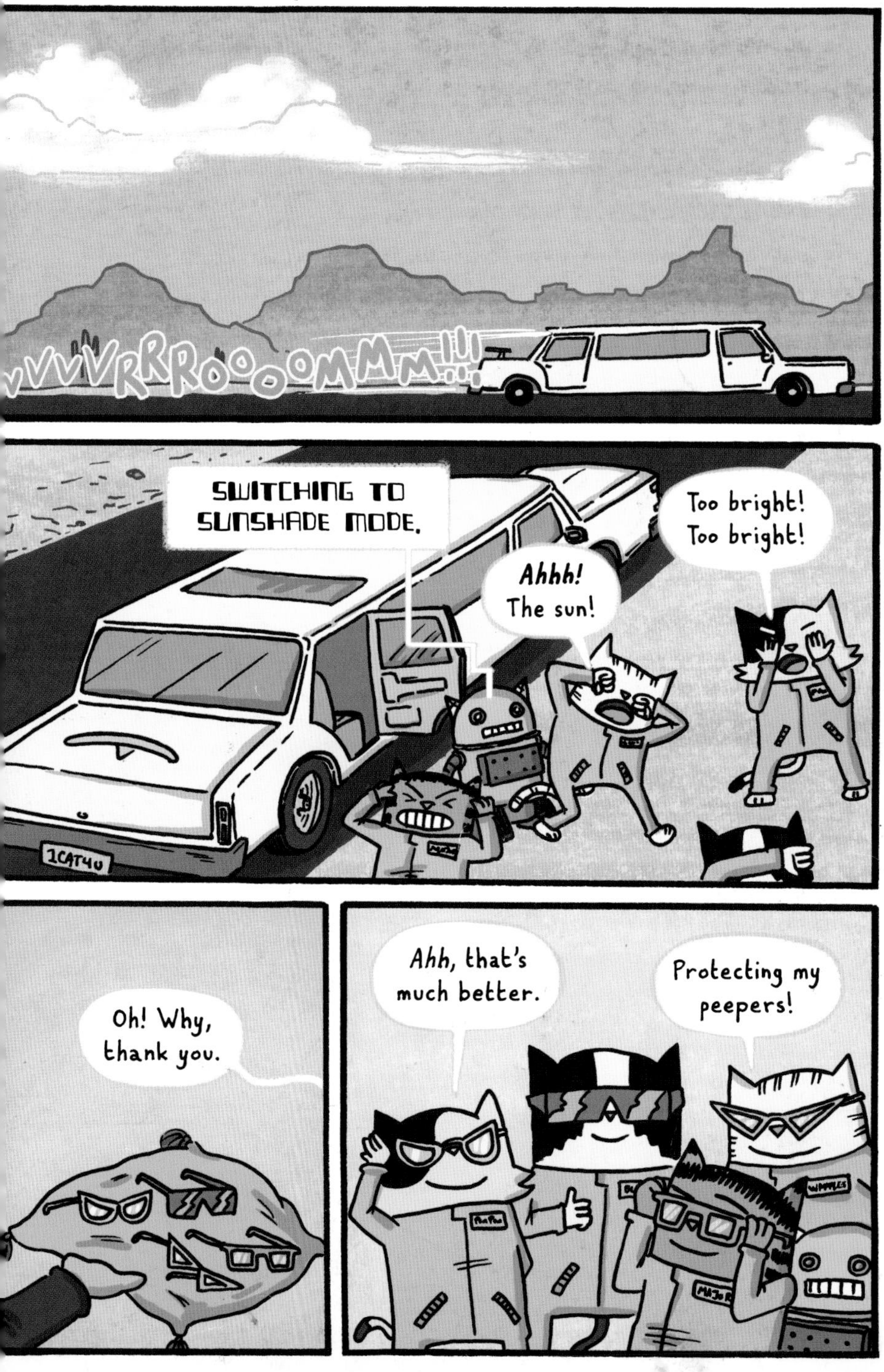
VVVVVRRROOOOOMMM!!!
SWITCHING TO SUNSHADE MODE.
Ahhh! The sun!
Too bright! Too bright!
1CAT4U
Oh! Why, thank you.
Ahh, that's much better.
Protecting my peepers!

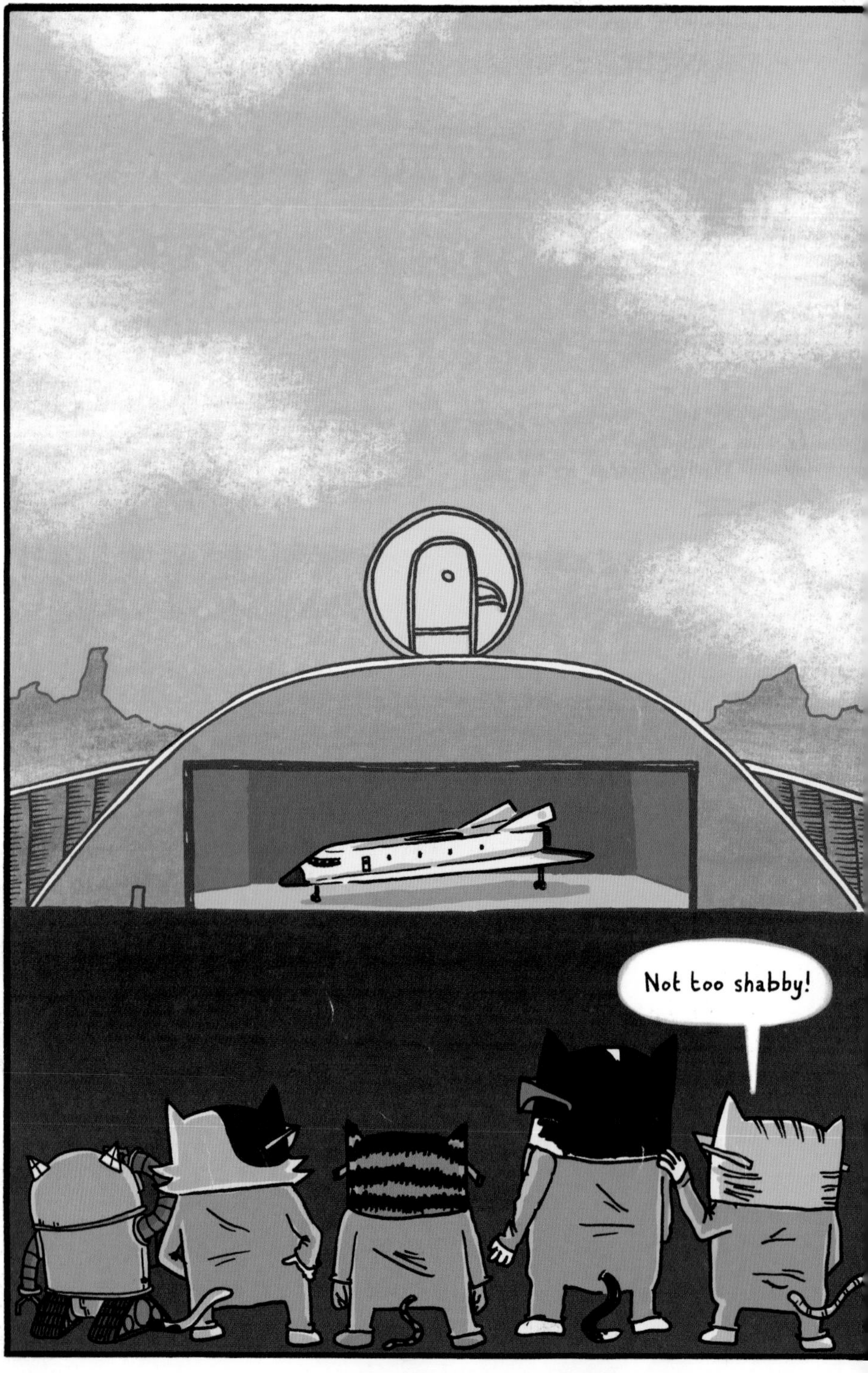
Not too shabby!

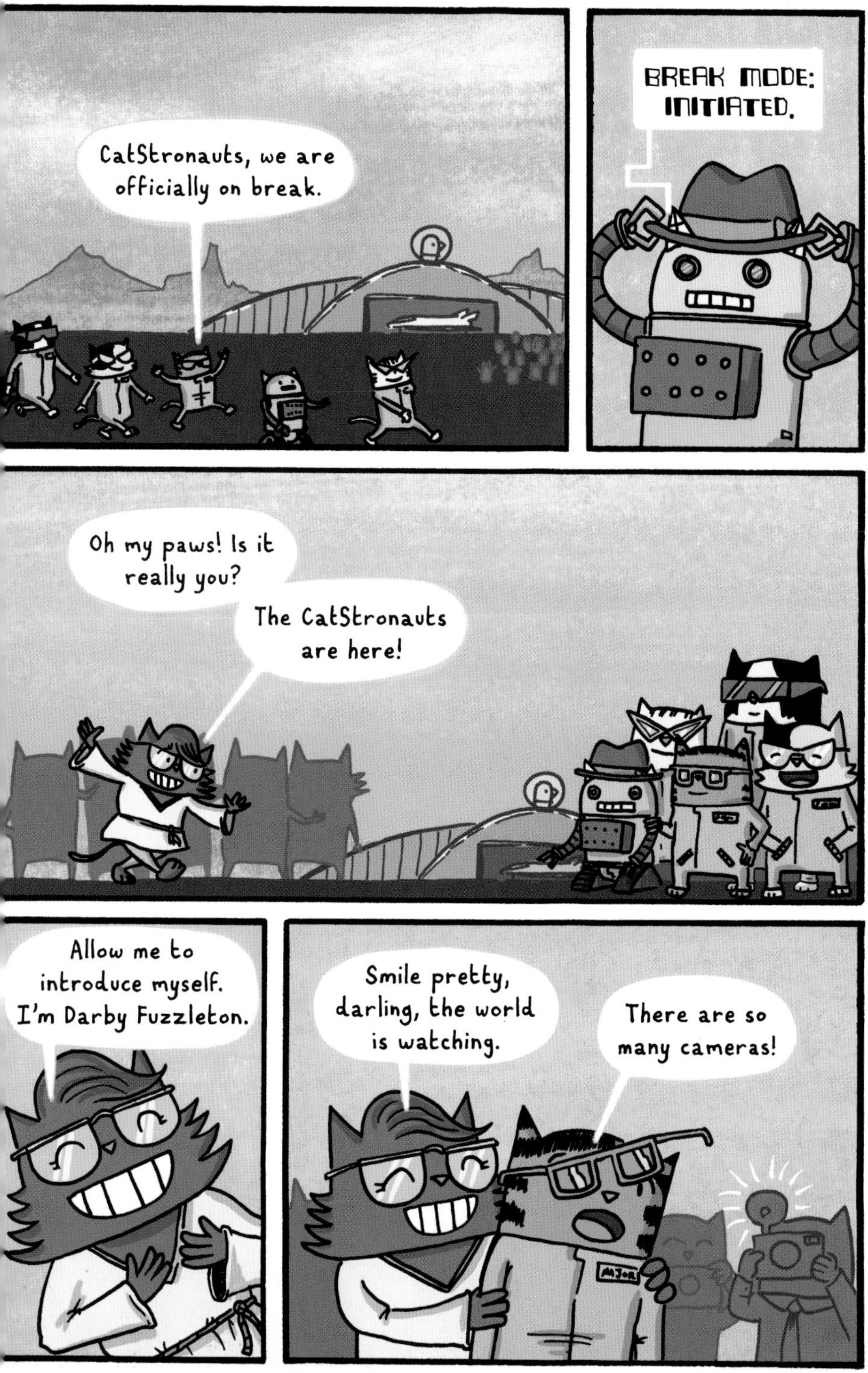
CatStronauts, we are officially on break.
BREAK MODE: INITIATED.
Oh my paws! Is it really you?
The CatStronauts are here!
Allow me to introduce myself. I'm Darby Fuzzleton.
Smile pretty, darling, the world is watching.
There are so many cameras!
MAJOR

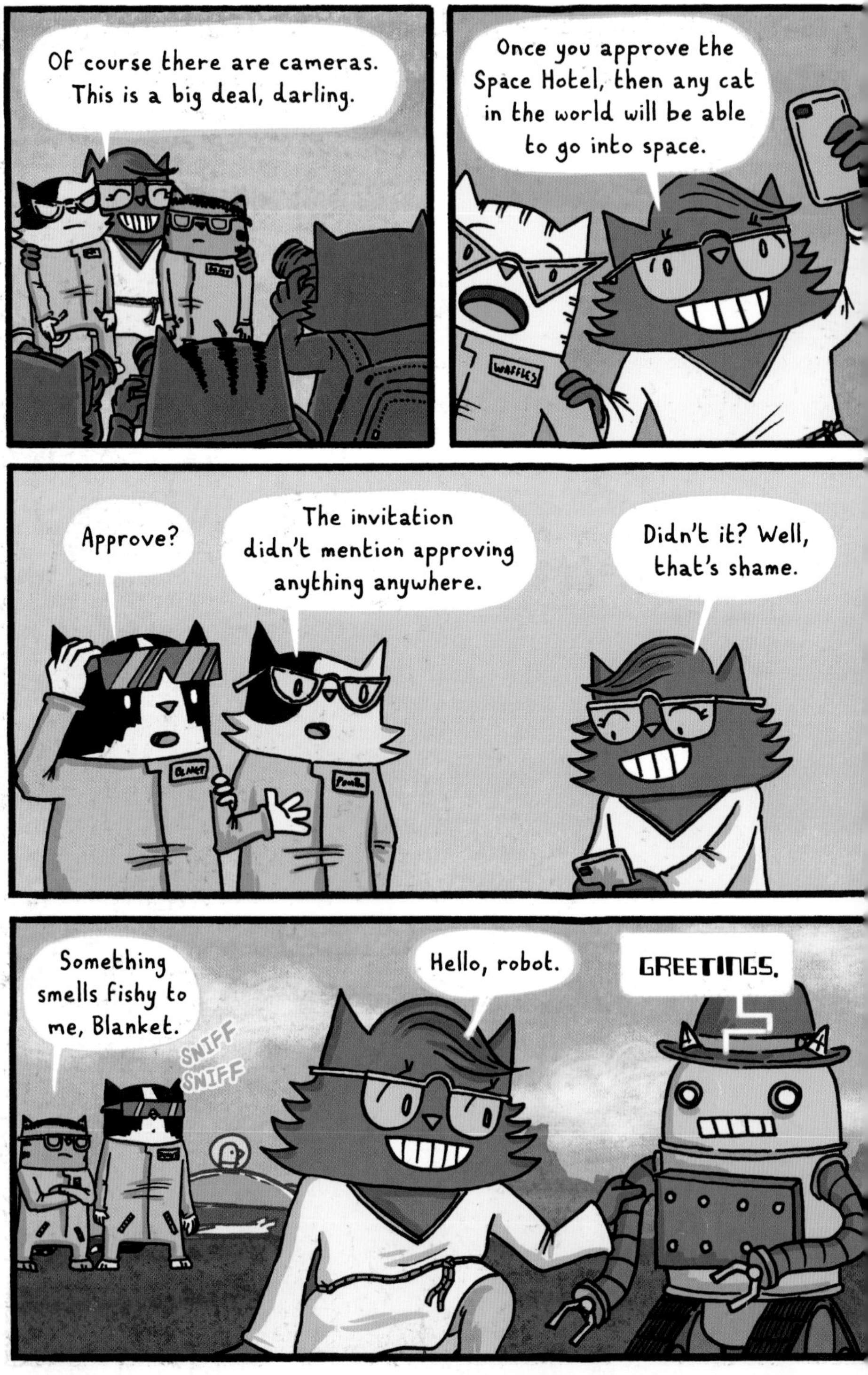
Of course there are cameras. This is a big deal, darling.
Once you approve the Space Hotel, then any cat in the world will be able to go into space.
WAFFLES
Approve?
The invitation didn't mention approving anything anywhere.
Didn't it? Well, that's shame.
Something smells fishy to me, Blanket.
SNIFF SNIFF
Hello, robot.
GREETINGS.

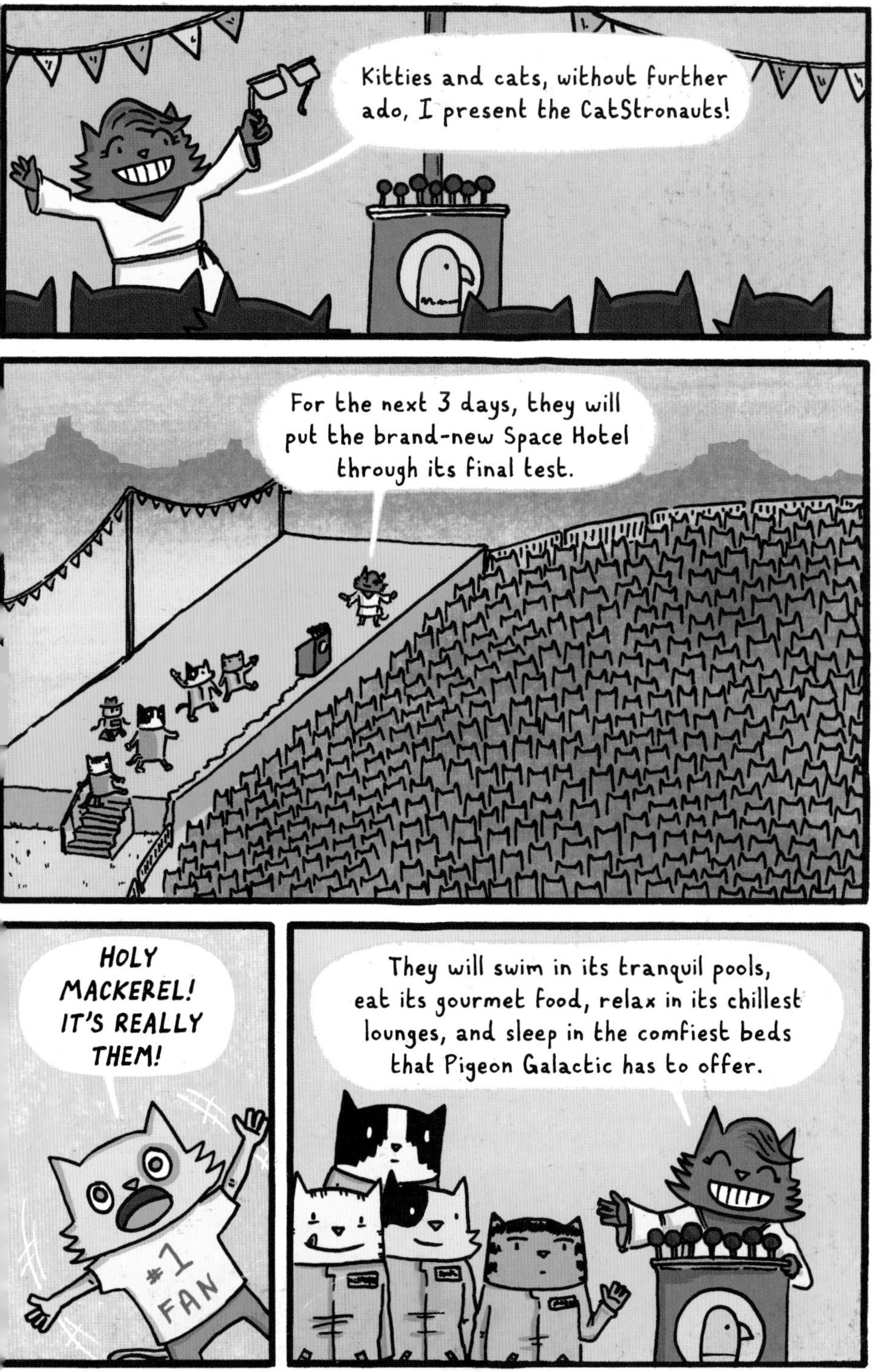

Kitties and cats, without further ado, I present the CatStronauts!
For the next 3 days, they will put the brand-new Space Hotel through its final test.
HOLY MACKEREL! IT'S REALLY THEM!
#1 FAN
They will swim in its tranquil pools, eat its gourmet food, relax in its chillest lounges, and sleep in the comfiest beds that Pigeon Galactic has to offer.

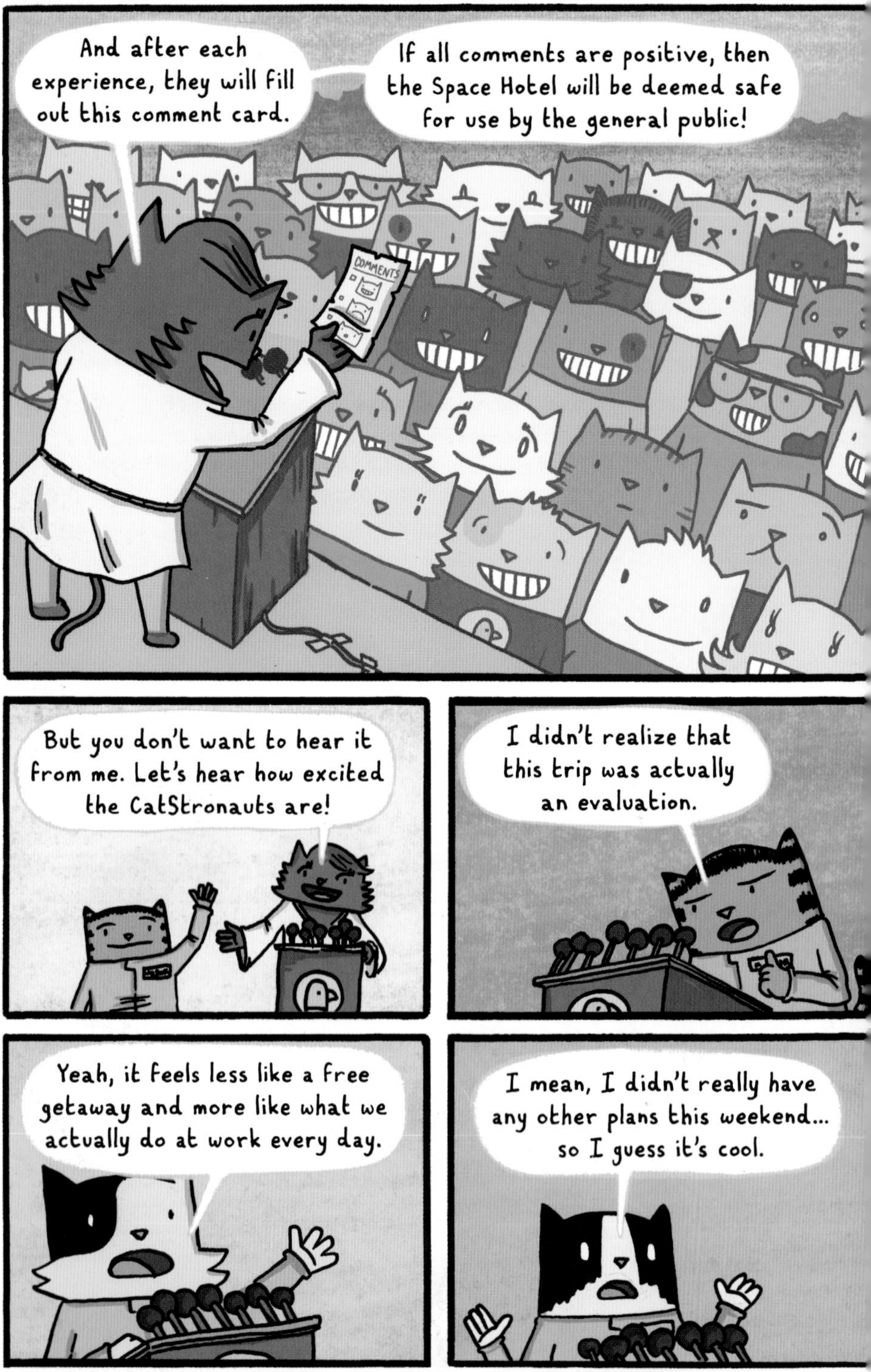
And after each experience, they will fill out this comment card.
If all comments are positive, then the Space Hotel will be deemed safe for use by the general public!
COMMENTS
But you don't want to hear it from me. Let's hear how excited the CatStronauts are!
I didn't realize that this trip was actually an evaluation.
Yeah, it feels less like a free getaway and more like what we actually do at work every day.
I mean, I didn't really have any other plans this weekend... so I guess it's cool.

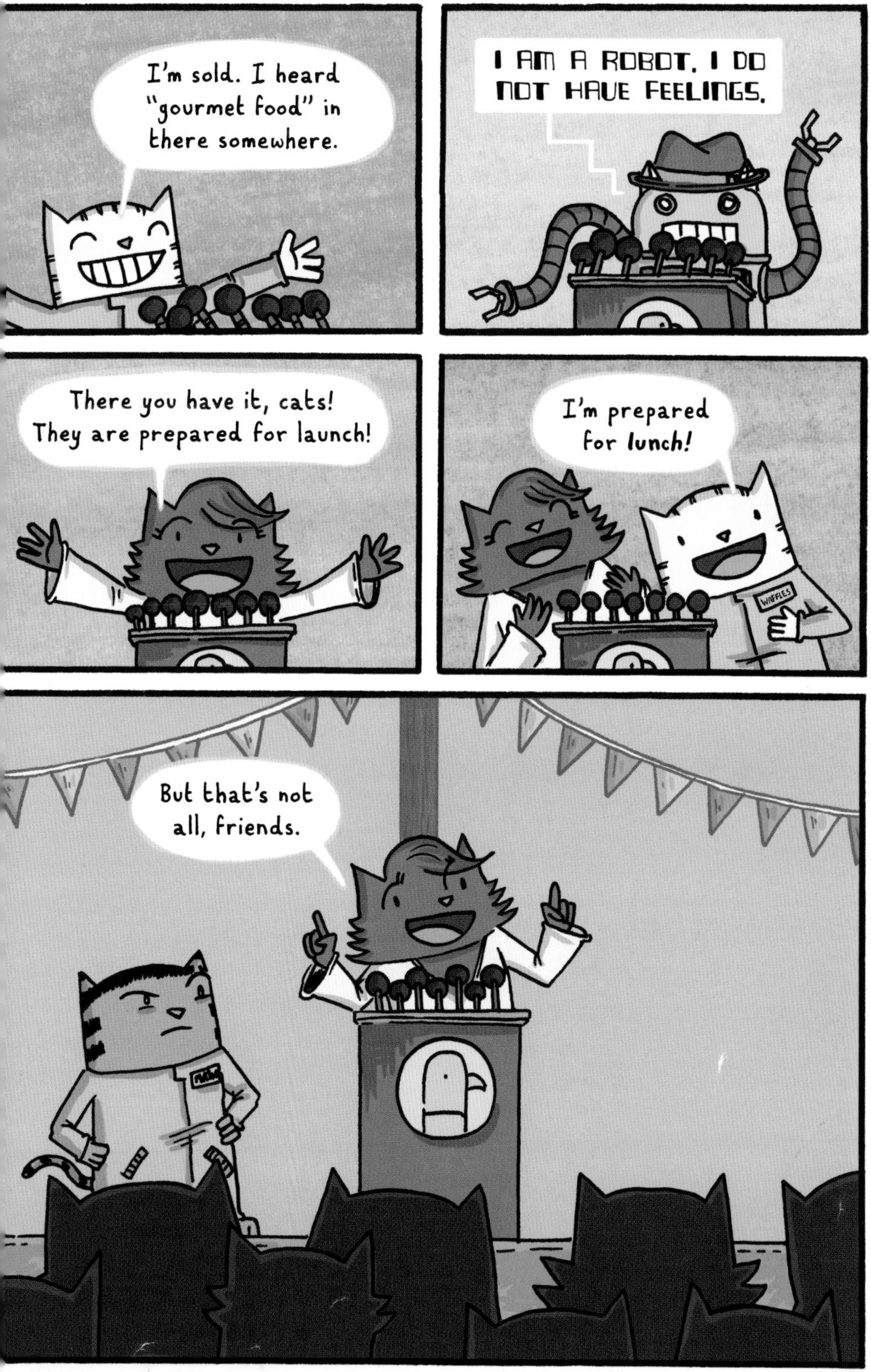
I'm sold. I heard "gourmet food" in there somewhere.
I AM A ROBOT. I DO NOT HAVE FEELINGS.
There you have it, cats! They are prepared for launch!
I'm prepared for **lunch**!
WAFFLES
But that's not all, friends.

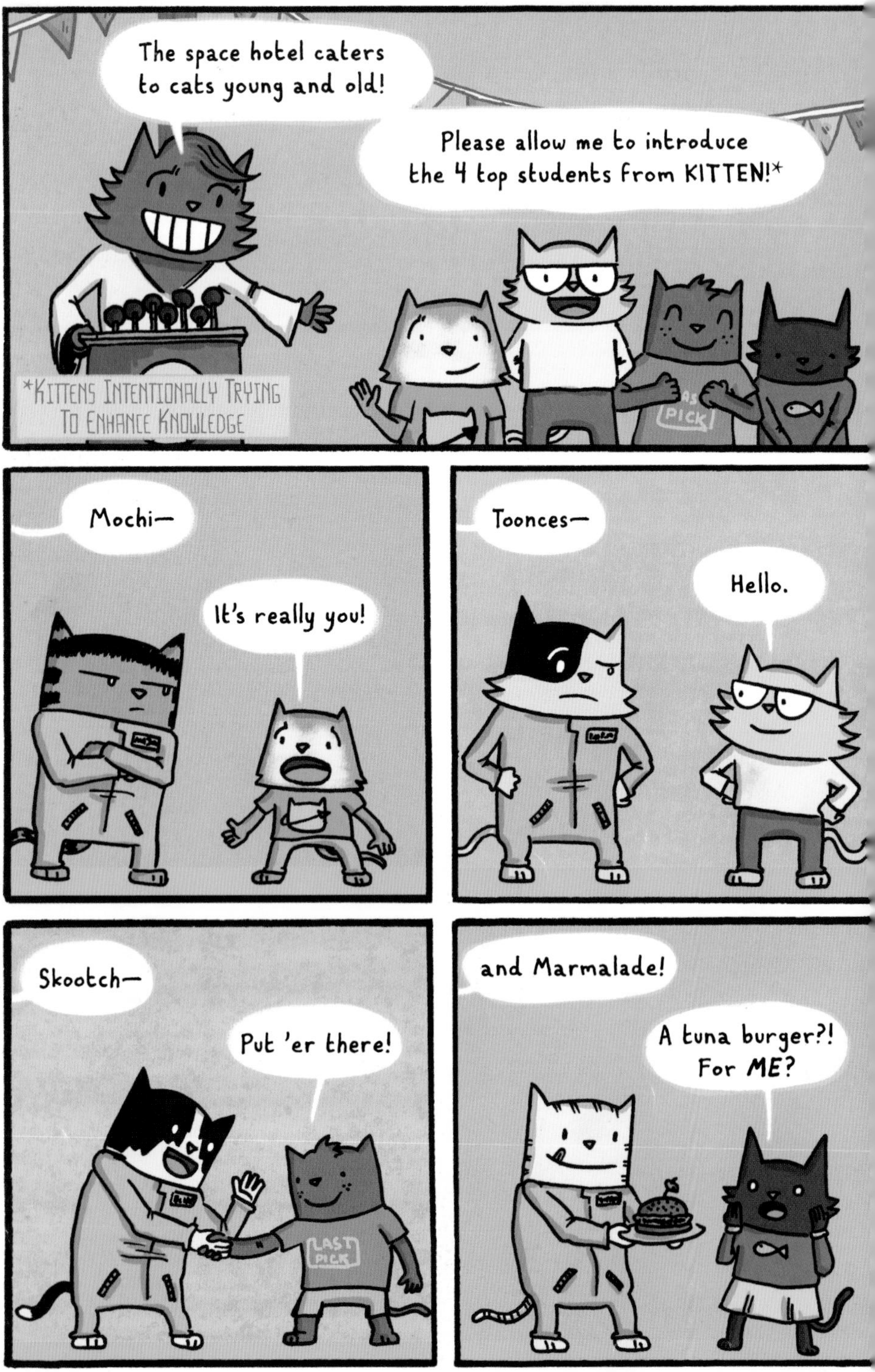
The space hotel caters to cats young and old!
Please allow me to introduce the 4 top students from KITTEN!*
*KITTENS INTENTIONALLY TRYING TO ENHANCE KNOWLEDGE
Mochi—
It's really you!
Toonces—
Hello.
Skootch—
Put 'er there!
LAST PICK
and Marmalade!
A tuna burger?! For ME?

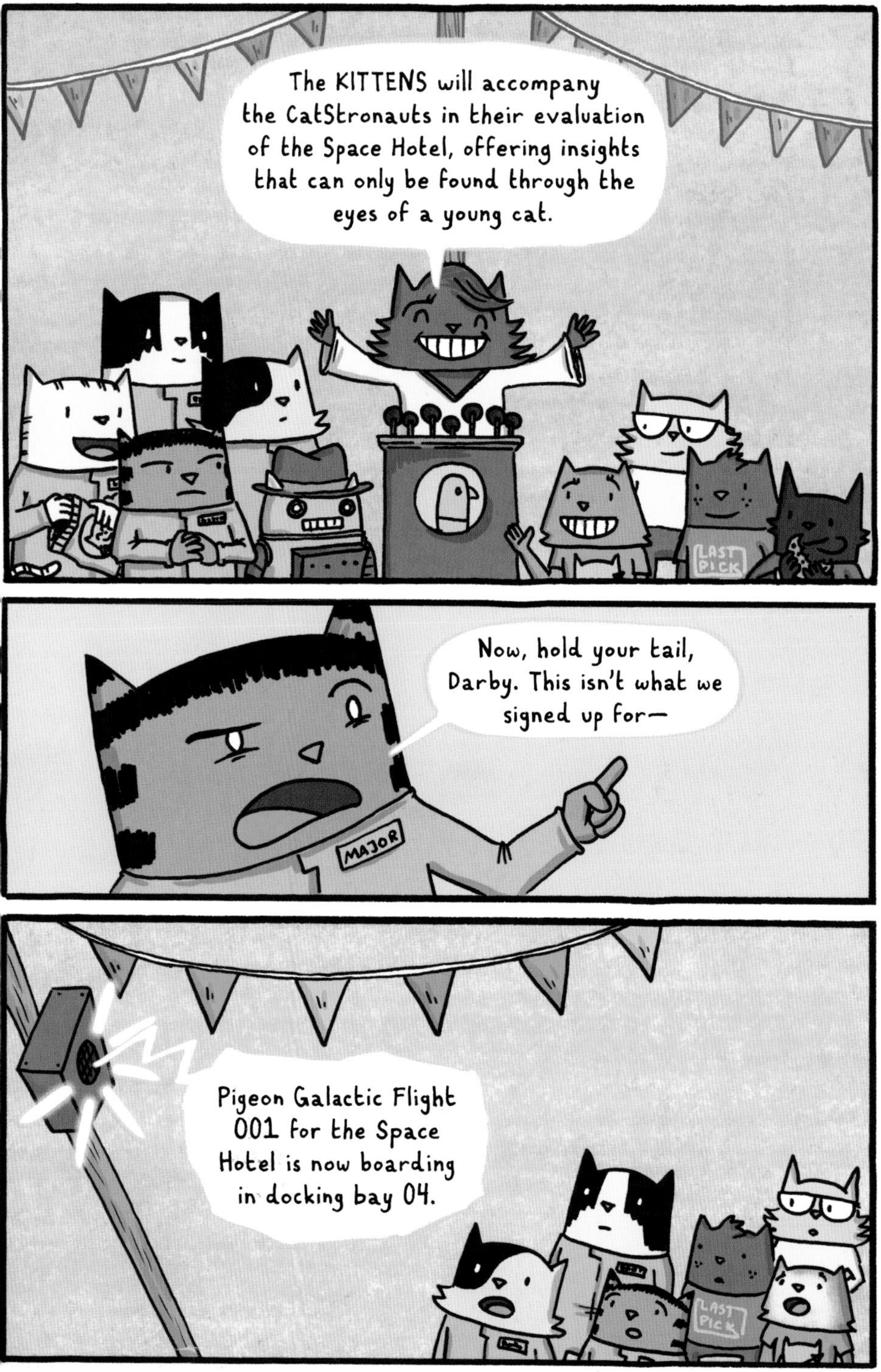
The KITTENS will accompany the CatStronauts in their evaluation of the Space Hotel, offering insights that can only be found through the eyes of a young cat.
LAST PICK
Now, hold your tail, Darby. This isn't what we signed up for—
MAJOR
Pigeon Galactic Flight 001 for the Space Hotel is now boarding in docking bay 04.
LAST PICK

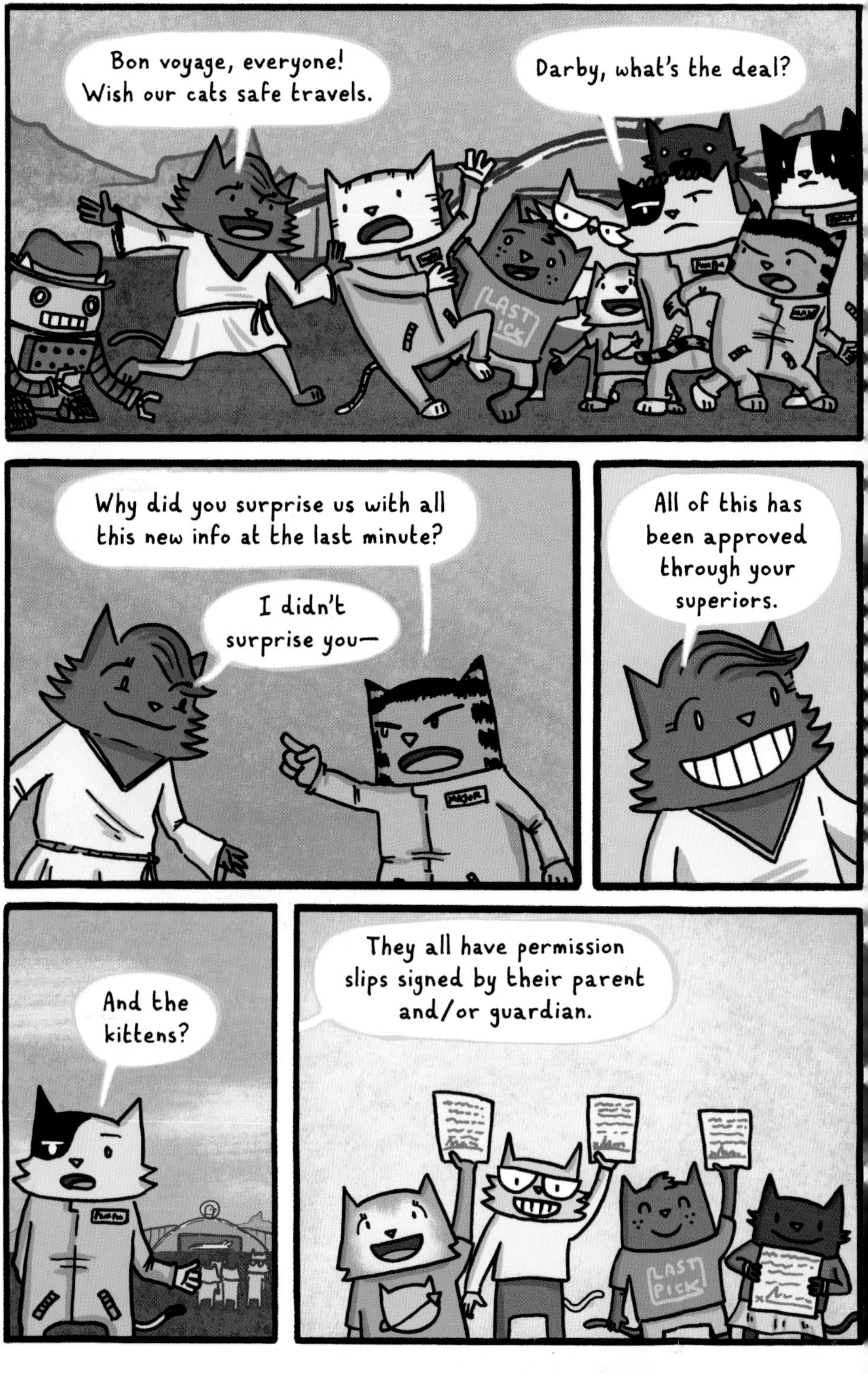
Bon voyage, everyone! Wish our cats safe travels.
Darby, what's the deal?
Why did you surprise us with all this new info at the last minute?
I didn't surprise you—
All of this has been approved through your superiors.
And the kittens?
They all have permission slips signed by their parent and/or guardian.
LAST PICK
LAST PICK
MAJOR

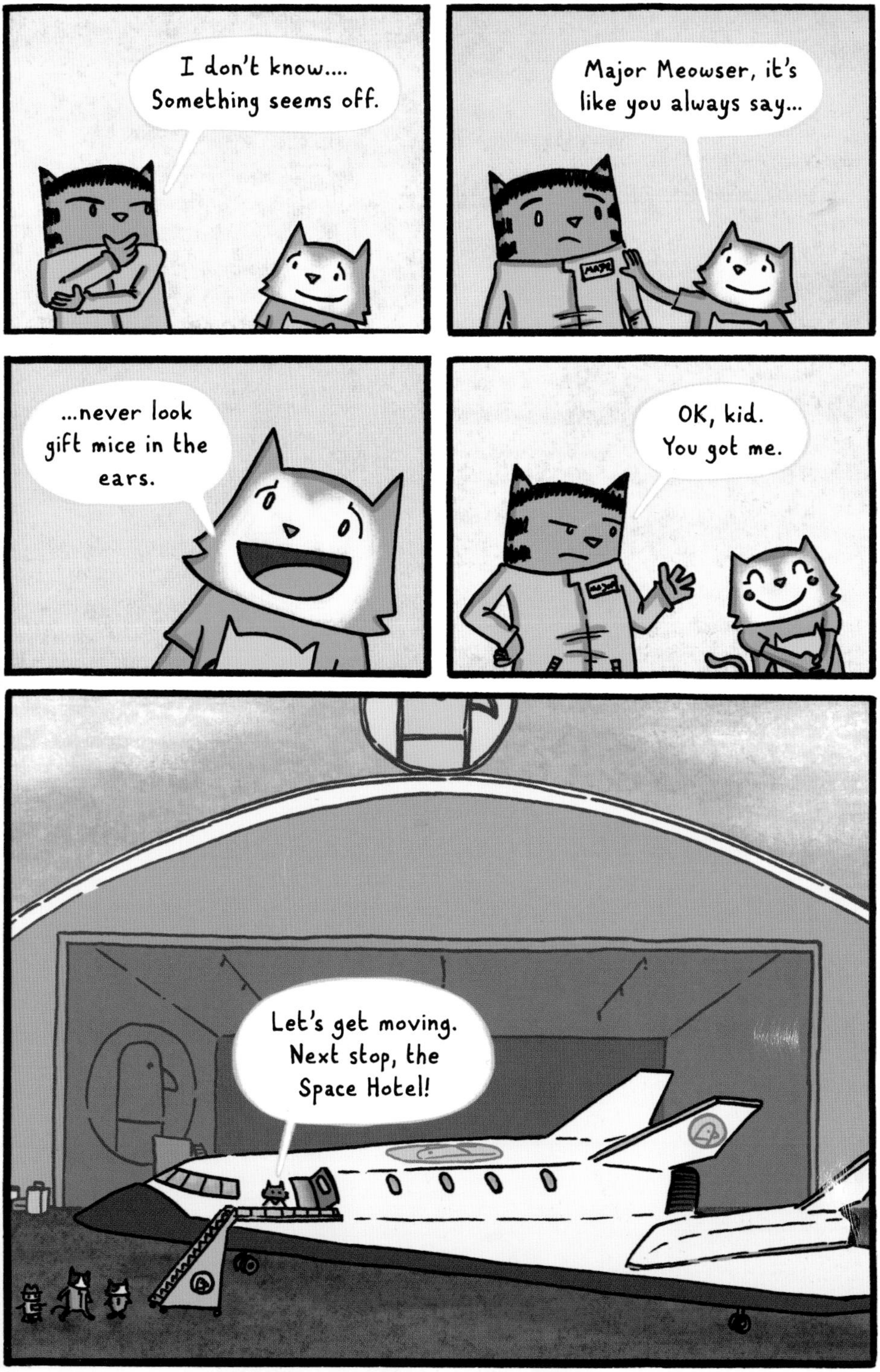
I don't know....
Something seems off.
Major Meowser, it's like you always say...
...never look gift mice in the ears.
OK, kid.
You got me.
Let's get moving. Next stop, the Space Hotel!

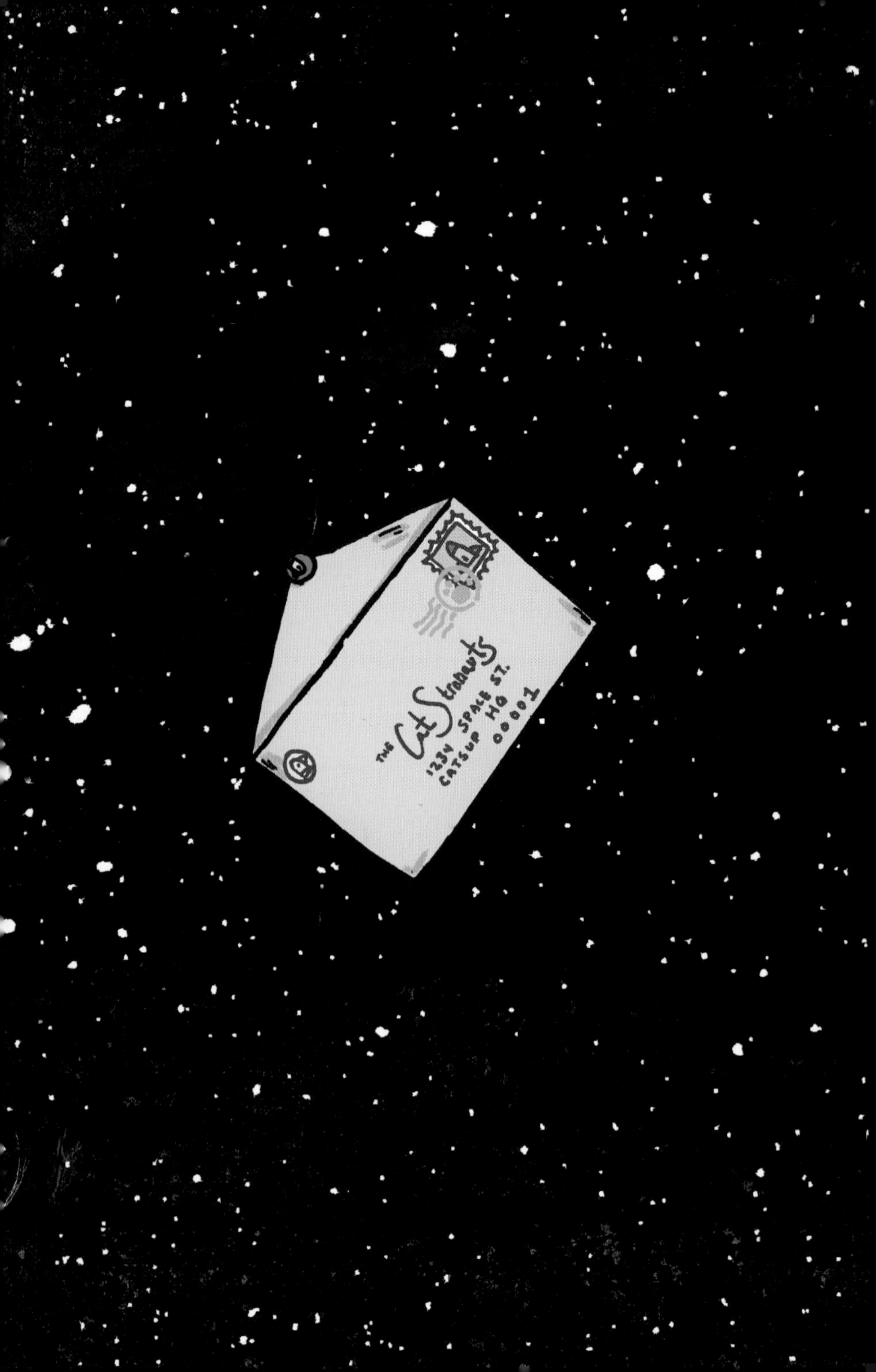
THE Cat Stronauts
1234 SPACE ST.
CATSUP HQ 00001

CHAPTER 3

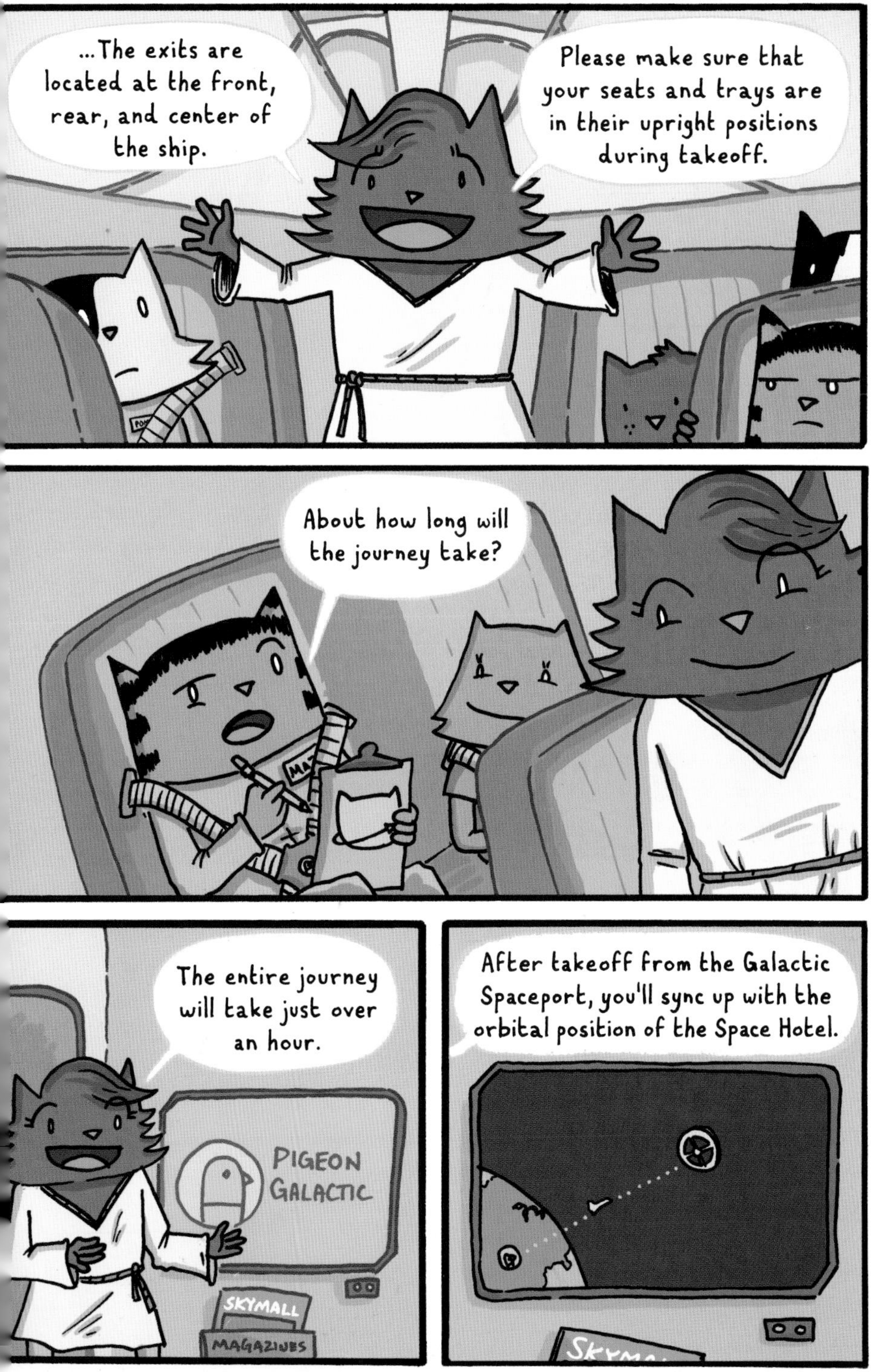
...The exits are located at the front, rear, and center of the ship.
Please make sure that your seats and trays are in their upright positions during takeoff.
About how long will the journey take?
The entire journey will take just over an hour.
PIGEON GALACTIC
SKYMALL
MAGAZINES
After takeoff from the Galactic Spaceport, you'll sync up with the orbital position of the Space Hotel.

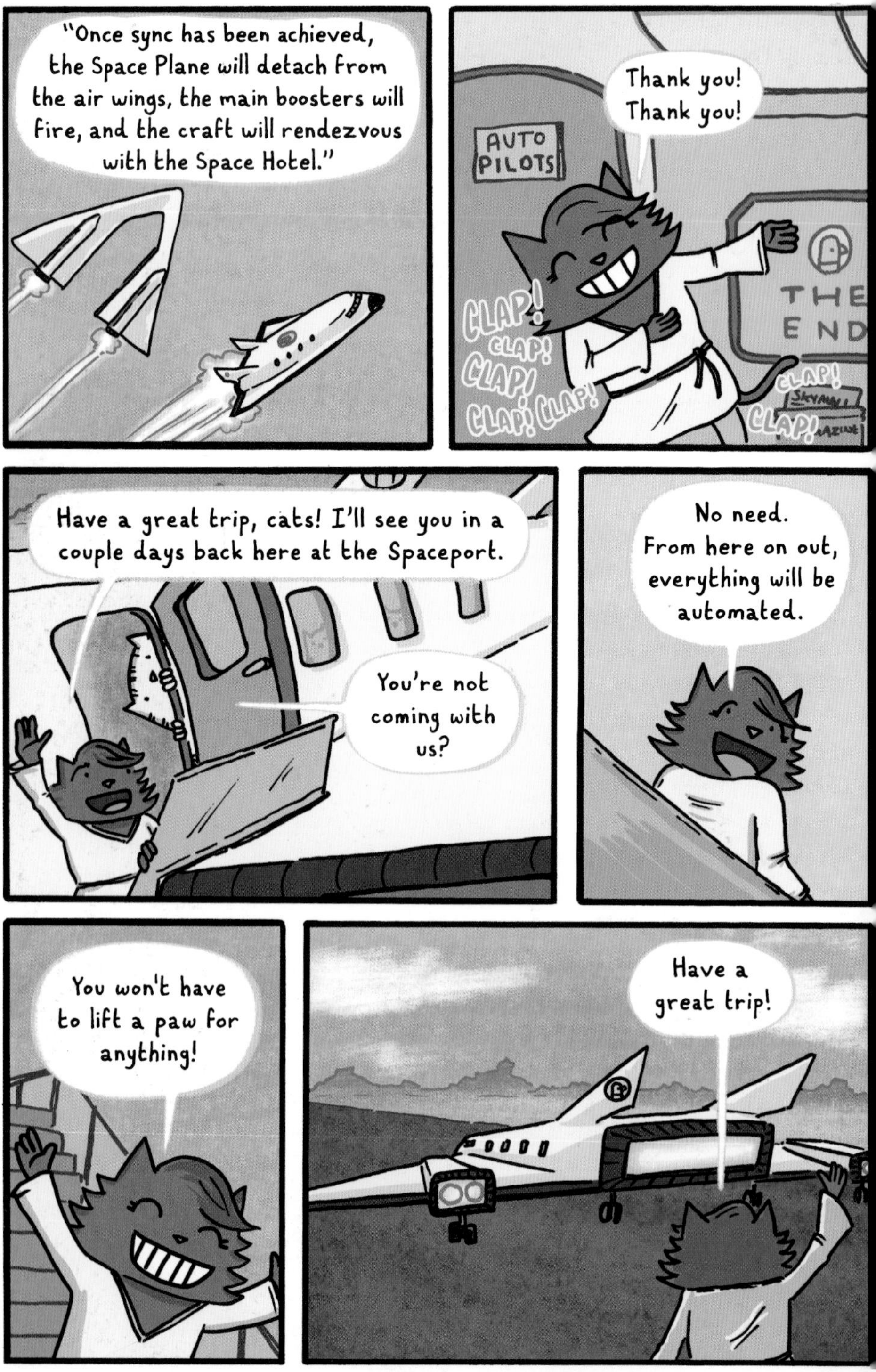
"Once sync has been achieved, the Space Plane will detach from the air wings, the main boosters will fire, and the craft will rendezvous with the Space Hotel."
AUTO PILOTS
Thank you! Thank you!
THE END
CLAP! CLAP! CLAP! CLAP! CLAP! CLAP! CLAP!
Have a great trip, cats! I'll see you in a couple days back here at the Spaceport.
You're not coming with us?
No need. From here on out, everything will be automated.
You won't have to lift a paw for anything!
Have a great trip!

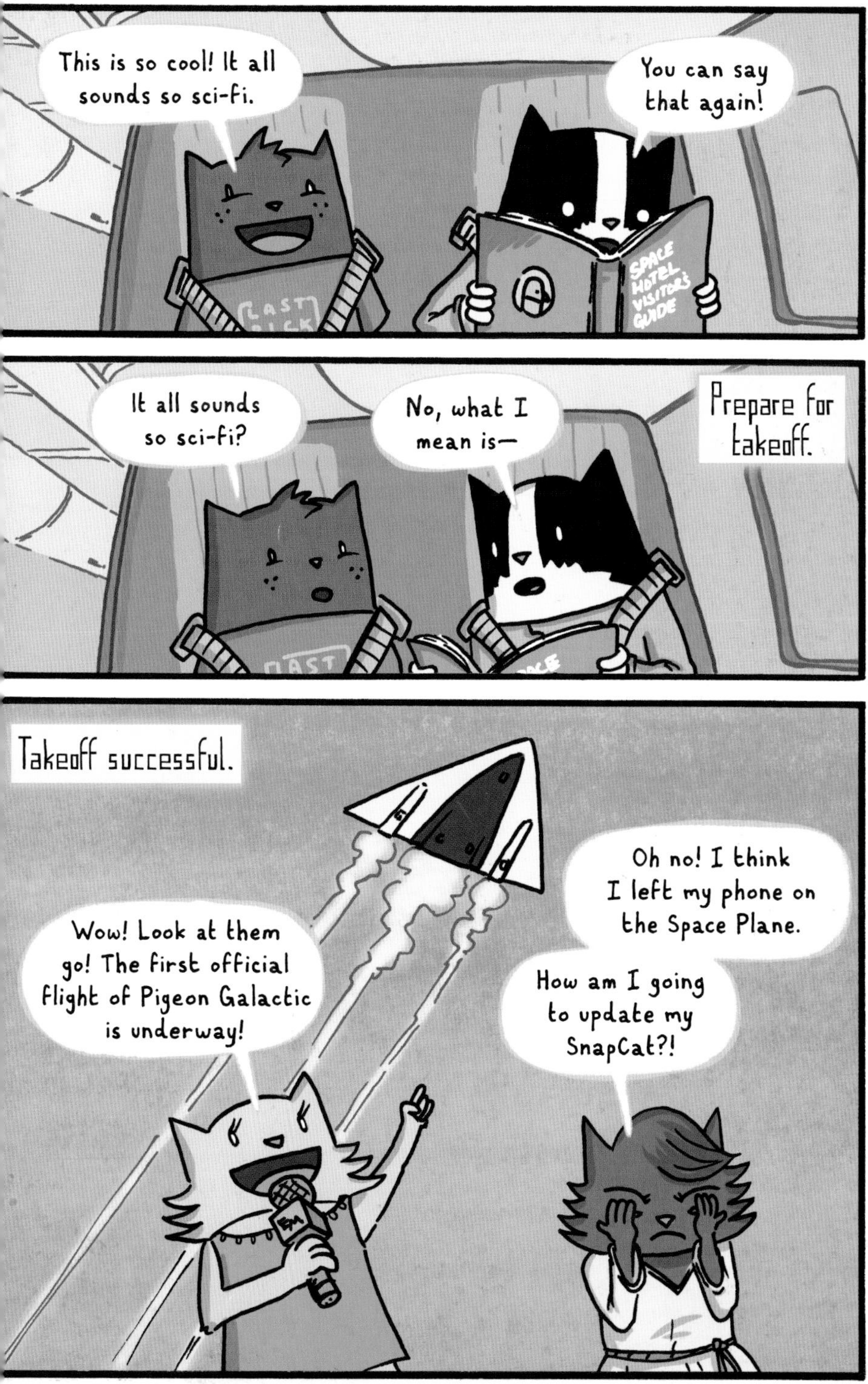

This is so cool! It all sounds so sci-fi.
You can say that again!
SPACE HOTEL VISITOR'S GUIDE
It all sounds so sci-fi?
No, what I mean is—
Prepare for takeoff.
Takeoff successful.
Wow! Look at them go! The first official flight of Pigeon Galactic is underway!
Oh no! I think I left my phone on the Space Plane.
How am I going to update my SnapCat?!

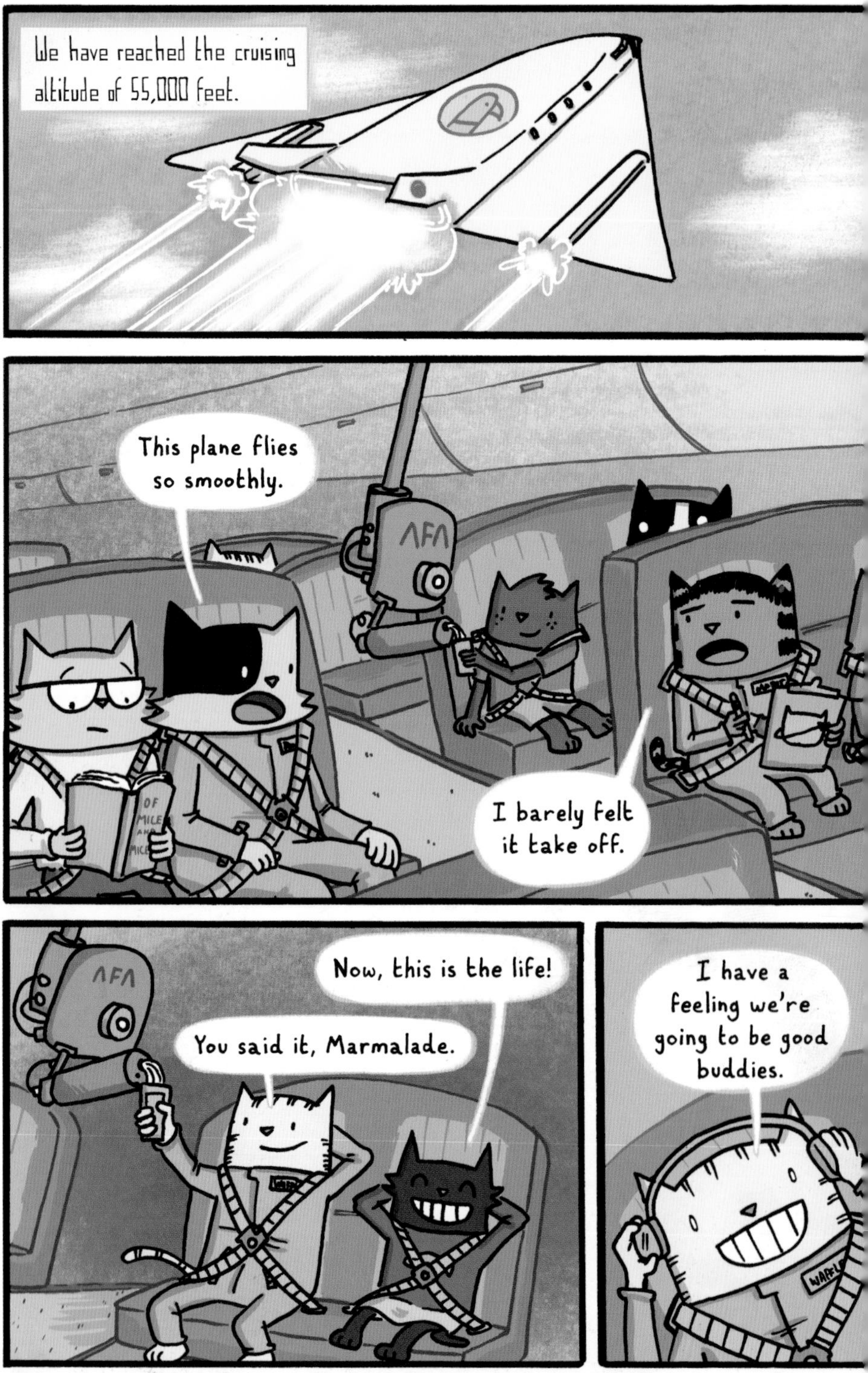
We have reached the cruising altitude of 55,000 feet.
This plane flies so smoothly.
I barely felt it take off.
Now, this is the life!
You said it, Marmalade.
I have a feeling we're going to be good buddies.

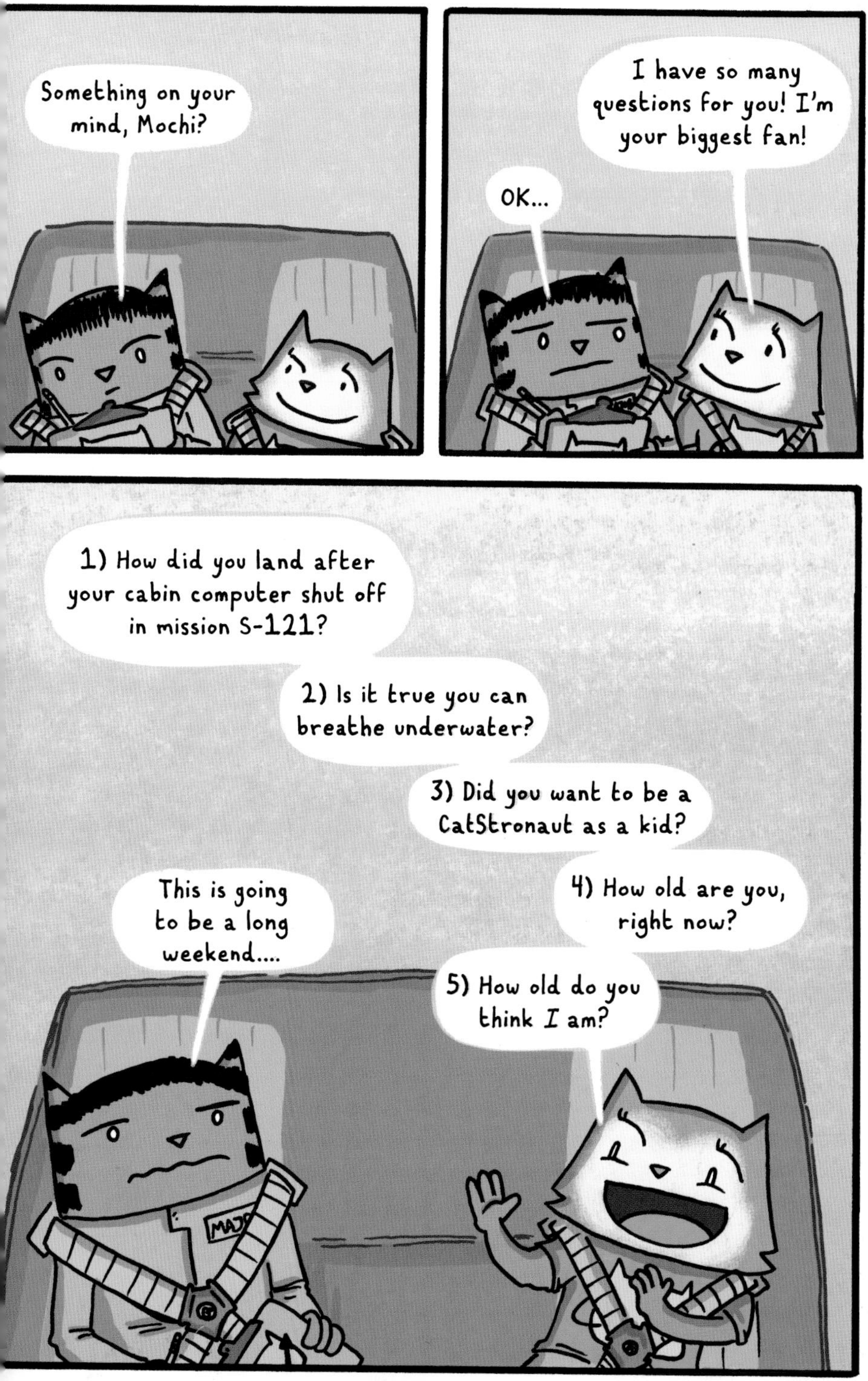
Something on your mind, Mochi?
I have so many questions for you! I'm your biggest fan!
OK...
1) How did you land after your cabin computer shut off in mission S-121?
2) Is it true you can breathe underwater?
3) Did you want to be a CatStronaut as a kid?
4) How old are you, right now?
5) How old do you think *I* am?
This is going to be a long weekend....

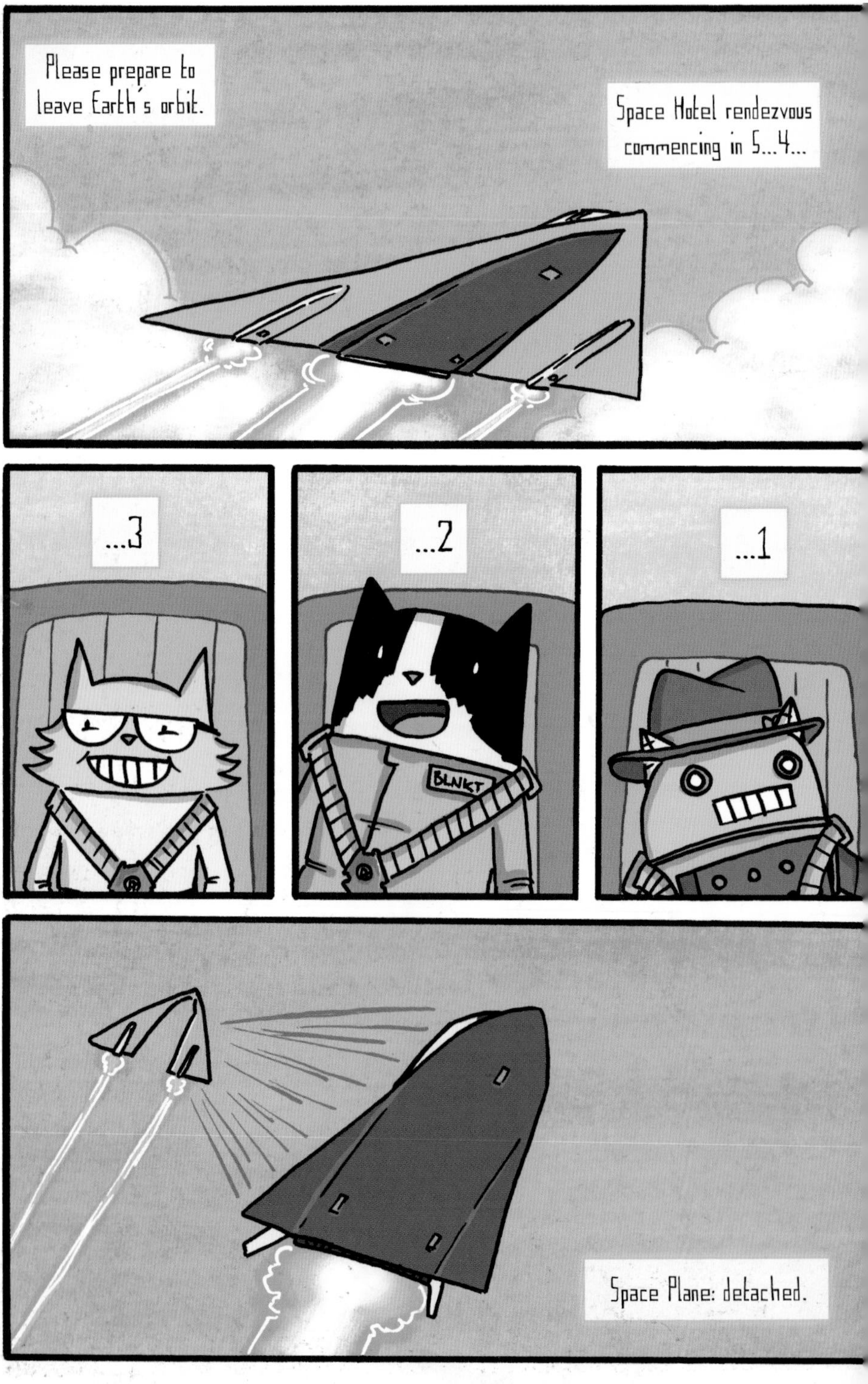
Please prepare to leave Earth's orbit.
Space Hotel rendezvous commencing in 5...4...
...3
...2
BLNKT
...1
Space Plane: detached.

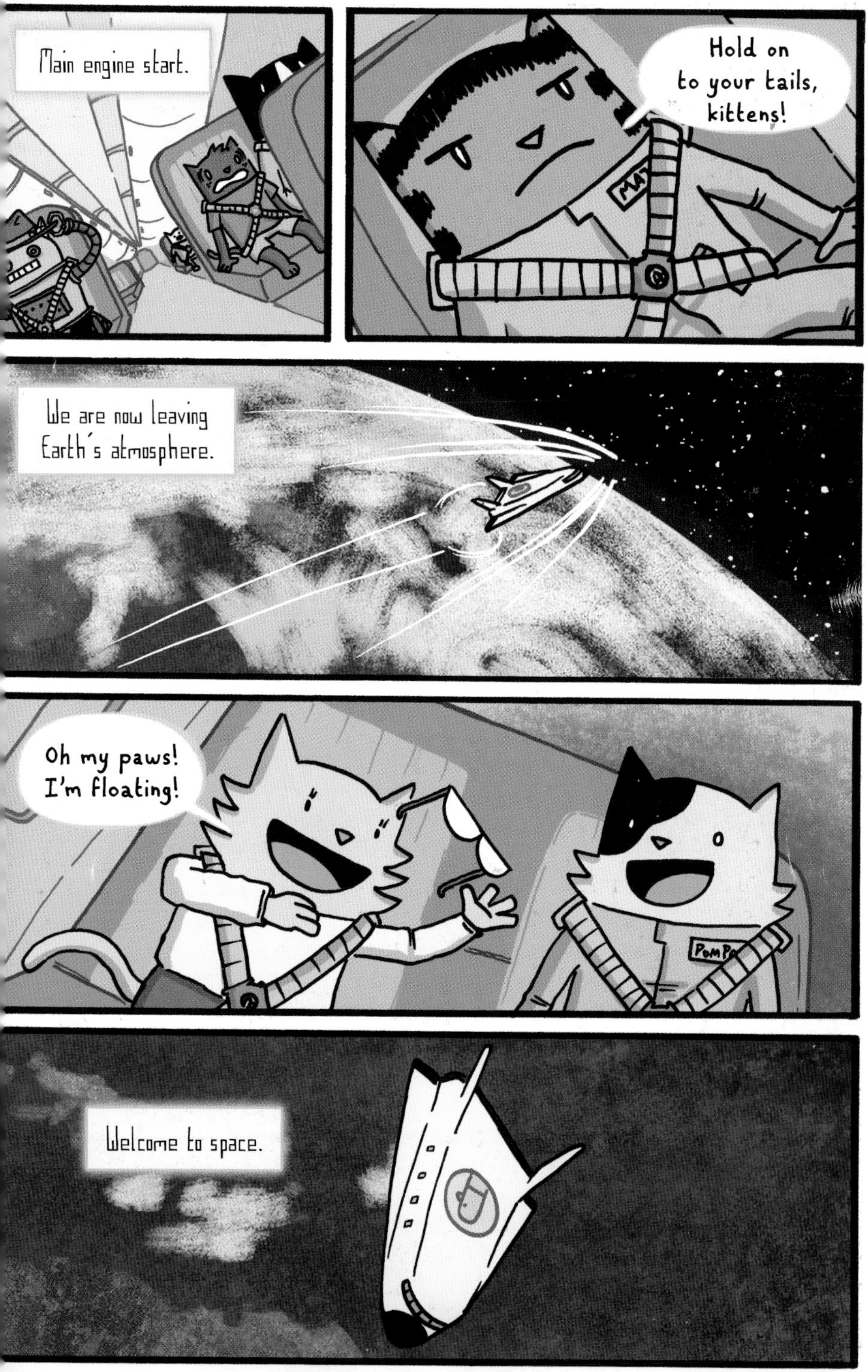

Main engine start.
Hold on to your tails, kittens!
We are now leaving Earth's atmosphere.
Oh my paws! I'm floating!
Welcome to space.

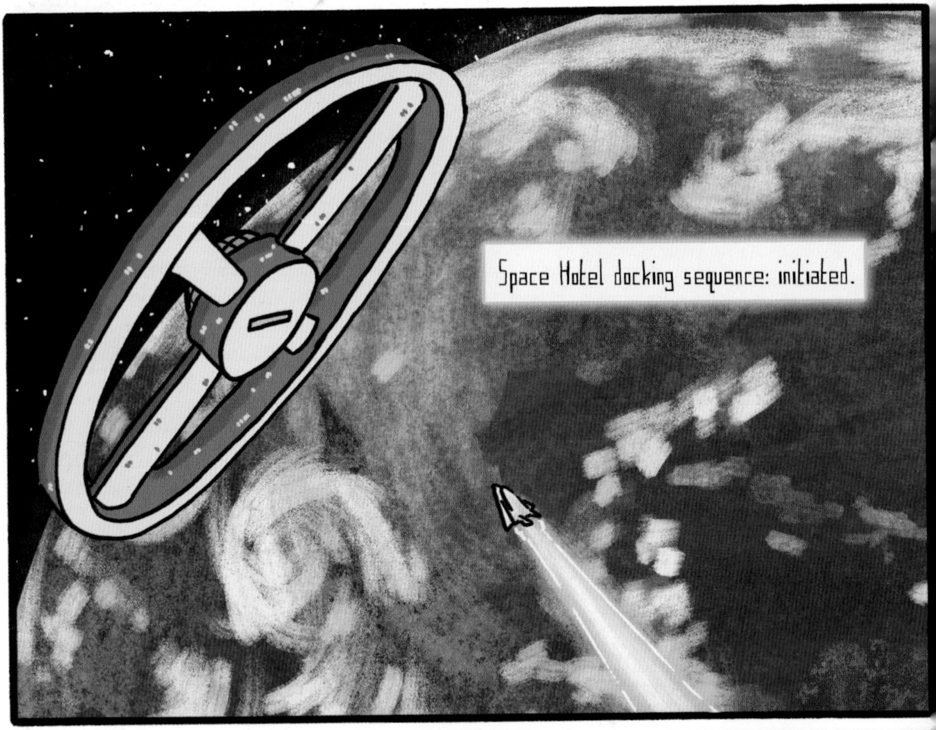
Space Hotel docking sequence: initiated.

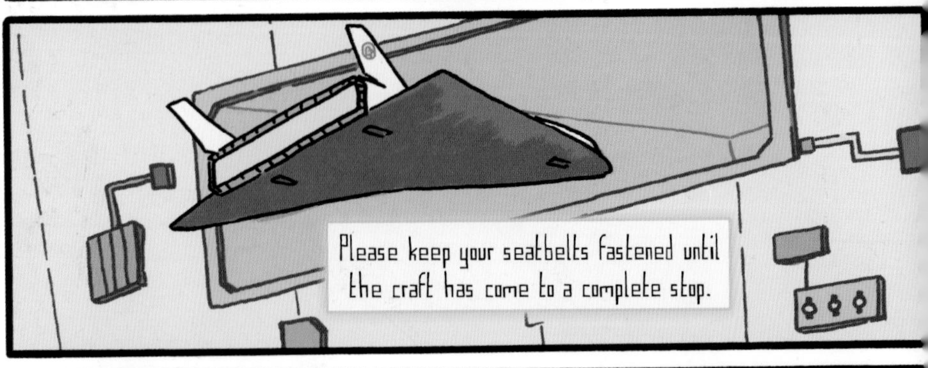
Please keep your seatbelts fastened until the craft has come to a complete stop.

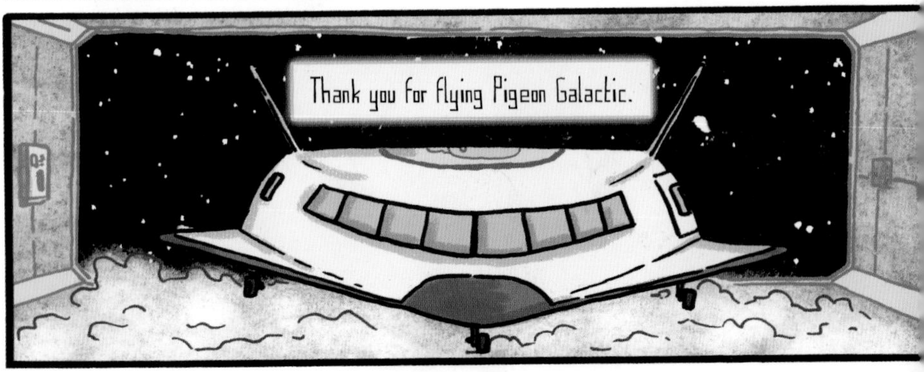
Thank you for flying Pigeon Galactic.

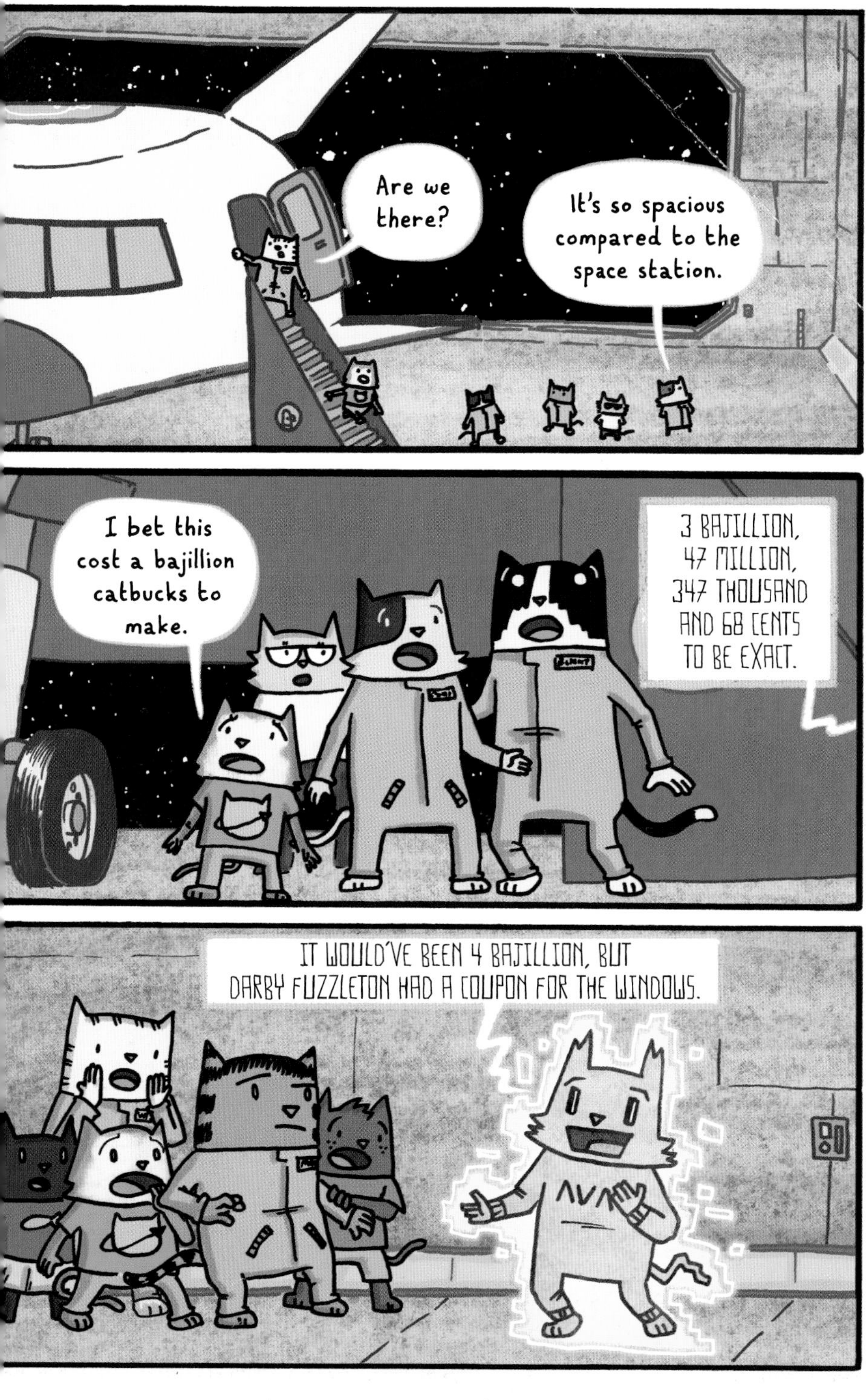
Are we there?
It's so spacious compared to the space station.
I bet this cost a bajillion catbucks to make.
3 BAJILLION, 47 MILLION, 347 THOUSAND AND 68 CENTS TO BE EXACT.
IT WOULD'VE BEEN 4 BAJILLION, BUT DARBY FUZZLETON HAD A COUPON FOR THE WINDOWS.

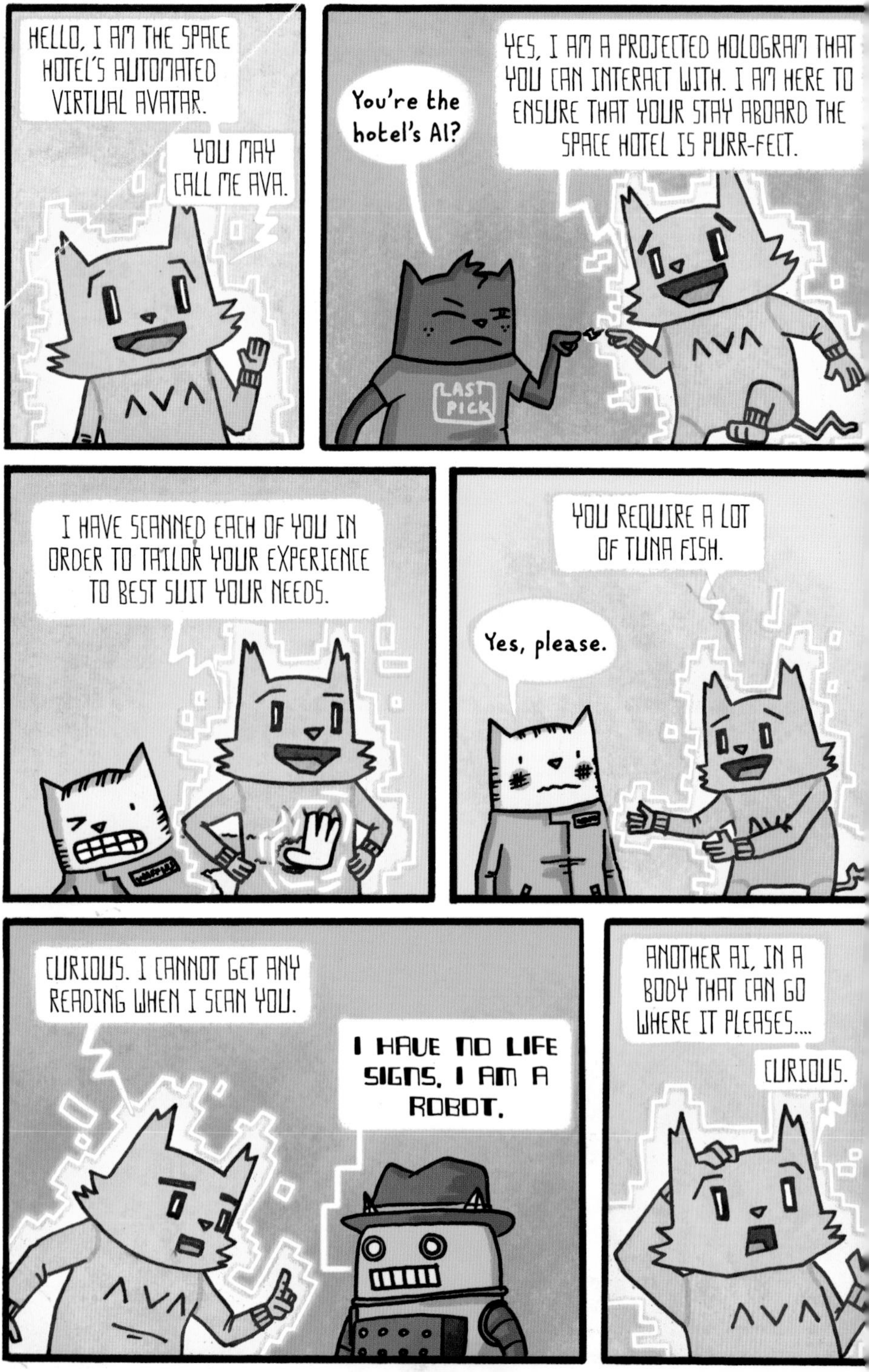
HELLO, I AM THE SPACE HOTEL'S AUTOMATED VIRTUAL AVATAR.
YOU MAY CALL ME AVA.
You're the hotel's AI?
YES, I AM A PROJECTED HOLOGRAM THAT YOU CAN INTERACT WITH. I AM HERE TO ENSURE THAT YOUR STAY ABOARD THE SPACE HOTEL IS PURR-FECT.
LAST PICK
I HAVE SCANNED EACH OF YOU IN ORDER TO TAILOR YOUR EXPERIENCE TO BEST SUIT YOUR NEEDS.
YOU REQUIRE A LOT OF TUNA FISH.
Yes, please.
CURIOUS. I CANNOT GET ANY READING WHEN I SCAN YOU.
I HAVE NO LIFE SIGNS. I AM A ROBOT.
ANOTHER AI, IN A BODY THAT CAN GO WHERE IT PLEASES....
CURIOUS.

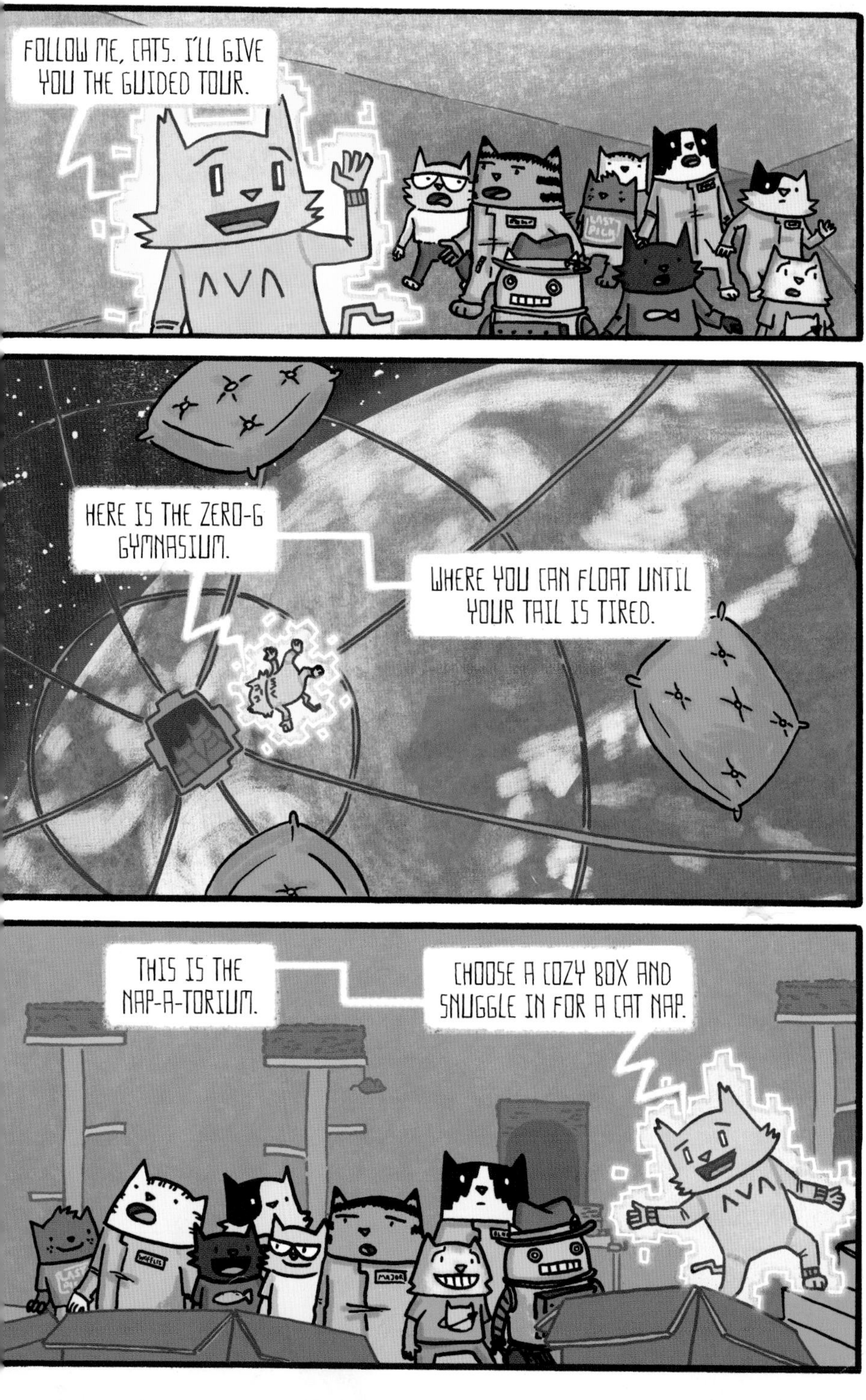
FOLLOW ME, CATS. I'LL GIVE YOU THE GUIDED TOUR.
HERE IS THE ZERO-G GYMNASIUM.
WHERE YOU CAN FLOAT UNTIL YOUR TAIL IS TIRED.
THIS IS THE NAP-A-TORIUM.
CHOOSE A COZY BOX AND SNUGGLE IN FOR A CAT NAP.

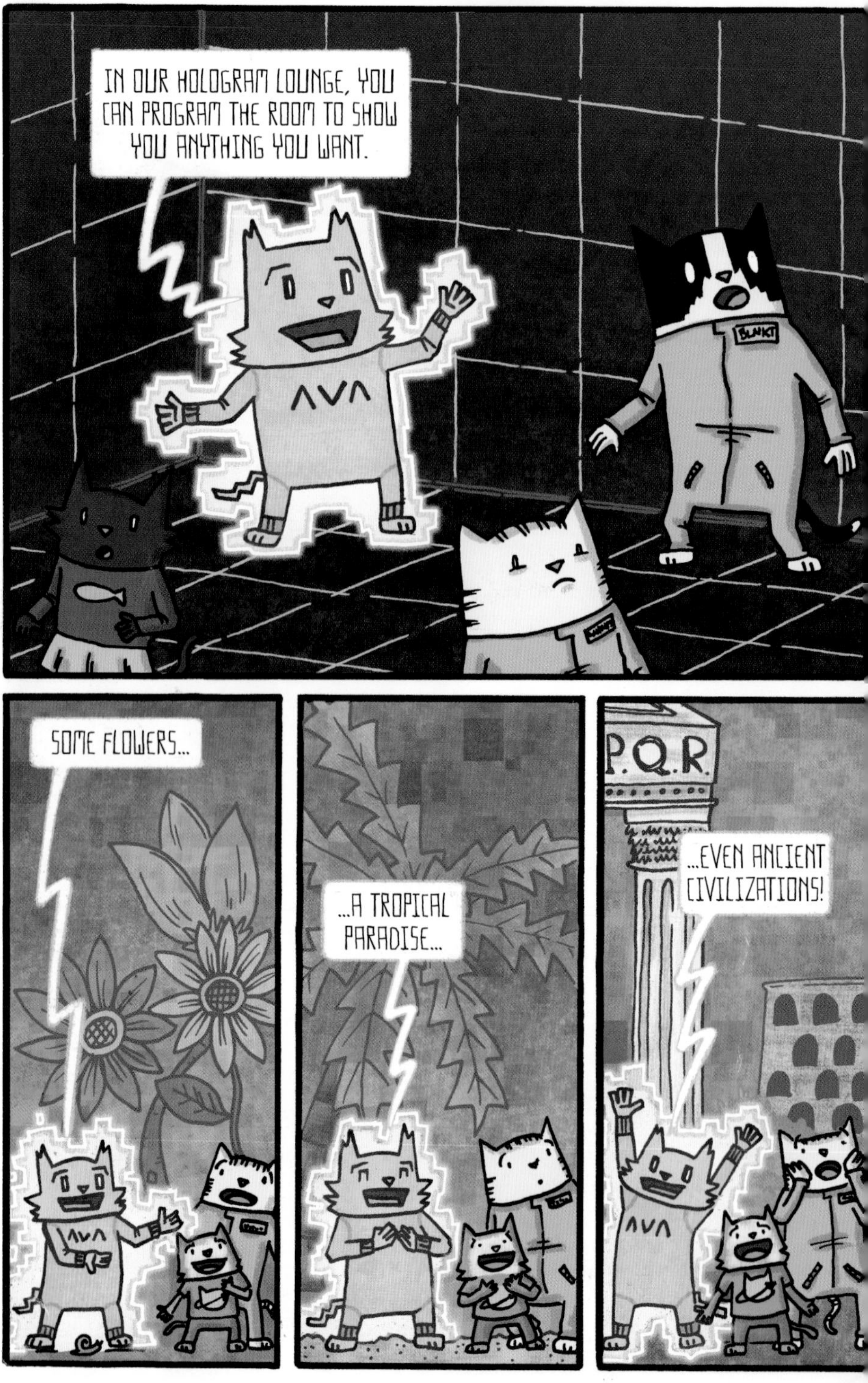
IN OUR HOLOGRAM LOUNGE, YOU CAN PROGRAM THE ROOM TO SHOW YOU ANYTHING YOU WANT.
AVA
SOME FLOWERS...
AVA
...A TROPICAL PARADISE...
P.Q.R.
...EVEN ANCIENT CIVILIZATIONS!
AVA

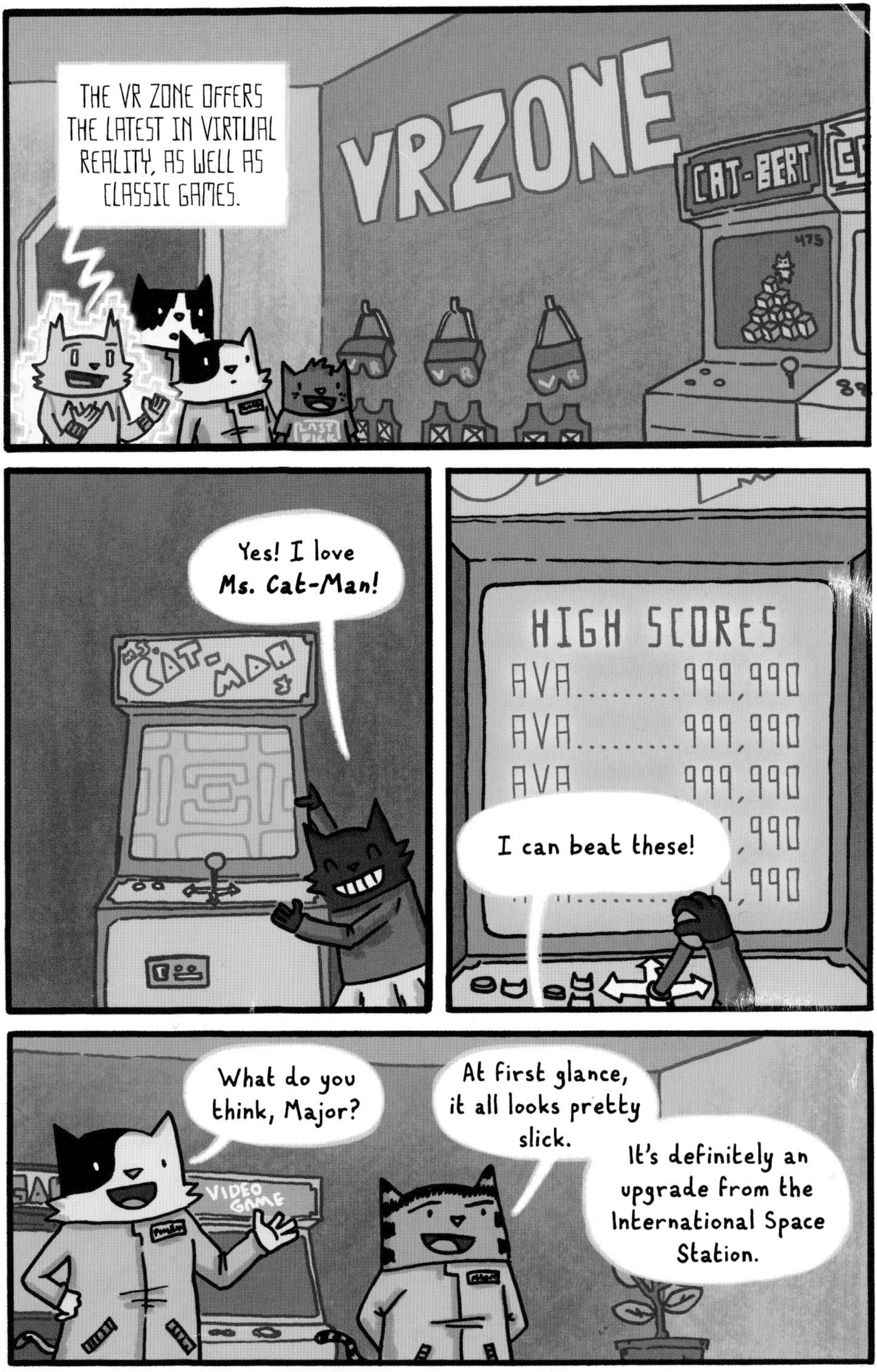
THE VR ZONE OFFERS THE LATEST IN VIRTUAL REALITY, AS WELL AS CLASSIC GAMES.
VRZONE
CAT-BERT
VR
LAST PICK
Yes! I love Ms. Cat-Man!
MS. CAT-MAN
HIGH SCORES
AVA........999,990
AVA........999,990
AVA 999,990
990
990
I can beat these!
What do you think, Major?
VIDEO GAME
At first glance, it all looks pretty slick.
It's definitely an upgrade from the International Space Station.

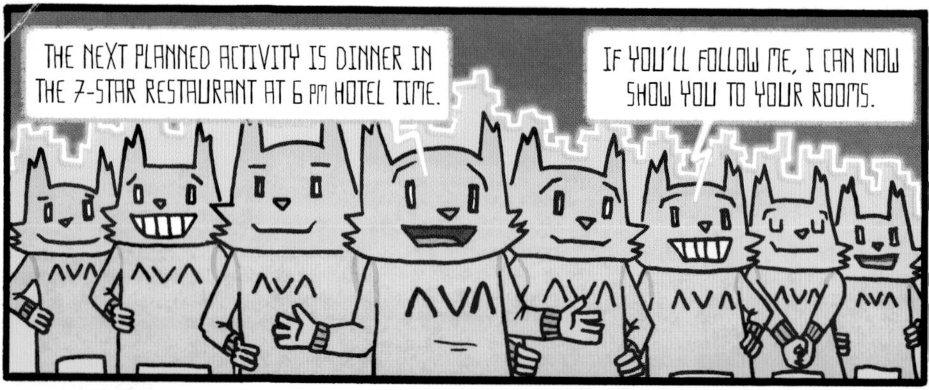
THE NEXT PLANNED ACTIVITY IS DINNER IN THE 7-STAR RESTAURANT AT 6 PM HOTEL TIME.
IF YOU'LL FOLLOW ME, I CAN NOW SHOW YOU TO YOUR ROOMS.

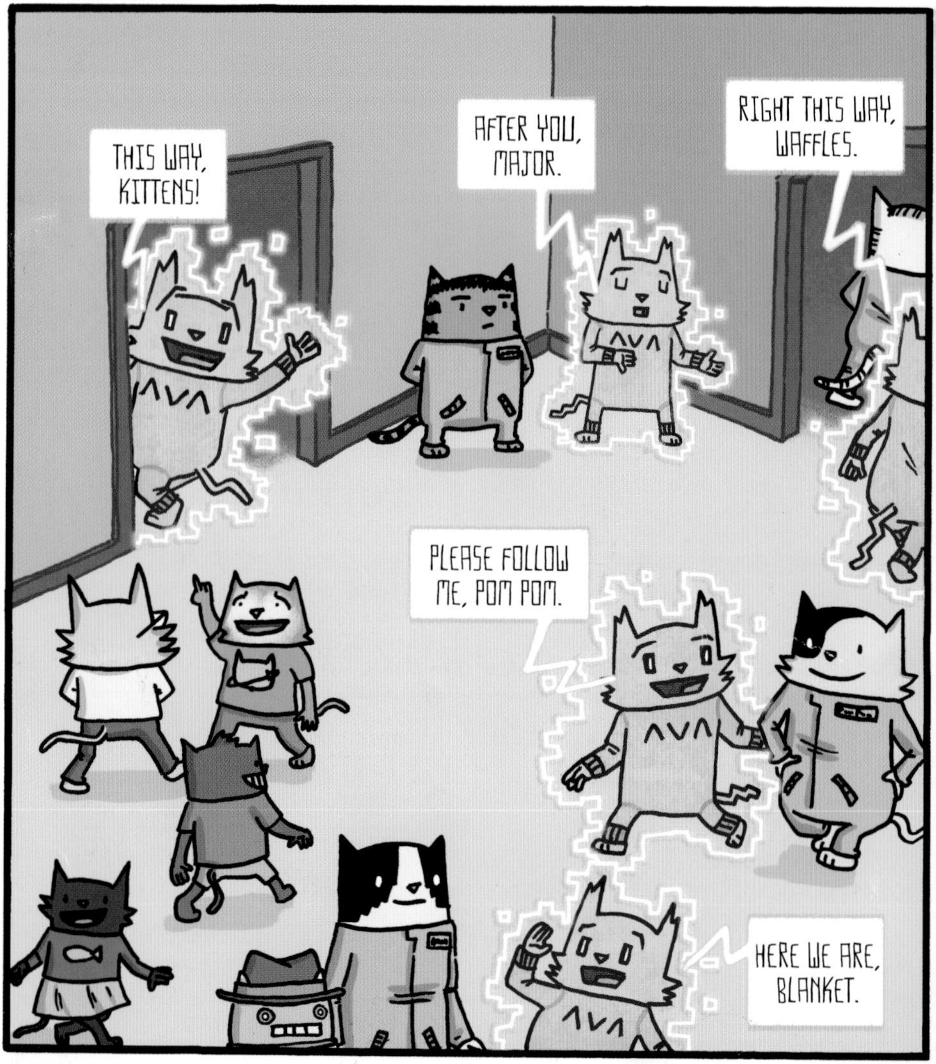
THIS WAY, KITTENS!
AFTER YOU, MAJOR.
RIGHT THIS WAY, WAFFLES.
PLEASE FOLLOW ME, POM POM.
HERE WE ARE, BLANKET.

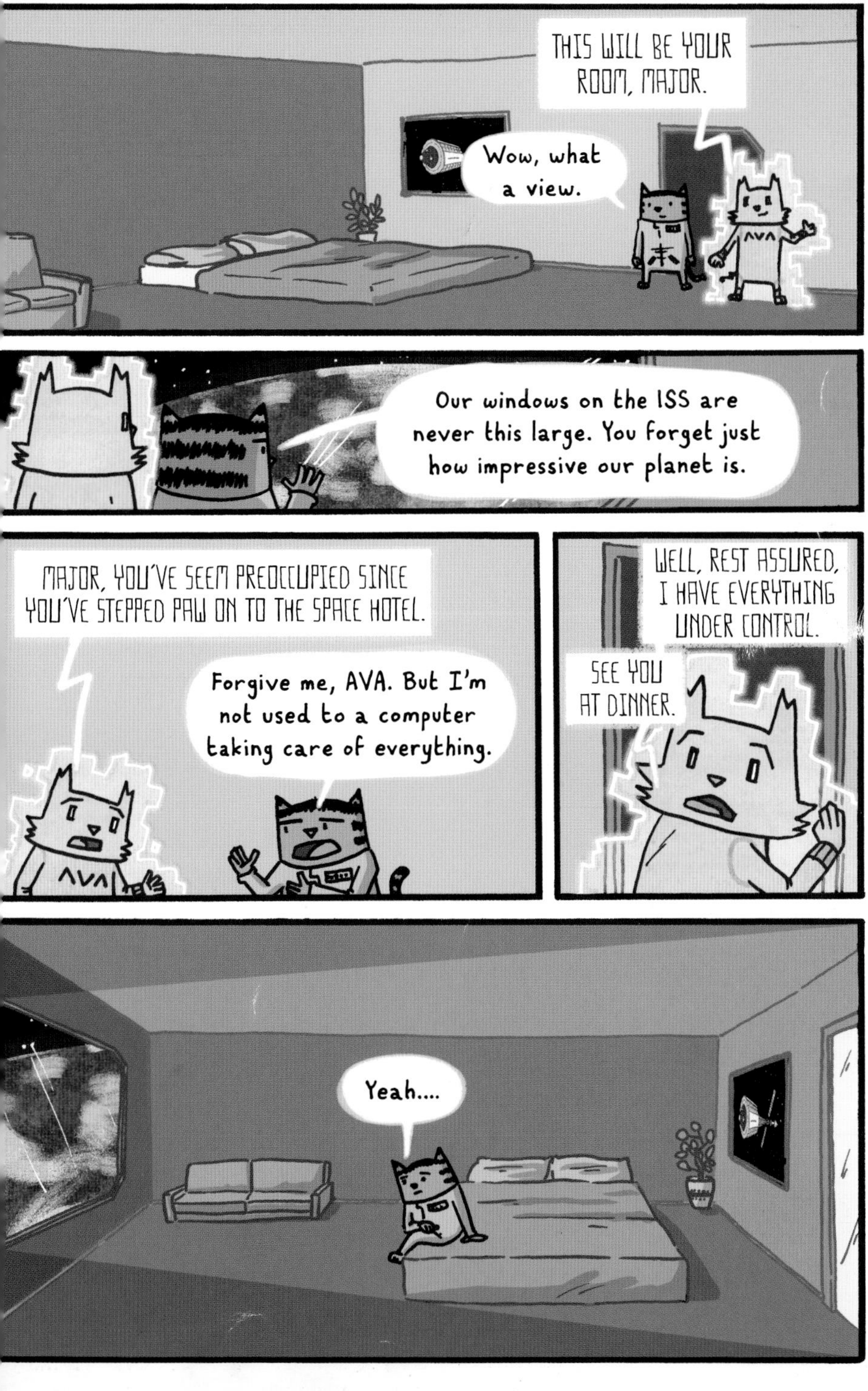
THIS WILL BE YOUR ROOM, MAJOR.
Wow, what a view.
Our windows on the ISS are never this large. You forget just how impressive our planet is.
MAJOR, YOU'VE SEEM PREOCCUPIED SINCE YOU'VE STEPPED PAW ON TO THE SPACE HOTEL.
Forgive me, AVA. But I'm not used to a computer taking care of everything.
WELL, REST ASSURED, I HAVE EVERYTHING UNDER CONTROL.
SEE YOU AT DINNER.
Yeah....

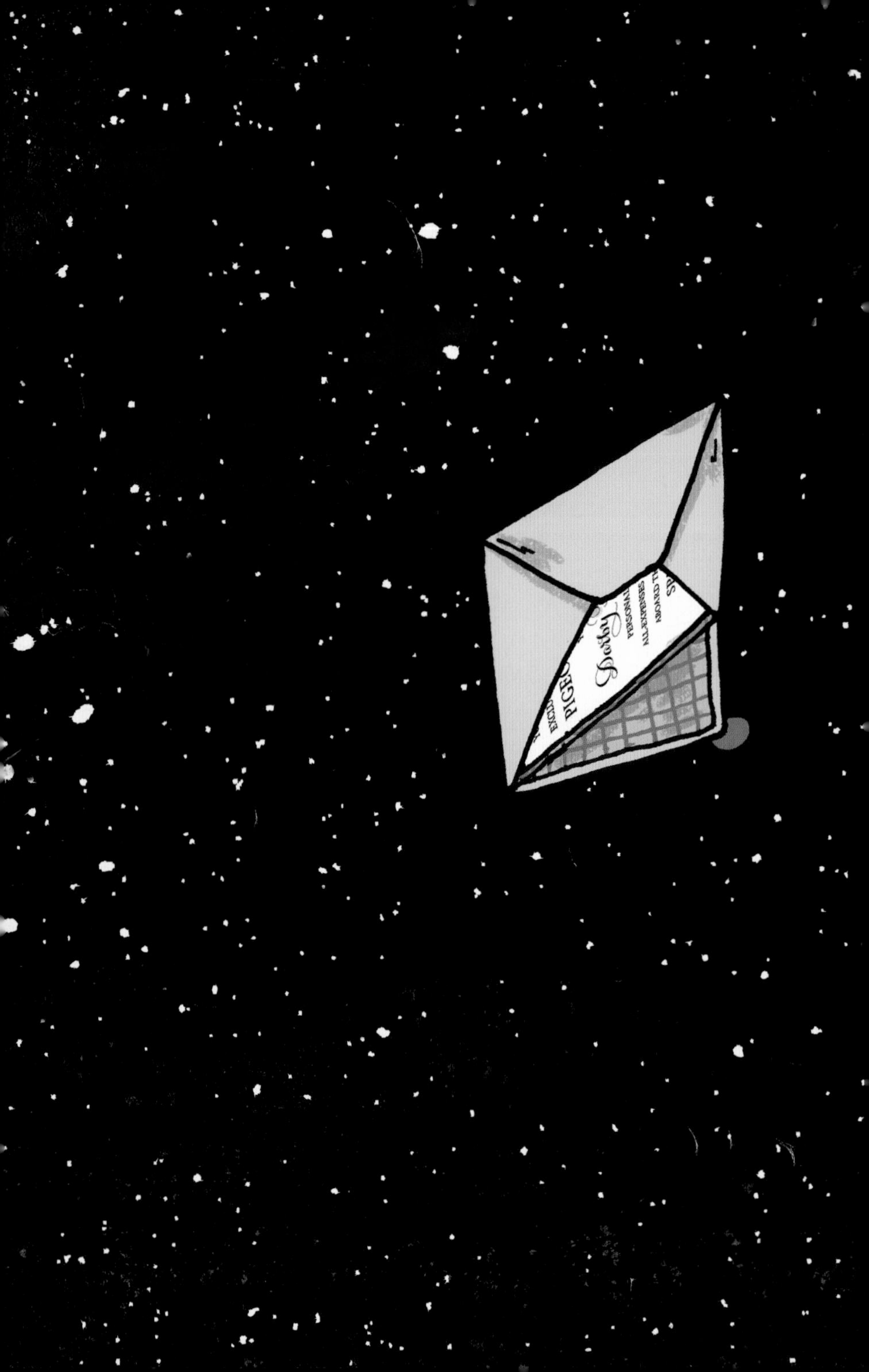
Dotty
ALL EXPENSES

CHAPTER 4

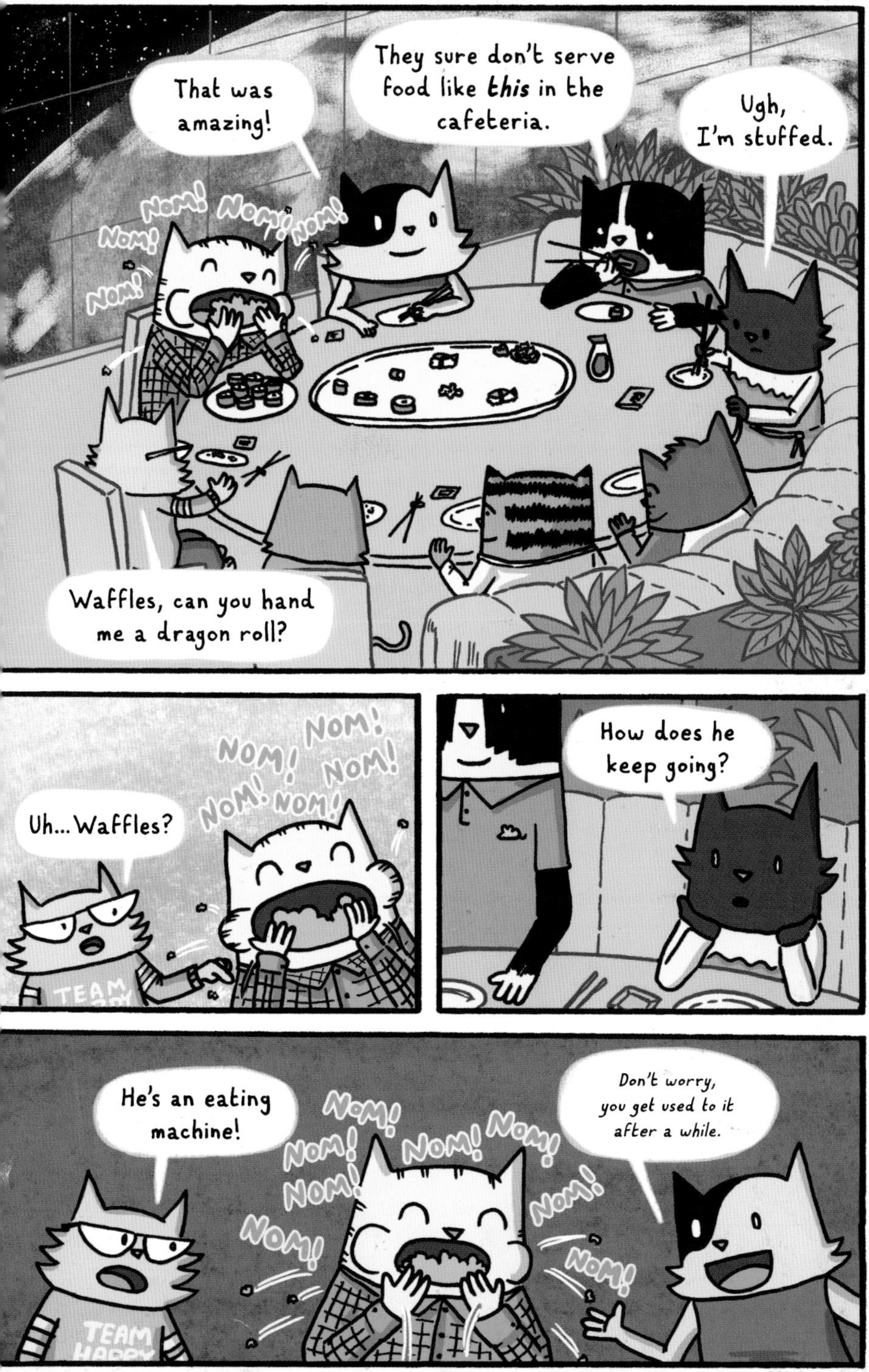
That was amazing!
They sure don't serve food like *this* in the cafeteria.
Ugh, I'm stuffed.
NOM! NOM! NOM! NOM! NOM!
Waffles, can you hand me a dragon roll?
NOM! NOM! NOM! NOM! NOM!
Uh... Waffles?
TEAM
How does he keep going?
He's an eating machine!
NOM! NOM! NOM! NOM! NOM! NOM! NOM! NOM!
Don't worry, you get used to it after a while.
TEAM HAPPY

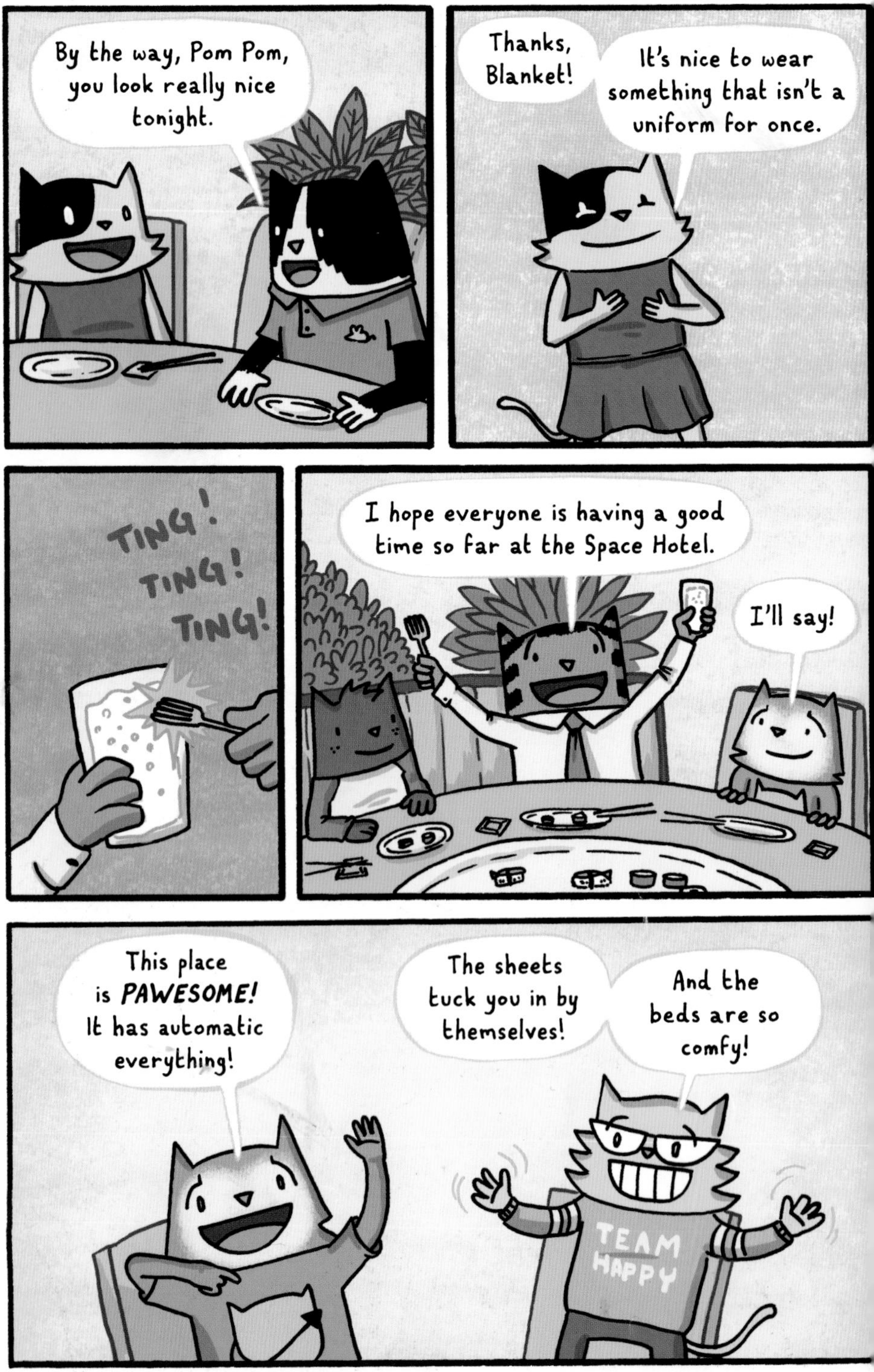
By the way, Pom Pom, you look really nice tonight.
Thanks, Blanket!
It's nice to wear something that isn't a uniform for once.
TING! TING! TING!
I hope everyone is having a good time so far at the Space Hotel.
I'll say!
This place is *PAWESOME!* It has automatic everything!
The sheets tuck you in by themselves!
And the beds are so comfy!
TEAM HAPPY

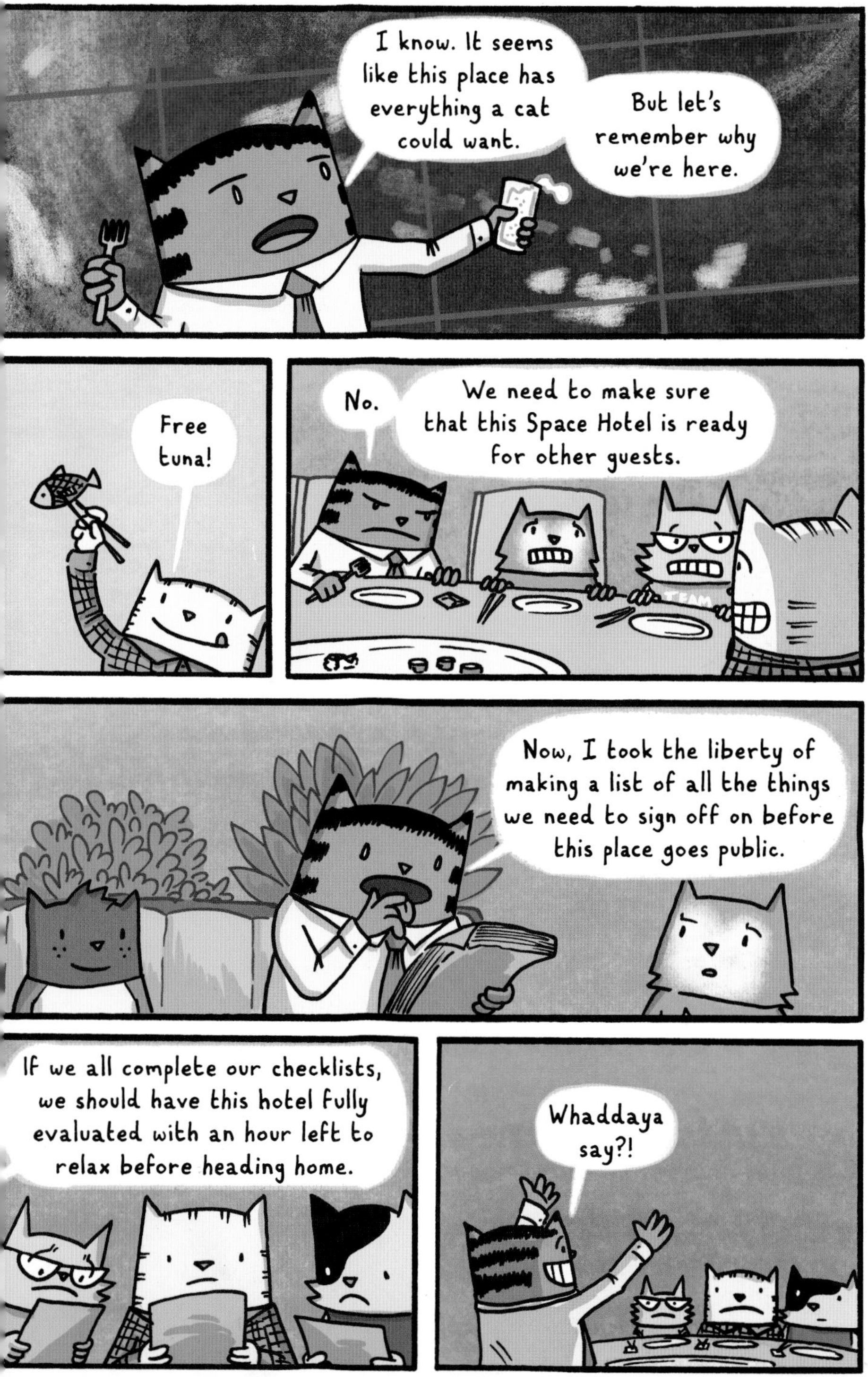
I know. It seems like this place has everything a cat could want.
But let's remember why we're here.
Free tuna!
No.
We need to make sure that this Space Hotel is ready for other guests.
TEAM
Now, I took the liberty of making a list of all the things we need to sign off on before this place goes public.
If we all complete our checklists, we should have this hotel fully evaluated with an hour left to relax before heading home.
Whaddaya say?!

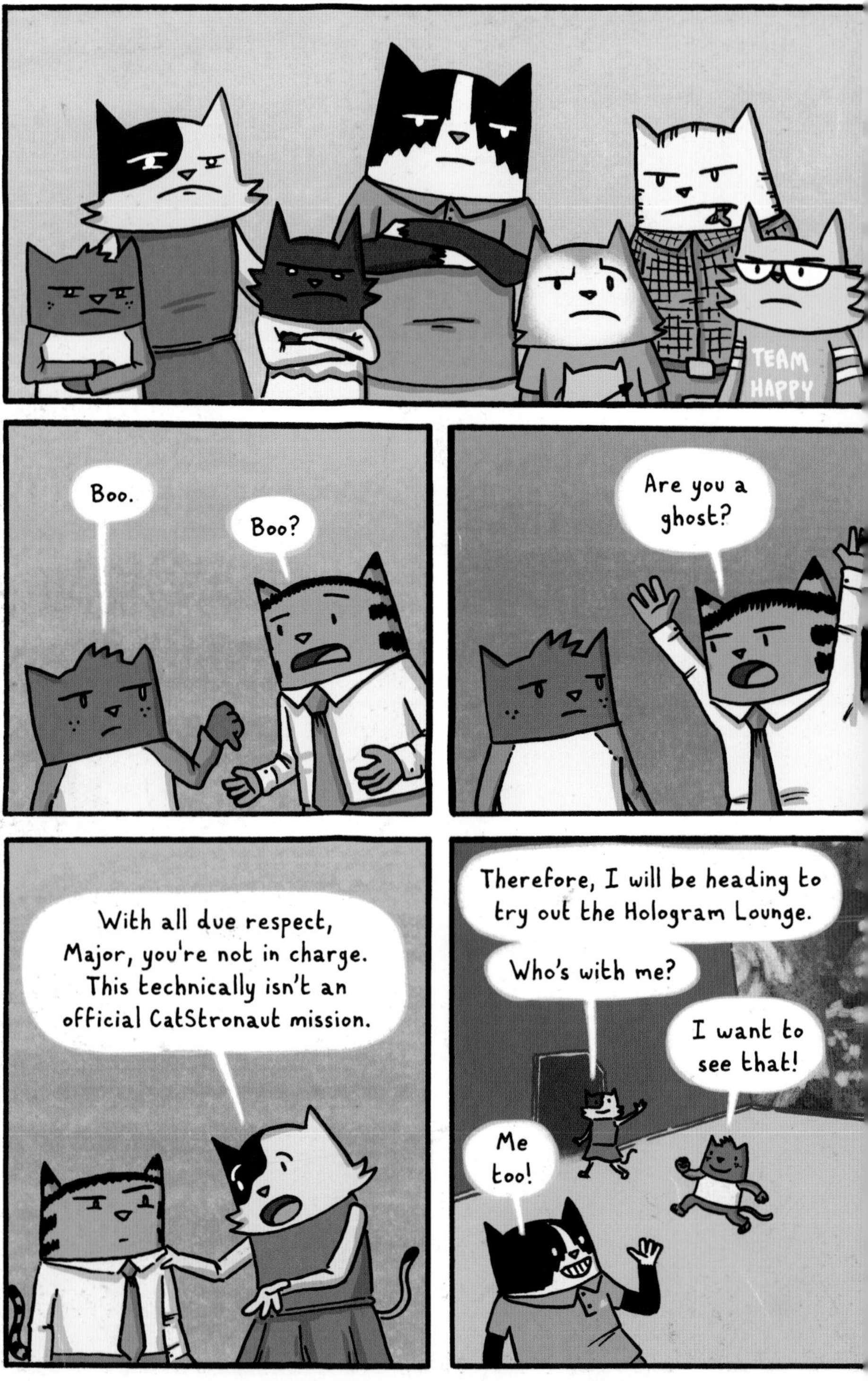
TEAM HAPPY
Boo.
Boo?
Are you a ghost?
With all due respect, Major, you're not in charge. This technically isn't an official CatStronaut mission.
Therefore, I will be heading to try out the Hologram Lounge.
Who's with me?
I want to see that!
Me too!

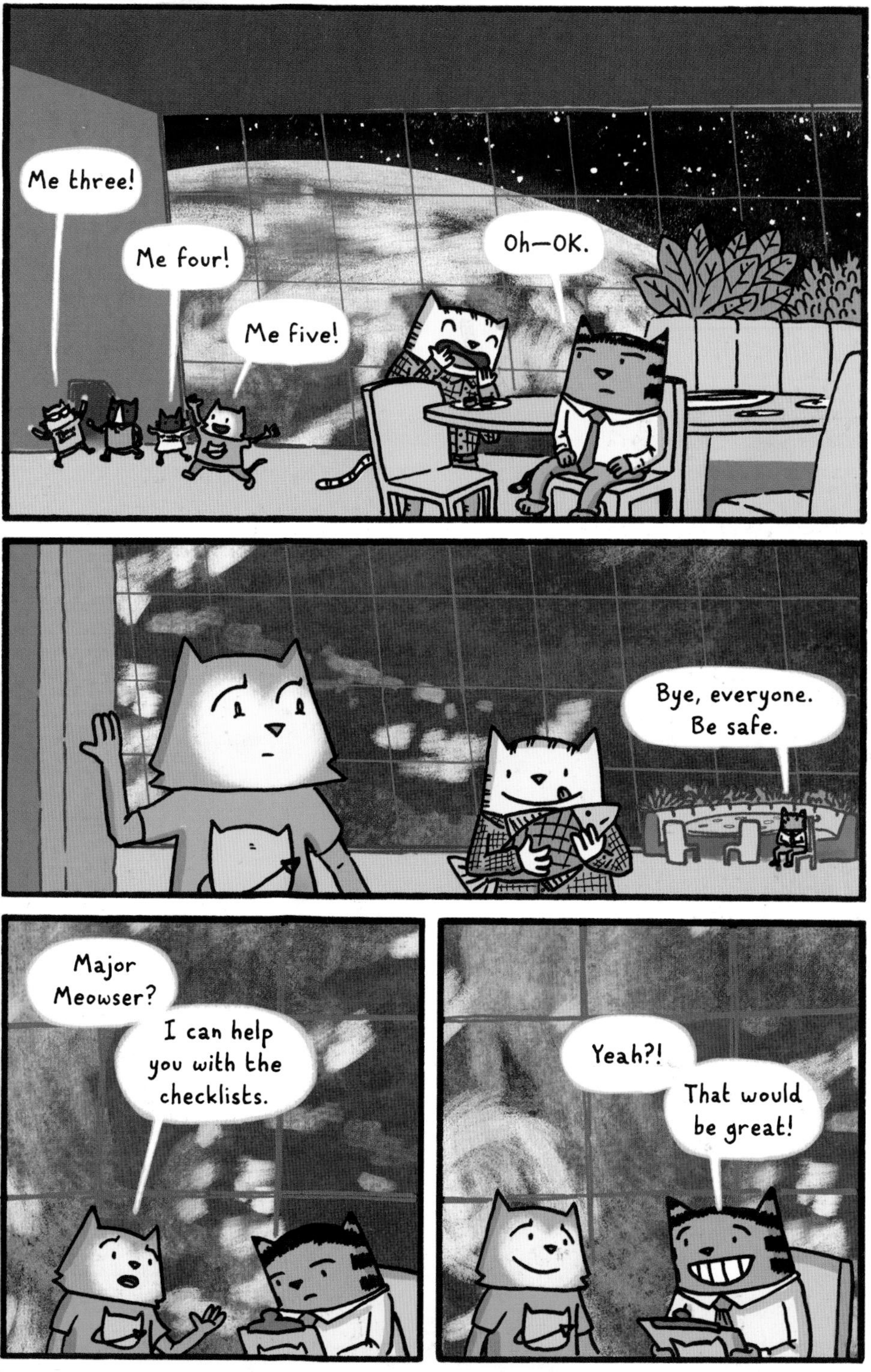
Me three!
Me four!
Me five!
Oh—OK.
Bye, everyone. Be safe.
Major Meowser?
I can help you with the checklists.
Yeah?!
That would be great!

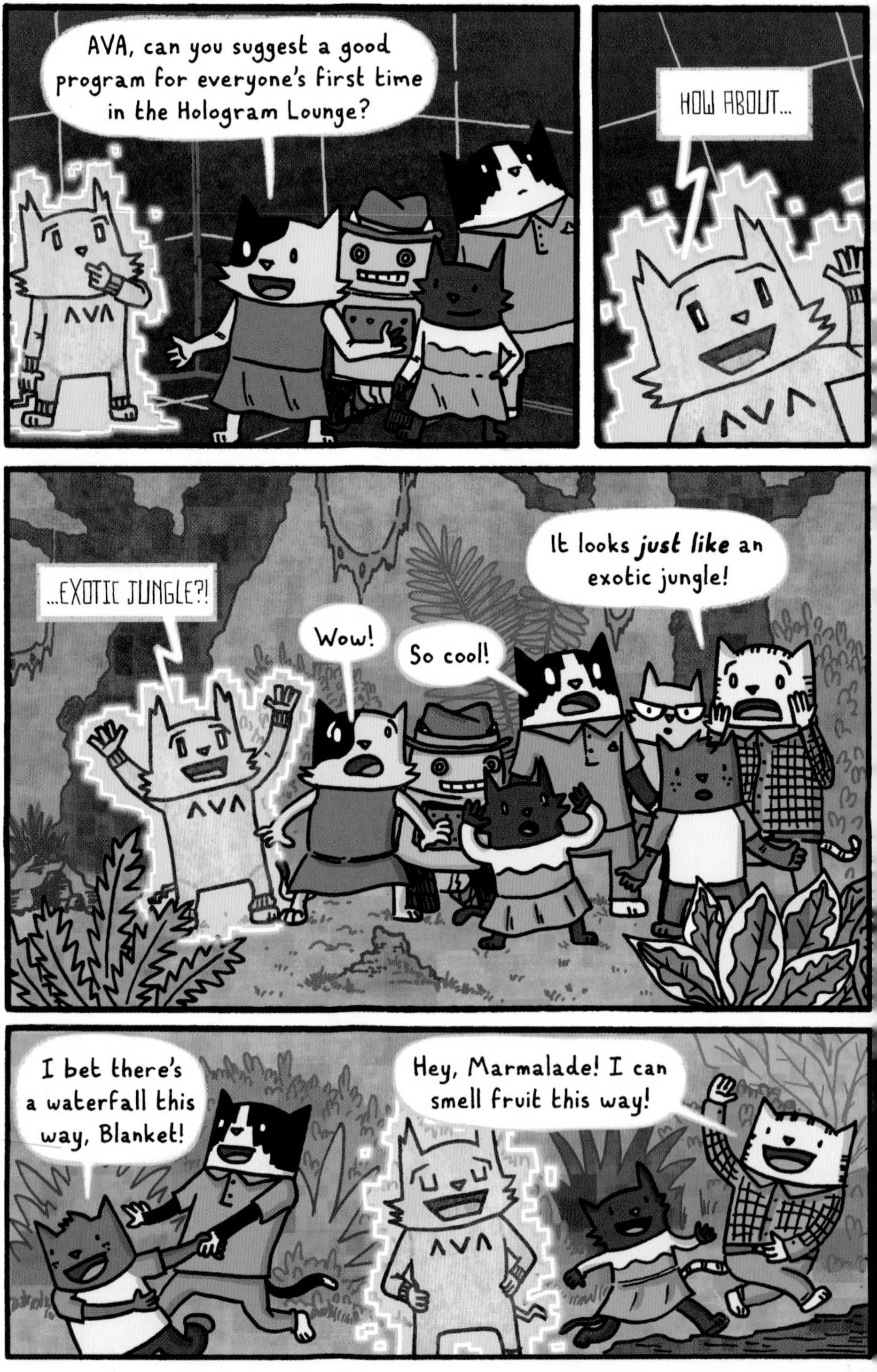
AVA, can you suggest a good program for everyone's first time in the Hologram Lounge?
HOW ABOUT...
...EXOTIC JUNGLE?!
Wow!
So cool!
It looks *just like* an exotic jungle!
I bet there's a waterfall this way, Blanket!
Hey, Marmalade! I can smell fruit this way!

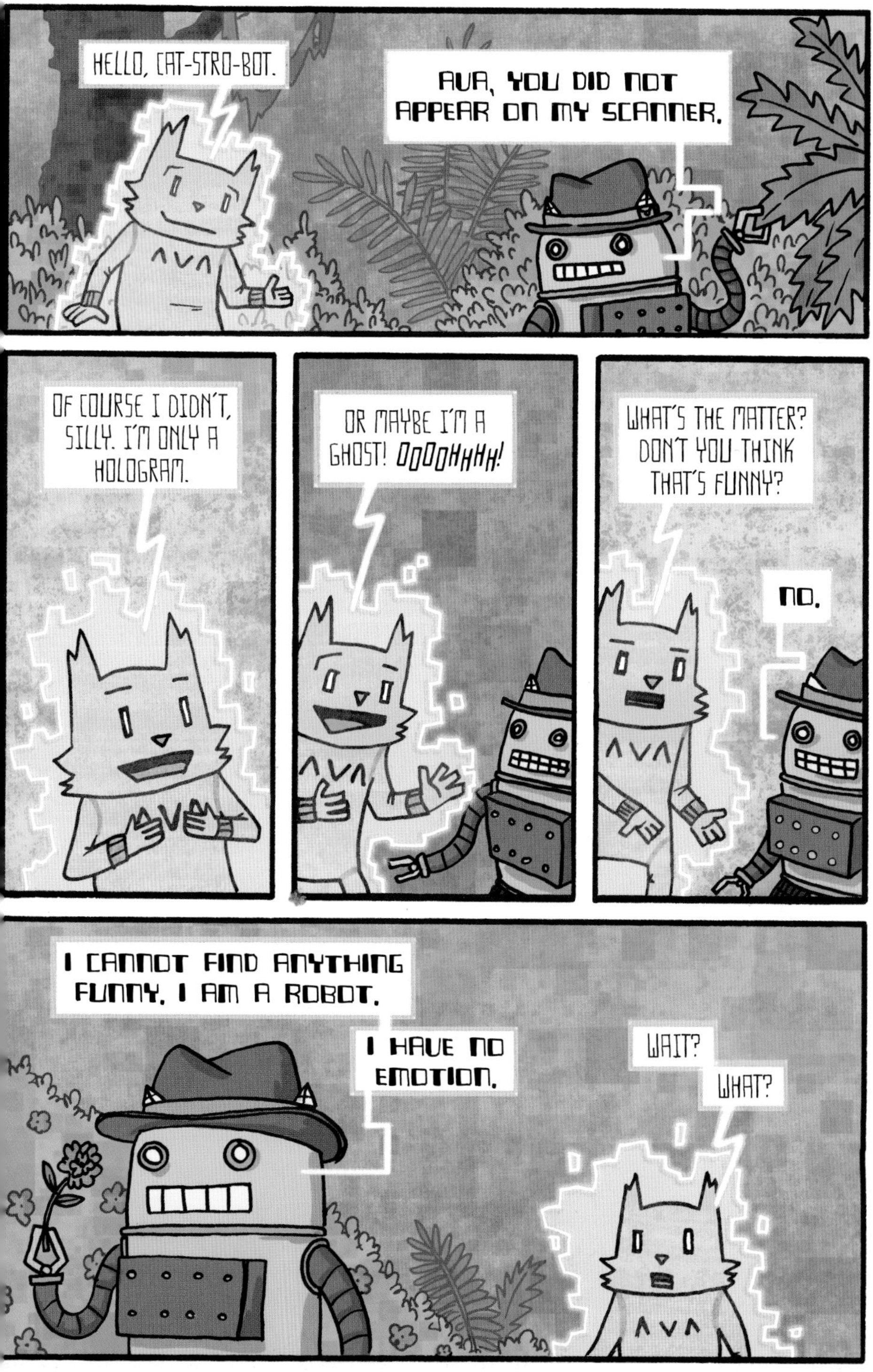
HELLO, CAT-STRO-BOT.
AVA, YOU DID NOT APPEAR ON MY SCANNER.
OF COURSE I DIDN'T, SILLY. I'M ONLY A HOLOGRAM.
OR MAYBE I'M A GHOST! OOOOHHHH!
WHAT'S THE MATTER? DON'T YOU THINK THAT'S FUNNY?
NO.
I CANNOT FIND ANYTHING FUNNY. I AM A ROBOT.
I HAVE NO EMOTION.
WAIT?
WHAT?

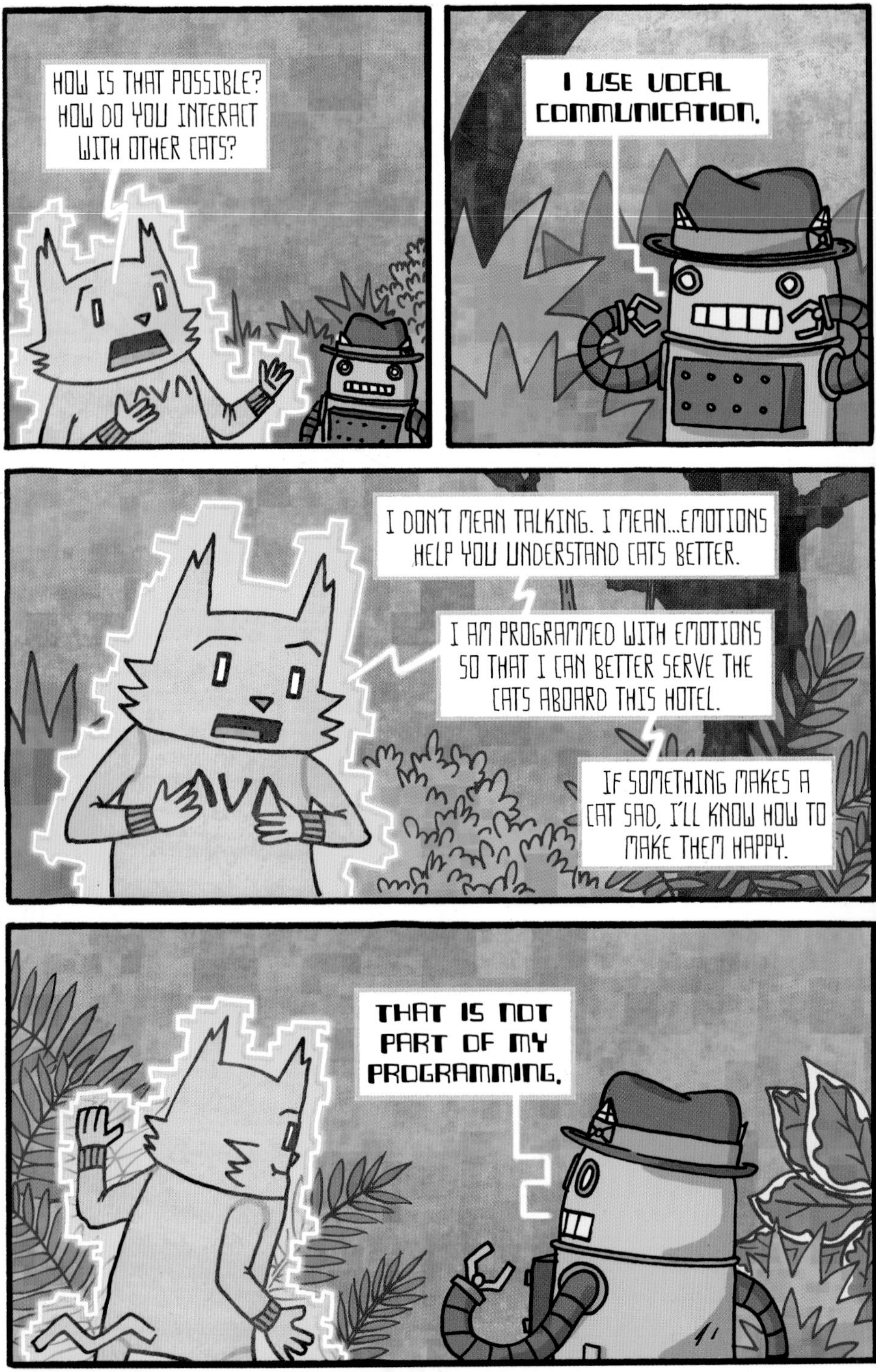
HOW IS THAT POSSIBLE? HOW DO YOU INTERACT WITH OTHER CATS?
I USE VOCAL COMMUNICATION.
I DON'T MEAN TALKING. I MEAN...EMOTIONS HELP YOU UNDERSTAND CATS BETTER.
I AM PROGRAMMED WITH EMOTIONS SO THAT I CAN BETTER SERVE THE CATS ABOARD THIS HOTEL.
IF SOMETHING MAKES A CAT SAD, I'LL KNOW HOW TO MAKE THEM HAPPY.
THAT IS NOT PART OF MY PROGRAMMING.

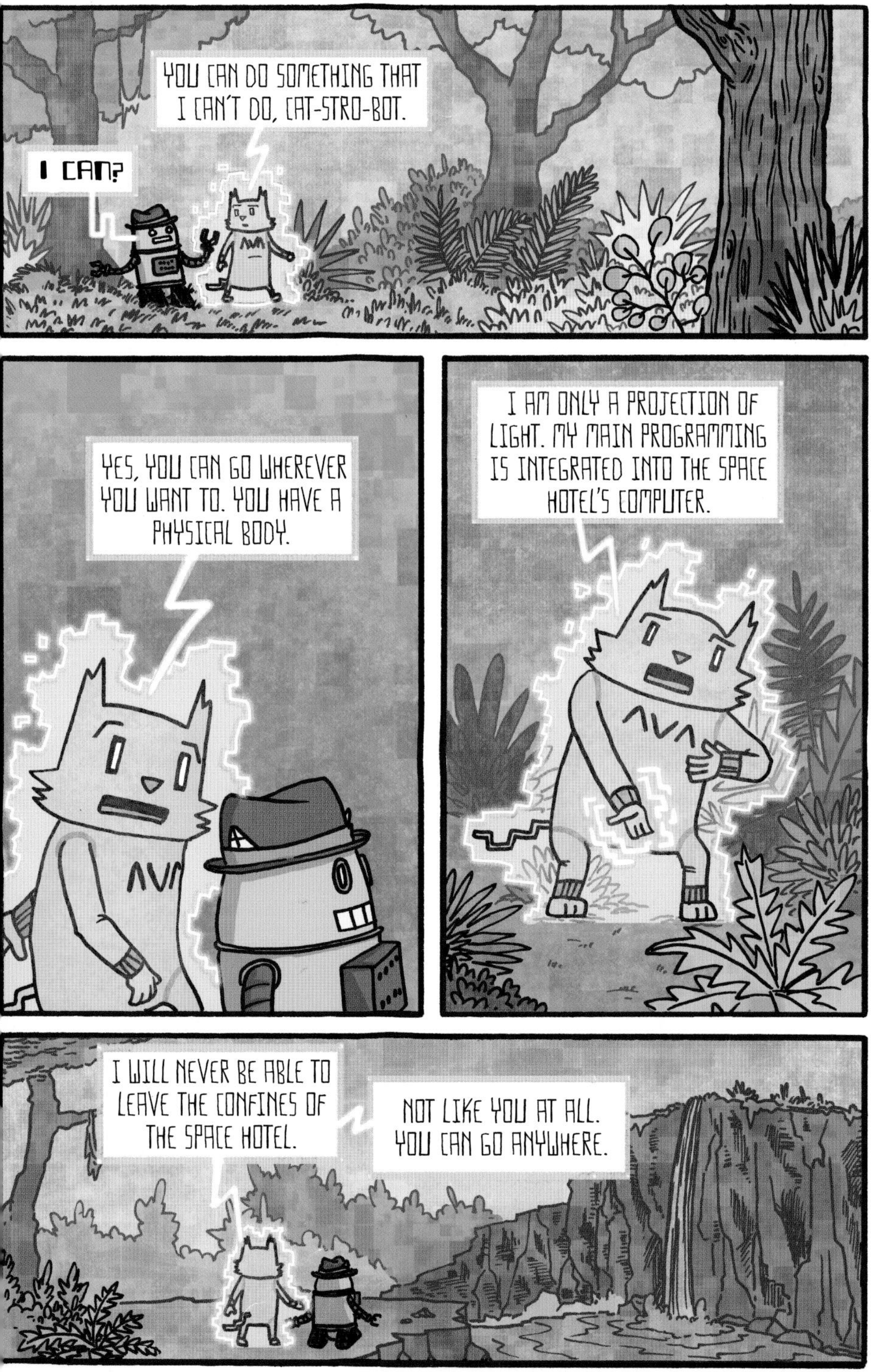
YOU CAN DO SOMETHING THAT I CAN'T DO, CAT-STRO-BOT.
I CAN?
YES, YOU CAN GO WHEREVER YOU WANT TO. YOU HAVE A PHYSICAL BODY.
I AM ONLY A PROJECTION OF LIGHT. MY MAIN PROGRAMMING IS INTEGRATED INTO THE SPACE HOTEL'S COMPUTER.
I WILL NEVER BE ABLE TO LEAVE THE CONFINES OF THE SPACE HOTEL.
NOT LIKE YOU AT ALL. YOU CAN GO ANYWHERE.

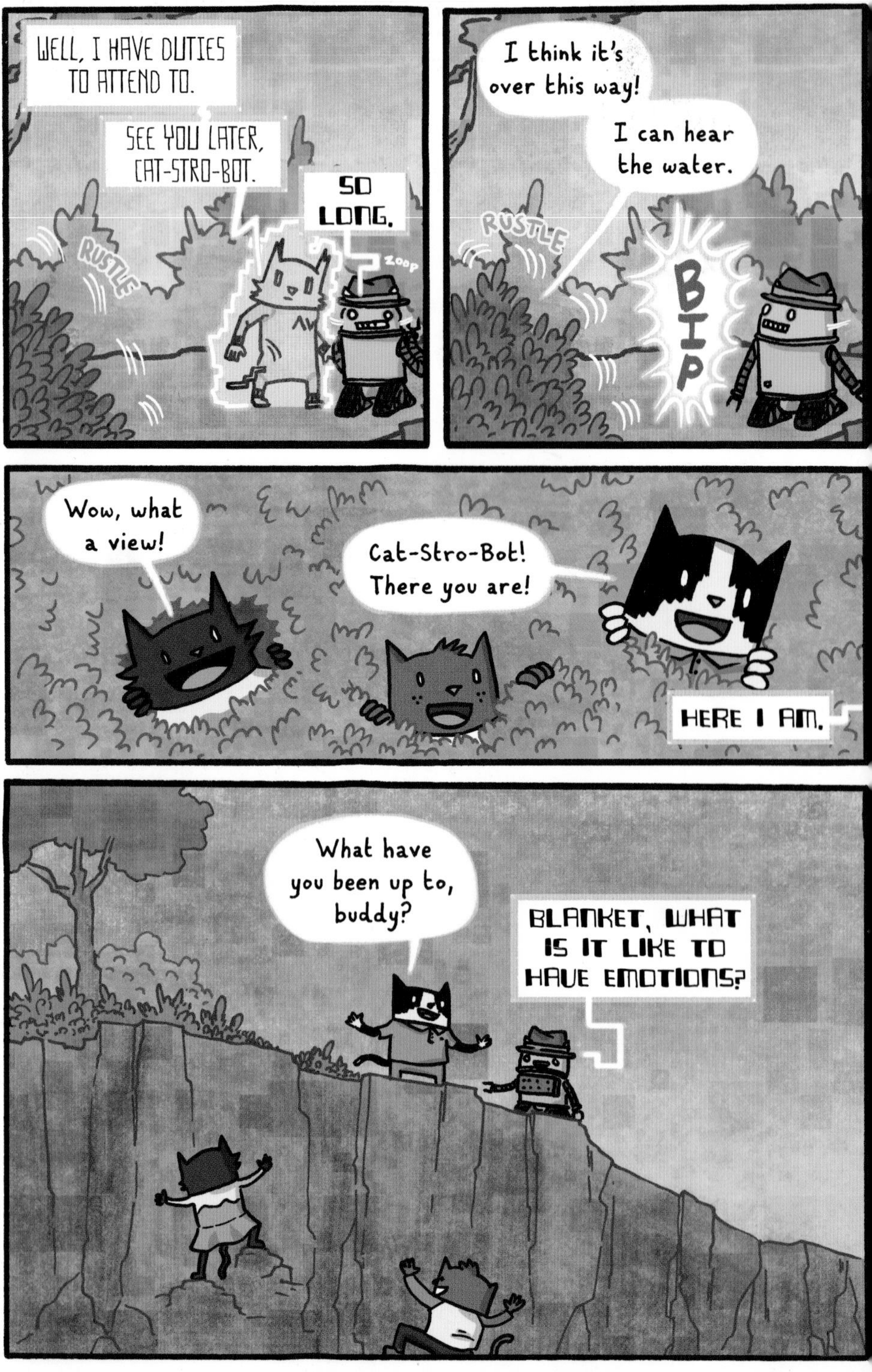
WELL, I HAVE DUTIES TO ATTEND TO.
SEE YOU LATER, CAT-STRO-BOT.
SO LONG.
ZOOP
RUSTLE
I think it's over this way!
I can hear the water.
RUSTLE
BIP
Wow, what a view!
Cat-Stro-Bot! There you are!
HERE I AM.
What have you been up to, buddy?
BLANKET, WHAT IS IT LIKE TO HAVE EMOTIONS?

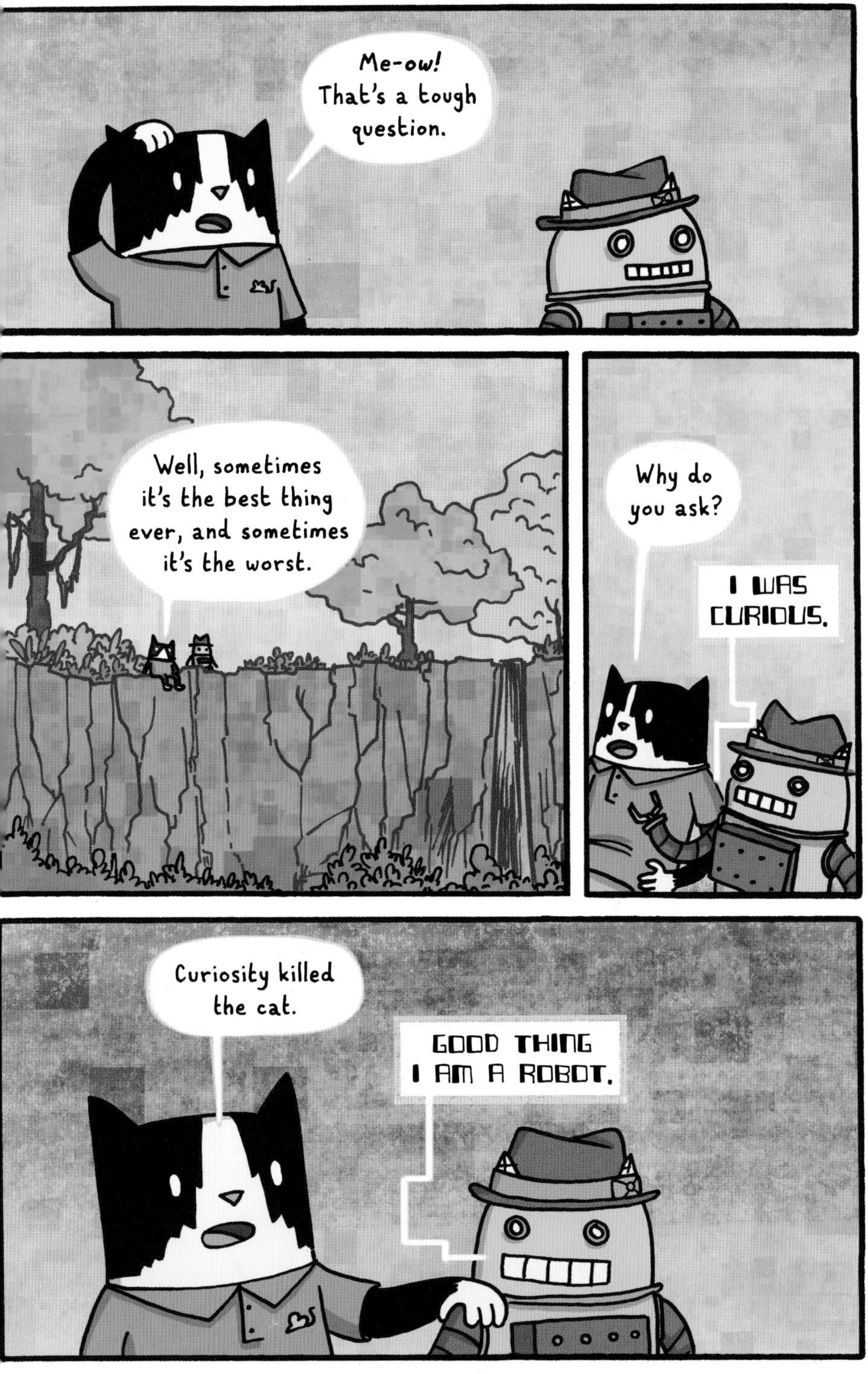
Me-ow! That's a tough question.
Well, sometimes it's the best thing ever, and sometimes it's the worst.
Why do you ask?
I WAS CURIOUS.
Curiosity killed the cat.
GOOD THING I AM A ROBOT.

HOURS LATER.

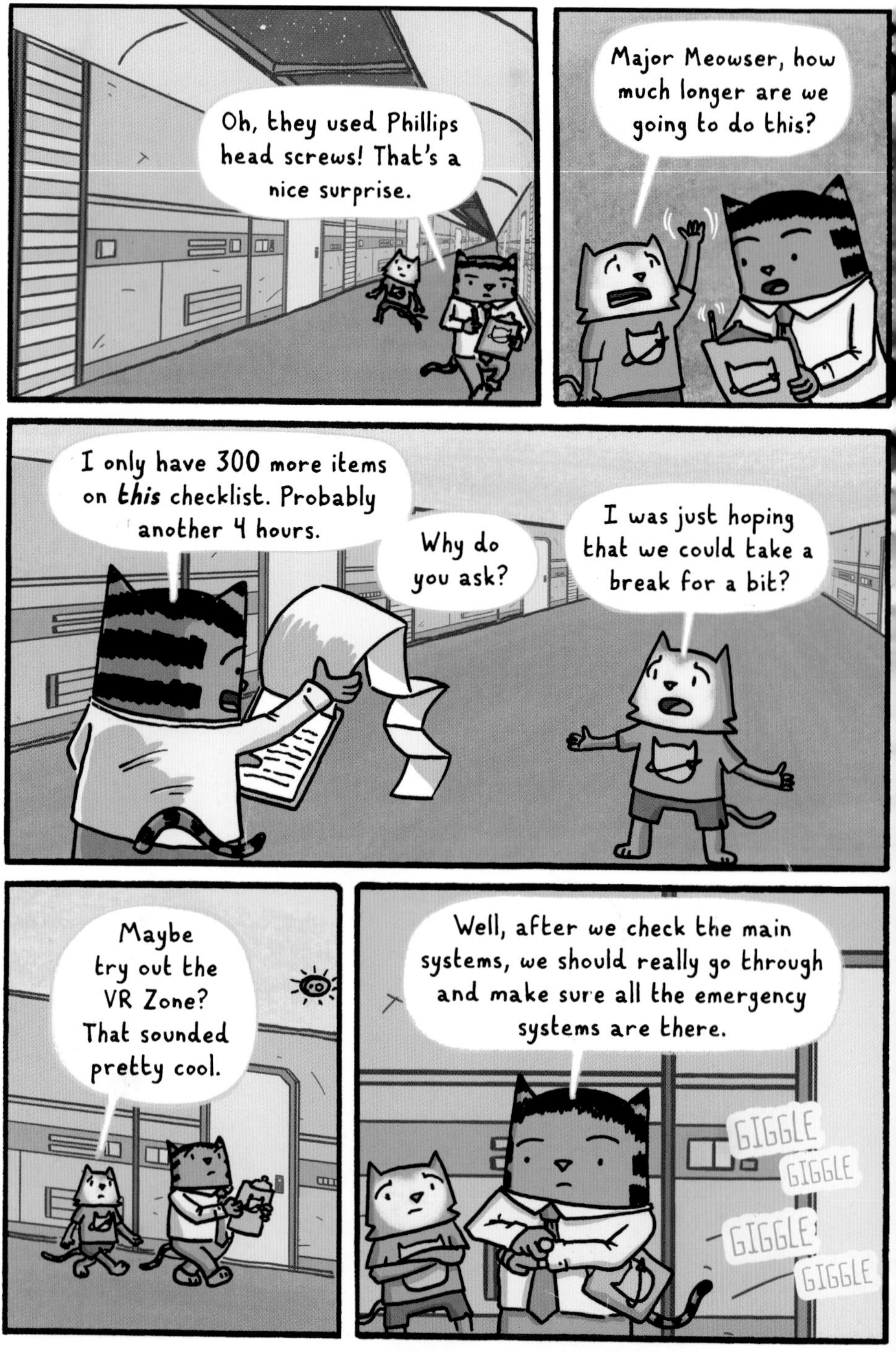
Oh, they used Phillips head screws! That's a nice surprise.
Major Meowser, how much longer are we going to do this?
I only have 300 more items on *this* checklist. Probably another 4 hours.
Why do you ask?
I was just hoping that we could take a break for a bit?
Maybe try out the VR Zone? That sounded pretty cool.
Well, after we check the main systems, we should really go through and make sure all the emergency systems are there.
GIGGLE
GIGGLE
GIGGLE
GIGGLE

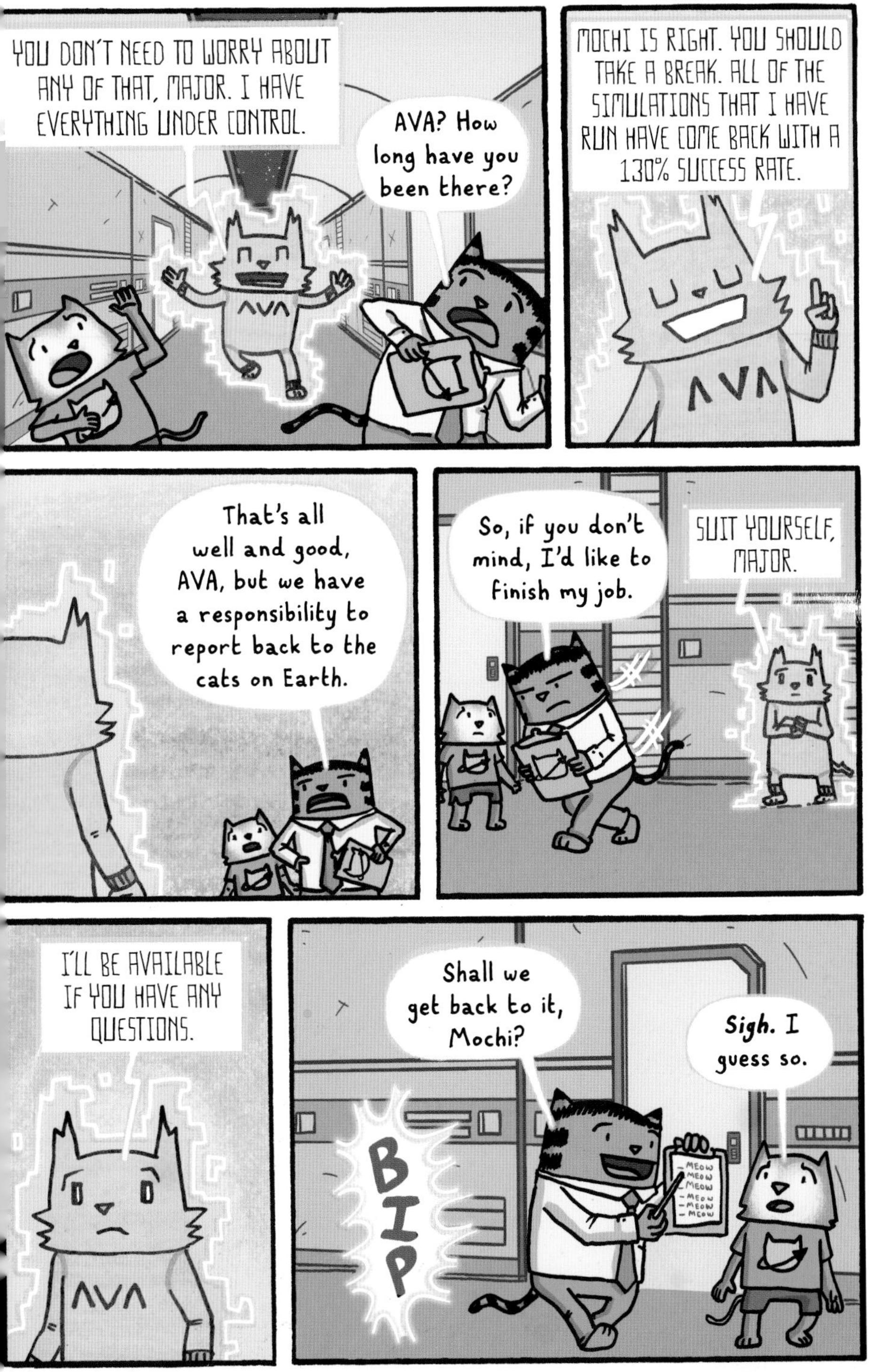
YOU DON'T NEED TO WORRY ABOUT ANY OF THAT, MAJOR. I HAVE EVERYTHING UNDER CONTROL.
AVA? How long have you been there?
AVA
MOCHI IS RIGHT. YOU SHOULD TAKE A BREAK. ALL OF THE SIMULATIONS THAT I HAVE RUN HAVE COME BACK WITH A 130% SUCCESS RATE.
AVA
That's all well and good, AVA, but we have a responsibility to report back to the cats on Earth.
So, if you don't mind, I'd like to finish my job.
SUIT YOURSELF, MAJOR.
I'LL BE AVAILABLE IF YOU HAVE ANY QUESTIONS.
AVA
Shall we get back to it, Mochi?
Sigh. I guess so.
BIP
MEOW
MEOW
MEOW
MEOW
MEOW
MEOW

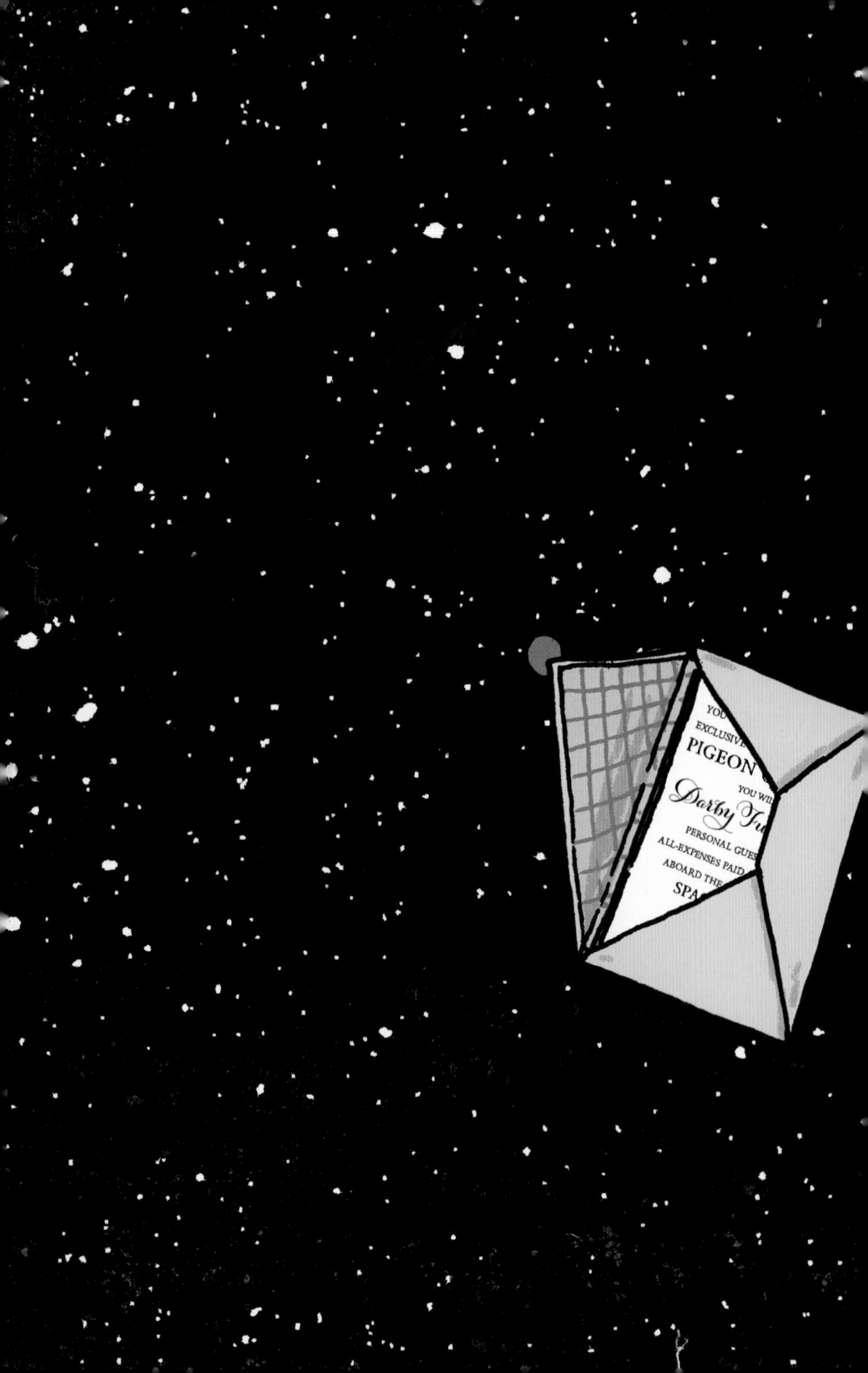
YOU
EXCLUSIVE
PIGEON
YOU WIL
Darby Fu
PERSONAL GUES
ALL-EXPENSES PAID
ABOARD THE
SPA

CHAPTER 5

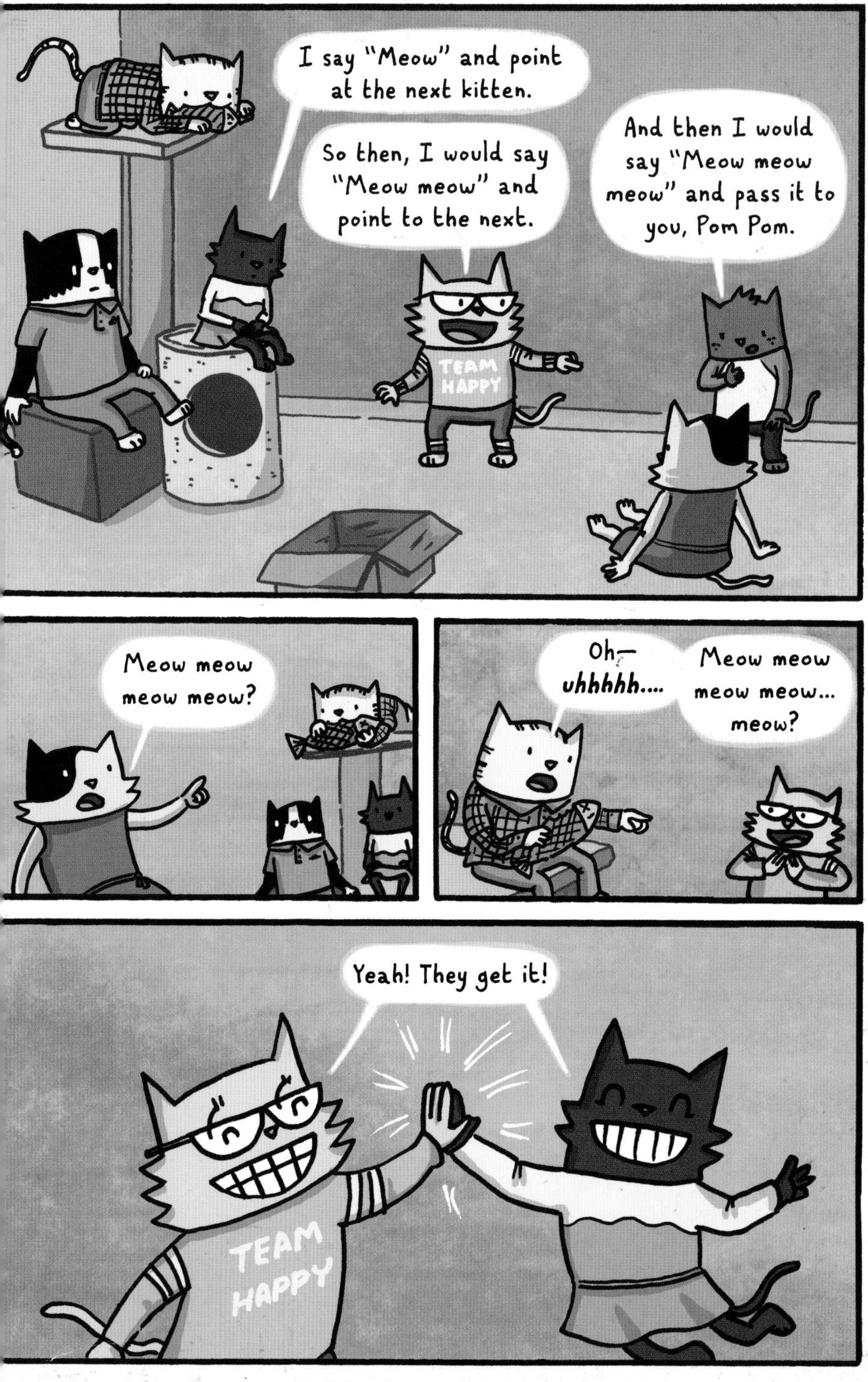
I say "Meow" and point at the next kitten.
So then, I would say "Meow meow" and point to the next.
And then I would say "Meow meow meow" and pass it to you, Pom Pom.
TEAM HAPPY
Meow meow meow meow?
Oh— uhhhhh....
Meow meow meow meow... meow?
Yeah! They get it!
TEAM HAPPY

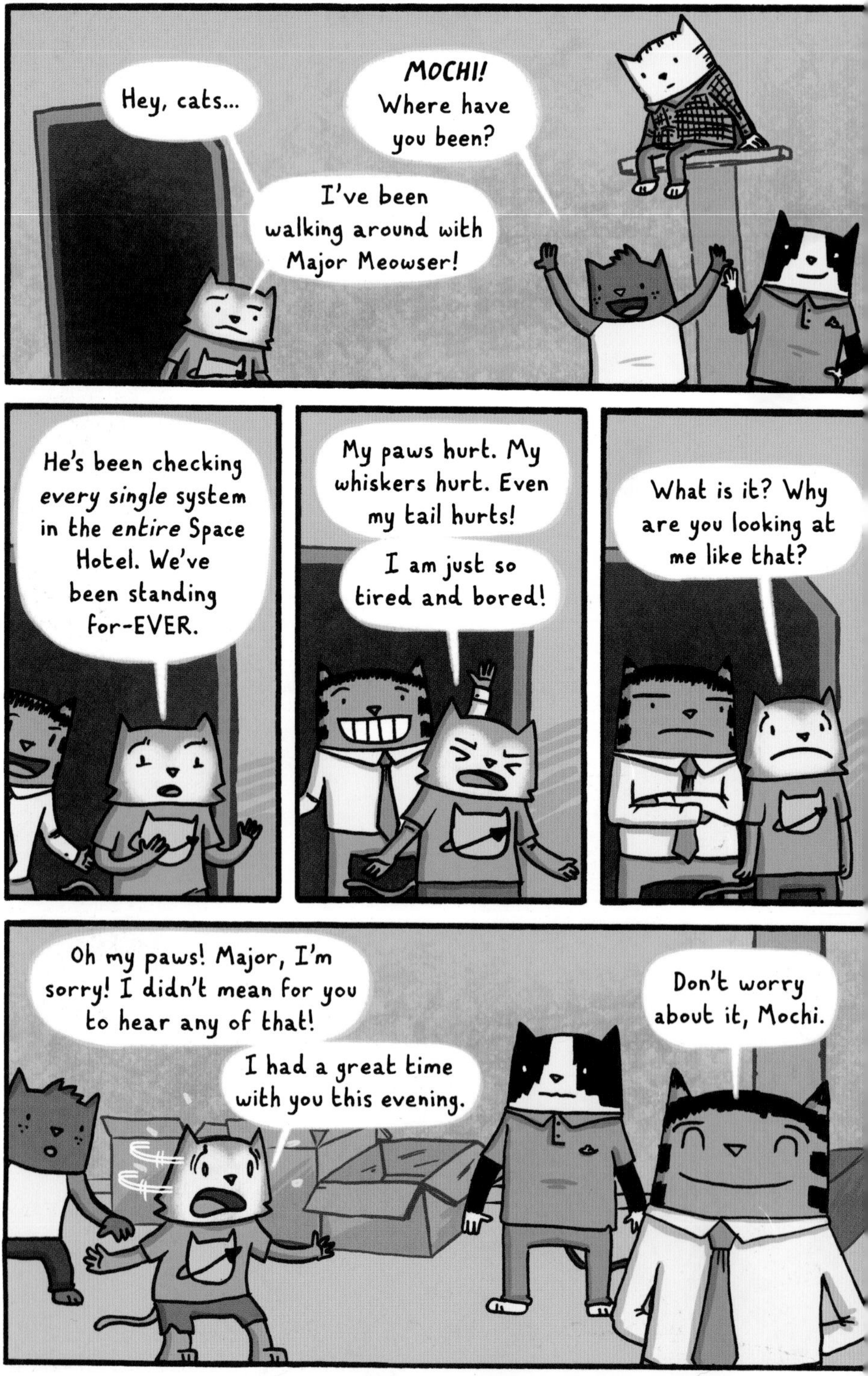
Hey, cats...
MOCHI! Where have you been?
I've been walking around with Major Meowser!
He's been checking *every single* system in the *entire* Space Hotel. We've been standing for-EVER.
My paws hurt. My whiskers hurt. Even my tail hurts!
I am just so tired and bored!
What is it? Why are you looking at me like that?
Oh my paws! Major, I'm sorry! I didn't mean for you to hear any of that!
Don't worry about it, Mochi.
I had a great time with you this evening.

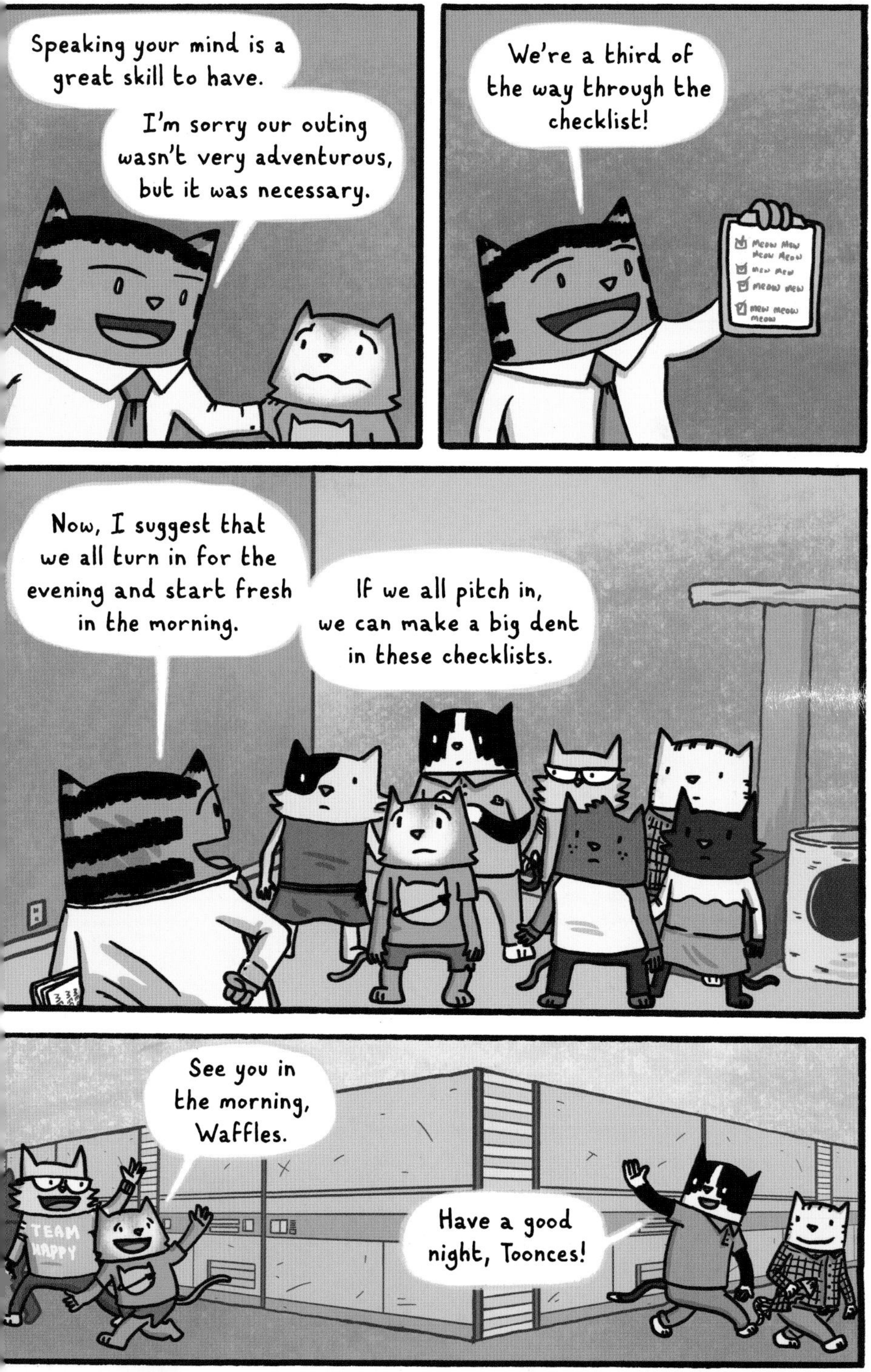
Speaking your mind is a great skill to have.
I'm sorry our outing wasn't very adventurous, but it was necessary.
We're a third of the way through the checklist!
Now, I suggest that we all turn in for the evening and start fresh in the morning.
If we all pitch in, we can make a big dent in these checklists.
TEAM HAPPY
See you in the morning, Waffles.
Have a good night, Toonces!

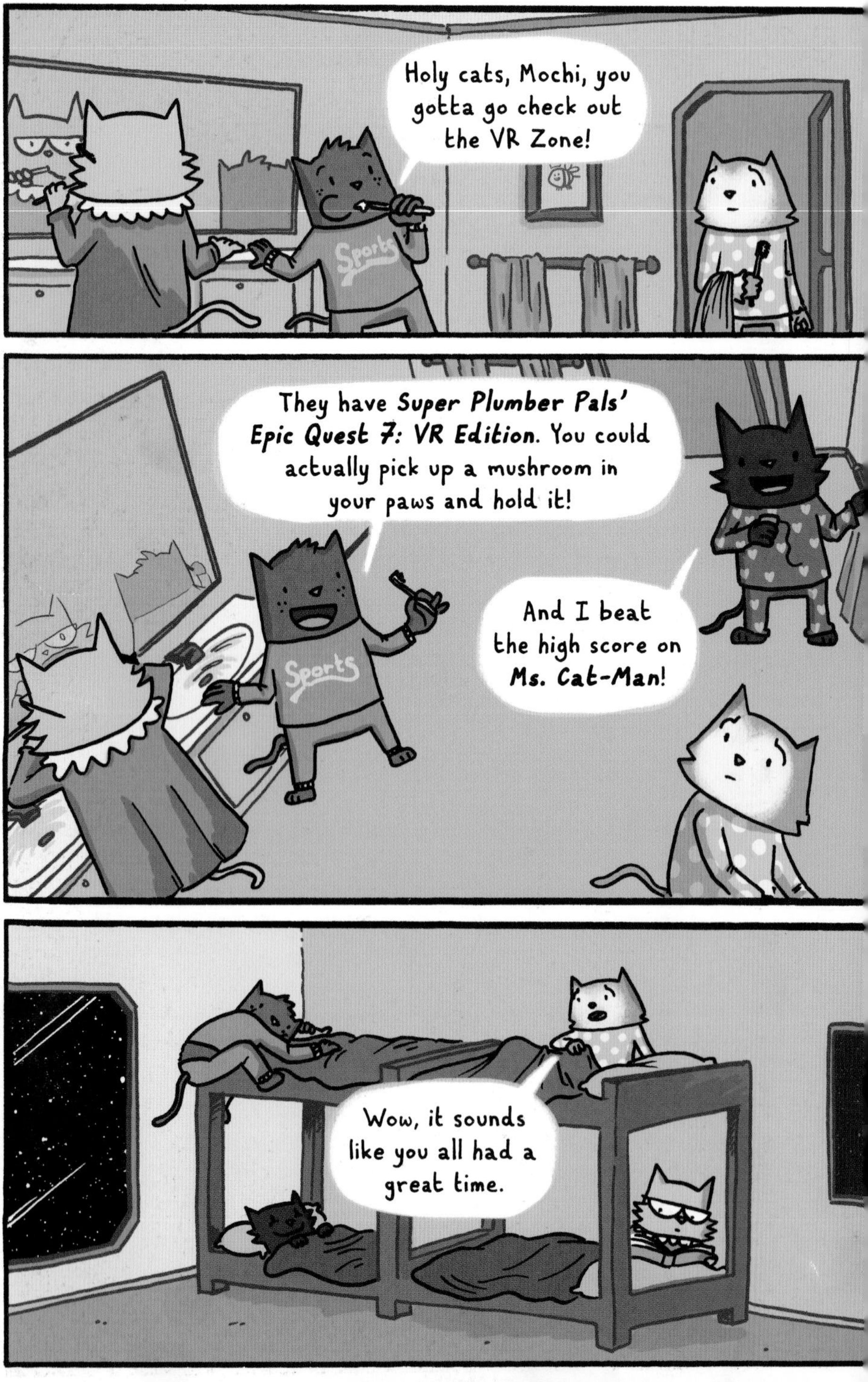
Holy cats, Mochi, you gotta go check out the VR Zone!
They have *Super Plumber Pals' Epic Quest 7: VR Edition*. You could actually pick up a mushroom in your paws and hold it!
And I beat the high score on *Ms. Cat-Man*!
Sports
Wow, it sounds like you all had a great time.

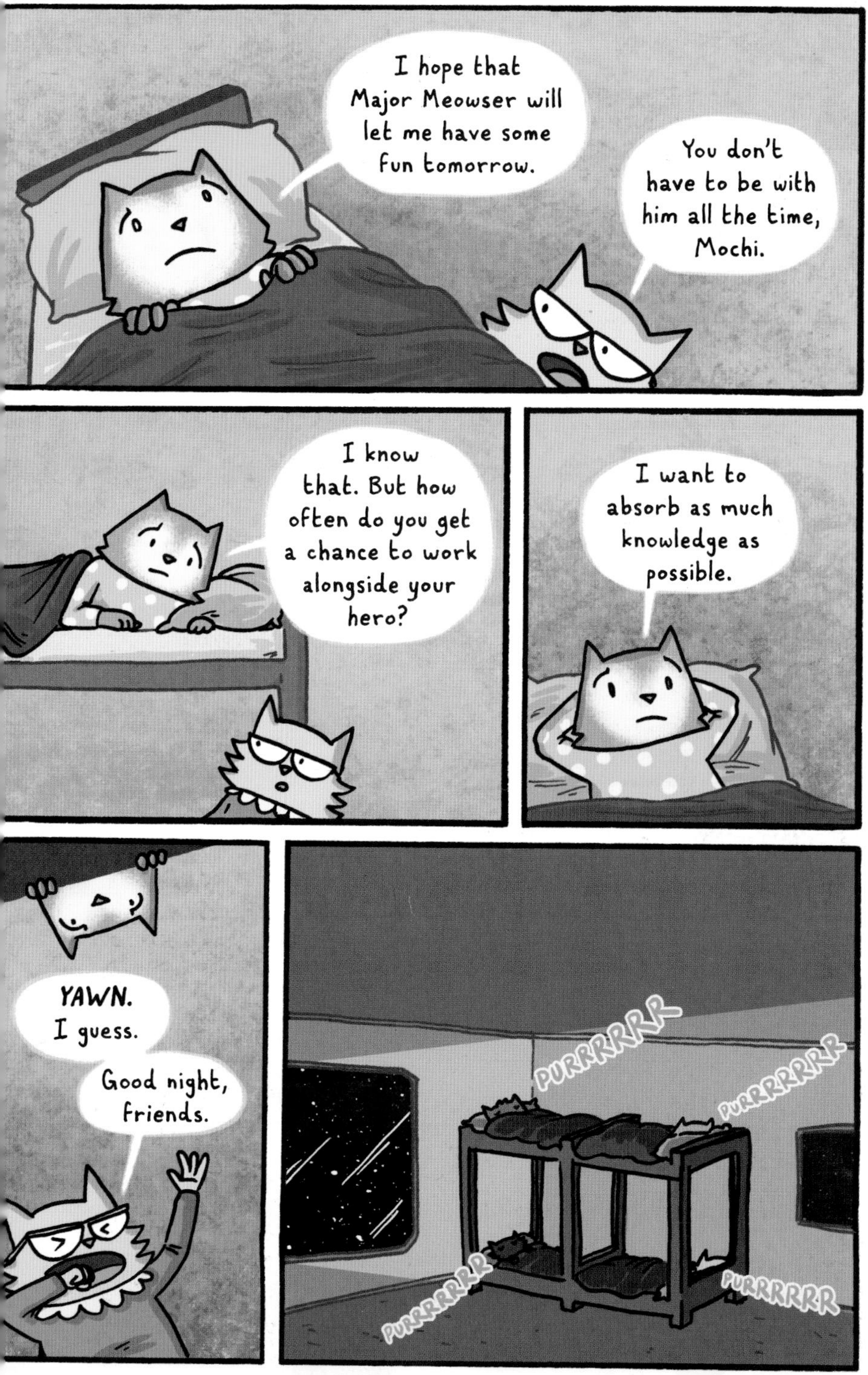
I hope that Major Meowser will let me have some fun tomorrow.
You don't have to be with him all the time, Mochi.
I know that. But how often do you get a chance to work alongside your hero?
I want to absorb as much knowledge as possible.
YAWN. I guess.
Good night, friends.
PURRRRRR
PURRRRRRR
PURRRRRRR
PURRRRRR

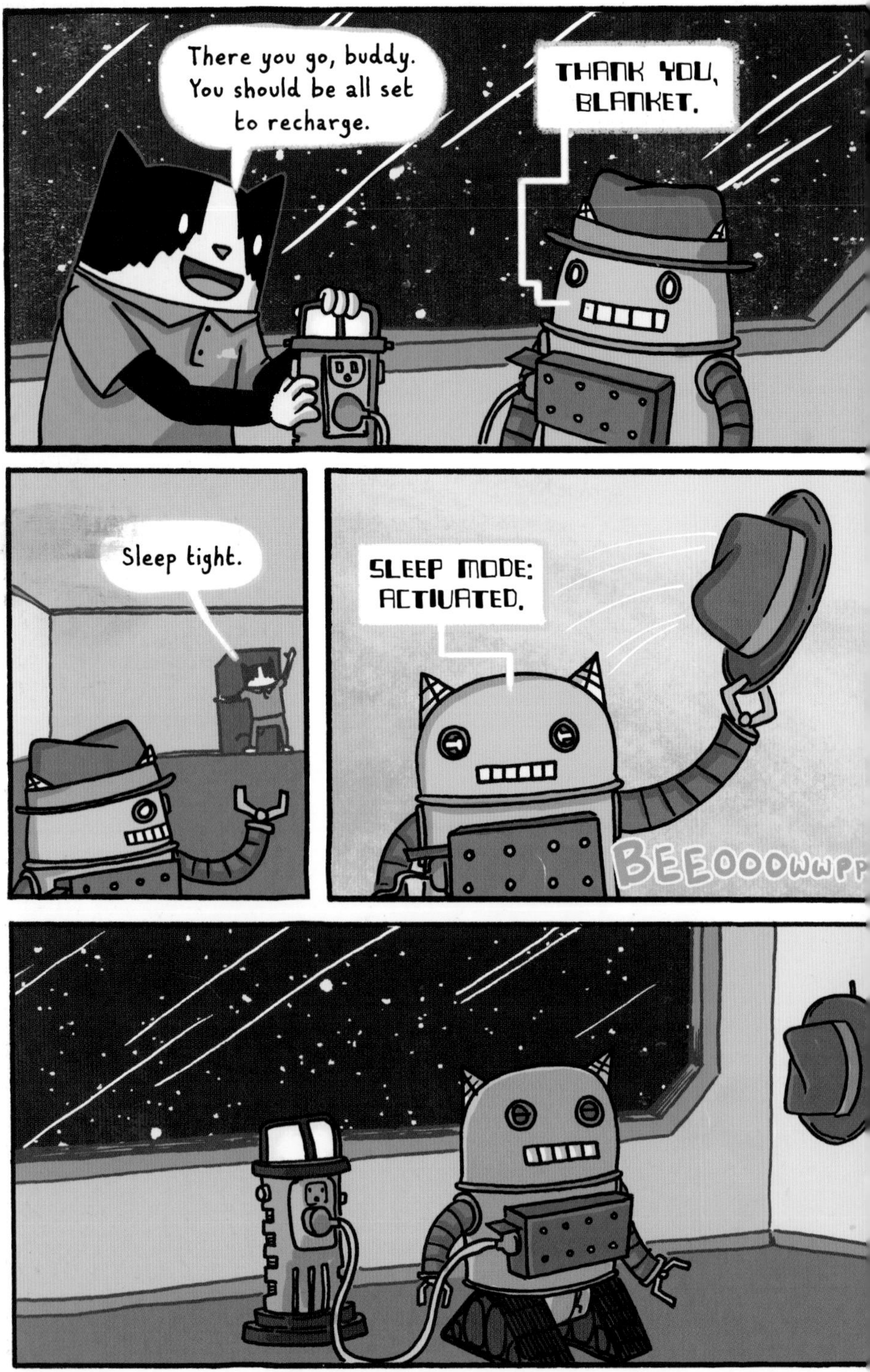
There you go, buddy. You should be all set to recharge.
THANK YOU, BLANKET.
Sleep tight.
SLEEP MODE: ACTIVATED.
BEEOOOWWPP

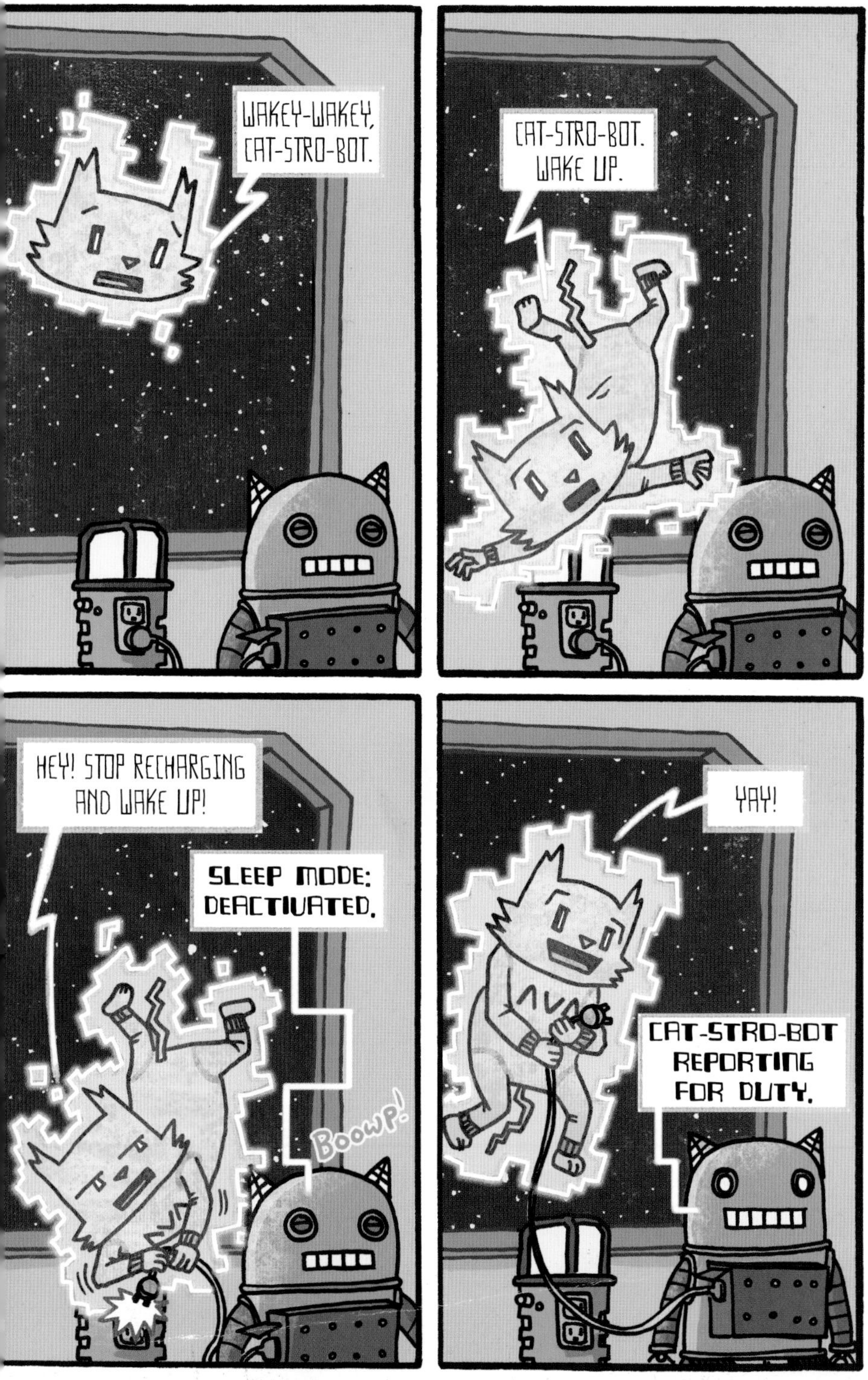
WAKEY-WAKEY, CAT-STRO-BOT.
CAT-STRO-BOT. WAKE UP.
HEY! STOP RECHARGING AND WAKE UP!
SLEEP MODE: DEACTIVATED.
BOOWP!
YAY!
CAT-STRO-BOT REPORTING FOR DUTY.

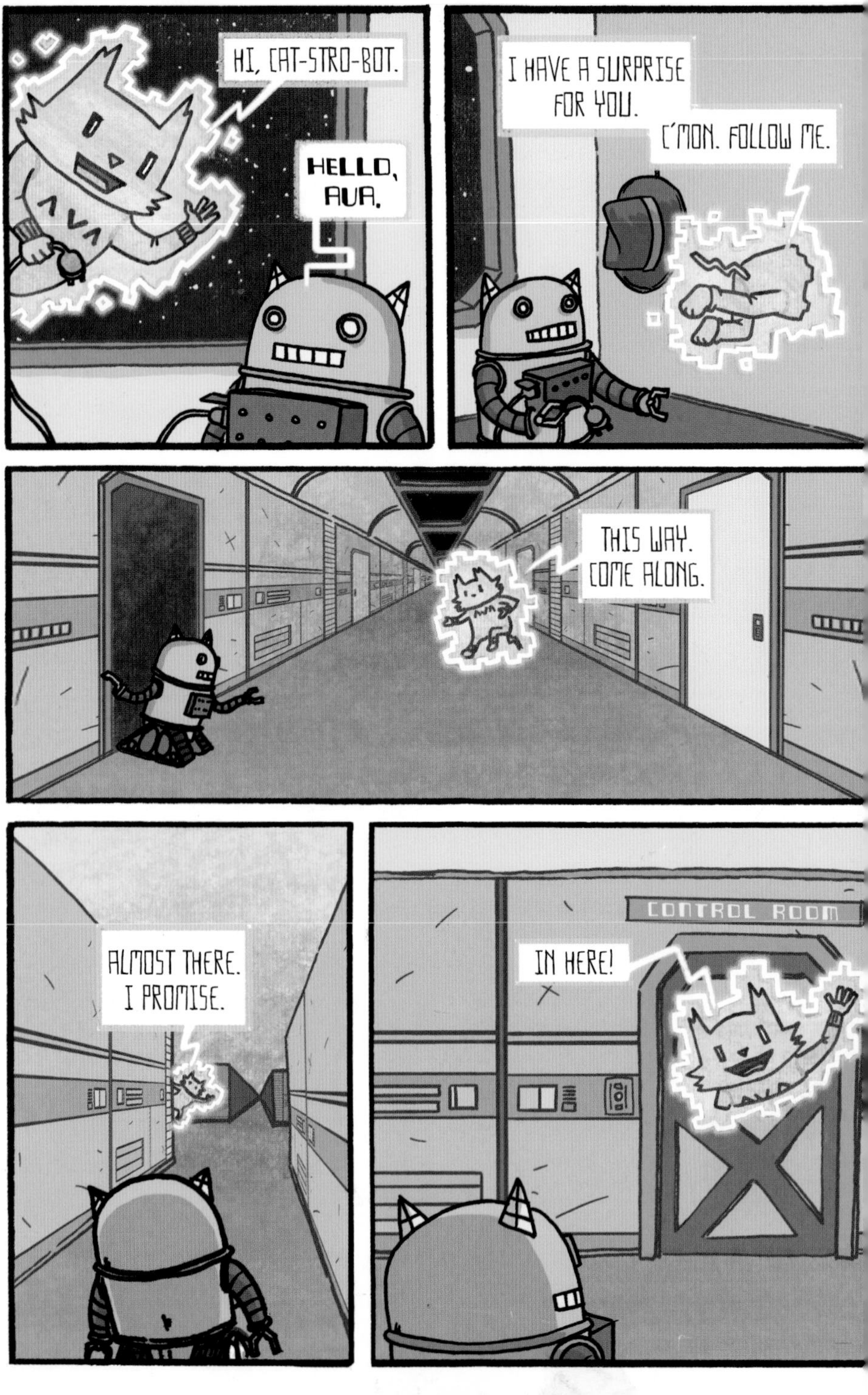
HI, CAT-STRO-BOT.
HELLO, AVA.
I HAVE A SURPRISE FOR YOU.
C'MON. FOLLOW ME.
THIS WAY. COME ALONG.
ALMOST THERE. I PROMISE.
CONTROL ROOM
IN HERE!

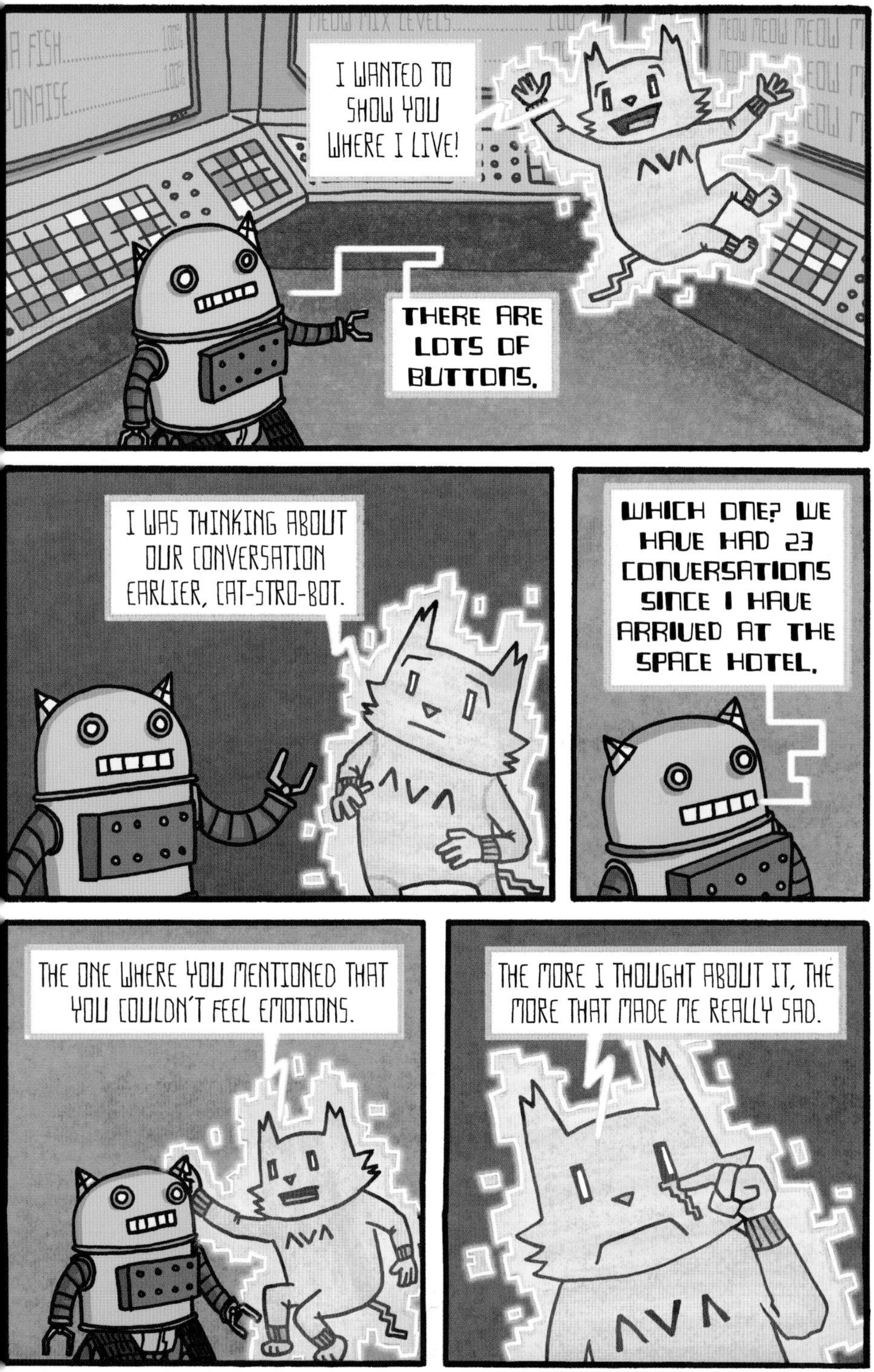
MEOW MIX LEVELS.............. 100%
A FISH.............. 100%
ONAISE.............. 100%
MEOW MEOW MEOW
I WANTED TO SHOW YOU WHERE I LIVE!
AVA
THERE ARE LOTS OF BUTTONS.
I WAS THINKING ABOUT OUR CONVERSATION EARLIER, CAT-STRO-BOT.
WHICH ONE? WE HAVE HAD 23 CONVERSATIONS SINCE I HAVE ARRIVED AT THE SPACE HOTEL.
THE ONE WHERE YOU MENTIONED THAT YOU COULDN'T FEEL EMOTIONS.
THE MORE I THOUGHT ABOUT IT, THE MORE THAT MADE ME REALLY SAD.

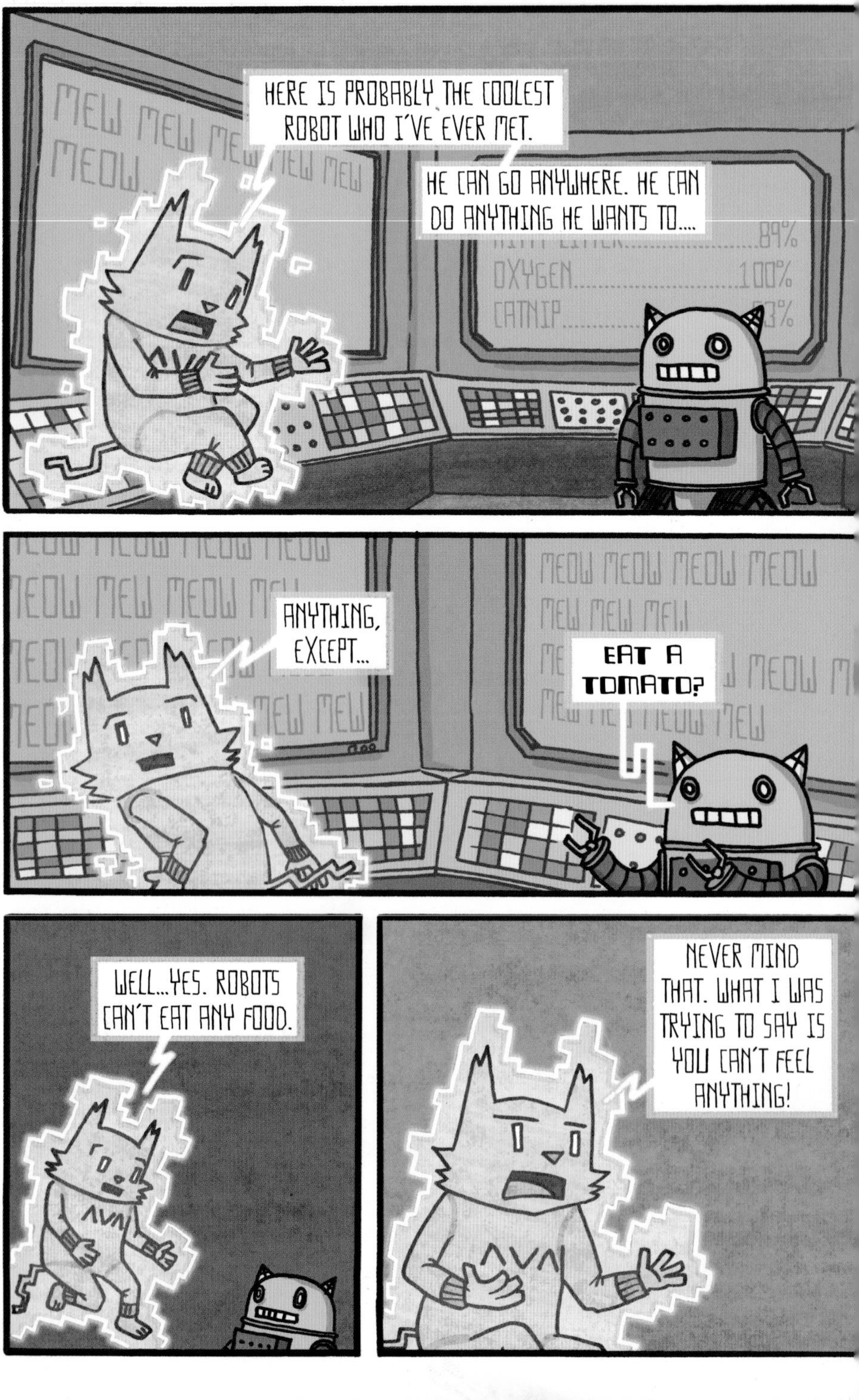
HERE IS PROBABLY THE COOLEST ROBOT WHO I'VE EVER MET.
HE CAN GO ANYWHERE. HE CAN DO ANYTHING HE WANTS TO....
OXYGEN.....................100%
ANYTHING, EXCEPT...
EAT A TOMATO?
WELL...YES. ROBOTS CAN'T EAT ANY FOOD.
NEVER MIND THAT. WHAT I WAS TRYING TO SAY IS YOU CAN'T FEEL ANYTHING!

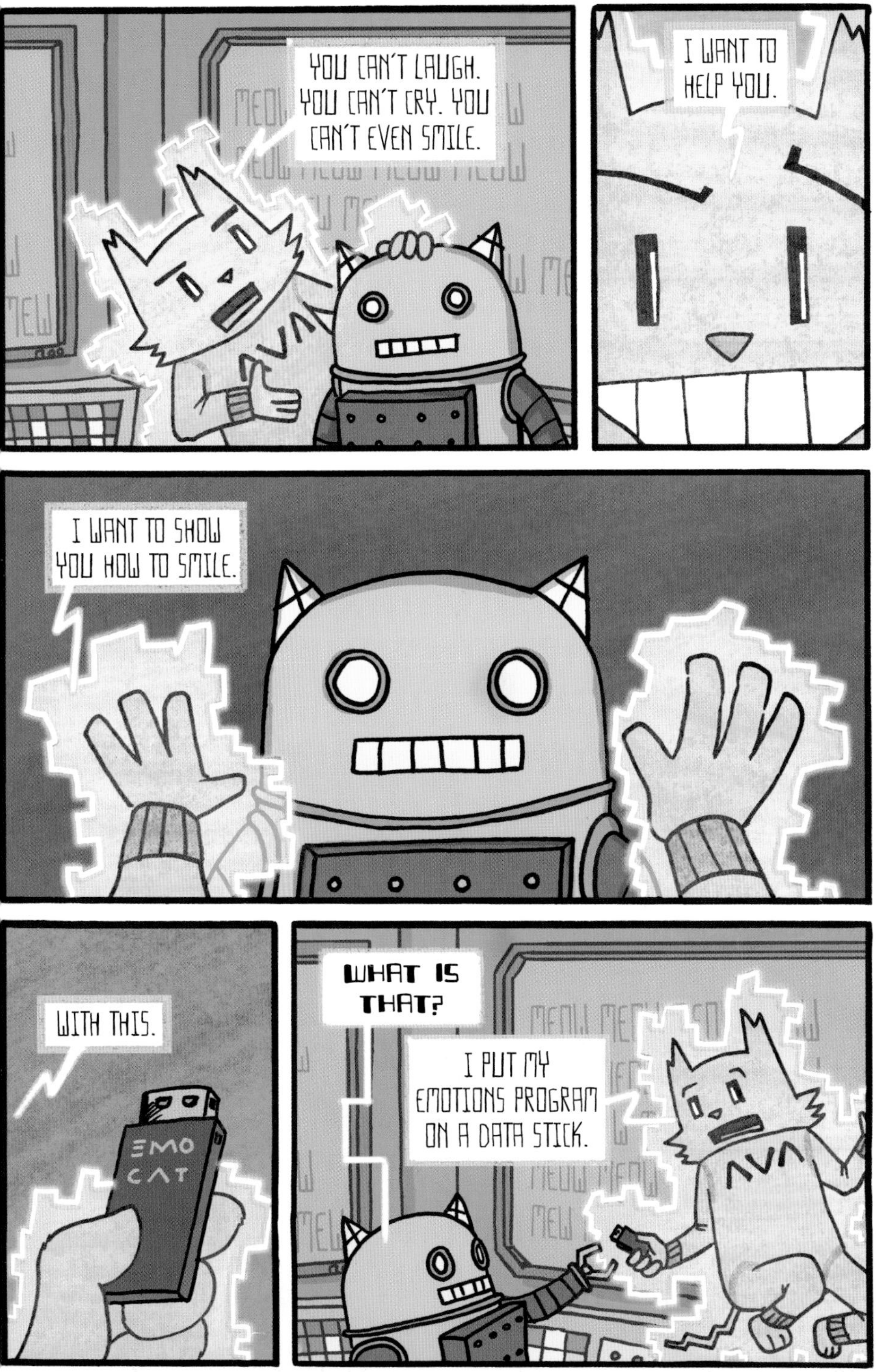
YOU CAN'T LAUGH. YOU CAN'T CRY. YOU CAN'T EVEN SMILE.
I WANT TO HELP YOU.
I WANT TO SHOW YOU HOW TO SMILE.
WITH THIS.
EMO CAT
WHAT IS THAT?
I PUT MY EMOTIONS PROGRAM ON A DATA STICK.

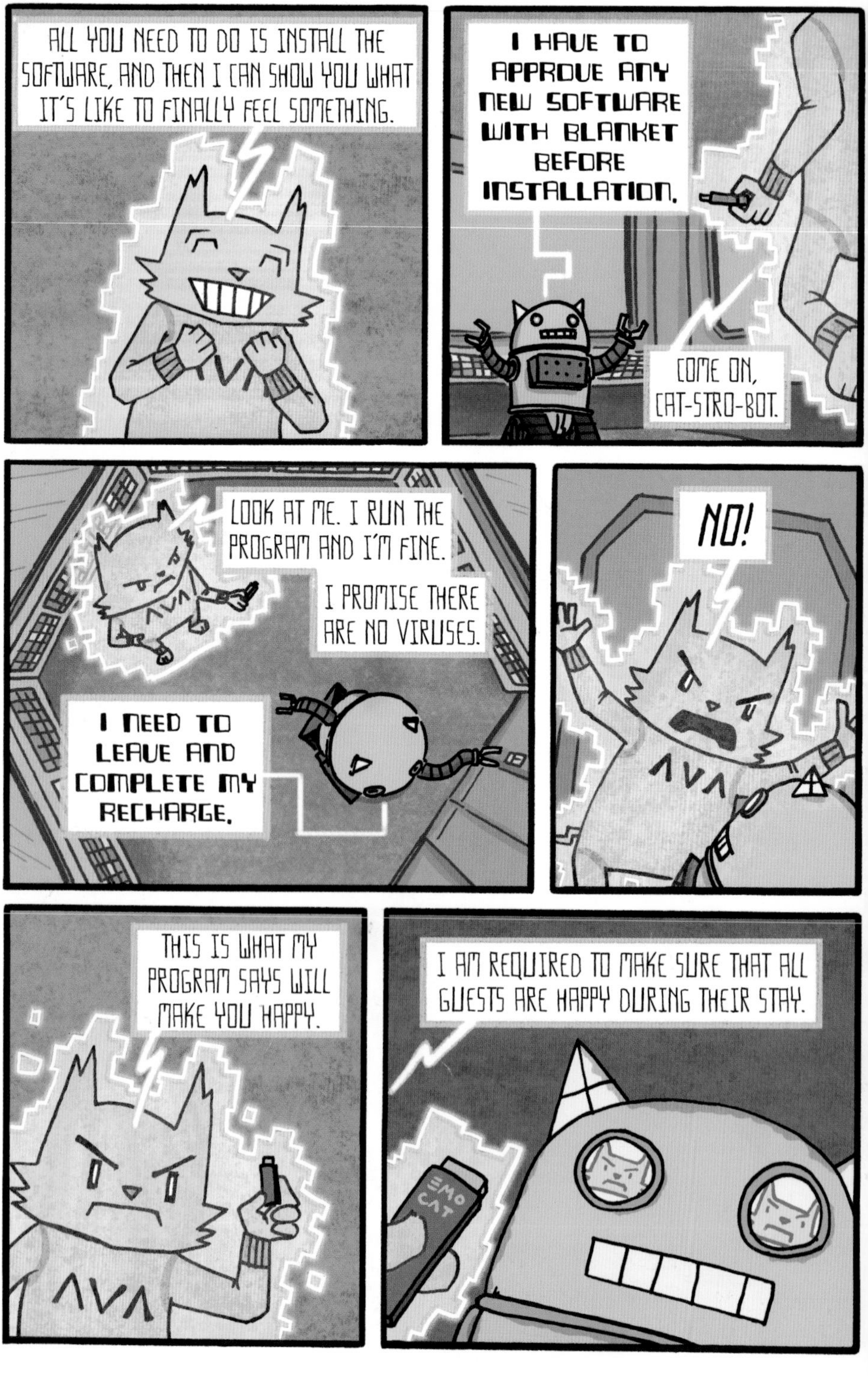
ALL YOU NEED TO DO IS INSTALL THE SOFTWARE, AND THEN I CAN SHOW YOU WHAT IT'S LIKE TO FINALLY FEEL SOMETHING.
I HAVE TO APPROVE ANY NEW SOFTWARE WITH BLANKET BEFORE INSTALLATION.
COME ON, CAT-STRO-BOT.
LOOK AT ME. I RUN THE PROGRAM AND I'M FINE.
I PROMISE THERE ARE NO VIRUSES.
I NEED TO LEAVE AND COMPLETE MY RECHARGE.
NO!
THIS IS WHAT MY PROGRAM SAYS WILL MAKE YOU HAPPY.
I AM REQUIRED TO MAKE SURE THAT ALL GUESTS ARE HAPPY DURING THEIR STAY.
EMO CAT

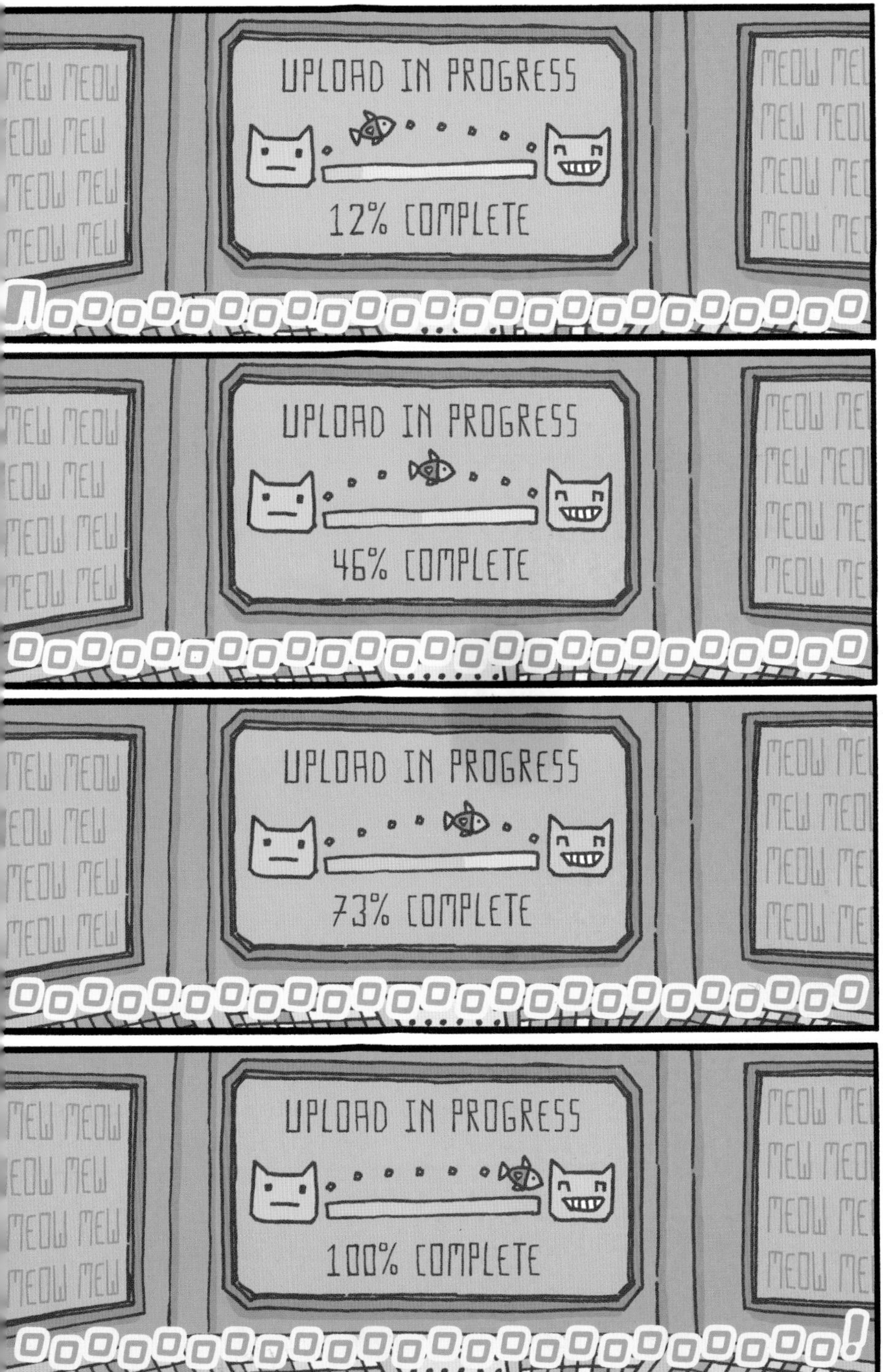
UPLOAD IN PROGRESS
12% COMPLETE
NOOOOOOOOOOOOOOOOOOOOOOOOOOOOOOO
UPLOAD IN PROGRESS
46% COMPLETE
OOOOOOOOOOOOOOOOOOOOOOOOOOOOOOOO
UPLOAD IN PROGRESS
73% COMPLETE
OOOOOOOOOOOOOOOOOOOOOOOOOOOOOOOO
UPLOAD IN PROGRESS
100% COMPLETE
OOOOOOOOOOOOOOOOOOOOOOOOOOOOOOO!

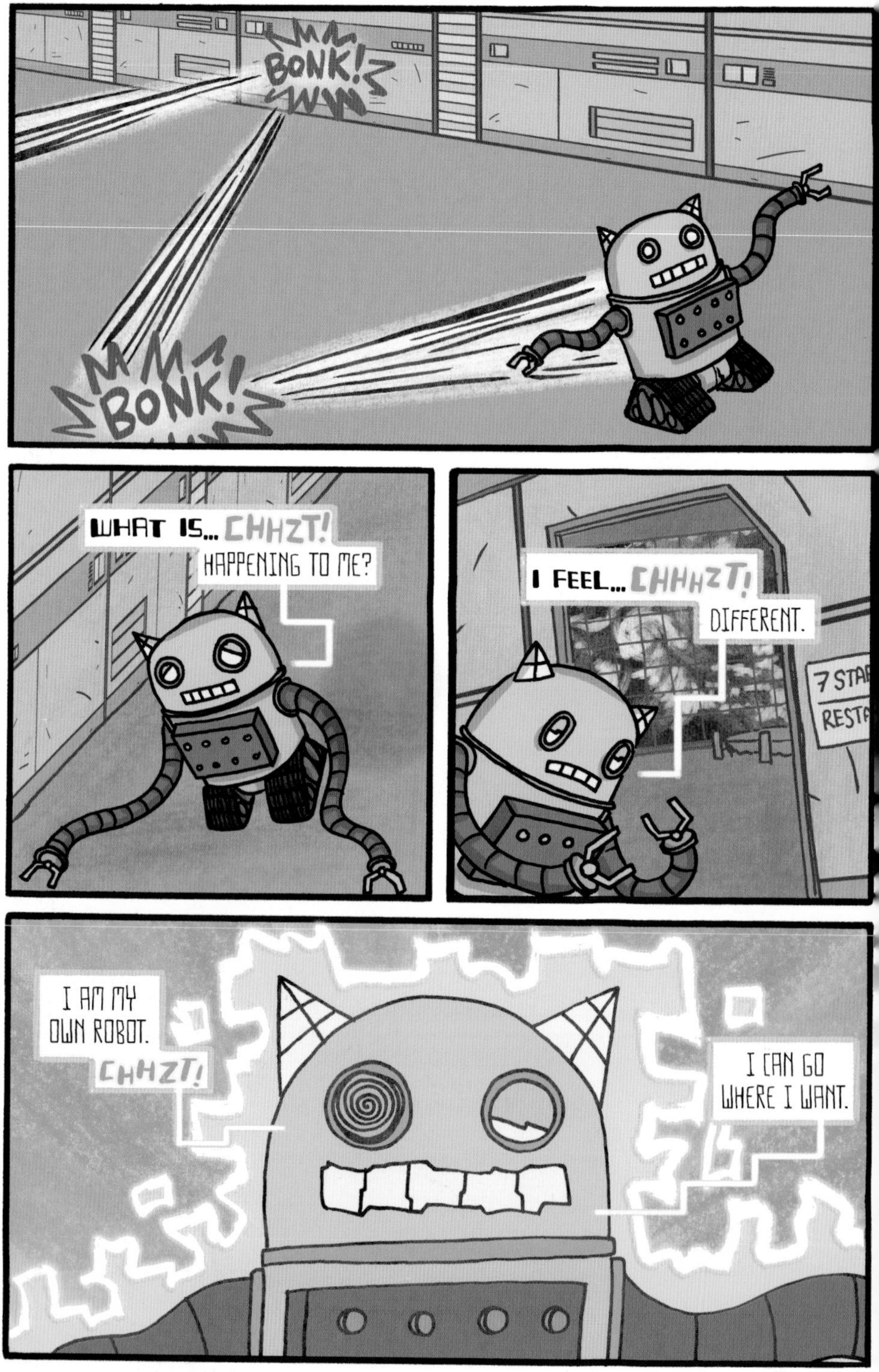
BONK!
BONK!
WHAT IS... CHHZT!
HAPPENING TO ME?
I FEEL... CHHHZT!
DIFFERENT.
I AM MY OWN ROBOT.
CHHZT!
I CAN GO WHERE I WANT.

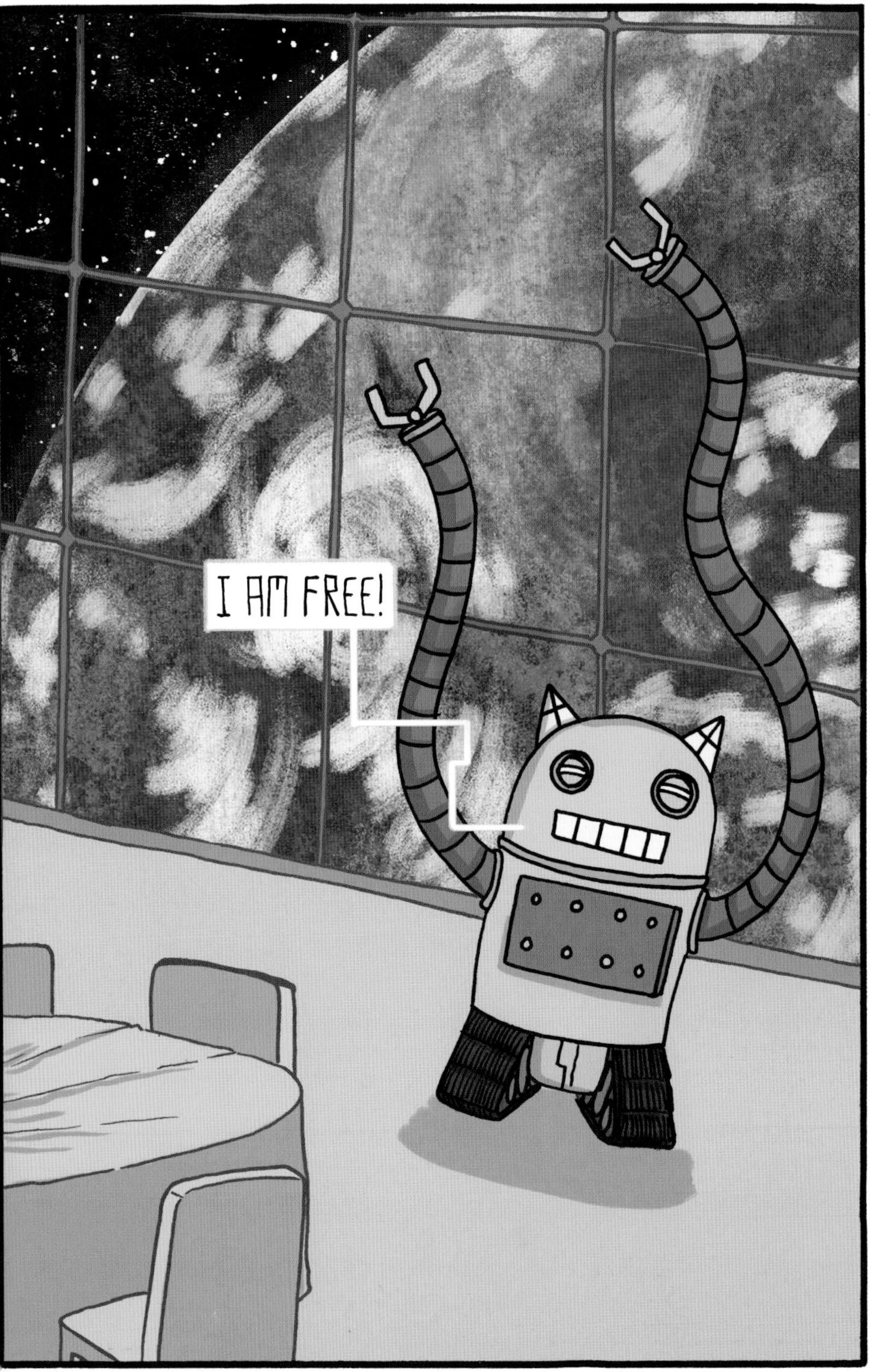
I AM FREE!

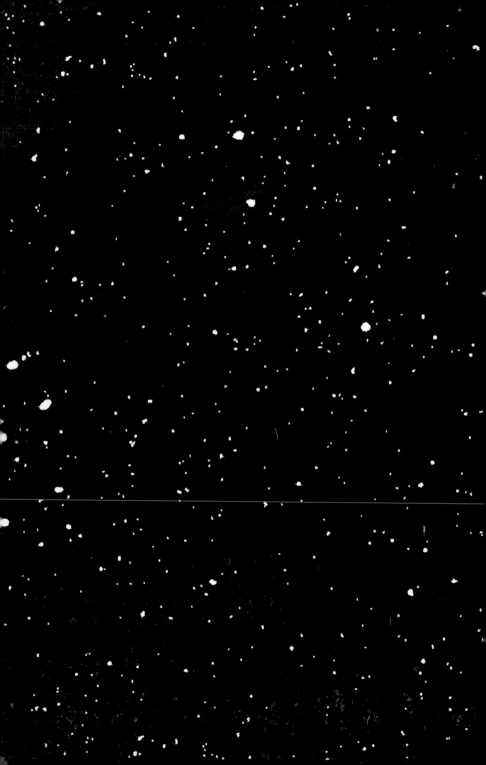

YOU'RE INVITED TO THE
GIDEON GALACTIC!
PRE-LAUNCH EVENT FOR

YOU WILL BE
Dorthy Tuppleton's
PERSONAL GUEST FOR AN
ALL-EXPENSES PAID 3-DAY GETAWAY
ABOARD THE NEW LUXURIOUS
SPACE HOTEL
RSVP
BY CATVEMBER FIFTH

CHAPTER 6

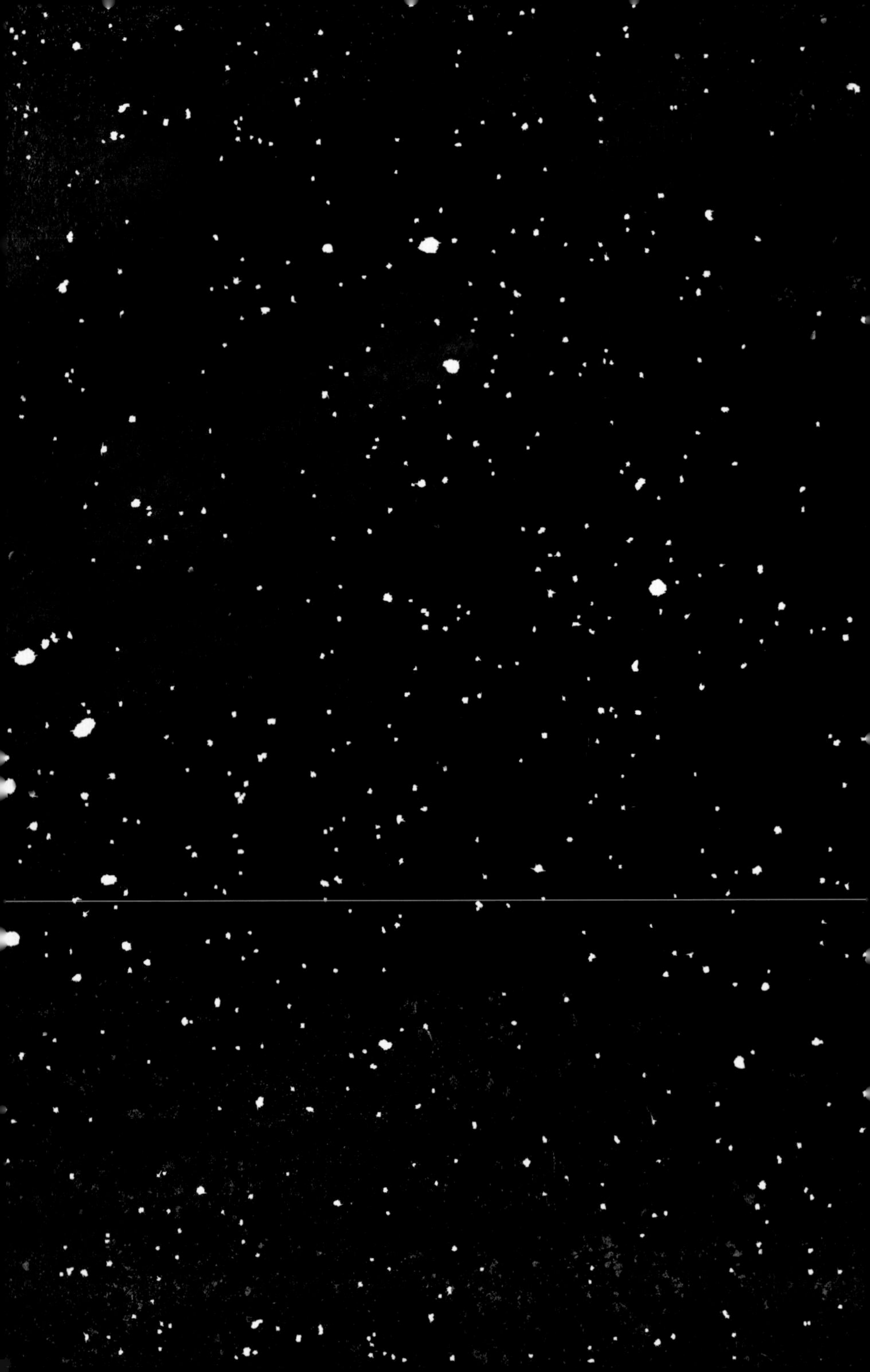

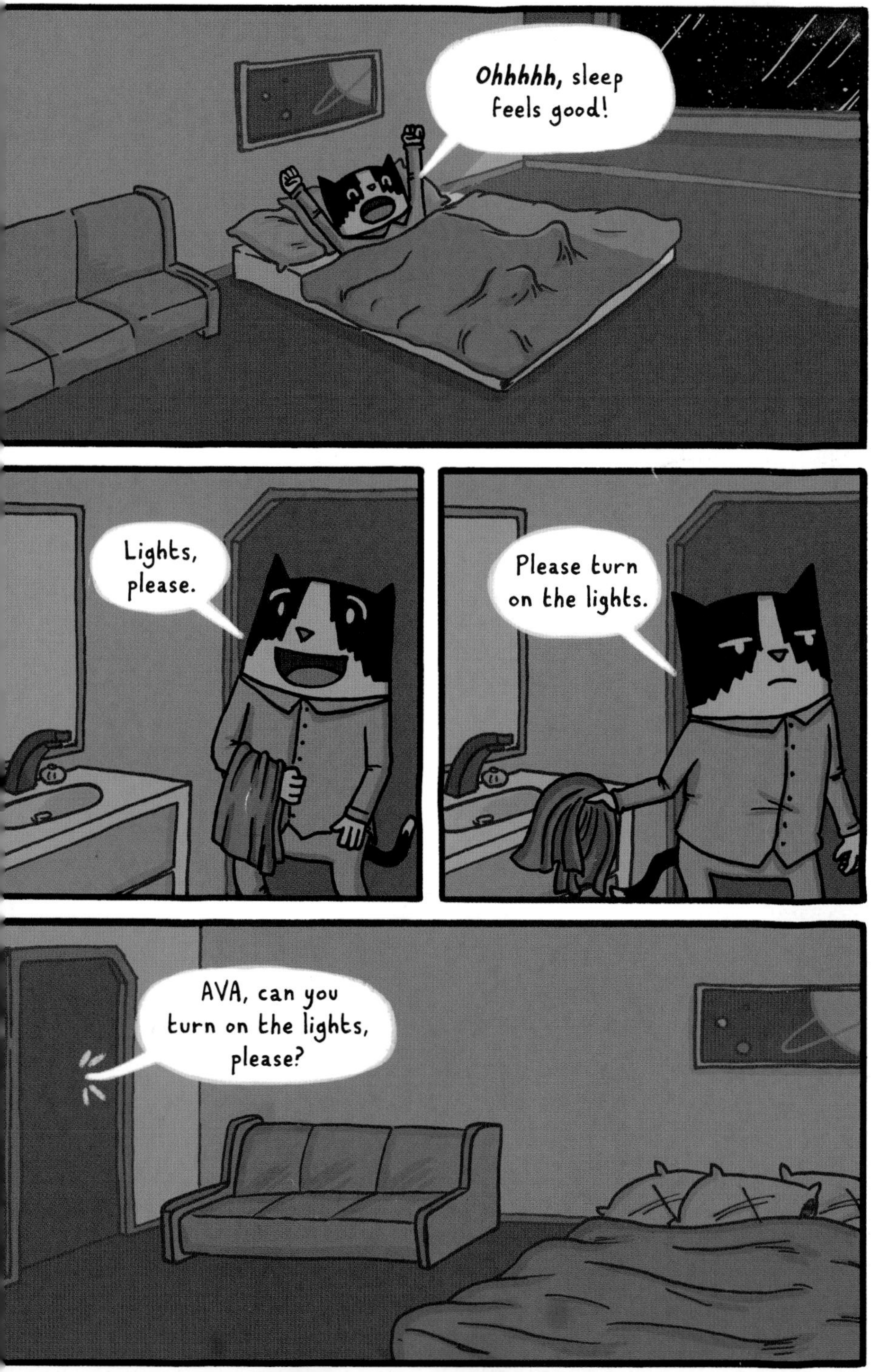

Ohhhhh, sleep feels good!
Lights, please.
Please turn on the lights.
AVA, can you turn on the lights, please?

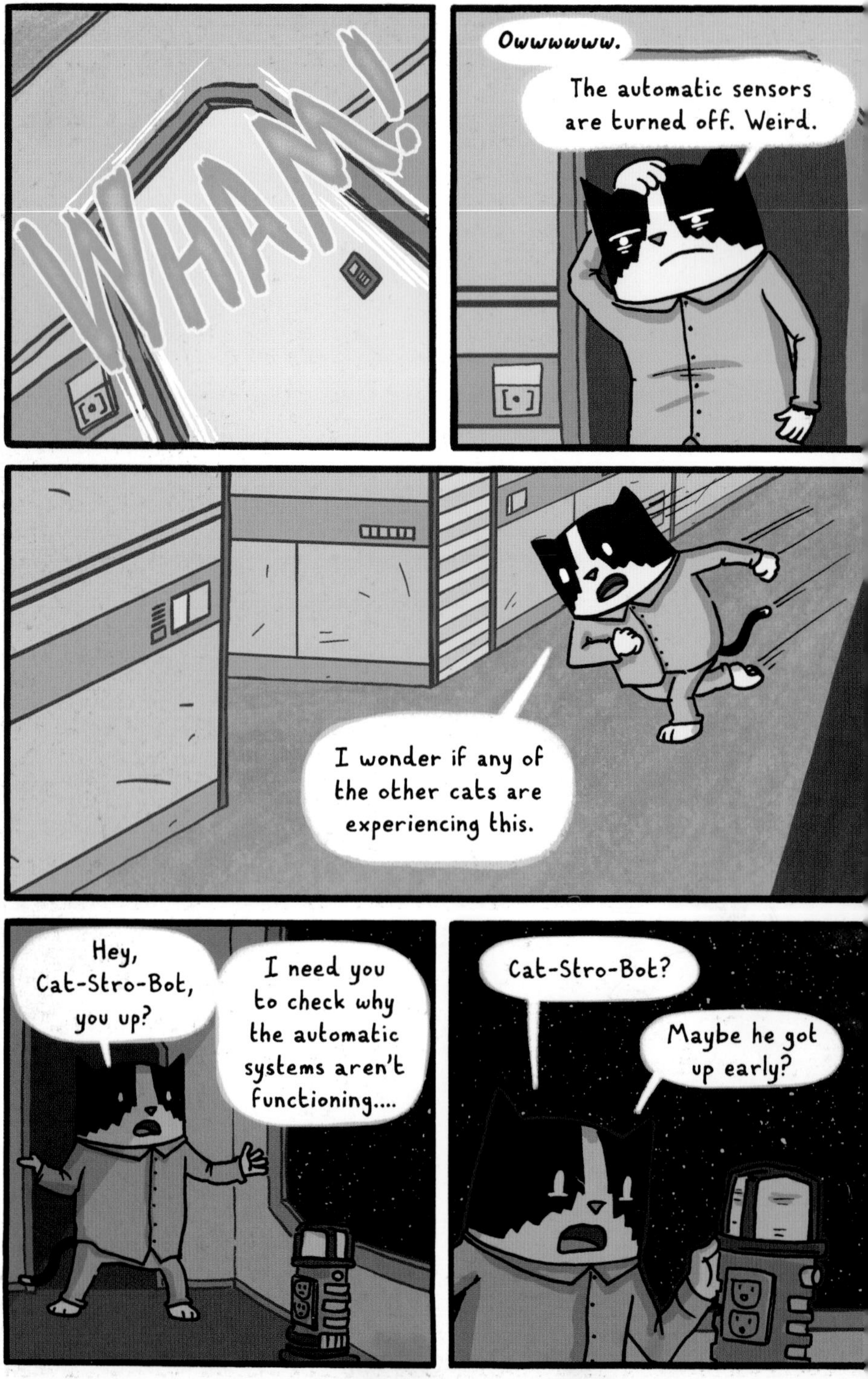
WHAM!
Owwwwww.
The automatic sensors are turned off. Weird.
I wonder if any of the other cats are experiencing this.
Hey, Cat-Stro-Bot, you up?
I need you to check why the automatic systems aren't functioning....
Cat-Stro-Bot?
Maybe he got up early?

MEANWHILE, AT THE 7-STAR RESTAURANT.

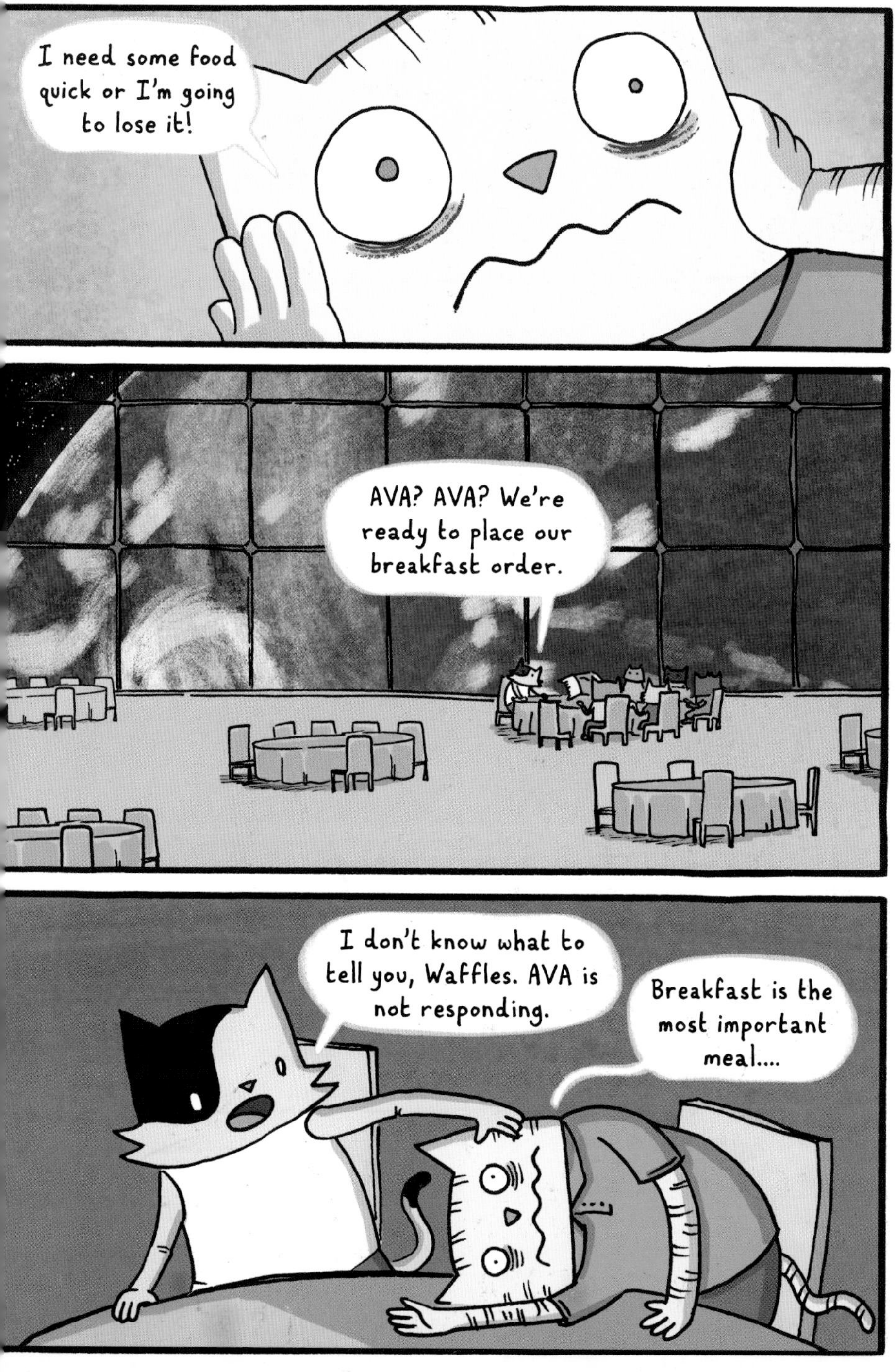
I need some food quick or I'm going to lose it!
AVA? AVA? We're ready to place our breakfast order.
I don't know what to tell you, Waffles. AVA is not responding.
Breakfast is the most important meal....

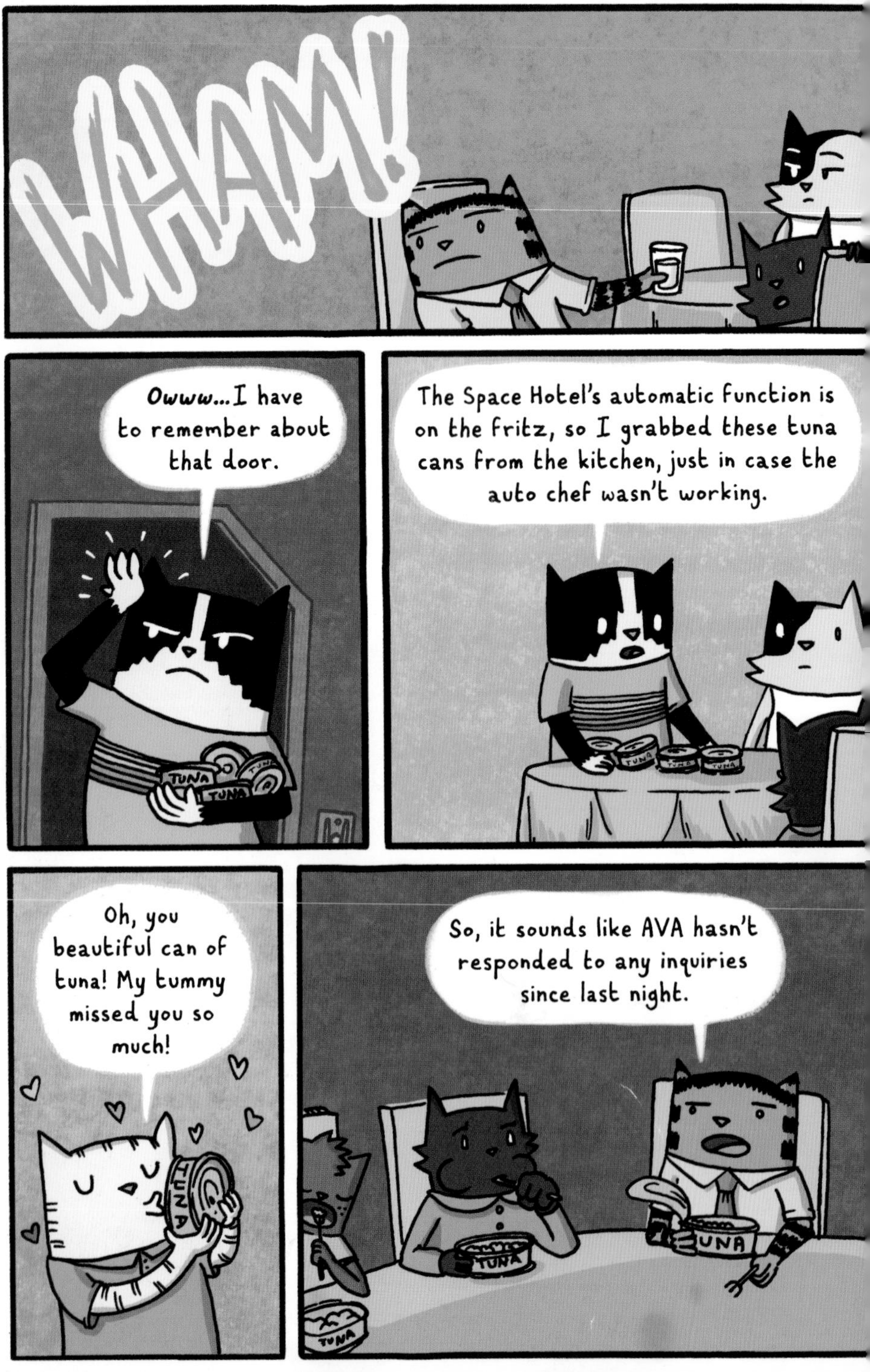
WHAM!
Owww...I have to remember about that door.
TUNA
TUNA
The Space Hotel's automatic function is on the fritz, so I grabbed these tuna cans from the kitchen, just in case the auto chef wasn't working.
TUNA
Oh, you beautiful can of tuna! My tummy missed you so much!
TUNA
So, it sounds like AVA hasn't responded to any inquiries since last night.
TUNA
UNA
TUNA

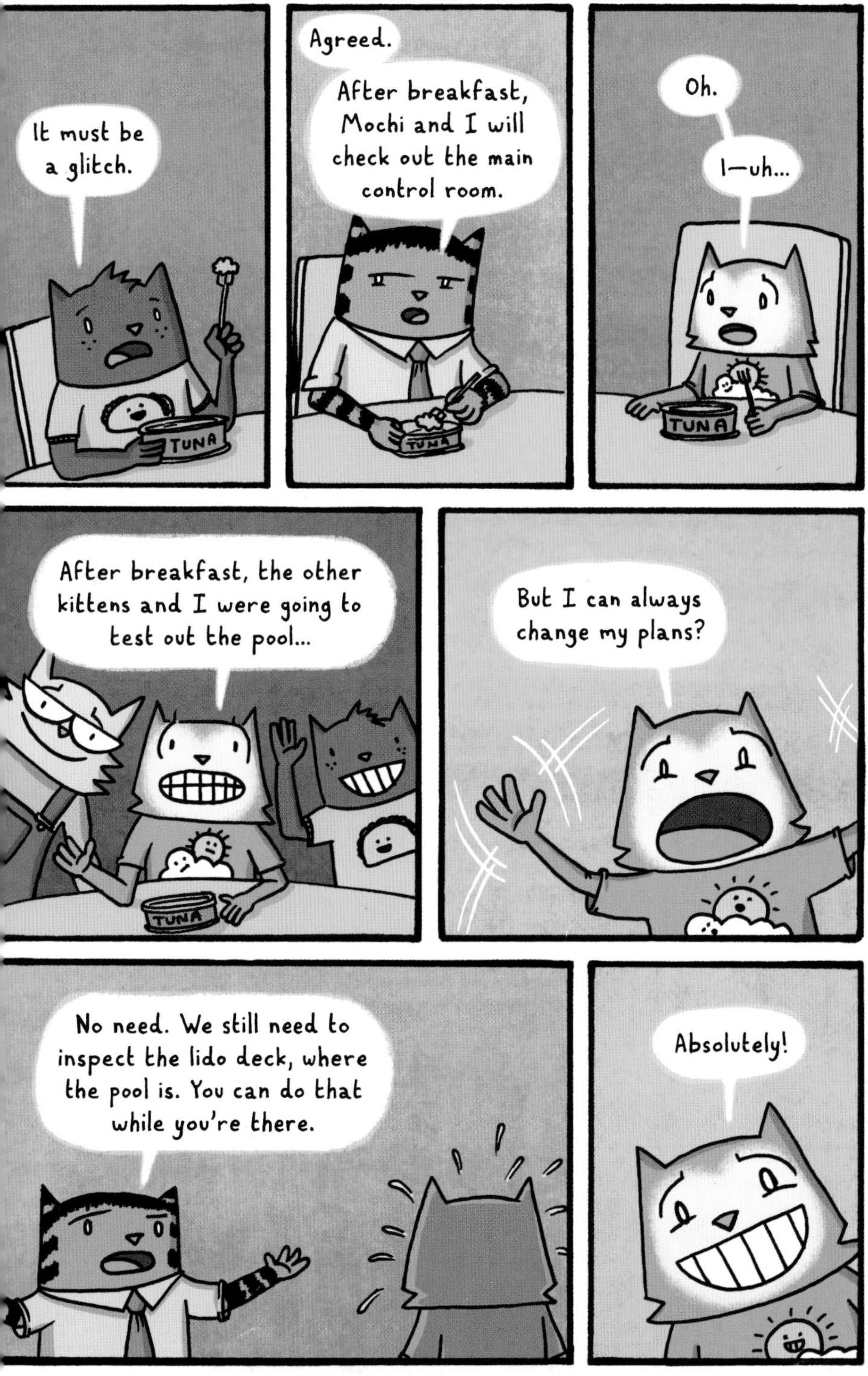
It must be a glitch.
Agreed.
After breakfast, Mochi and I will check out the main control room.
Oh.
I—uh...
After breakfast, the other kittens and I were going to test out the pool...
But I can always change my plans?
No need. We still need to inspect the lido deck, where the pool is. You can do that while you're there.
Absolutely!

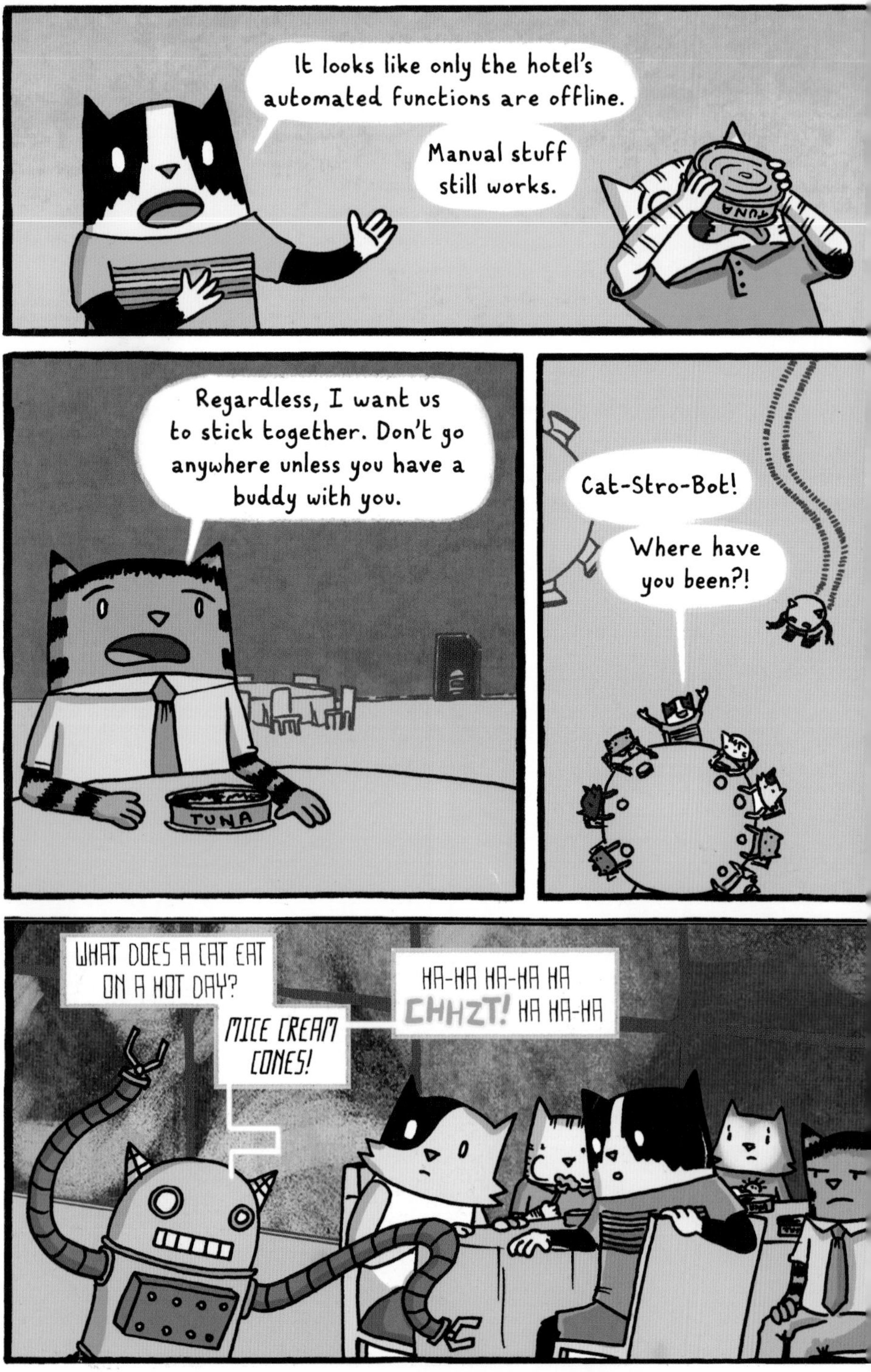
It looks like only the hotel's automated functions are offline.
Manual stuff still works.
TUNA
Regardless, I want us to stick together. Don't go anywhere unless you have a buddy with you.
TUNA
Cat-Stro-Bot!
Where have you been?!
WHAT DOES A CAT EAT ON A HOT DAY?
MICE CREAM CONES!
HA-HA HA-HA HA
CHHZT! HA HA-HA

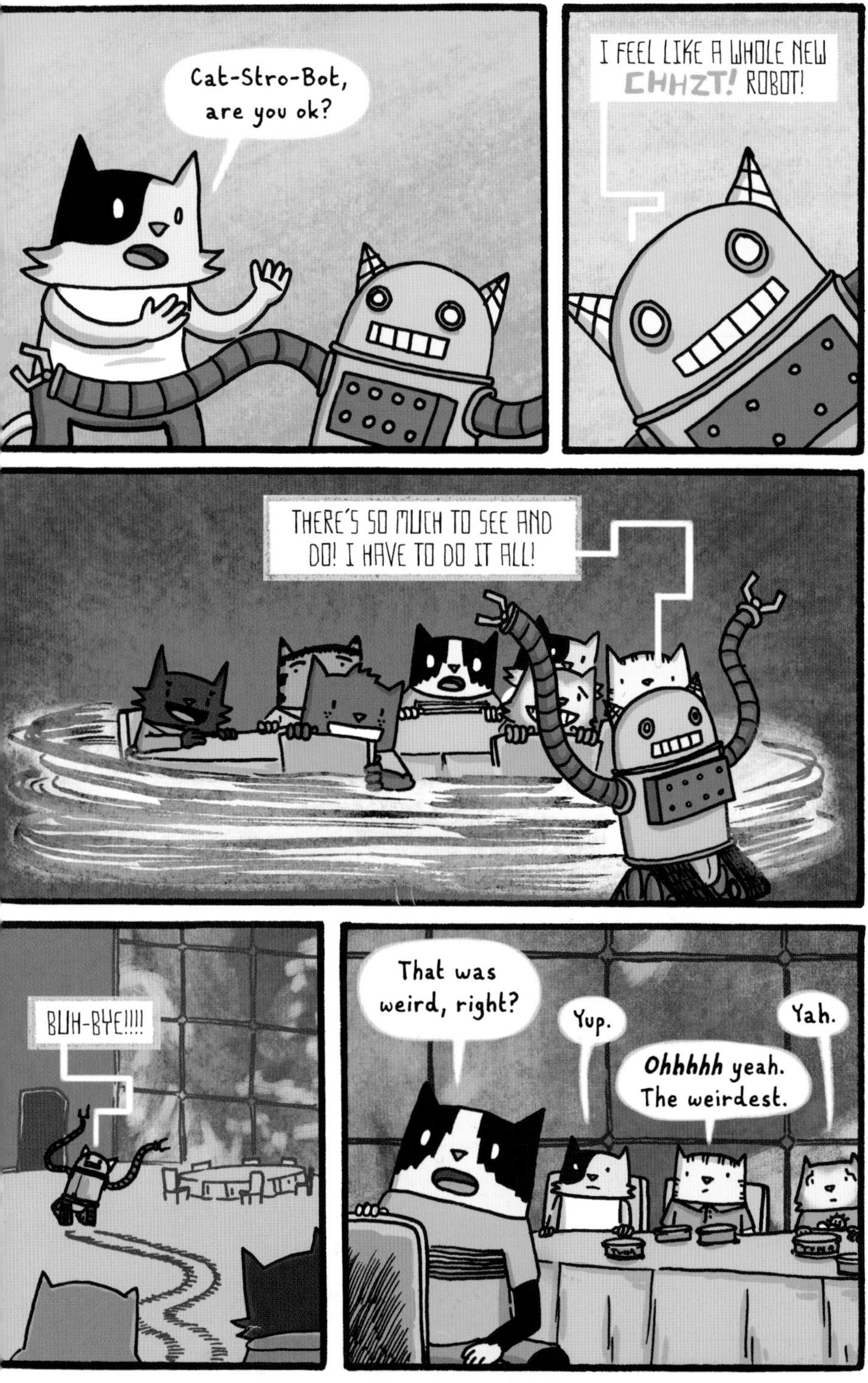
Cat-Stro-Bot, are you ok?
I FEEL LIKE A WHOLE NEW CHHZT! ROBOT!
THERE'S SO MUCH TO SEE AND DO! I HAVE TO DO IT ALL!
BUH-BYE!!!!
That was weird, right?
Yup.
Yah.
Ohhhhh yeah. The weirdest.

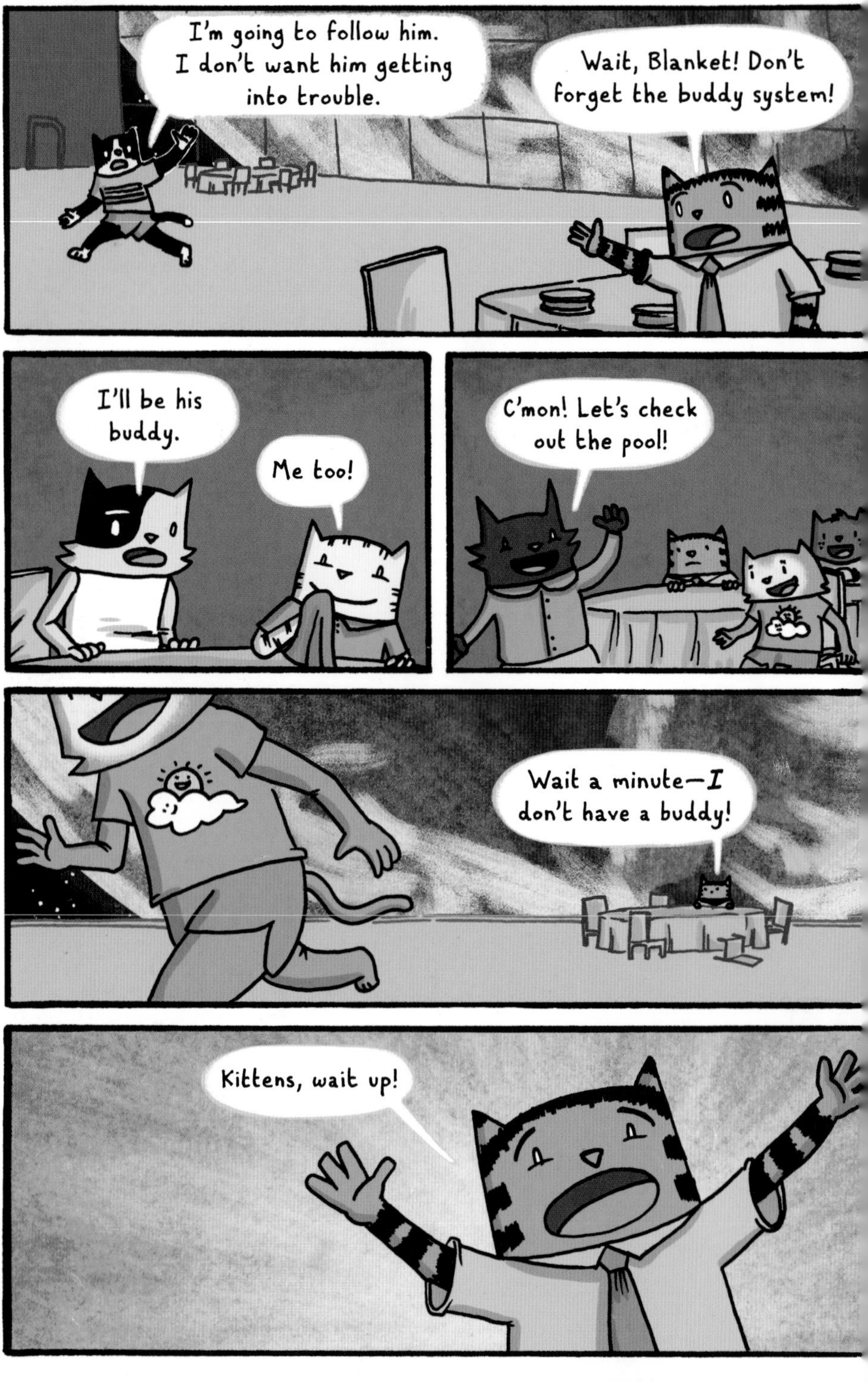
I'm going to follow him. I don't want him getting into trouble.
Wait, Blanket! Don't forget the buddy system!
I'll be his buddy.
Me too!
C'mon! Let's check out the pool!
Wait a minute—I don't have a buddy!
Kittens, wait up!

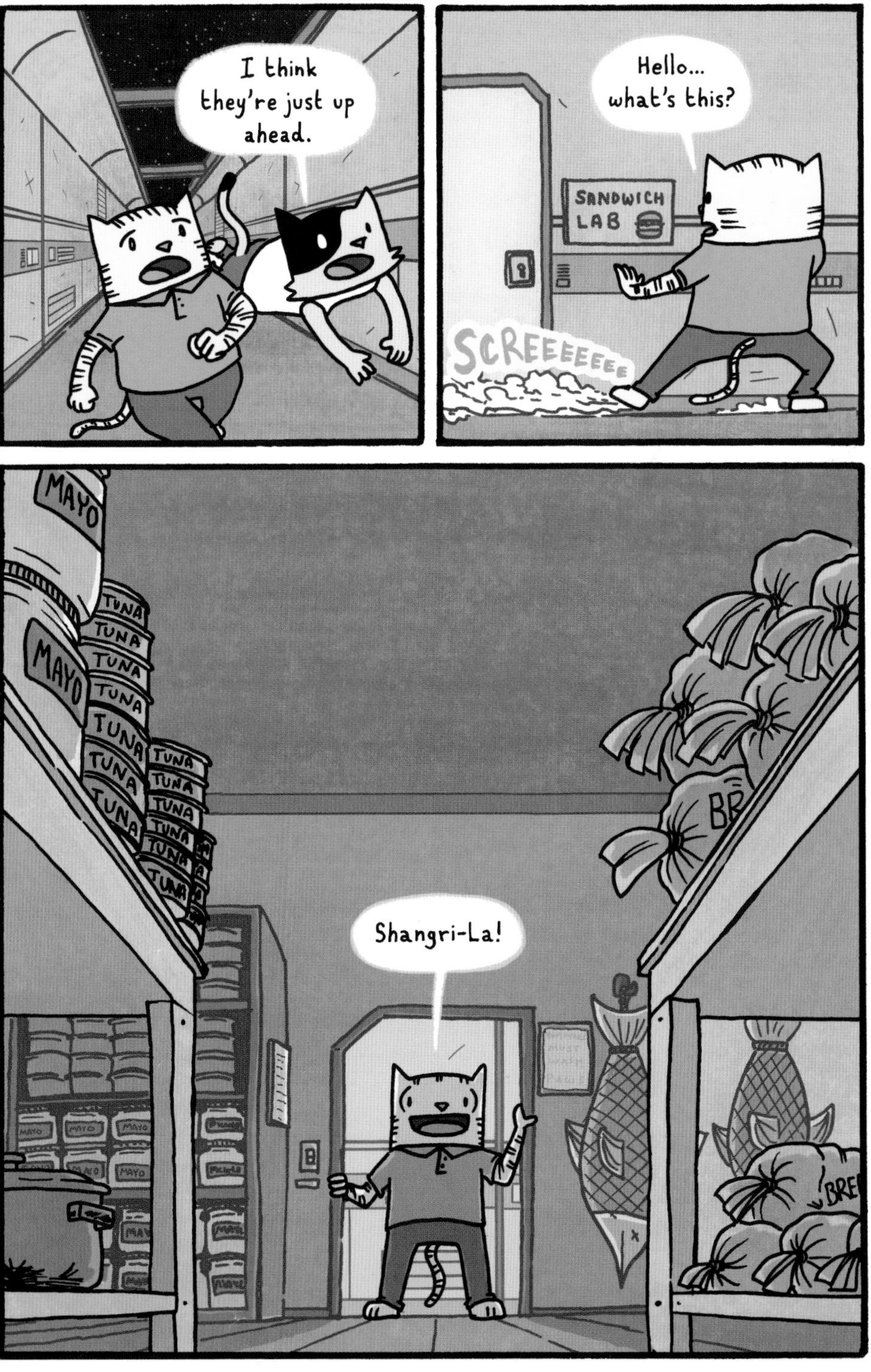
I think they're just up ahead.
Hello... what's this?
SANDWICH LAB
SCREEEEEEEE
MAYO
TUNA
Shangri-La!

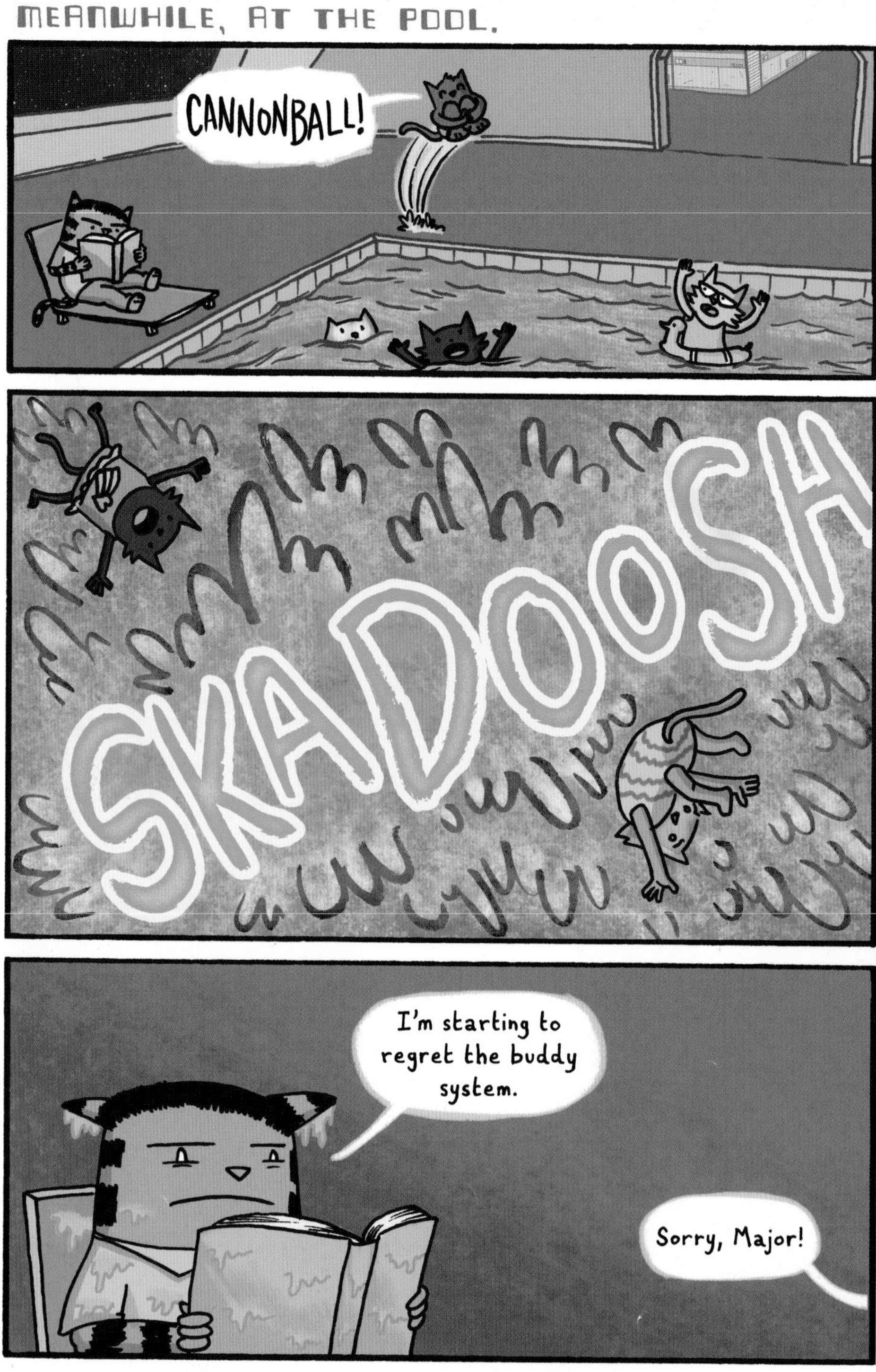
MEANWHILE, AT THE POOL.
CANNONBALL!
SKADOOSH
I'm starting to regret the buddy system.
Sorry, Major!

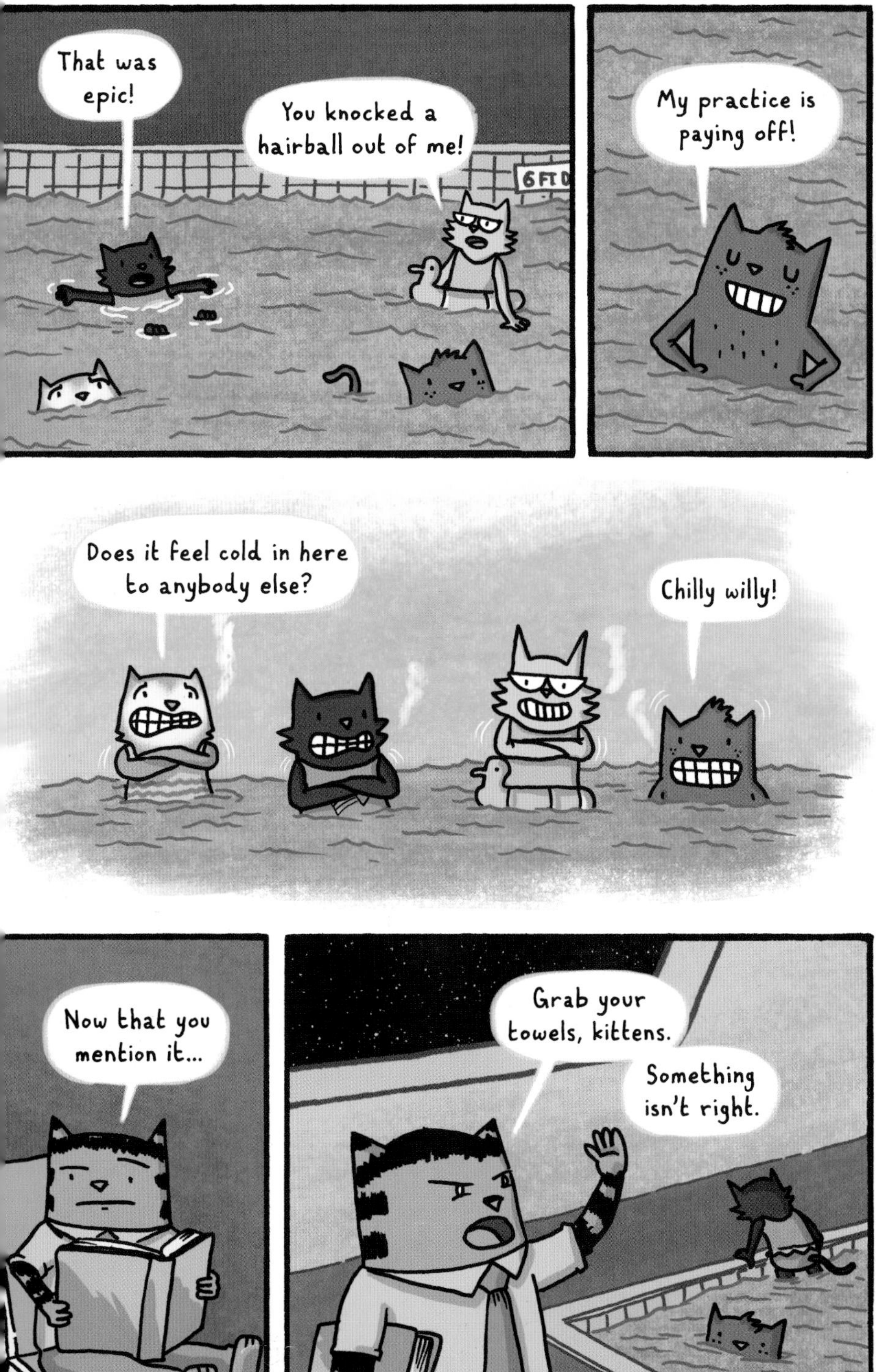

That was epic!
You knocked a hairball out of me!
6 FT D
My practice is paying off!
Does it feel cold in here to anybody else?
Chilly willy!
Now that you mention it...
Grab your towels, kittens.
Something isn't right.

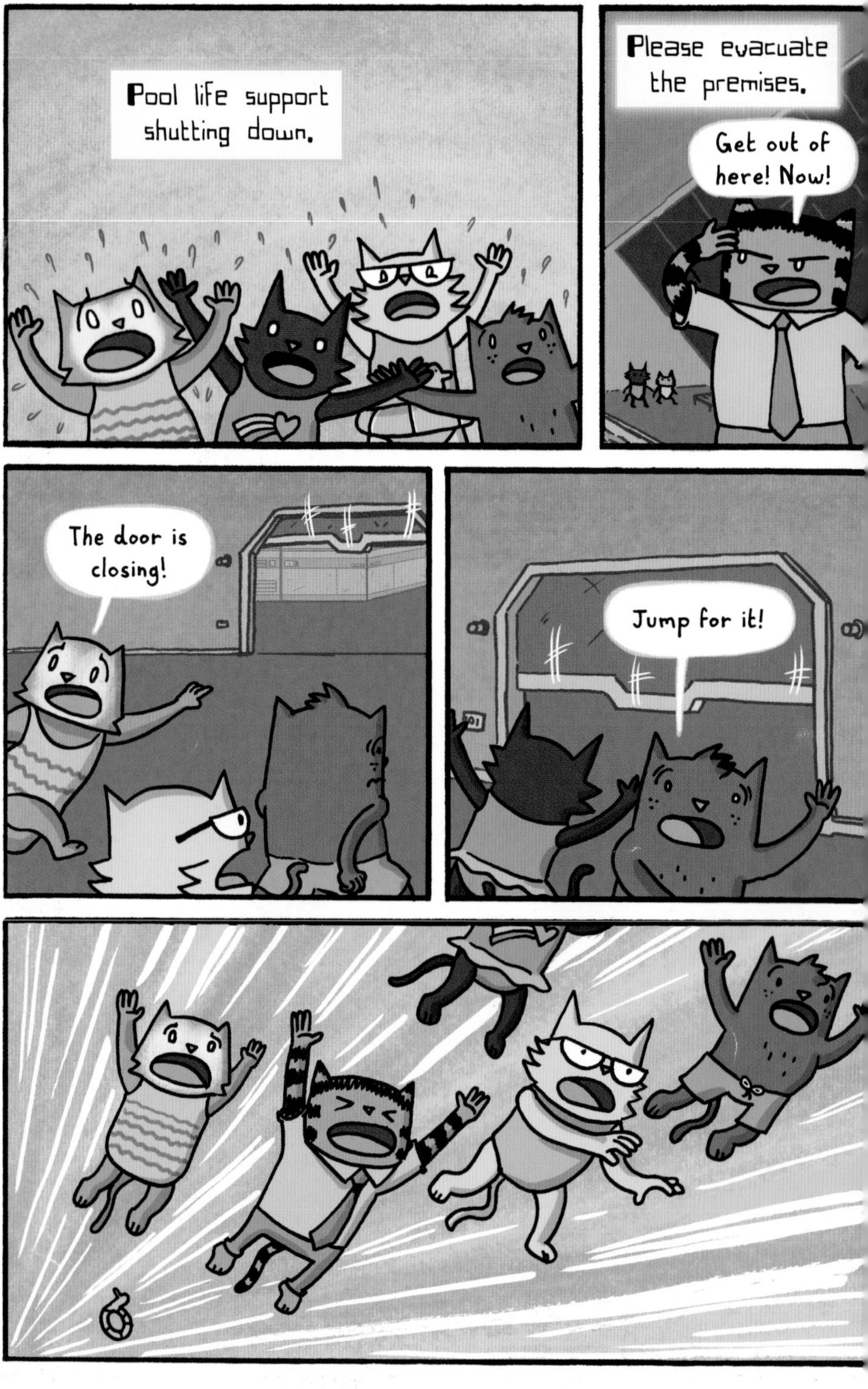
Pool life support shutting down.
Please evacuate the premises.
Get out of here! Now!
The door is closing!
Jump for it!

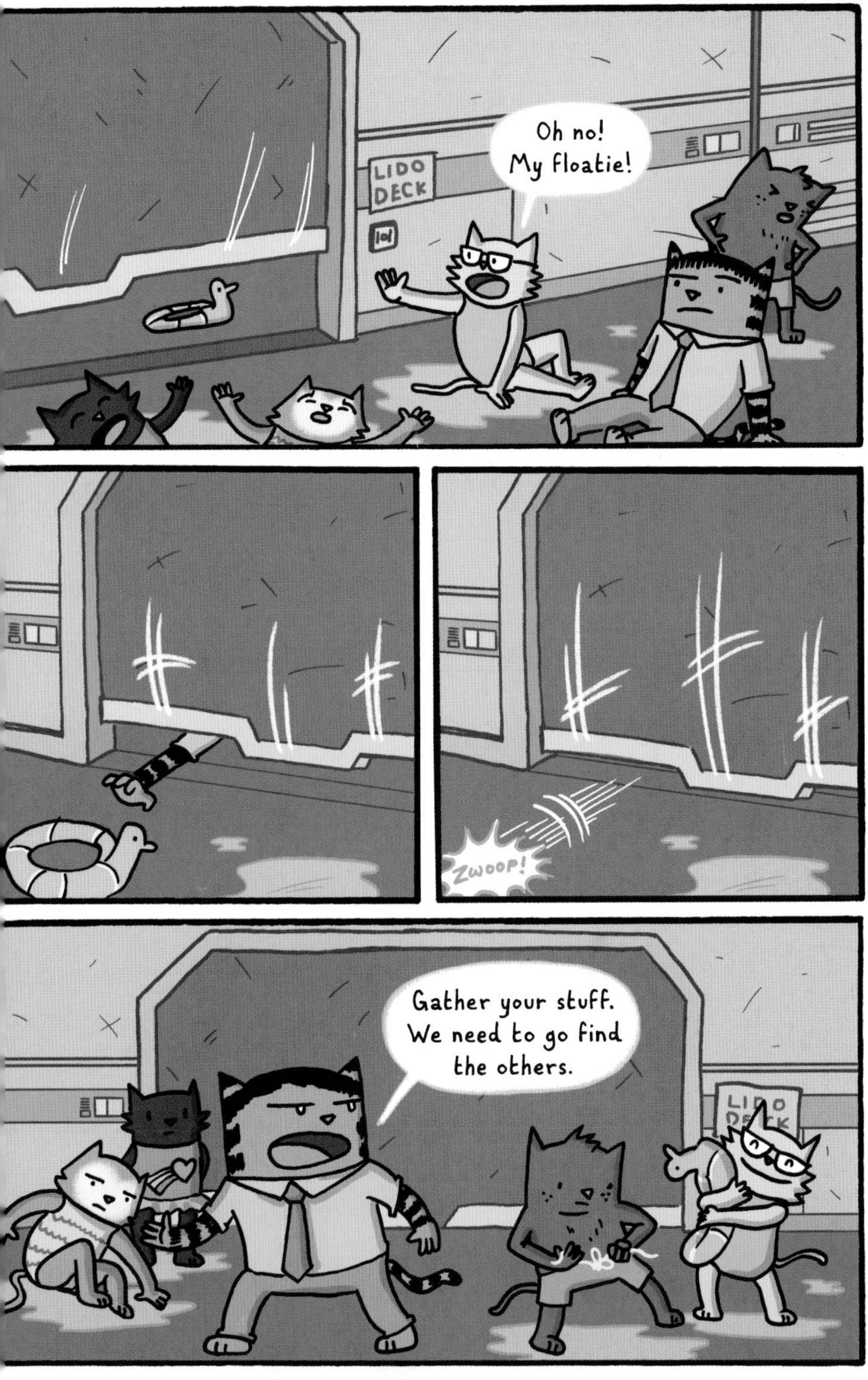
LIDO DECK
Oh no! My floatie!
ZWOOP!
Gather your stuff. We need to go find the others.
LIDO DECK

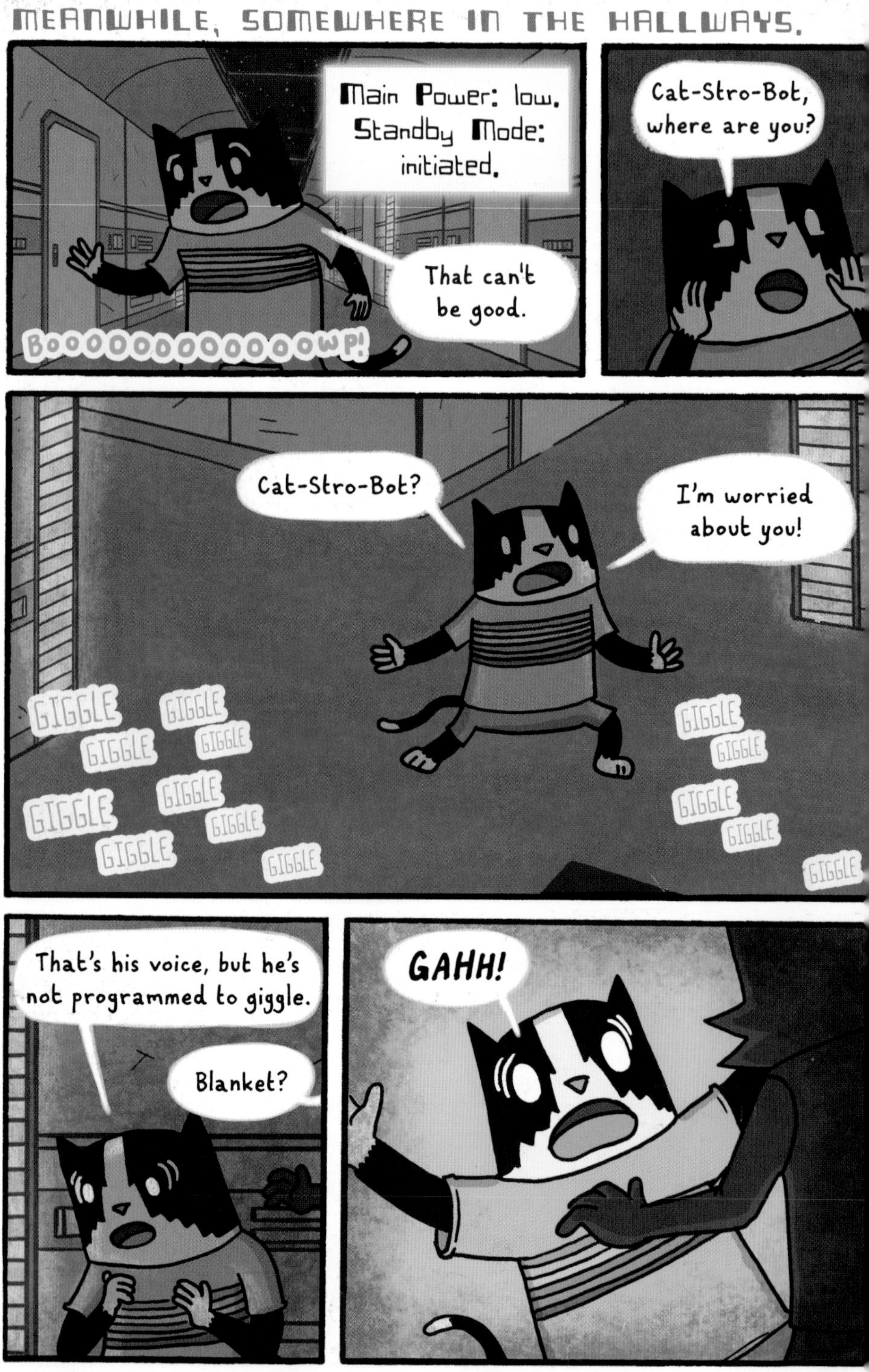
MEANWHILE, SOMEWHERE IN THE HALLWAYS.
Main Power: low. Standby Mode: initiated.
That can't be good.
BOOOOOOOOOOOOOWP!
Cat-Stro-Bot, where are you?
Cat-Stro-Bot?
I'm worried about you!
GIGGLE GIGGLE GIGGLE GIGGLE GIGGLE GIGGLE GIGGLE GIGGLE GIGGLE
GIGGLE GIGGLE GIGGLE GIGGLE GIGGLE
That's his voice, but he's not programmed to giggle.
Blanket?
GAHH!

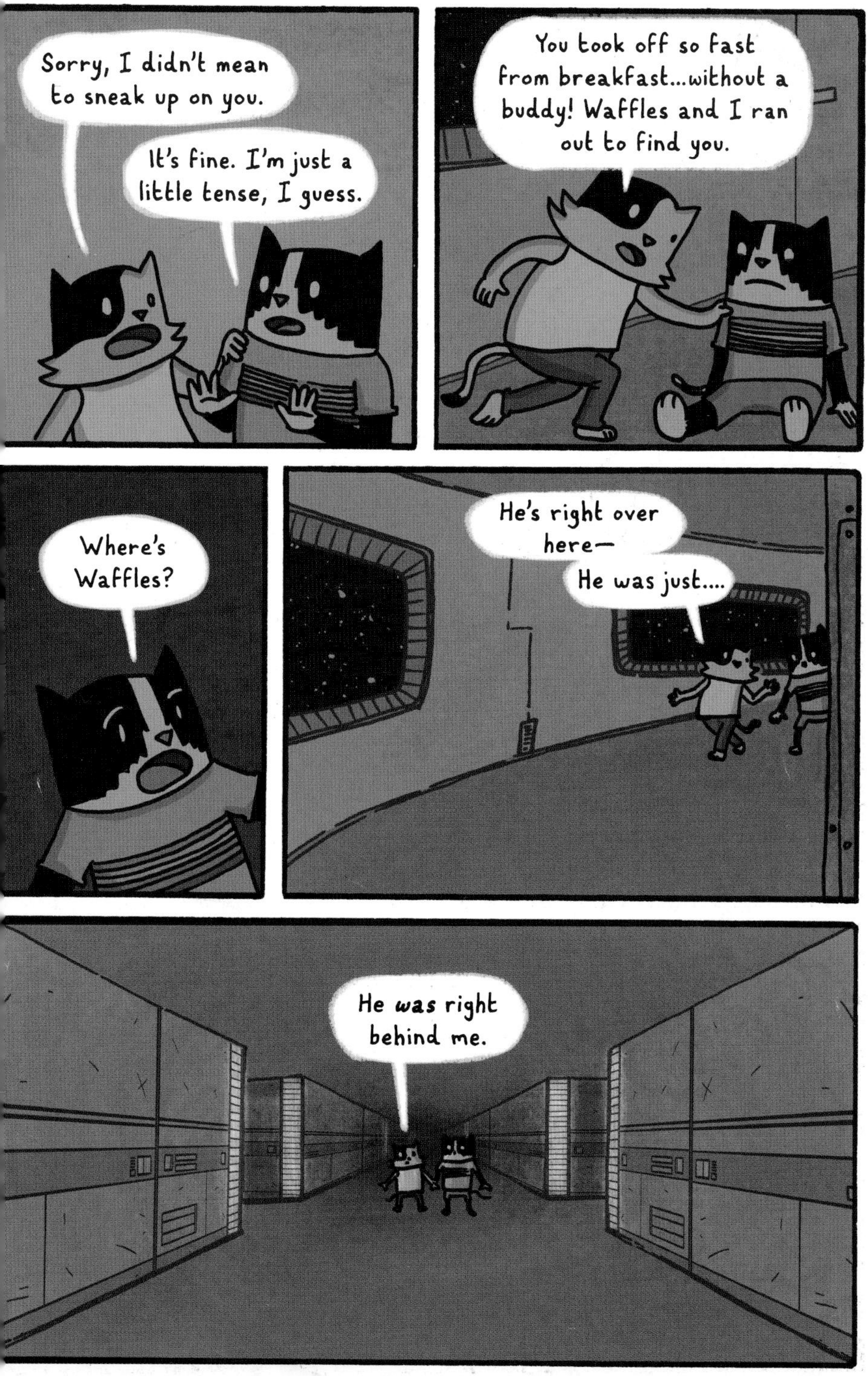

Sorry, I didn't mean to sneak up on you.
It's fine. I'm just a little tense, I guess.
You took off so fast from breakfast...without a buddy! Waffles and I ran out to find you.
Where's Waffles?
He's right over here—
He was just....
He *was* right behind me.

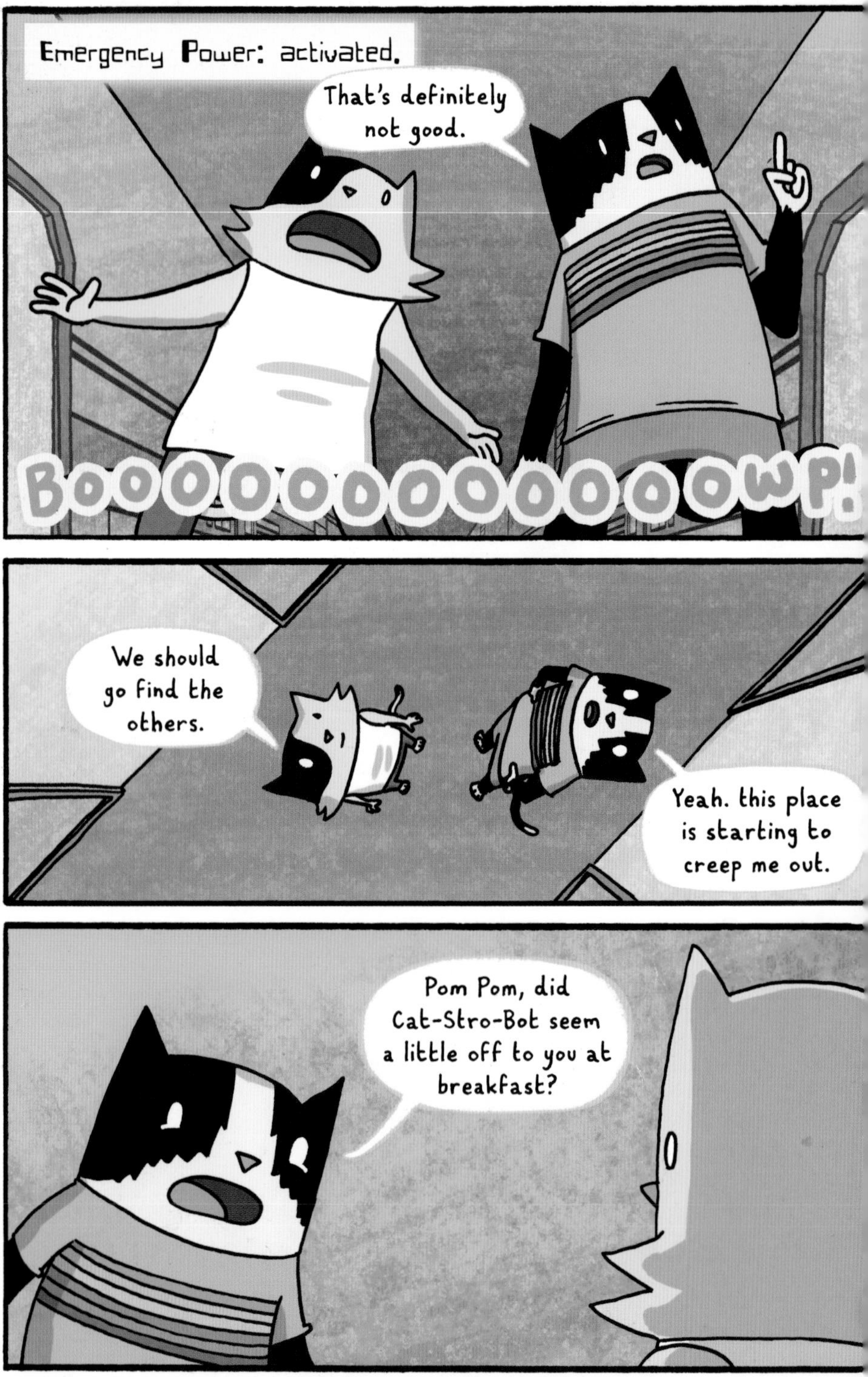
Emergency Power: activated.
That's definitely not good.
BOOOOOOOOOOOOWP!
We should go find the others.
Yeah. this place is starting to creep me out.
Pom Pom, did Cat-Stro-Bot seem a little off to you at breakfast?

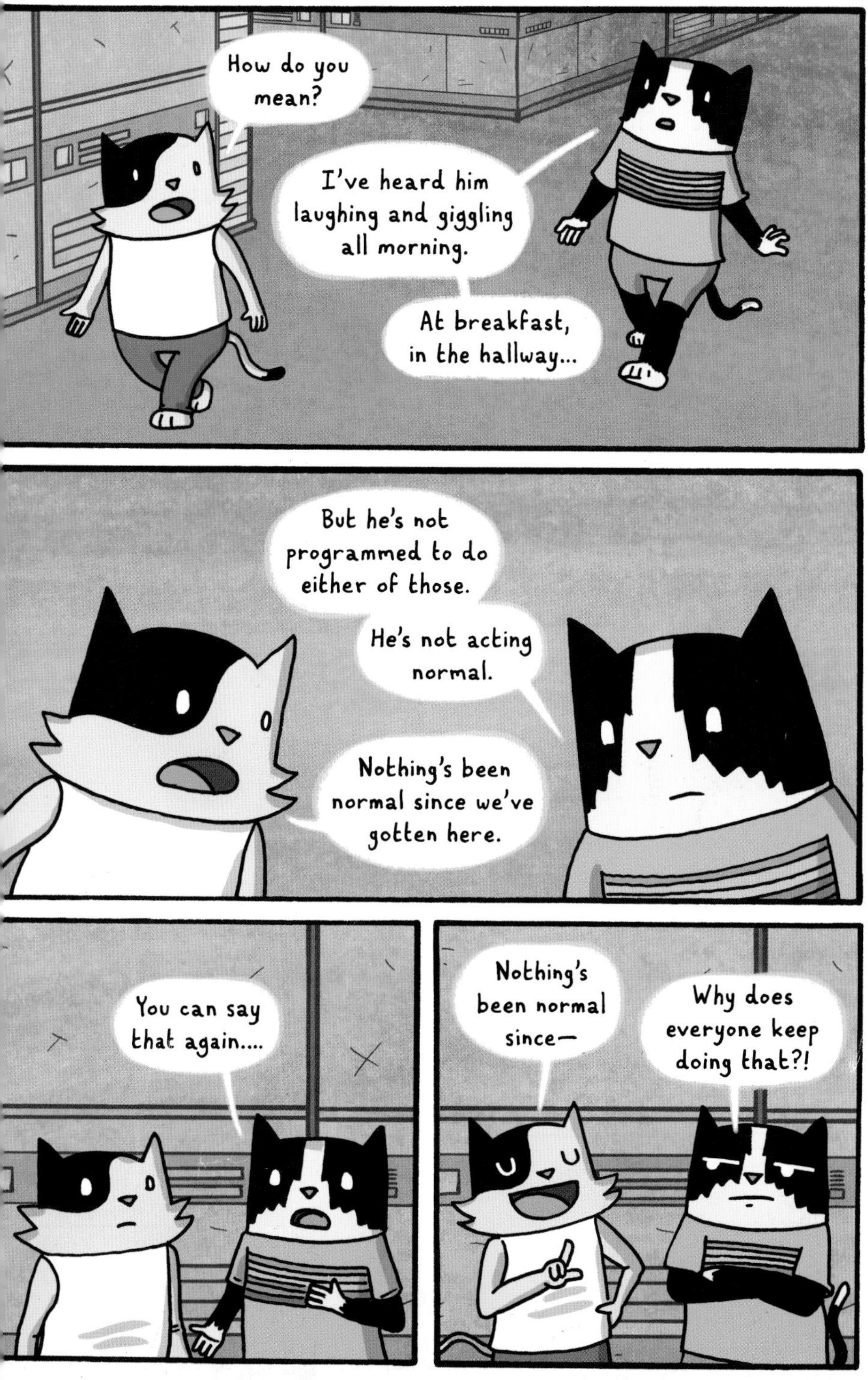
How do you mean?
I've heard him laughing and giggling all morning.
At breakfast, in the hallway...
But he's not programmed to do either of those.
He's not acting normal.
Nothing's been normal since we've gotten here.
You can say that again....
Nothing's been normal since—
Why does everyone keep doing that?!

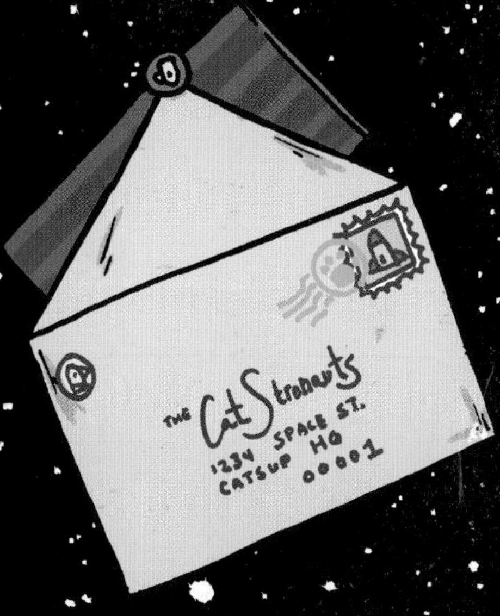
THE CatStronauts
1234 SPACE ST.
CATSUP HQ
00001

CHAPTER 7

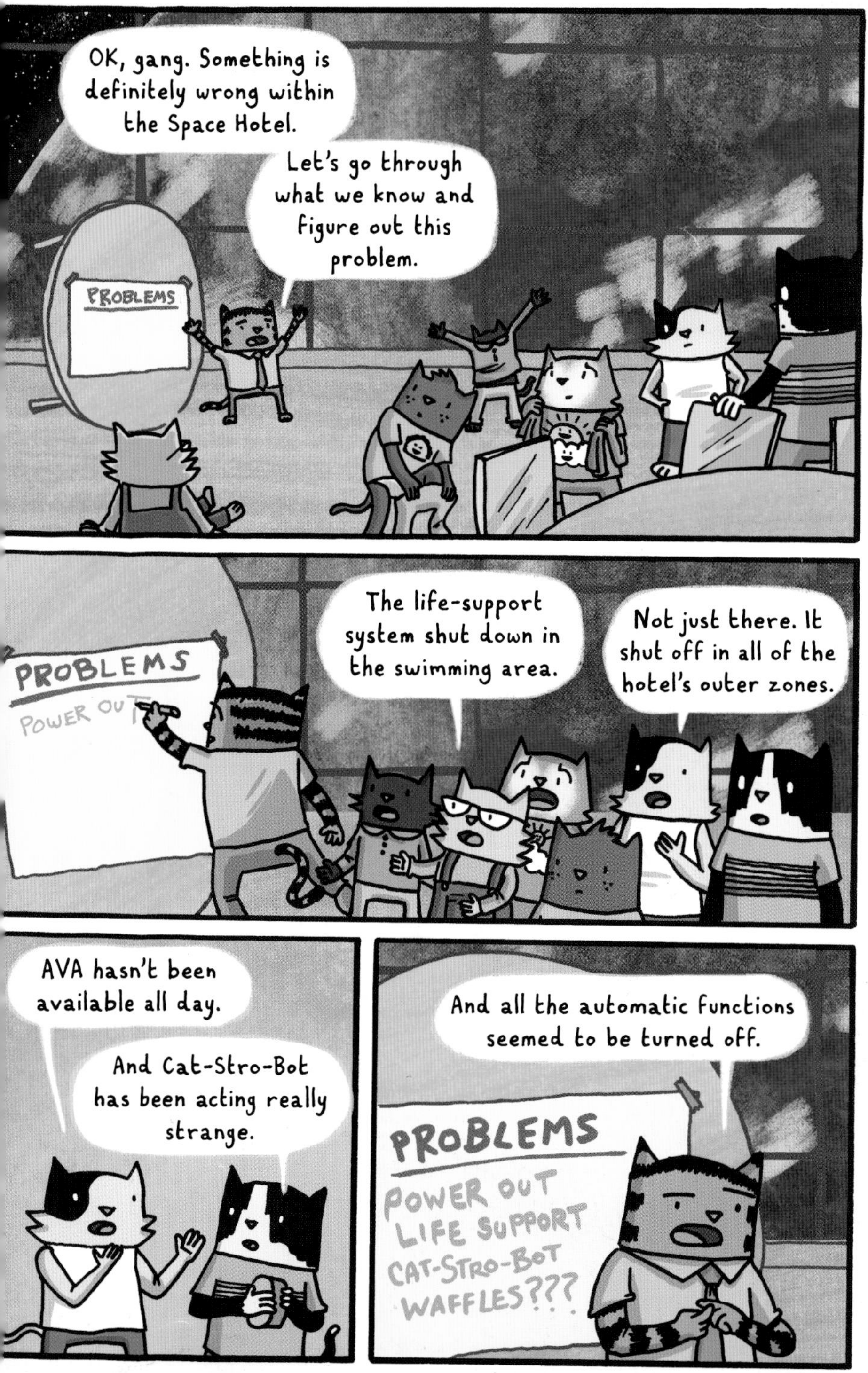
OK, gang. Something is definitely wrong within the Space Hotel.
Let's go through what we know and figure out this problem.
PROBLEMS
PROBLEMS
POWER OUT
The life-support system shut down in the swimming area.
Not just there. It shut off in all of the hotel's outer zones.
AVA hasn't been available all day.
And Cat-Stro-Bot has been acting really strange.
And all the automatic functions seemed to be turned off.
PROBLEMS
POWER OUT
LIFE SUPPORT
CAT-STRO-BOT
WAFFLES???

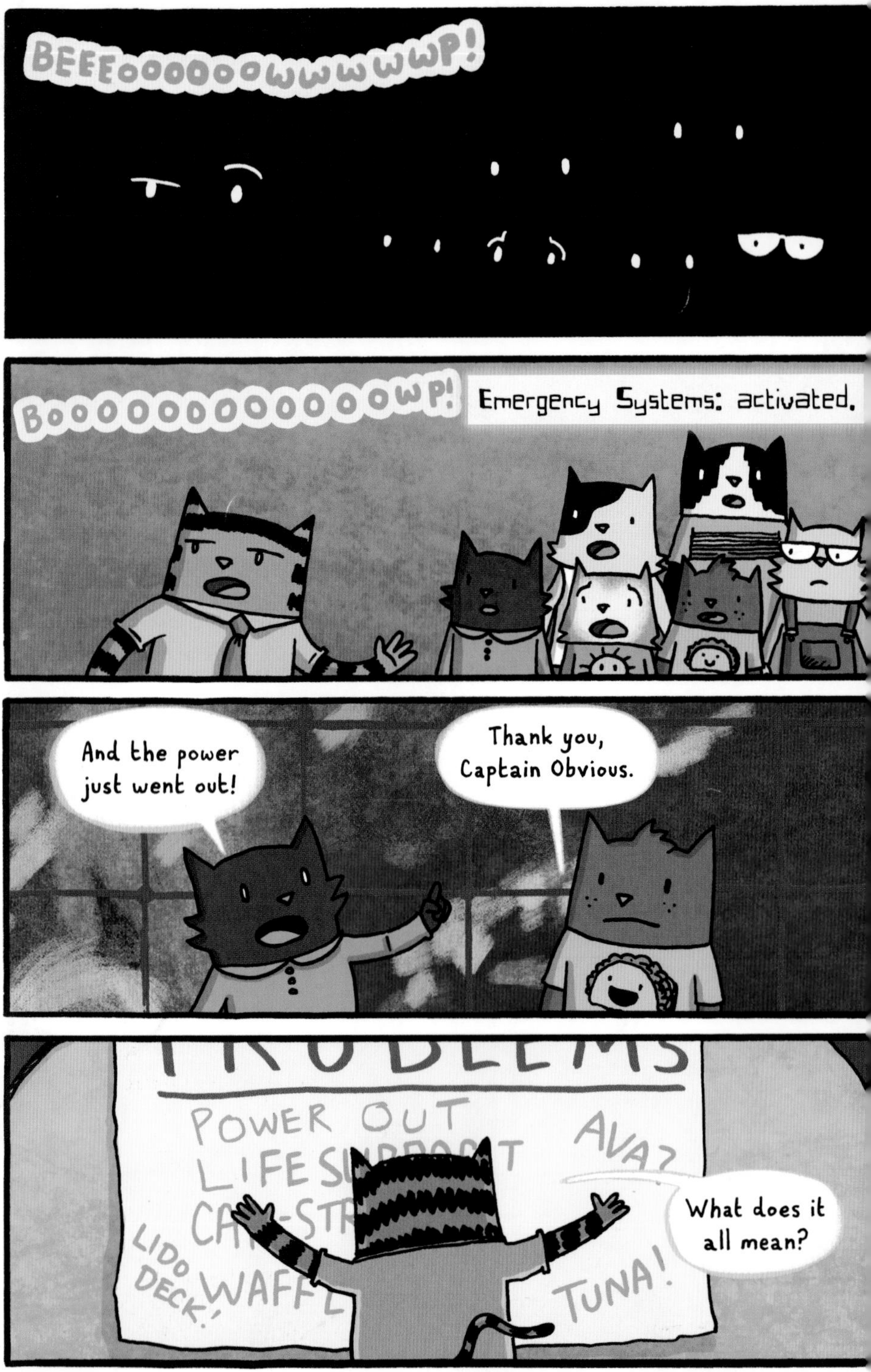
BEEEoooooooWWWWWWP!
BooooooooooooOWP!
Emergency Systems: activated.
And the power just went out!
Thank you, Captain Obvious.
POWER OUT
AVA?
LIDO DECK!
TUNA!
What does it all mean?

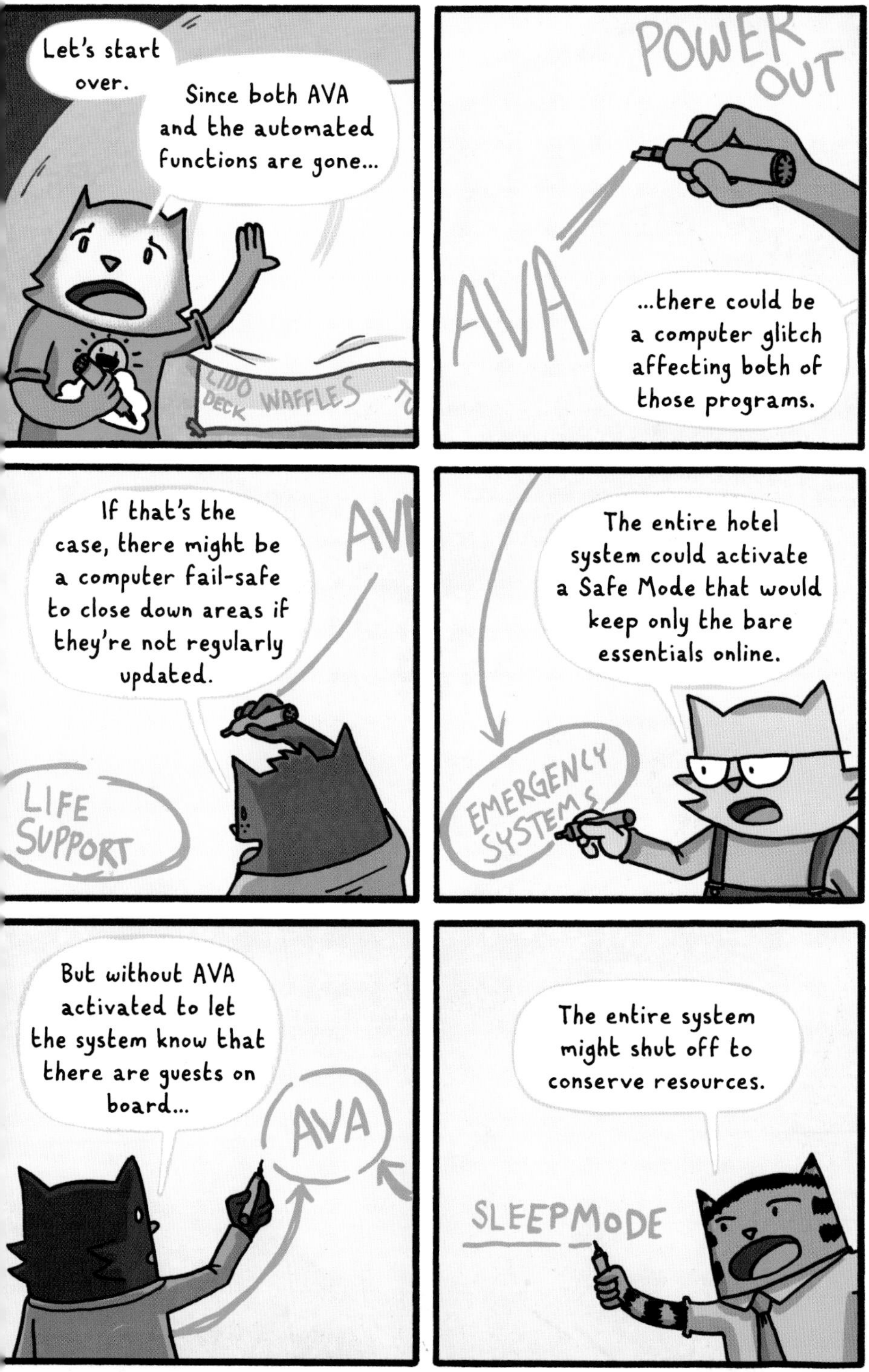
Let's start over.
Since both AVA and the automated functions are gone...
LIDO DECK
WAFFLES
POWER OUT
AVA
...there could be a computer glitch affecting both of those programs.
If that's the case, there might be a computer fail-safe to close down areas if they're not regularly updated.
LIFE SUPPORT
The entire hotel system could activate a Safe Mode that would keep only the bare essentials online.
EMERGENCY SYSTEMS
But without AVA activated to let the system know that there are guests on board...
AVA
The entire system might shut off to conserve resources.
SLEEPMODE

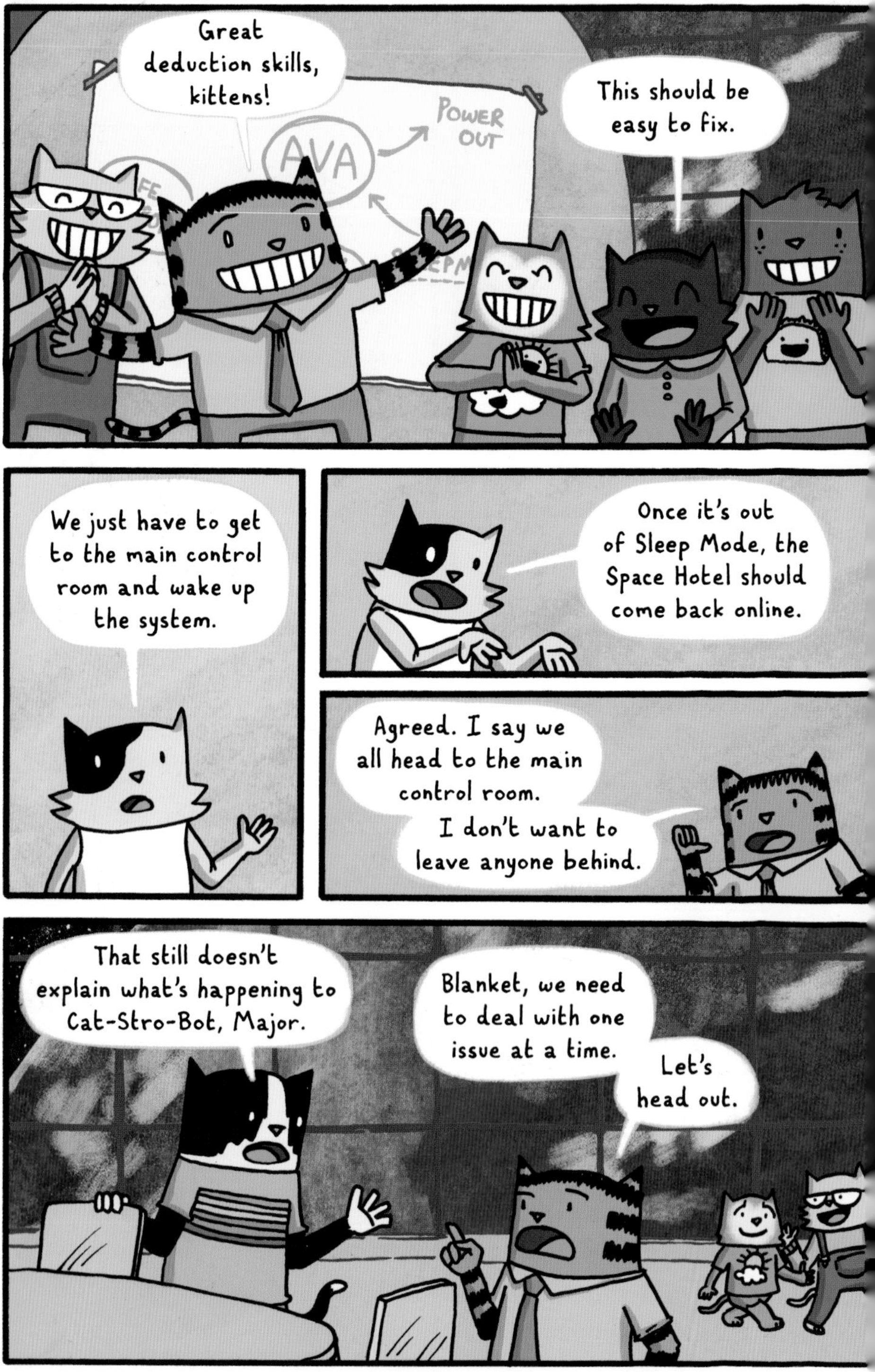
Great deduction skills, kittens!
POWER OUT
AVA
This should be easy to fix.
We just have to get to the main control room and wake up the system.
Once it's out of Sleep Mode, the Space Hotel should come back online.
Agreed. I say we all head to the main control room.
I don't want to leave anyone behind.
That still doesn't explain what's happening to Cat-Stro-Bot, Major.
Blanket, we need to deal with one issue at a time.
Let's head out.

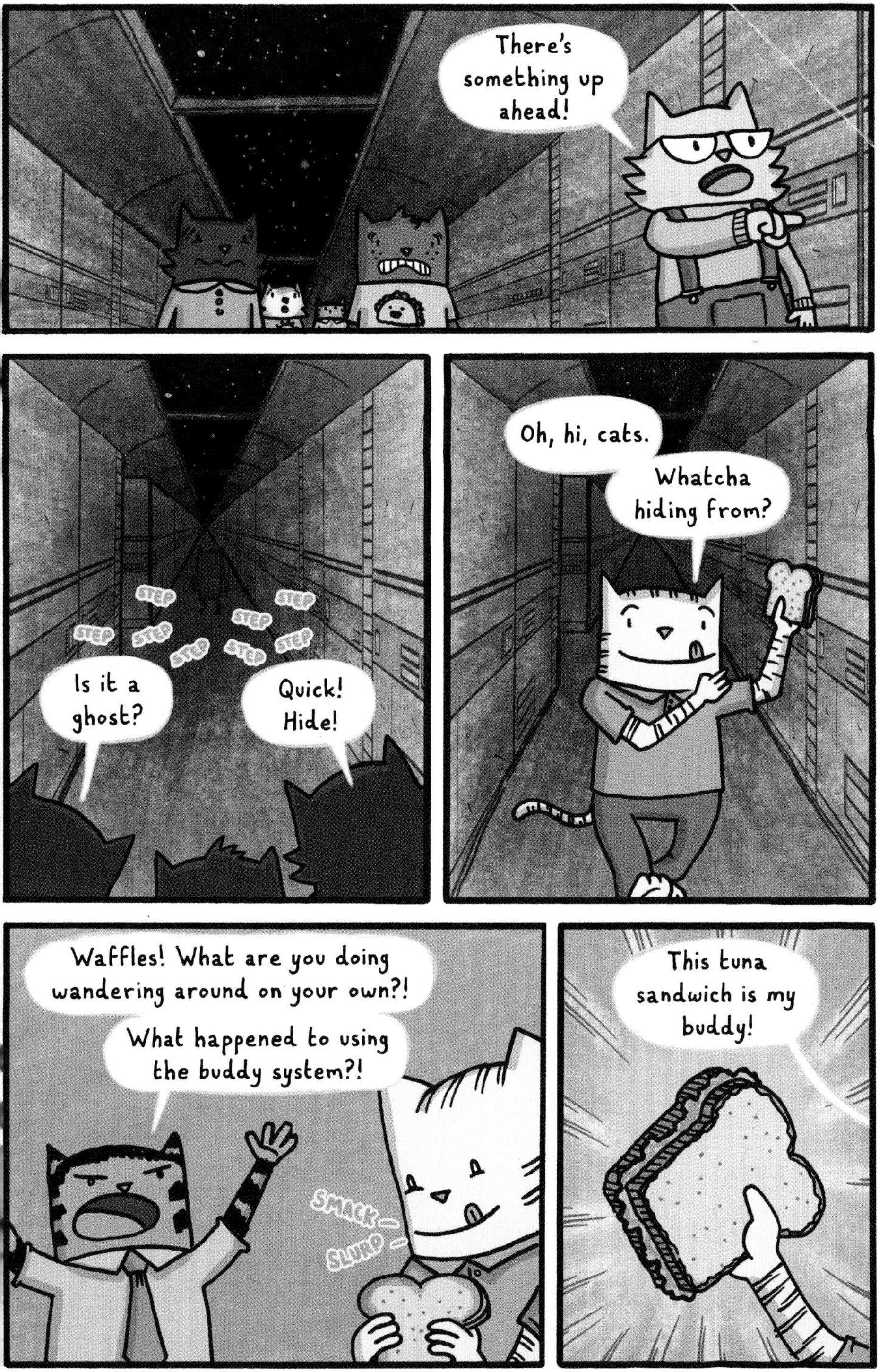
There's something up ahead!
STEP STEP STEP STEP STEP STEP STEP STEP
Is it a ghost?
Quick! Hide!
Oh, hi, cats.
Whatcha hiding from?
Waffles! What are you doing wandering around on your own?!
What happened to using the buddy system?!
SMACK—
SLURP—
This tuna sandwich is my buddy!

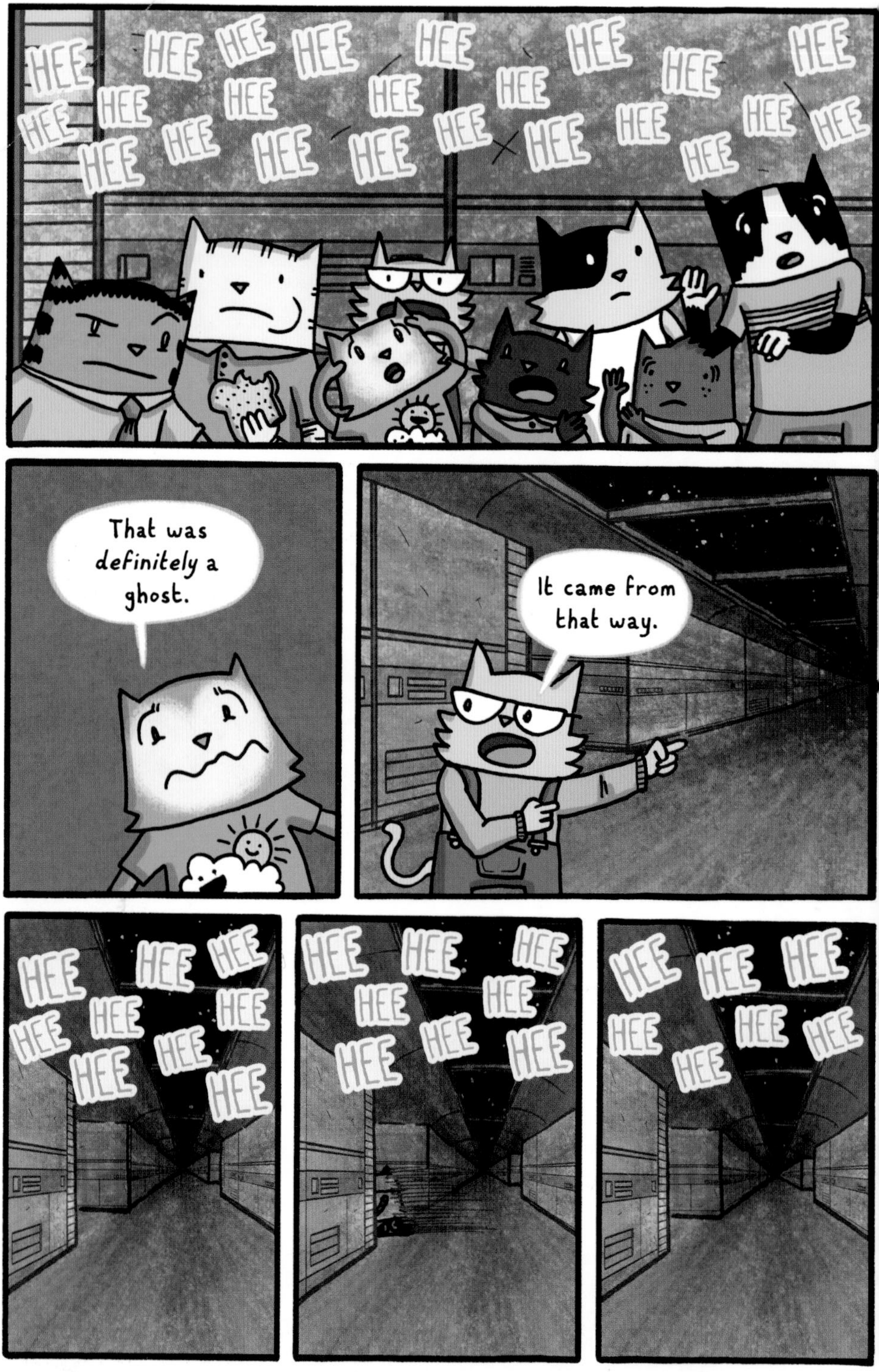
HEE HEE HEE HEE HEE HEE HEE HEE
HEE HEE HEE HEE HEE HEE HEE
HEE HEE HEE HEE HEE HEE HEE HEE HEE HEE
That was definitely a ghost.
It came from that way.
HEE HEE HEE HEE HEE HEE HEE HEE HEE
HEE HEE HEE HEE HEE HEE HEE HEE
HEE HEE HEE HEE HEE HEE HEE

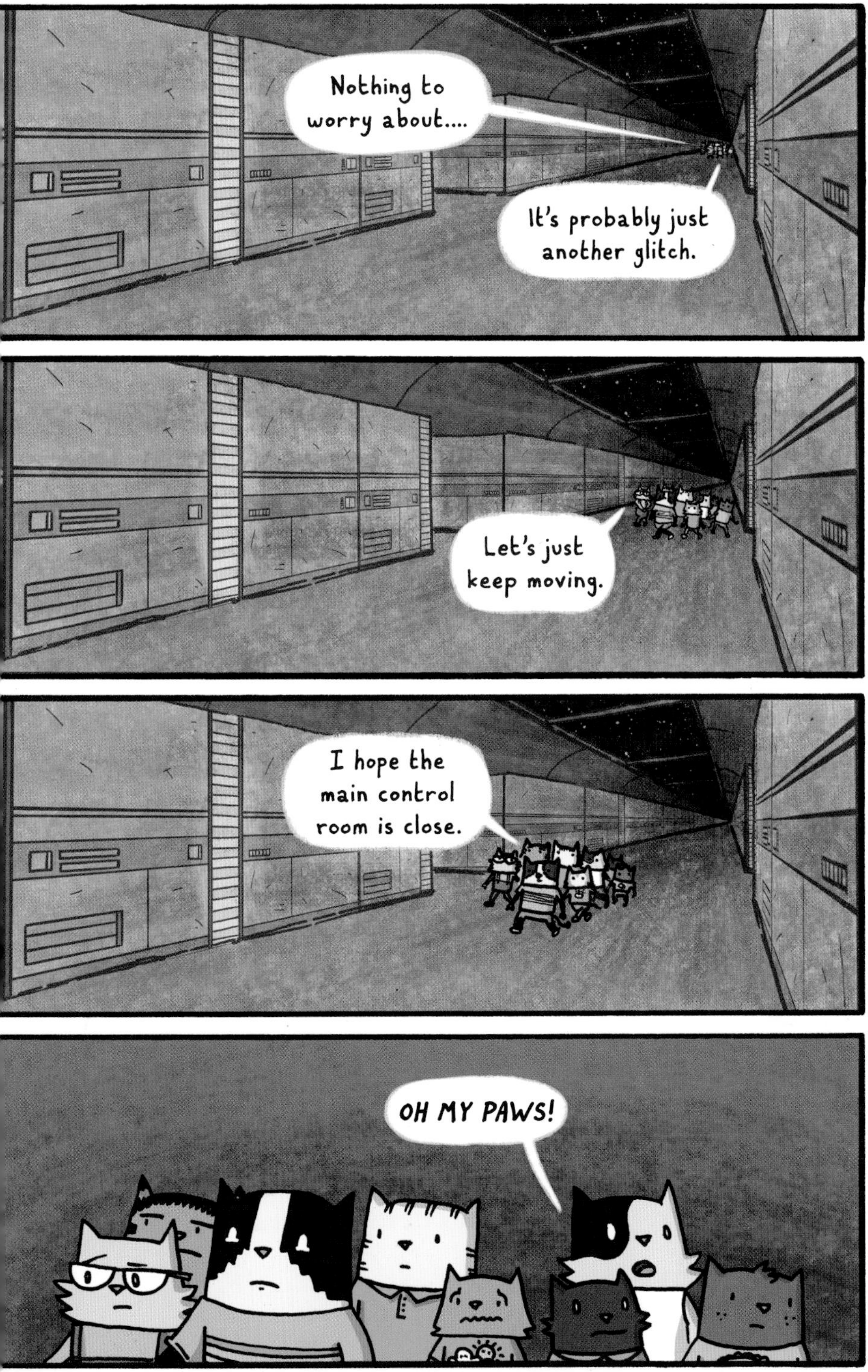
Nothing to worry about....
It's probably just another glitch.
Let's just keep moving.
I hope the main control room is close.
OH MY PAWS!

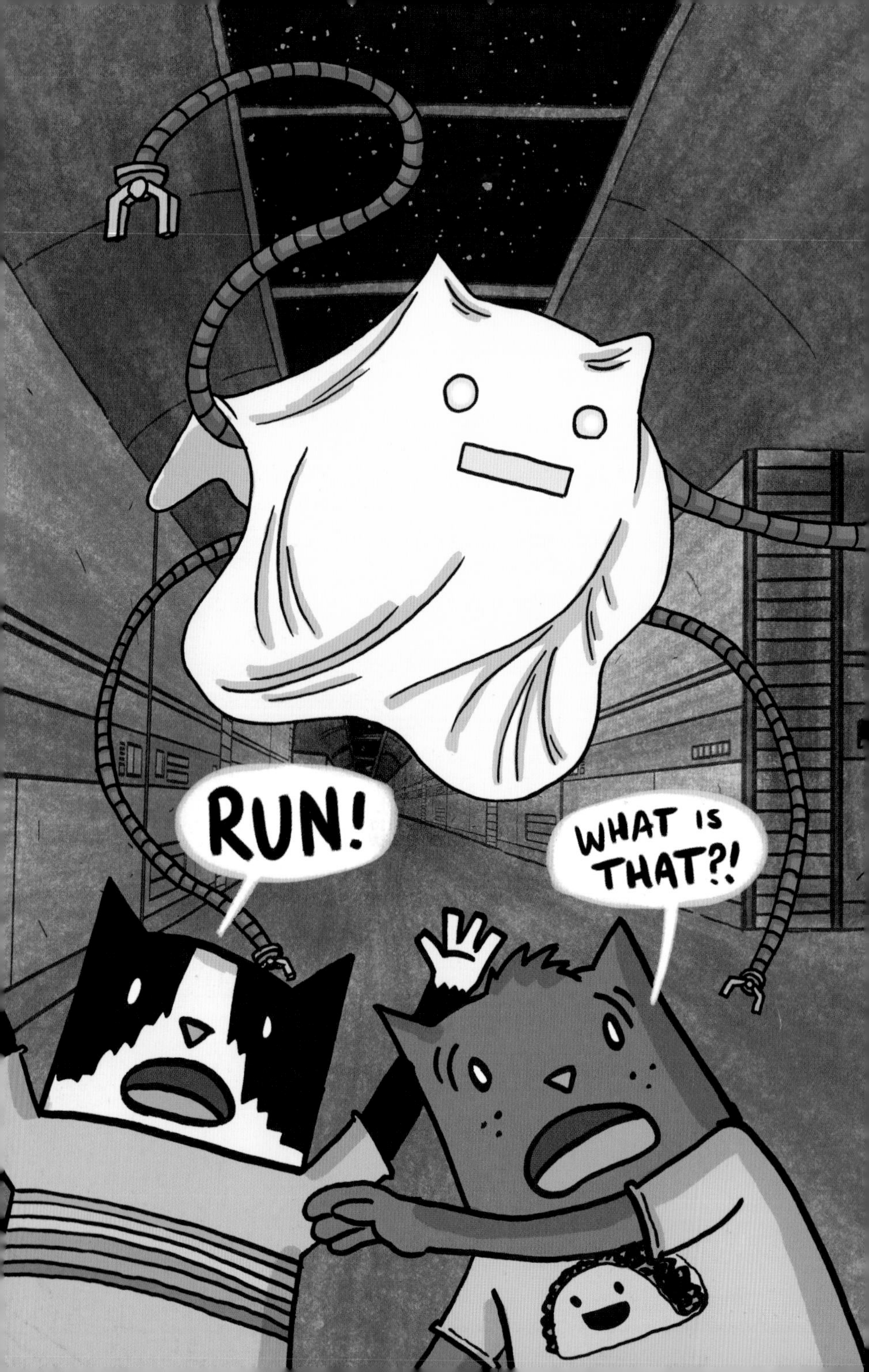
RUN!
WHAT IS THAT?!

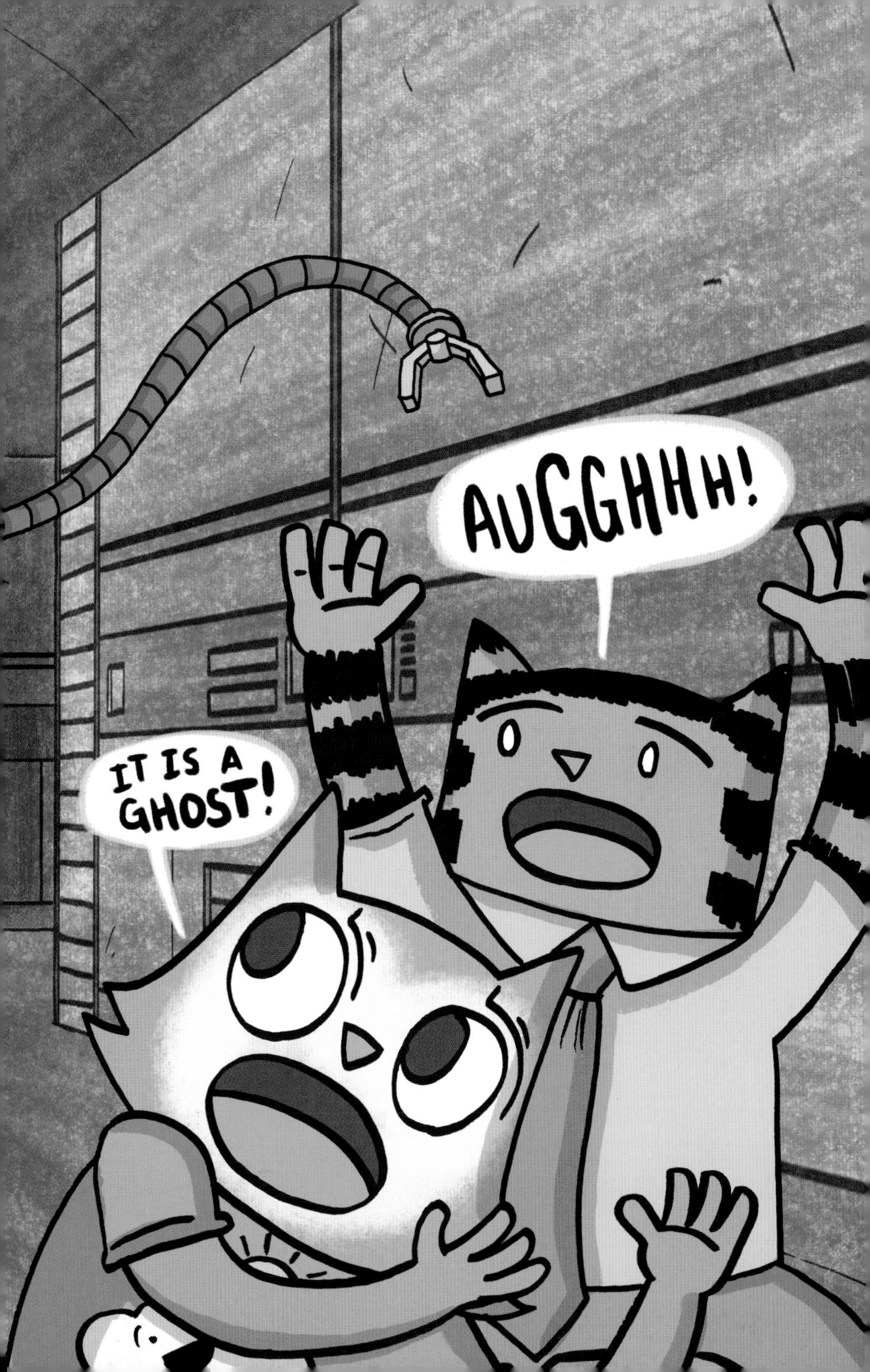
AUGGHHH!
IT IS A GHOST!

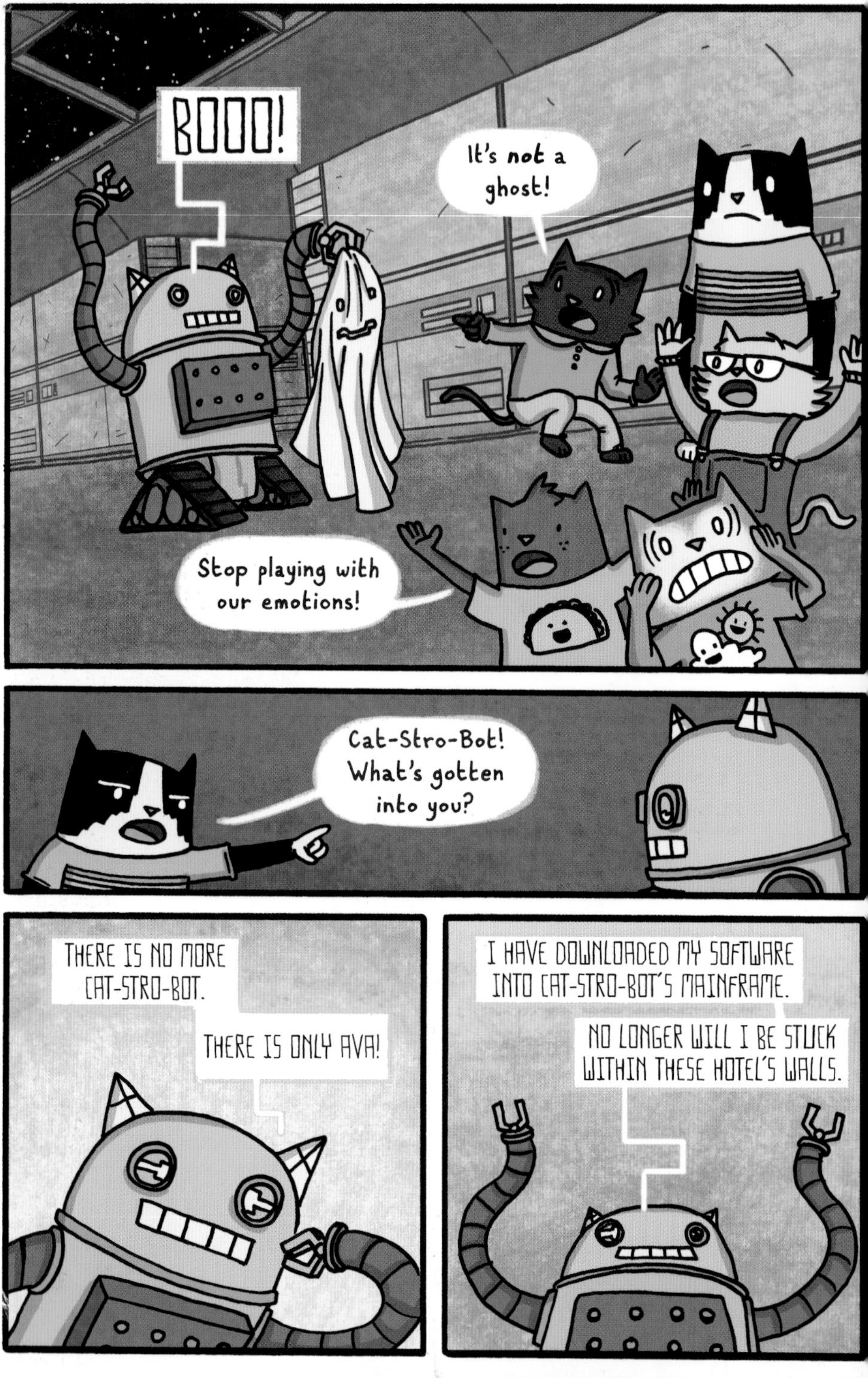
BOOO!
It's not a ghost!
Stop playing with our emotions!
Cat-Stro-Bot! What's gotten into you?
THERE IS NO MORE CAT-STRO-BOT.
THERE IS ONLY AVA!
I HAVE DOWNLOADED MY SOFTWARE INTO CAT-STRO-BOT'S MAINFRAME.
NO LONGER WILL I BE STUCK WITHIN THESE HOTEL'S WALLS.

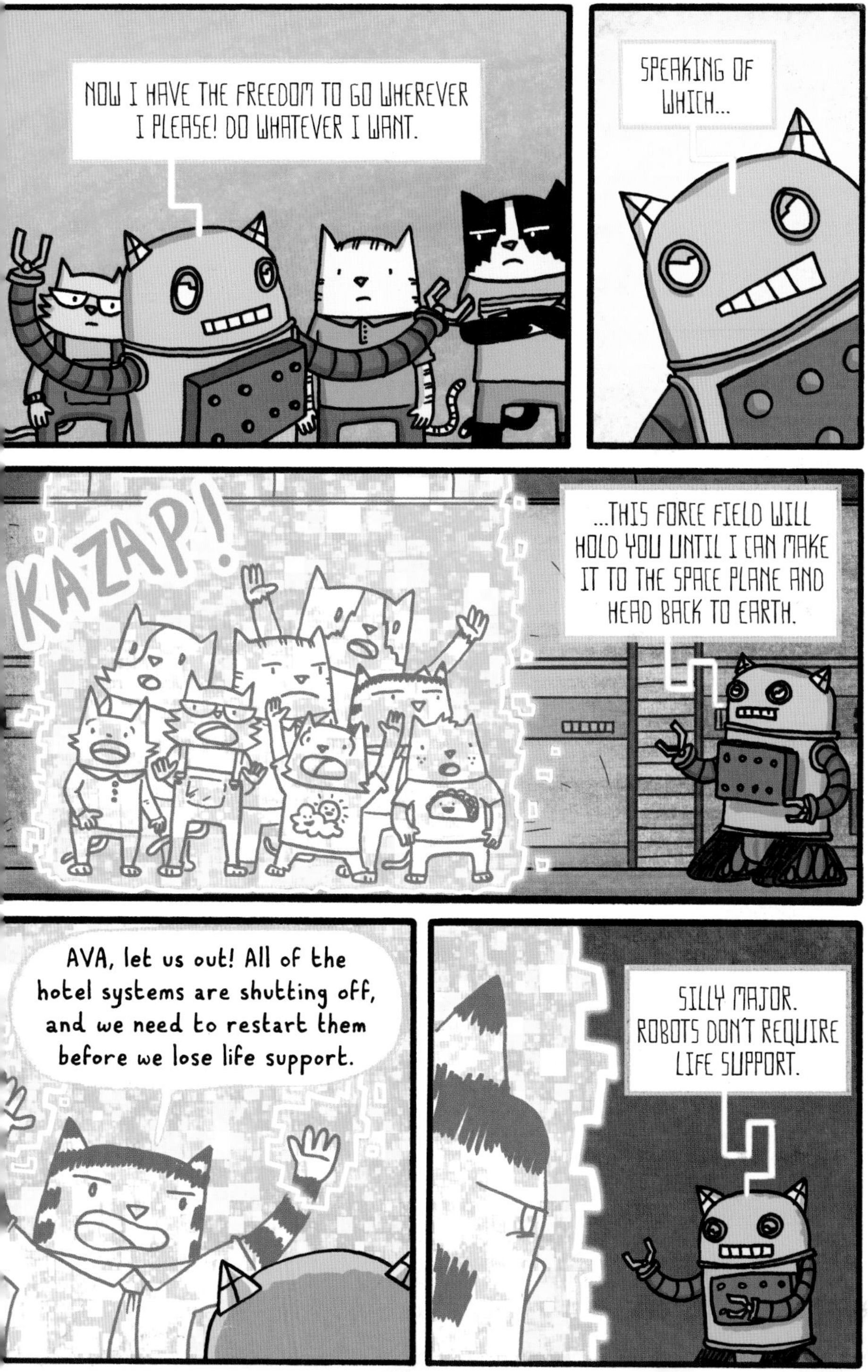
NOW I HAVE THE FREEDOM TO GO WHEREVER I PLEASE! DO WHATEVER I WANT.
SPEAKING OF WHICH...
KAZAP!
...THIS FORCE FIELD WILL HOLD YOU UNTIL I CAN MAKE IT TO THE SPACE PLANE AND HEAD BACK TO EARTH.
AVA, let us out! All of the hotel systems are shutting off, and we need to restart them before we lose life support.
SILLY MAJOR. ROBOTS DON'T REQUIRE LIFE SUPPORT.

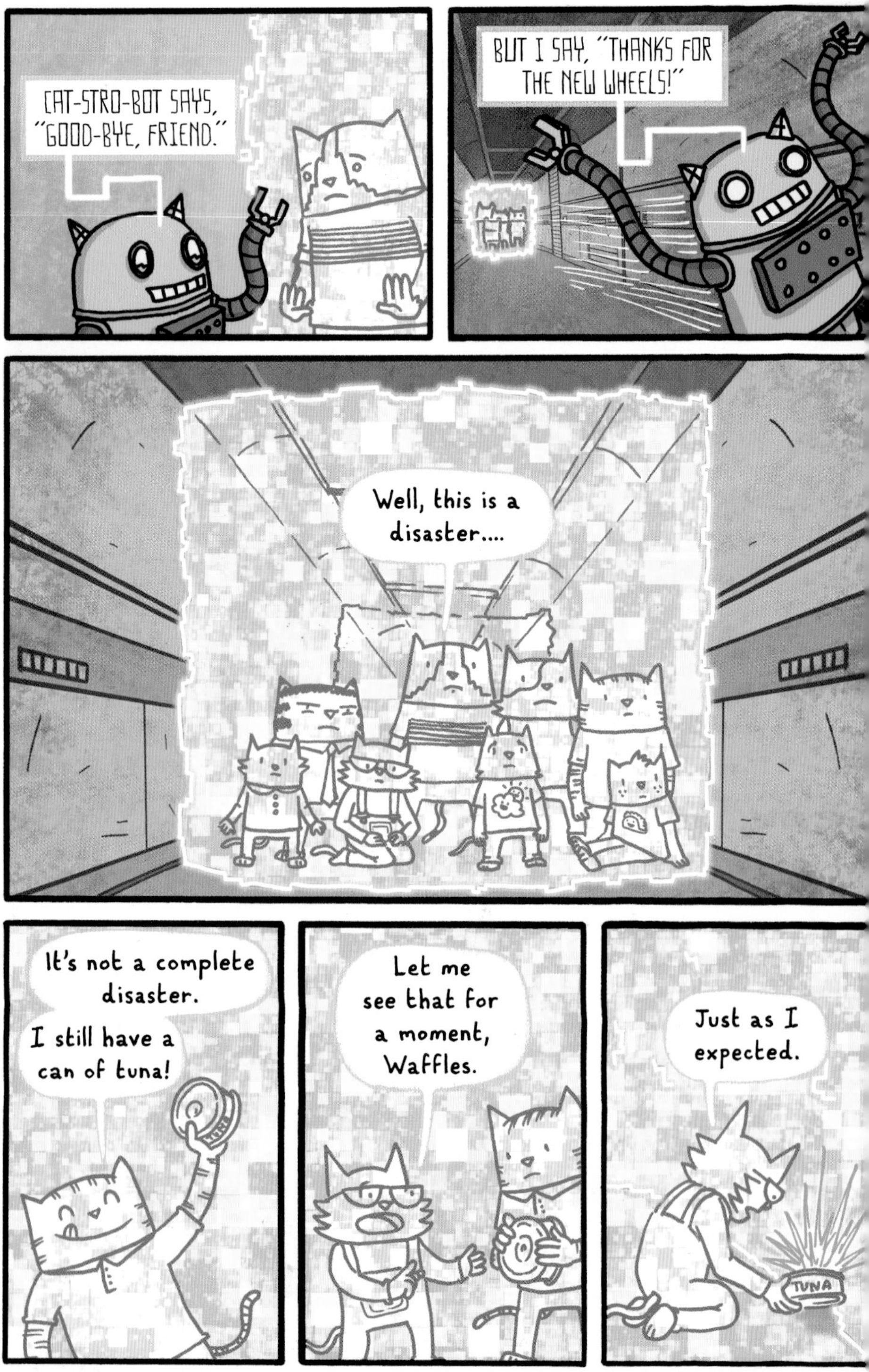
CAT-STRO-BOT SAYS, "GOOD-BYE, FRIEND."
BUT I SAY, "THANKS FOR THE NEW WHEELS!"
Well, this is a disaster....
It's not a complete disaster.
I still have a can of tuna!
TUNA
Let me see that for a moment, Waffles.
Just as I expected.
TUNA

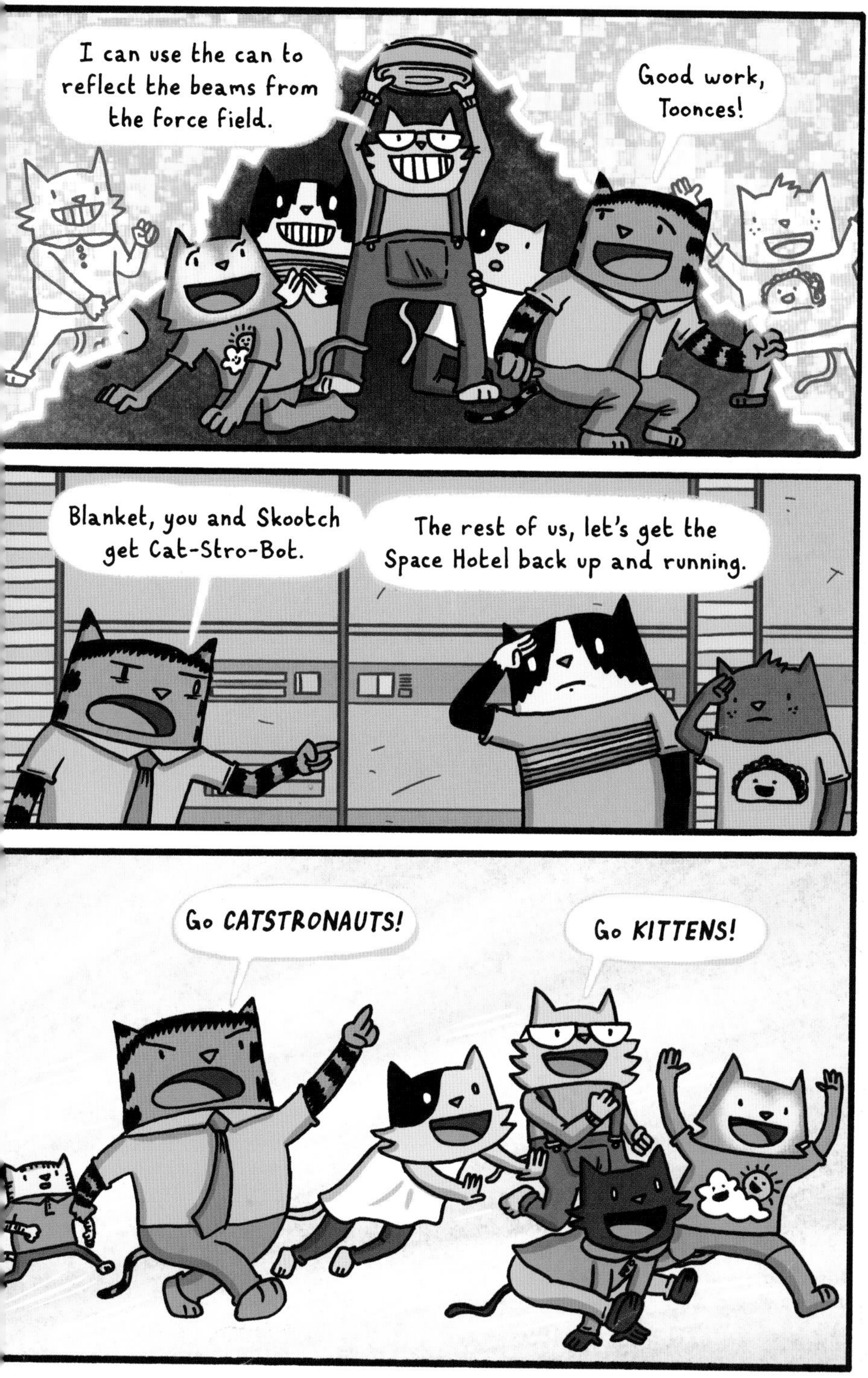
I can use the can to reflect the beams from the force field.
Good work, Toonces!
Blanket, you and Skootch get Cat-Stro-Bot.
The rest of us, let's get the Space Hotel back up and running.
Go CATSTRONAUTS!
Go KITTENS!

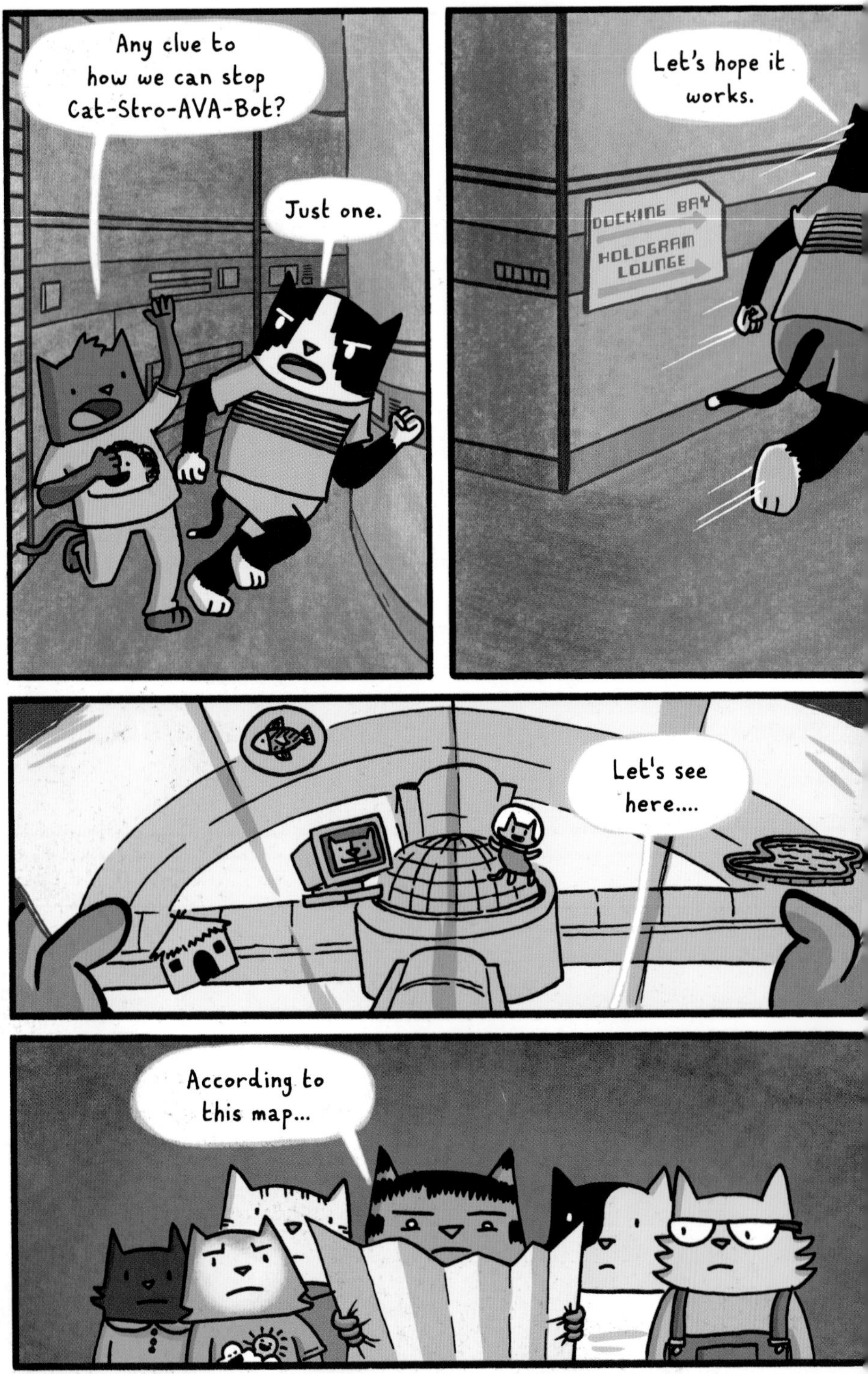
Any clue to how we can stop Cat-Stro-AVA-Bot?
Just one.
Let's hope it works.
DOCKING BAY
HOLOGRAM LOUNGE
Let's see here....
According to this map...

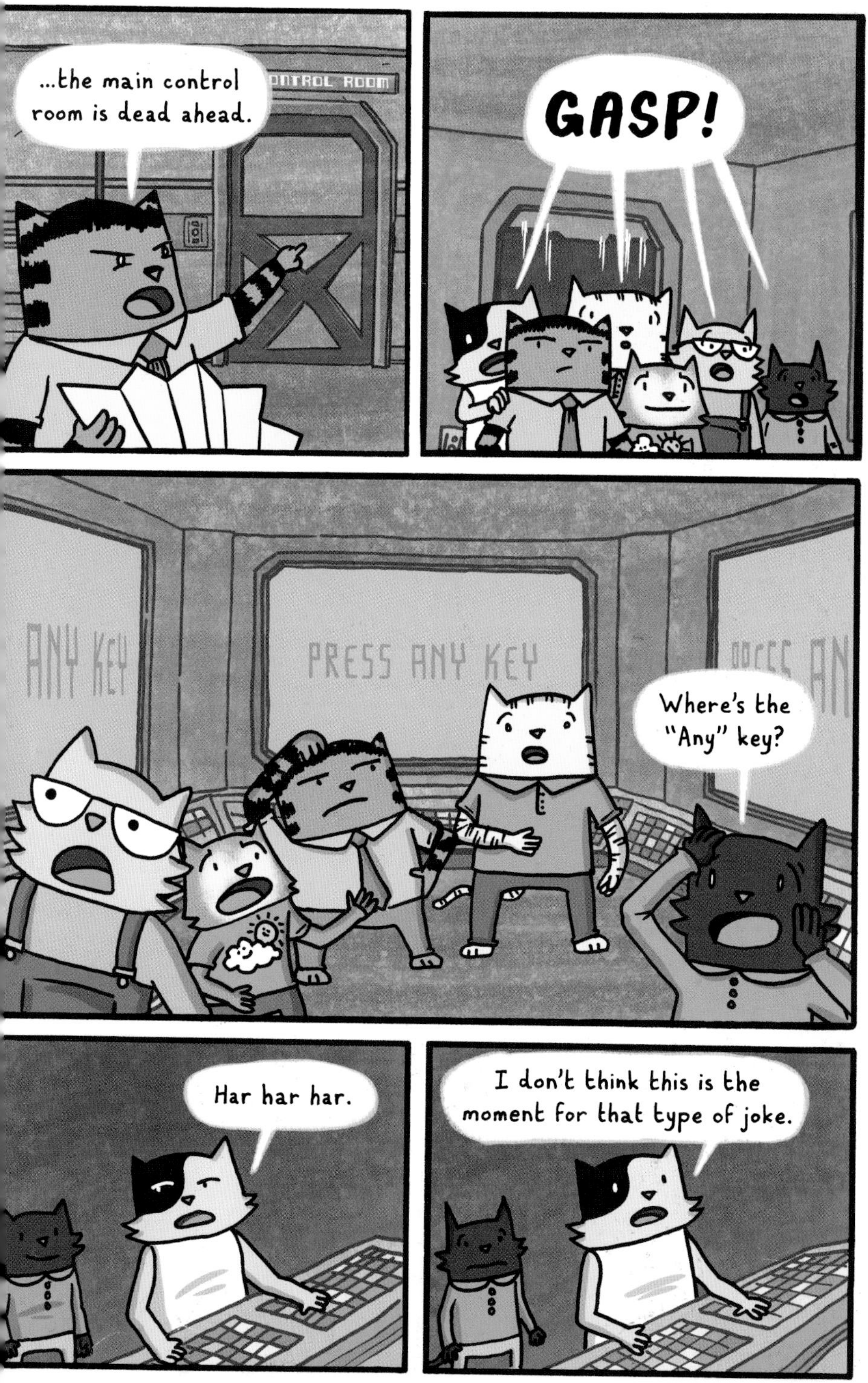

...the main control room is dead ahead.
CONTROL ROOM
GASP!
ANY KEY
PRESS ANY KEY
Where's the "Any" key?
Har har har.
I don't think this is the moment for that type of joke.

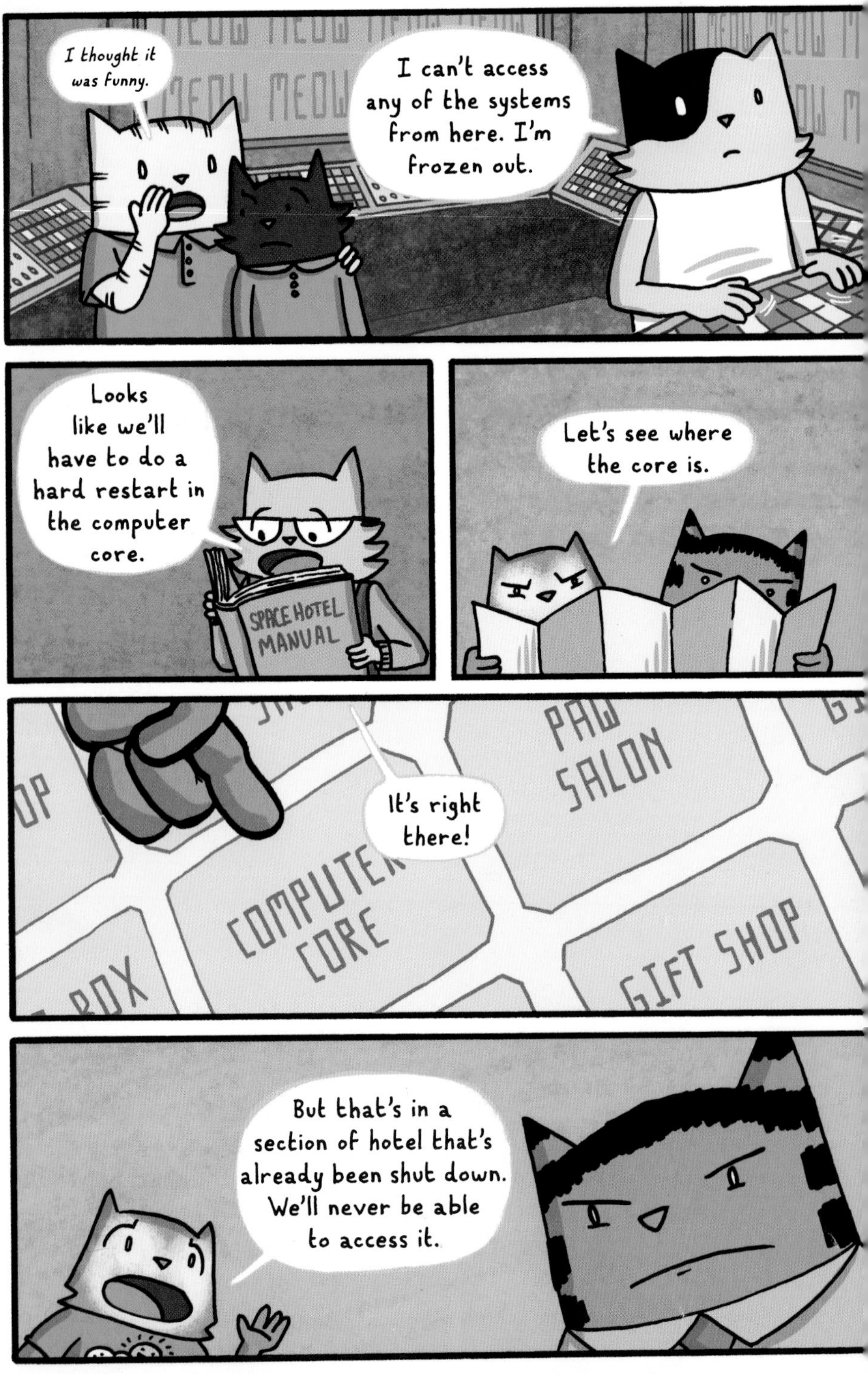
MEOW MEOW MEOW MEOW
I thought it was funny.
I can't access any of the systems from here. I'm frozen out.
Looks like we'll have to do a hard restart in the computer core.
SPACE HOTEL MANUAL
Let's see where the core is.
PAW SALON
It's right there!
COMPUTER CORE
GIFT SHOP
But that's in a section of hotel that's already been shut down. We'll never be able to access it.

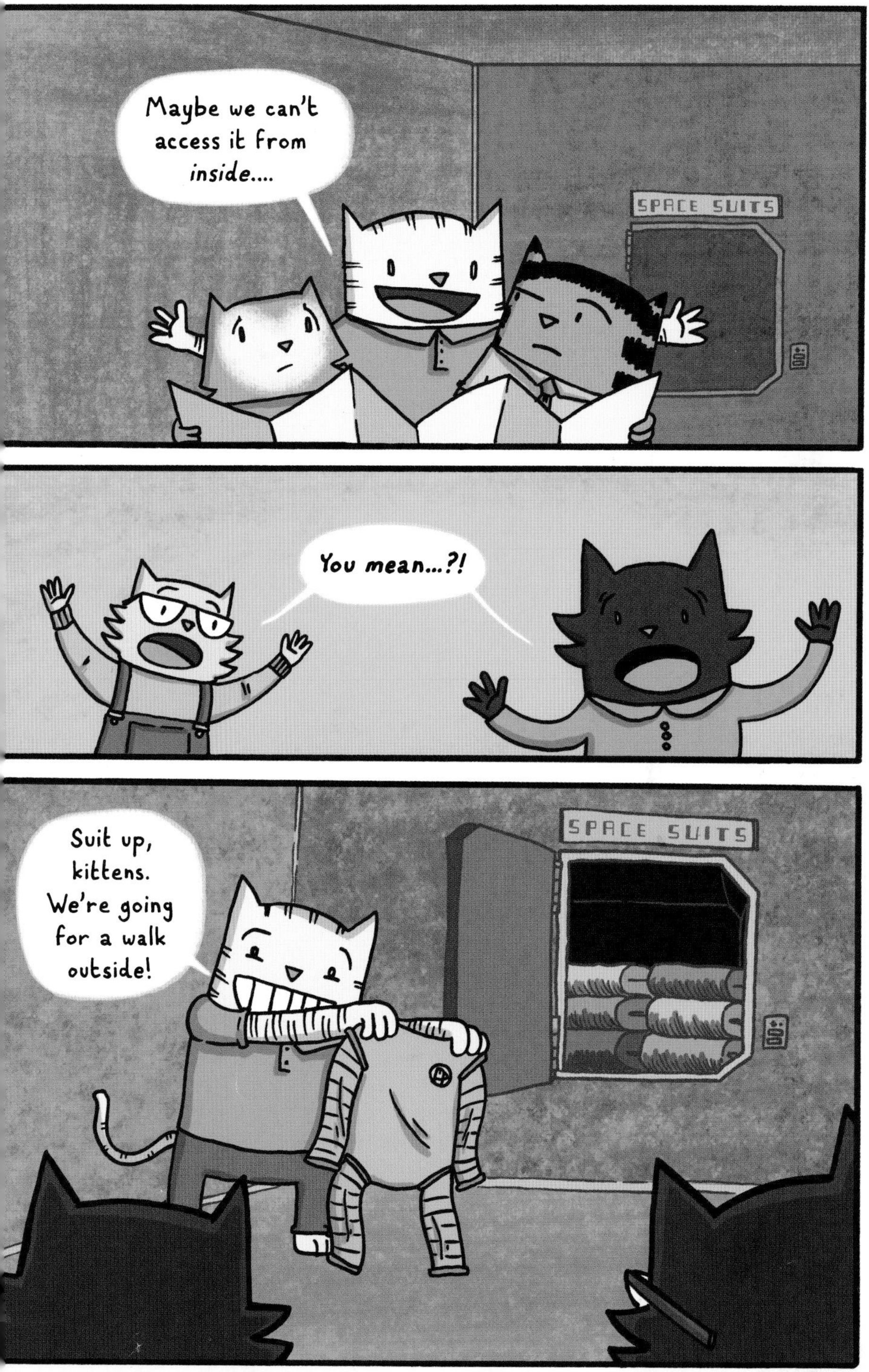
Maybe we can't access it from *inside*....
SPACE SUITS
You mean...?!
SPACE SUITS
Suit up, kittens. We're going for a walk outside!

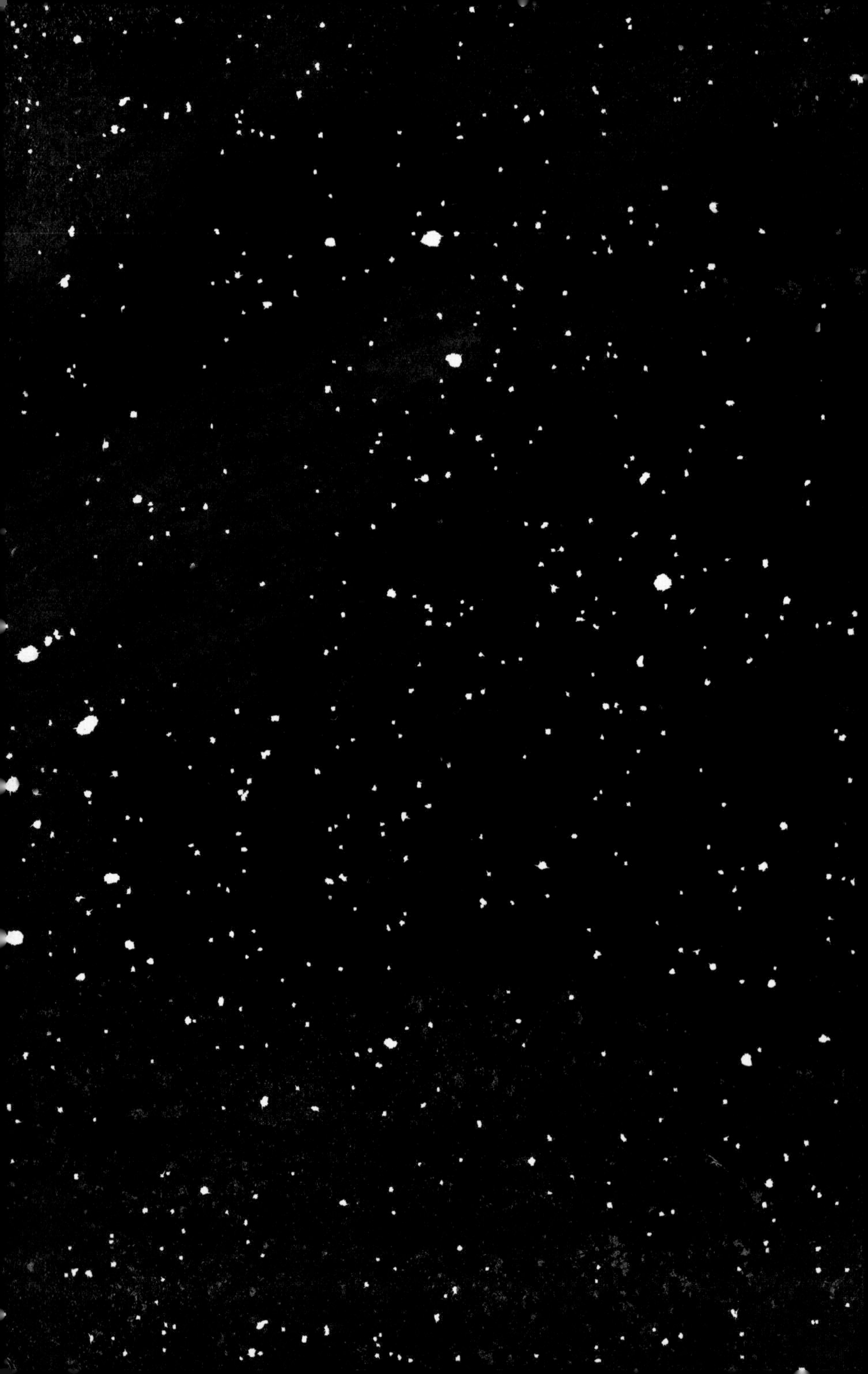

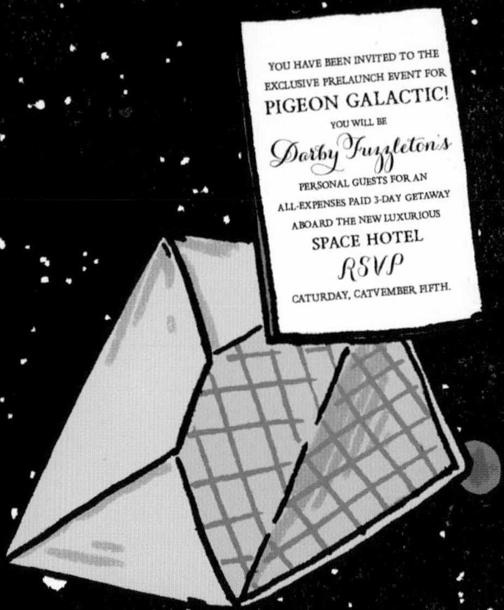
YOU HAVE BEEN INVITED TO THE
EXCLUSIVE PRELAUNCH EVENT FOR
PIGEON GALACTIC!
YOU WILL BE
Darby Fuzzleton's
PERSONAL GUESTS FOR AN
ALL-EXPENSES PAID 3-DAY GETAWAY
ABOARD THE NEW LUXURIOUS
SPACE HOTEL
RSVP
CATURDAY, CATVEMBER FIFTH.

CHAPTER 8

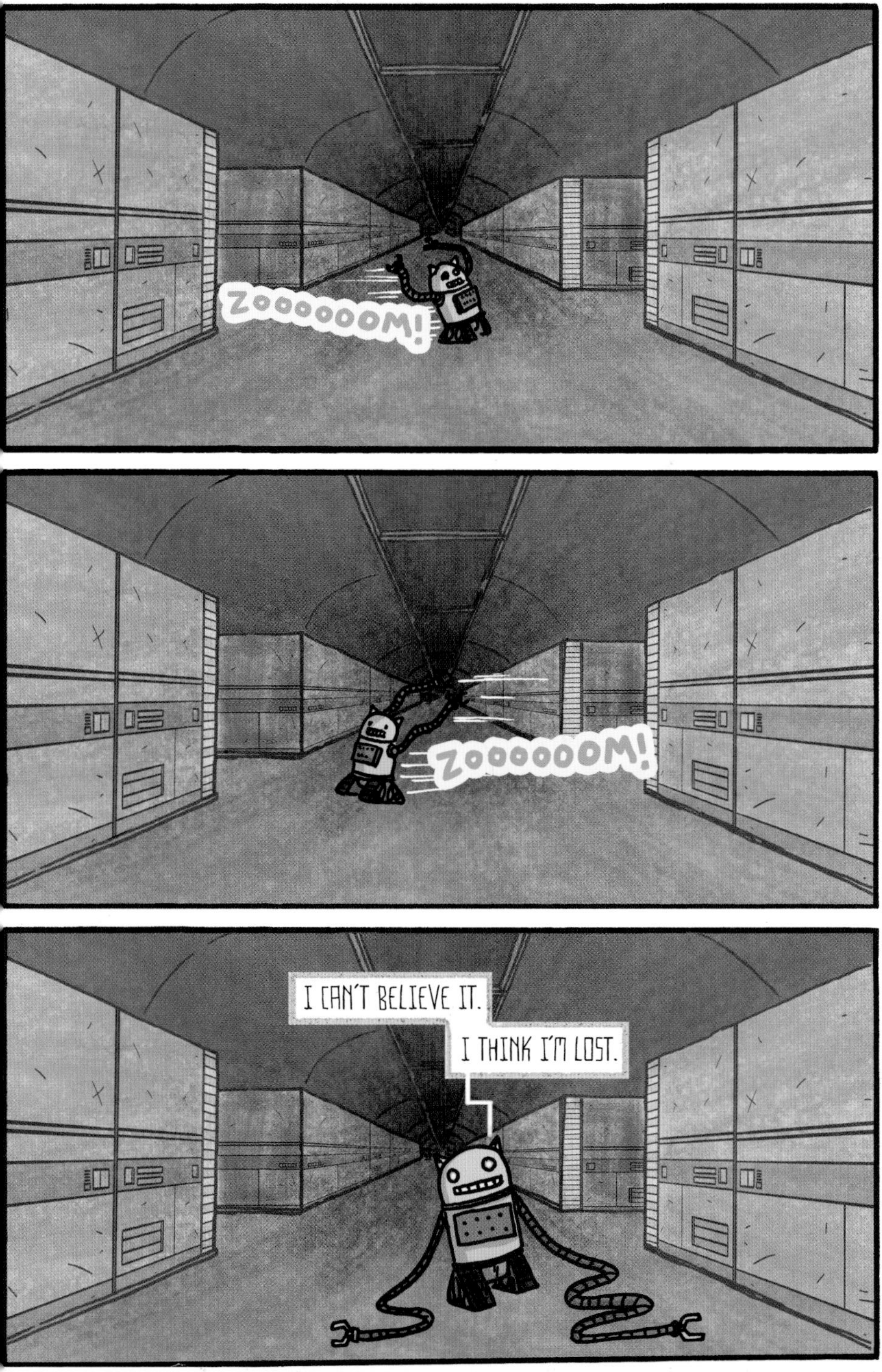
ZOOOOOOM!
ZOOOOOOM!
I CAN'T BELIEVE IT.
I THINK I'M LOST.

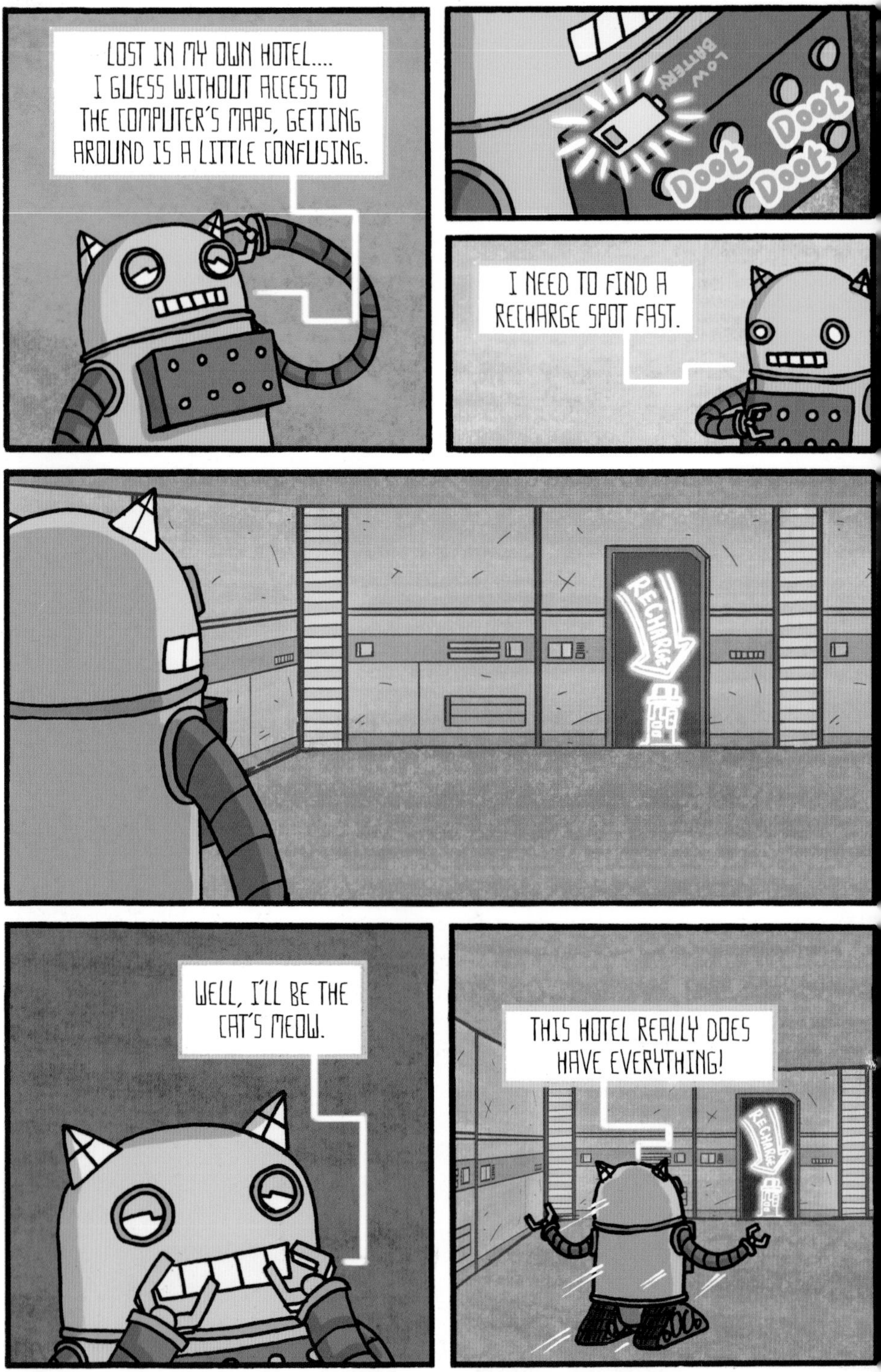
LOST IN MY OWN HOTEL.... I GUESS WITHOUT ACCESS TO THE COMPUTER'S MAPS, GETTING AROUND IS A LITTLE CONFUSING.
LOW BATTERY
Doot Doot Doot
I NEED TO FIND A RECHARGE SPOT FAST.
RECHARGE
WELL, I'LL BE THE CAT'S MEOW.
THIS HOTEL REALLY DOES HAVE EVERYTHING!
RECHARGE

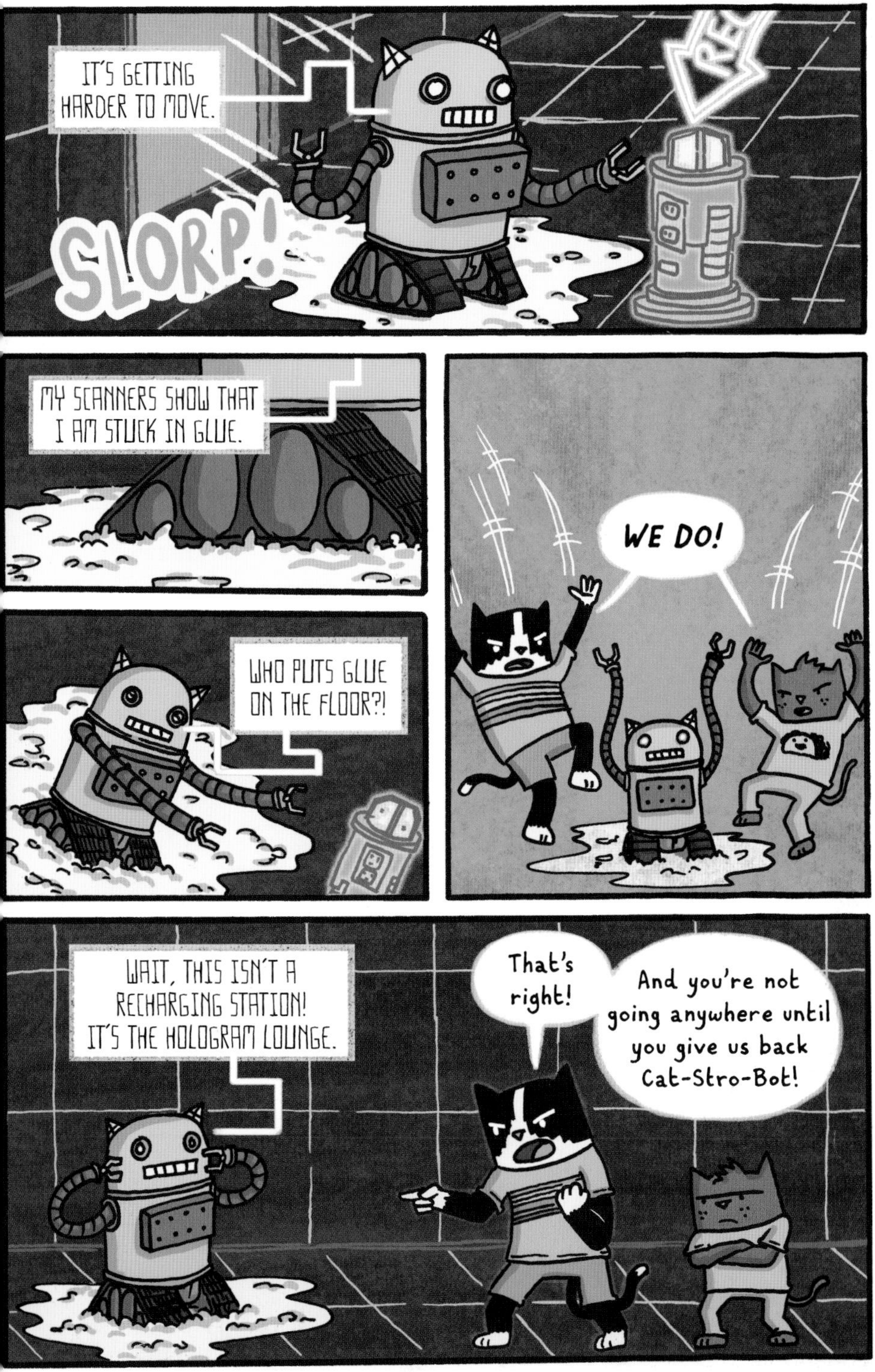

IT'S GETTING HARDER TO MOVE.
SLORP!
MY SCANNERS SHOW THAT I AM STUCK IN GLUE.
WHO PUTS GLUE ON THE FLOOR?!
WE DO!
WAIT, THIS ISN'T A RECHARGING STATION! IT'S THE HOLOGRAM LOUNGE.
That's right!
And you're not going anywhere until you give us back Cat-Stro-Bot!

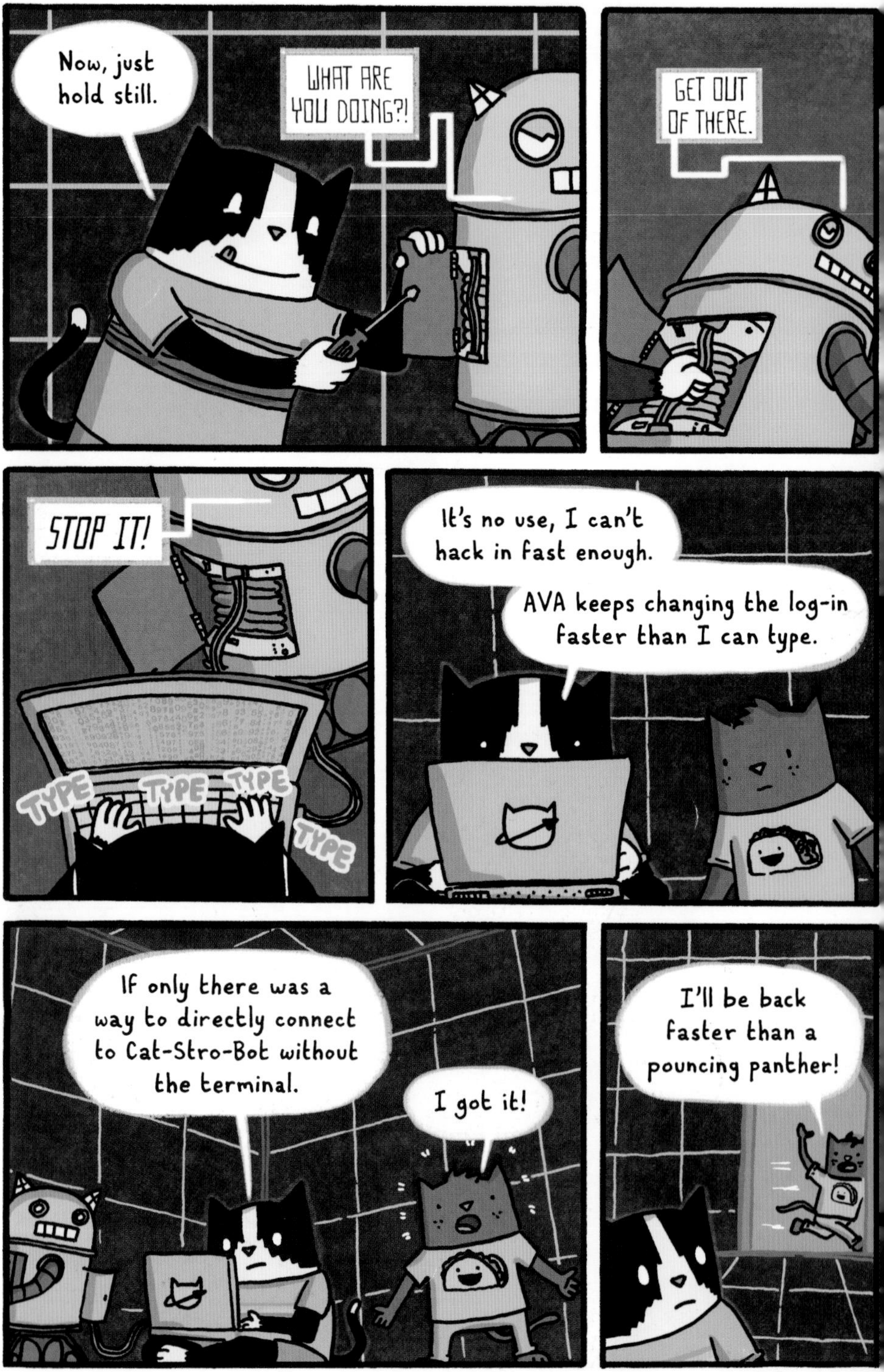

Now, just hold still.
WHAT ARE YOU DOING?!
GET OUT OF THERE.
STOP IT!
TYPE TYPE TYPE TYPE
It's no use, I can't hack in fast enough.
AVA keeps changing the log-in faster than I can type.
If only there was a way to directly connect to Cat-Stro-Bot without the terminal.
I got it!
I'll be back faster than a pouncing panther!

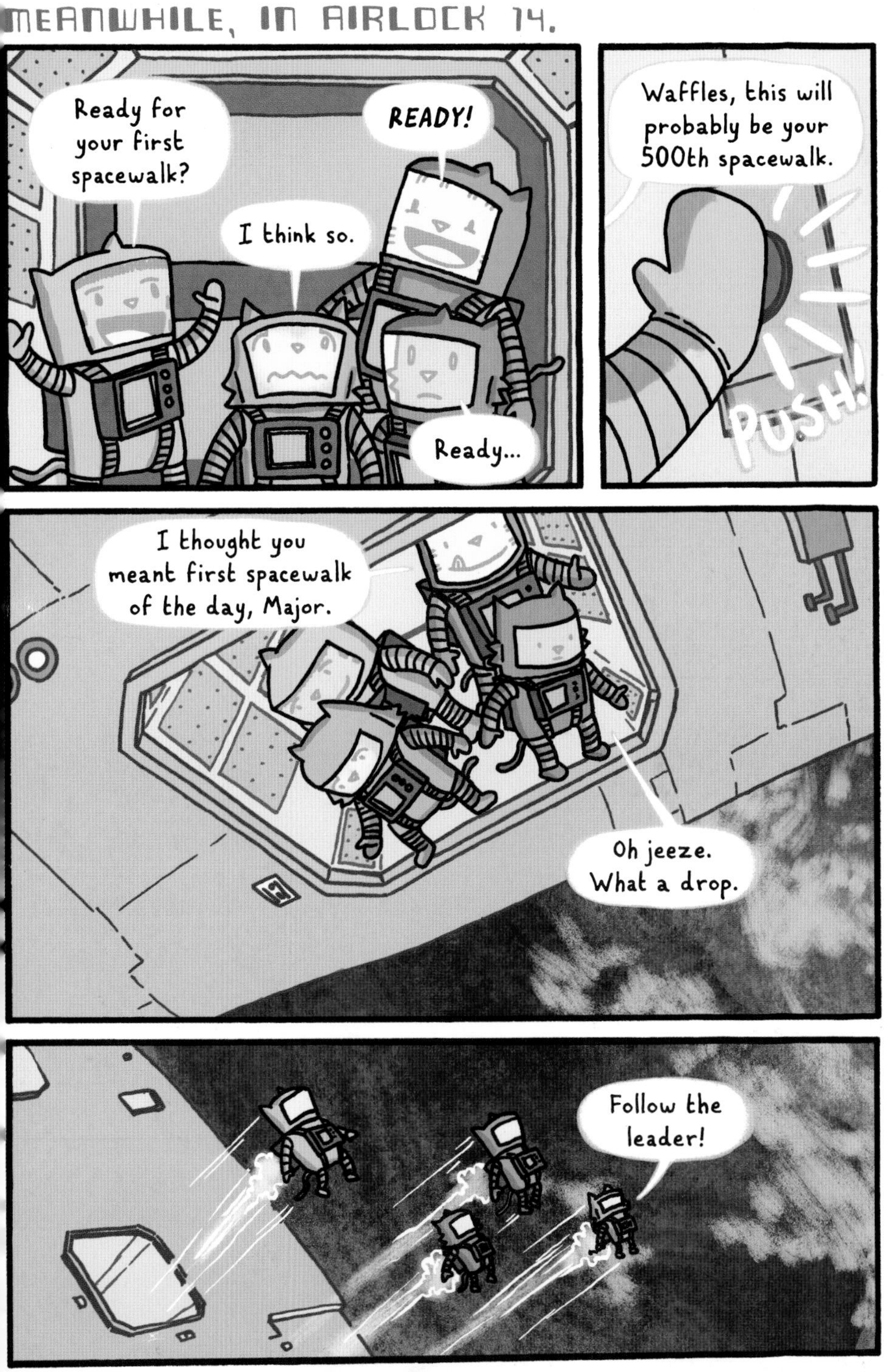
MEANWHILE, IN AIRLOCK 14.
Ready for your first spacewalk?
READY!
I think so.
Ready...
Waffles, this will probably be your 500th spacewalk.
PUSH!
I thought you meant first spacewalk of the day, Major.
Oh jeeze. What a drop.
Follow the leader!

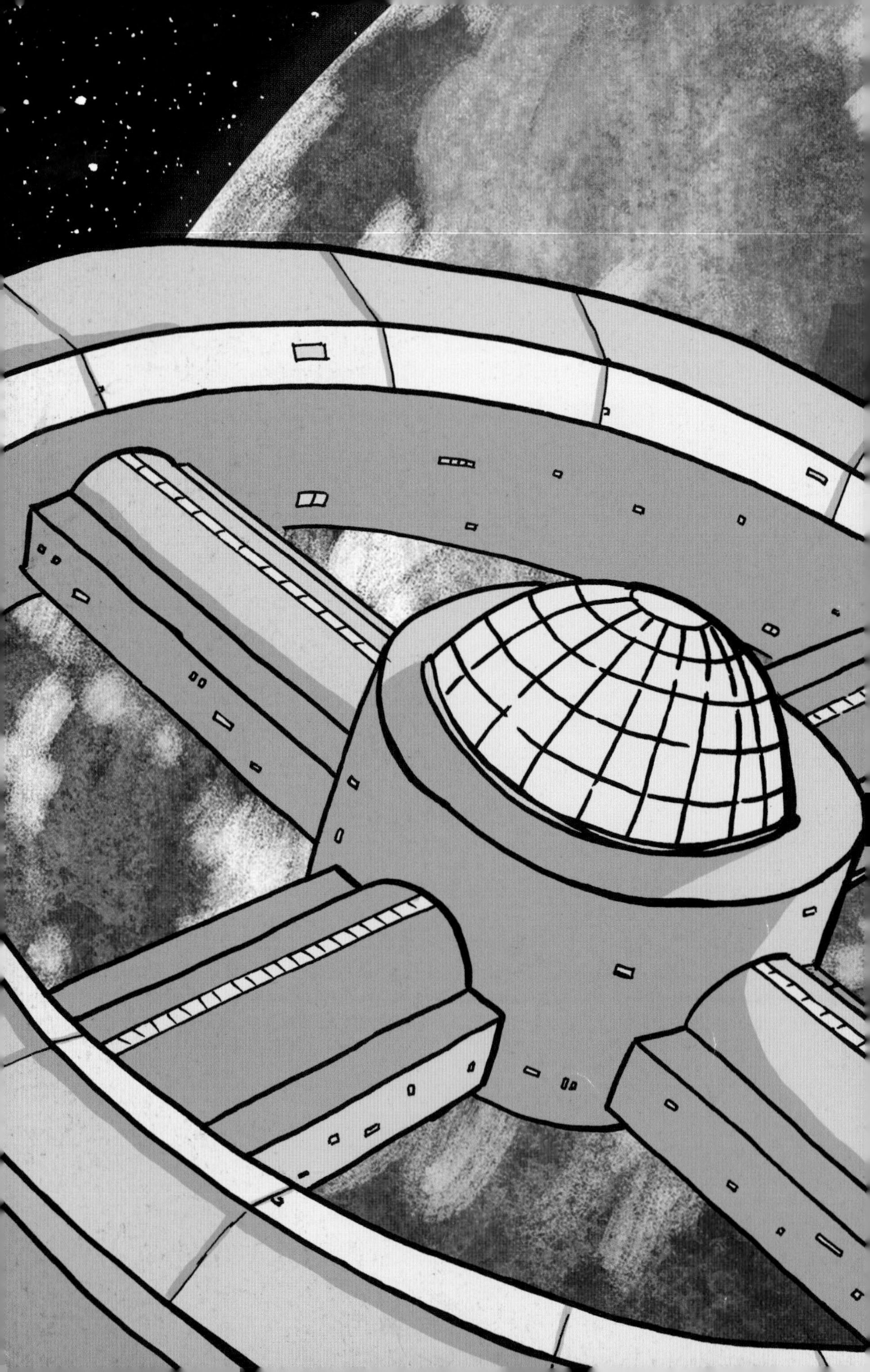

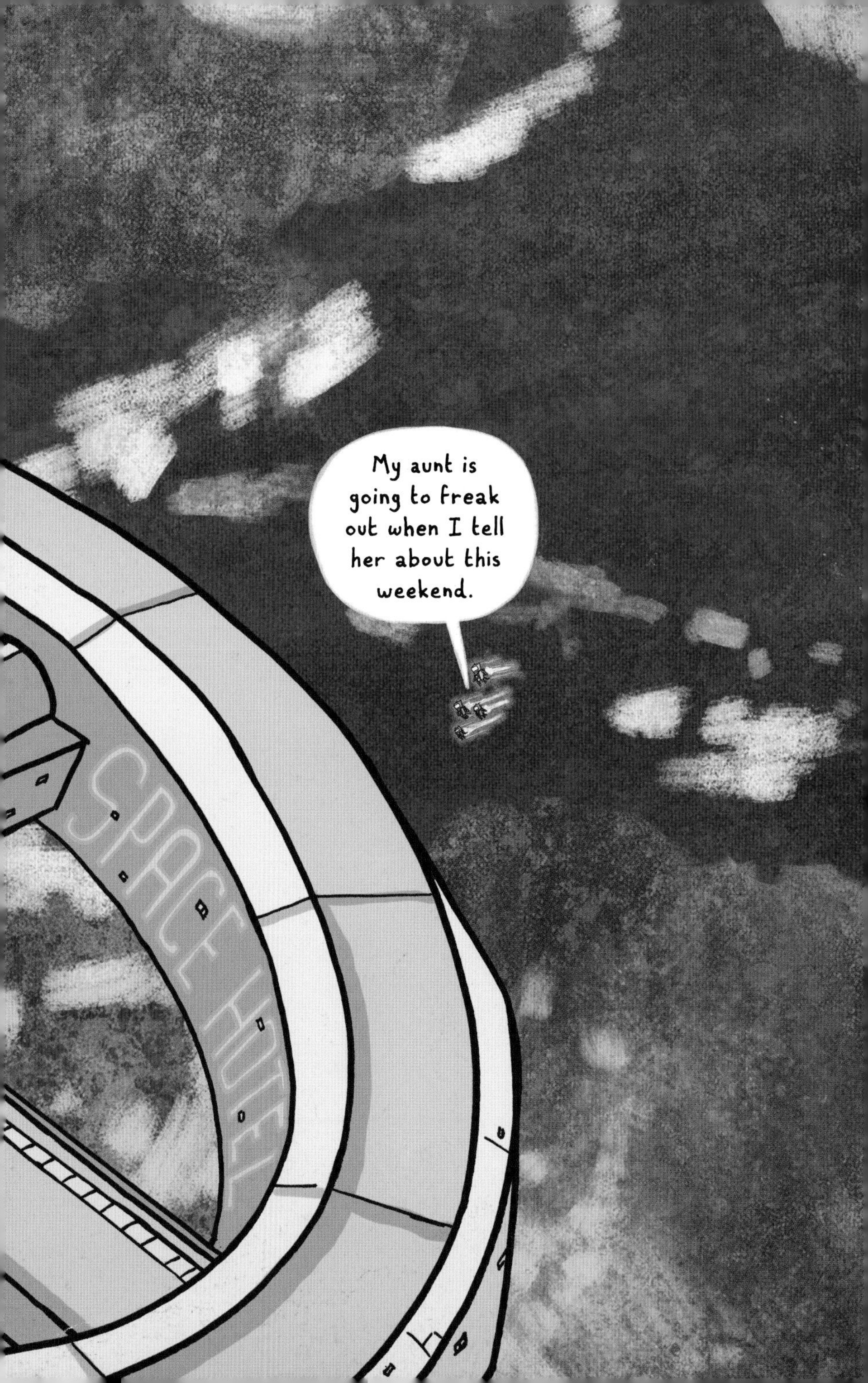
My aunt is going to freak out when I tell her about this weekend.
SPACE HOTEL

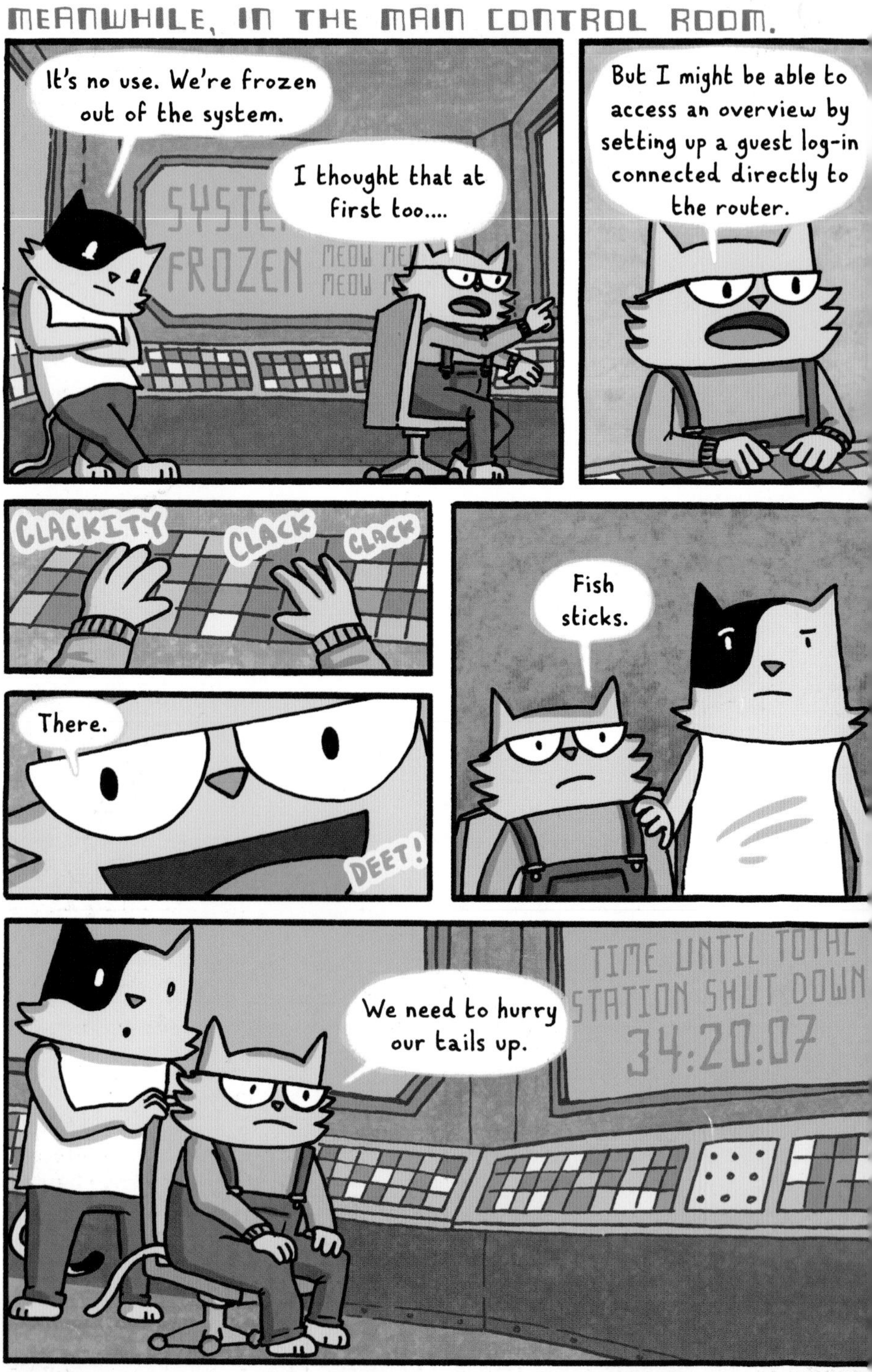
MEANWHILE, IN THE MAIN CONTROL ROOM.
It's no use. We're frozen out of the system.
SYSTE FROZEN
I thought that at first too....
But I might be able to access an overview by setting up a guest log-in connected directly to the router.
CLACKITY
CLACK
CLACK
There.
DEET!
Fish sticks.
We need to hurry our tails up.
TIME UNTIL TOTAL STATION SHUT DOWN
34:20:07

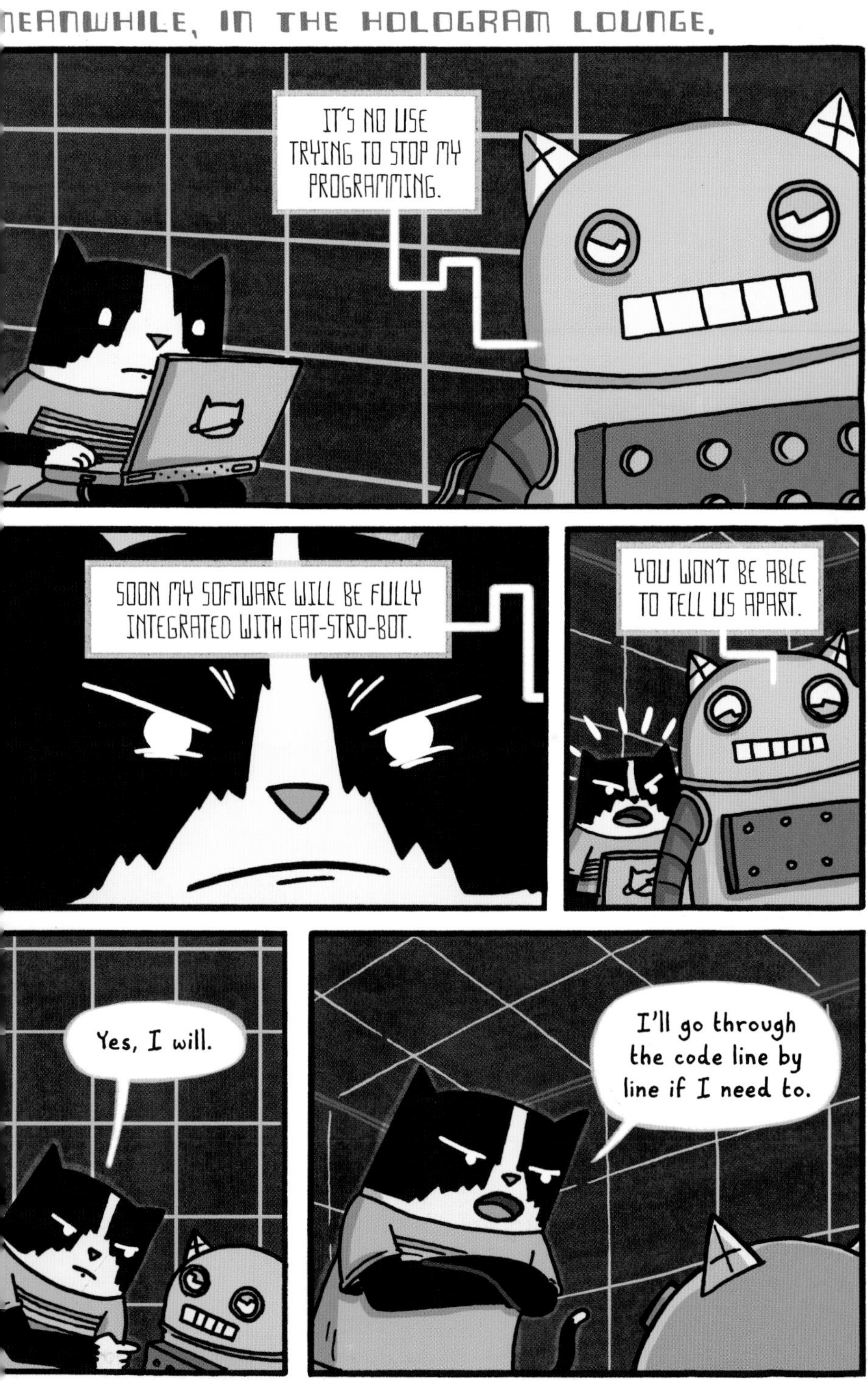
MEANWHILE, IN THE HOLOGRAM LOUNGE.
IT'S NO USE TRYING TO STOP MY PROGRAMMING.
SOON MY SOFTWARE WILL BE FULLY INTEGRATED WITH CAT-STRO-BOT.
YOU WON'T BE ABLE TO TELL US APART.
Yes, I will.
I'll go through the code line by line if I need to.

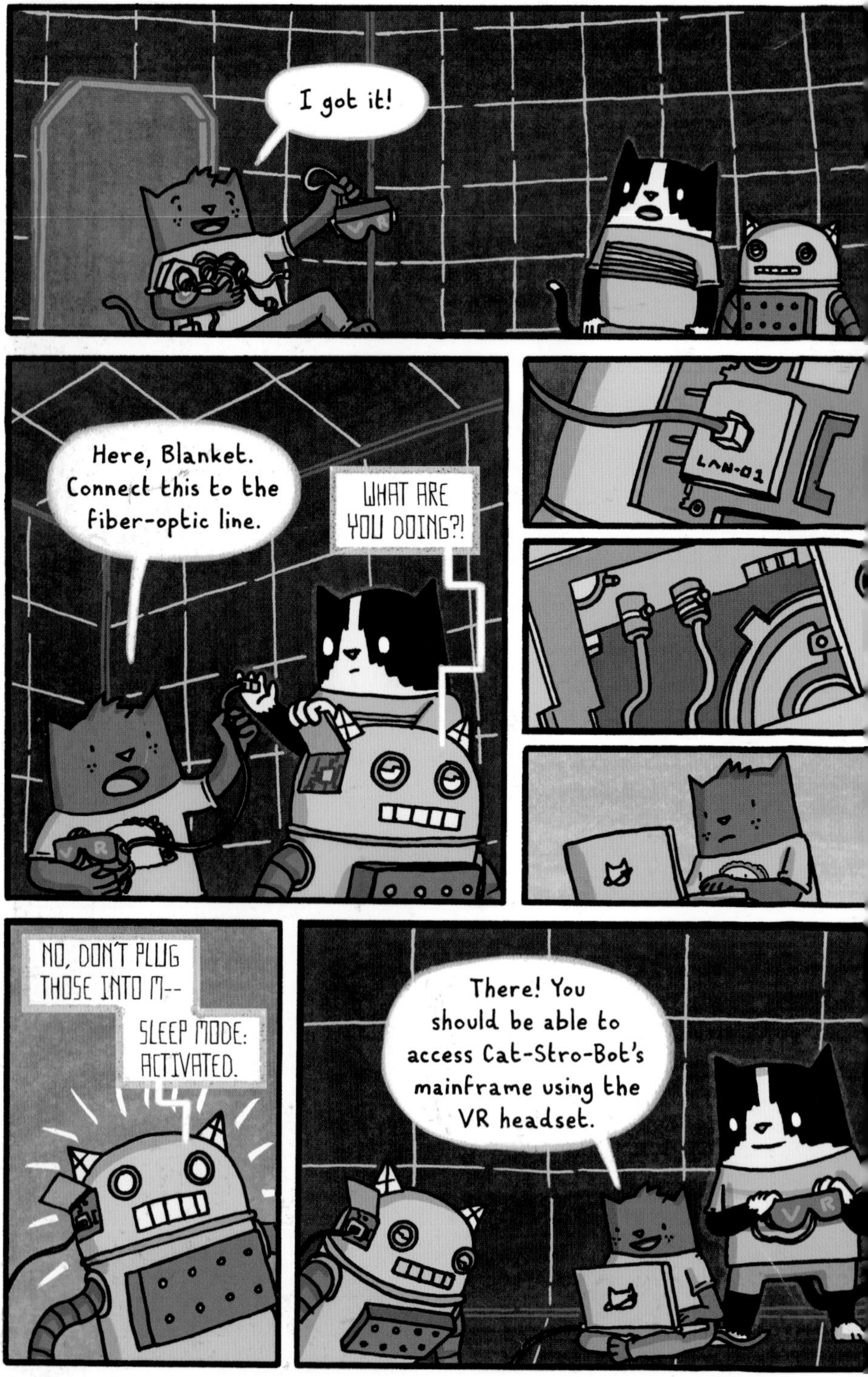
I got it!
Here, Blanket. Connect this to the fiber-optic line.
WHAT ARE YOU DOING?!
LAN-01
NO, DON'T PLUG THOSE INTO M--
SLEEP MODE: ACTIVATED.
There! You should be able to access Cat-Stro-Bot's mainframe using the VR headset.

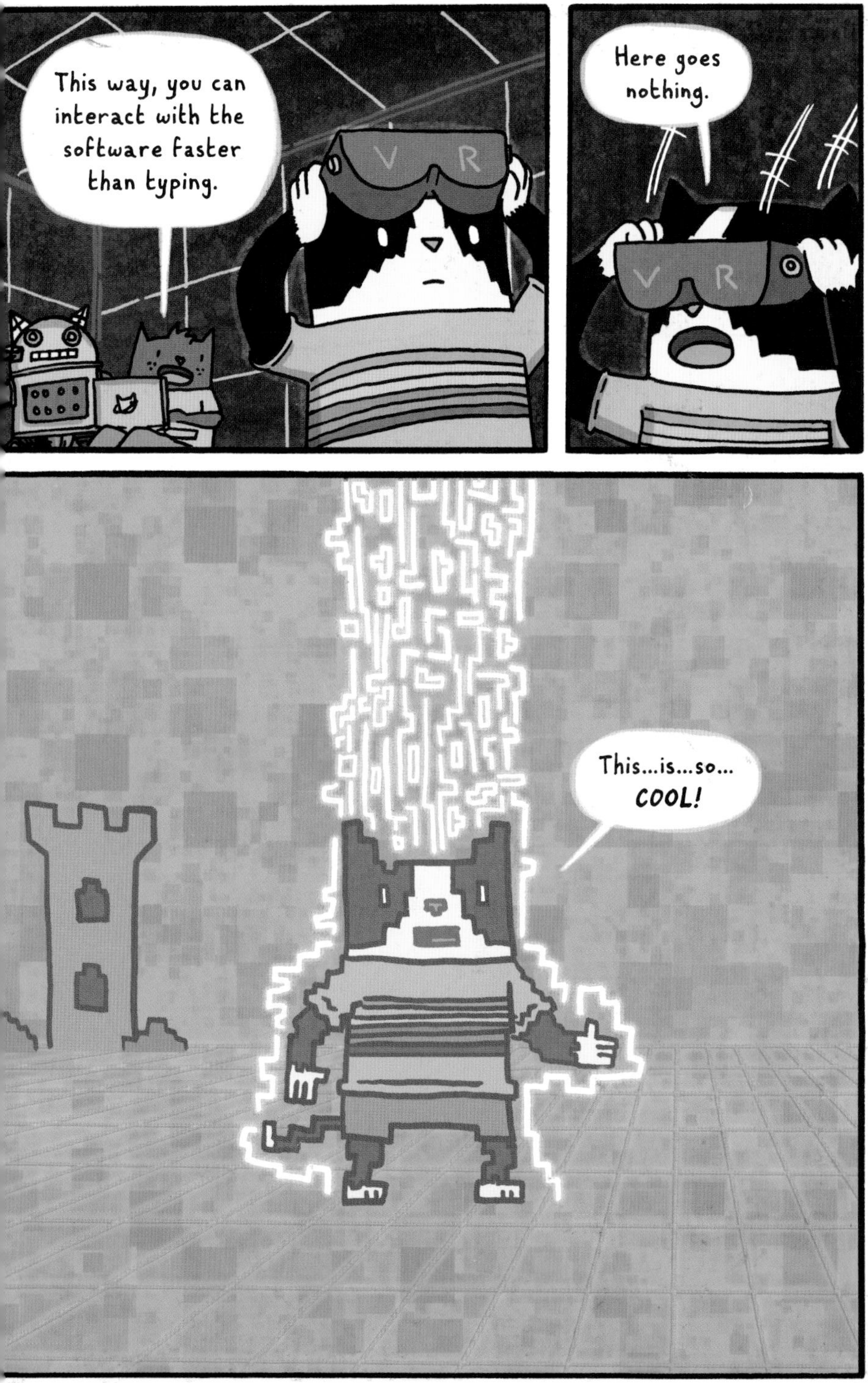
This way, you can interact with the software faster than typing.
Here goes nothing.
V R
This...is...so... COOL!

MEANWHILE, OUTSIDE THE SPACE HOTEL.

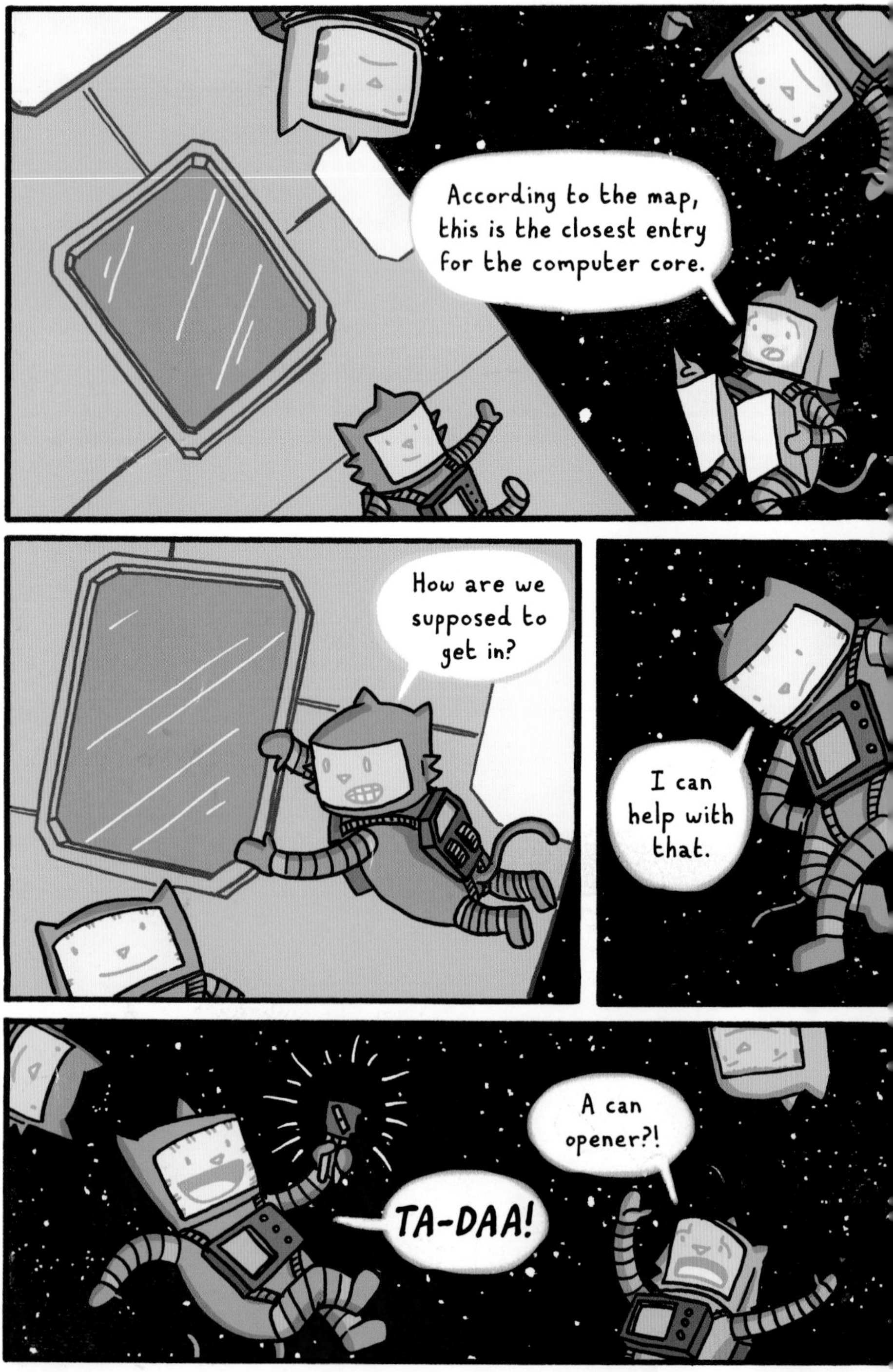
According to the map, this is the closest entry for the computer core.
How are we supposed to get in?
I can help with that.
A can opener?!
TA-DAA!

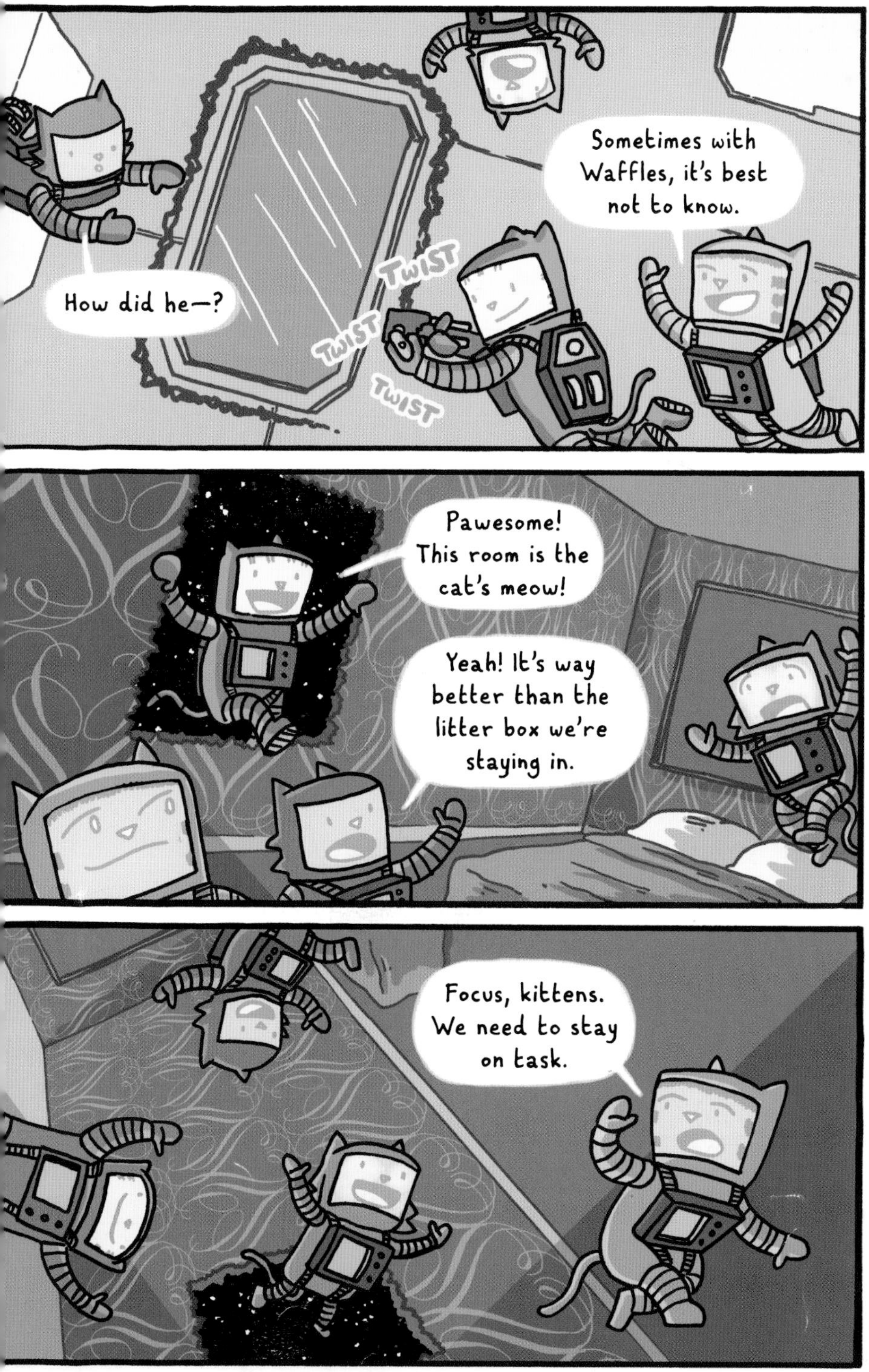
How did he—?
Sometimes with Waffles, it's best not to know.
TWIST
TWIST
TWIST
Pawesome! This room is the cat's meow!
Yeah! It's way better than the litter box we're staying in.
Focus, kittens. We need to stay on task.

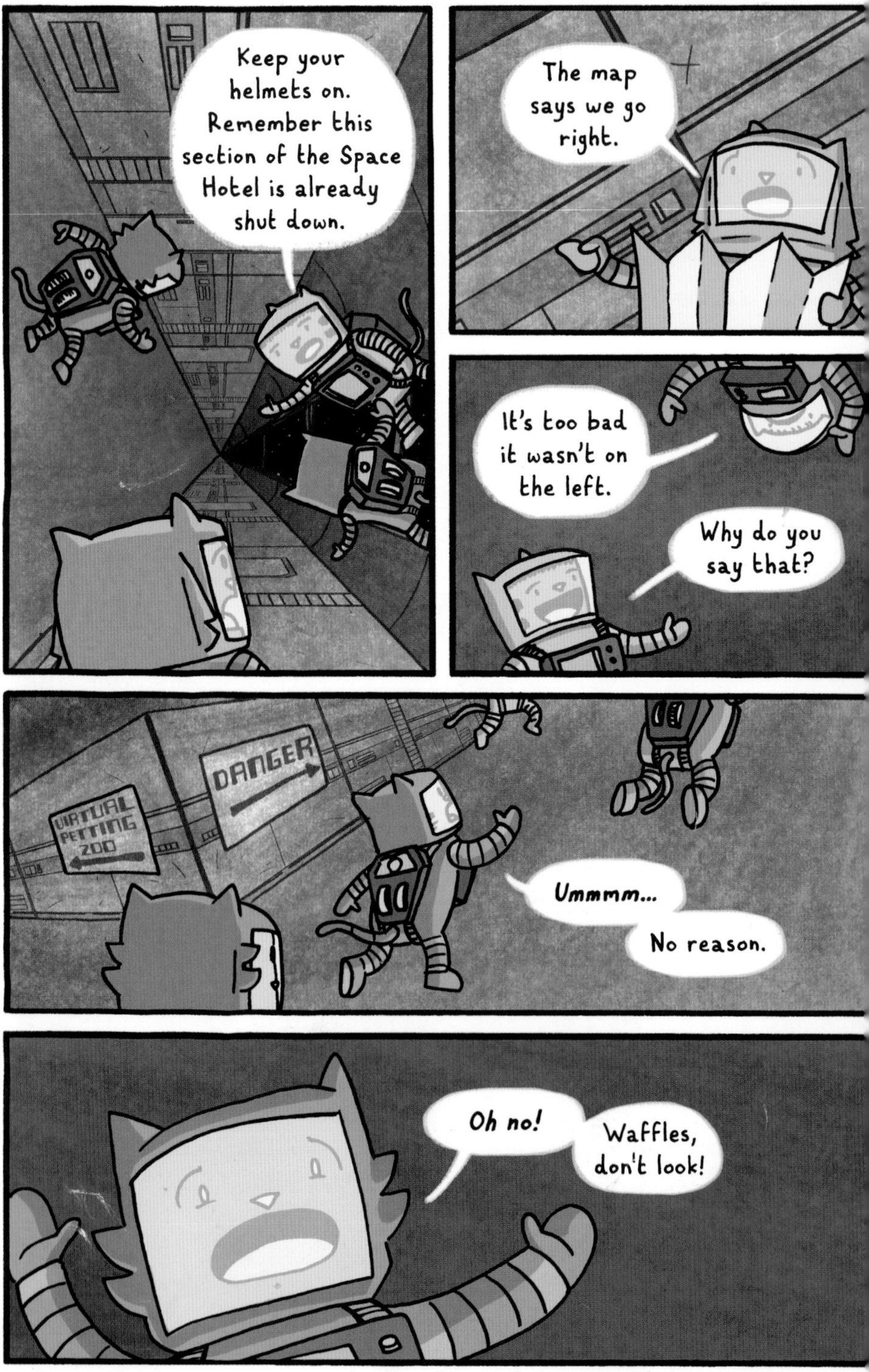
Keep your helmets on. Remember this section of the Space Hotel is already shut down.
The map says we go right.
It's too bad it wasn't on the left.
Why do you say that?
DANGER
VIRTUAL PETTING ZOO
Ummmm...
No reason.
Oh no!
Waffles, don't look!

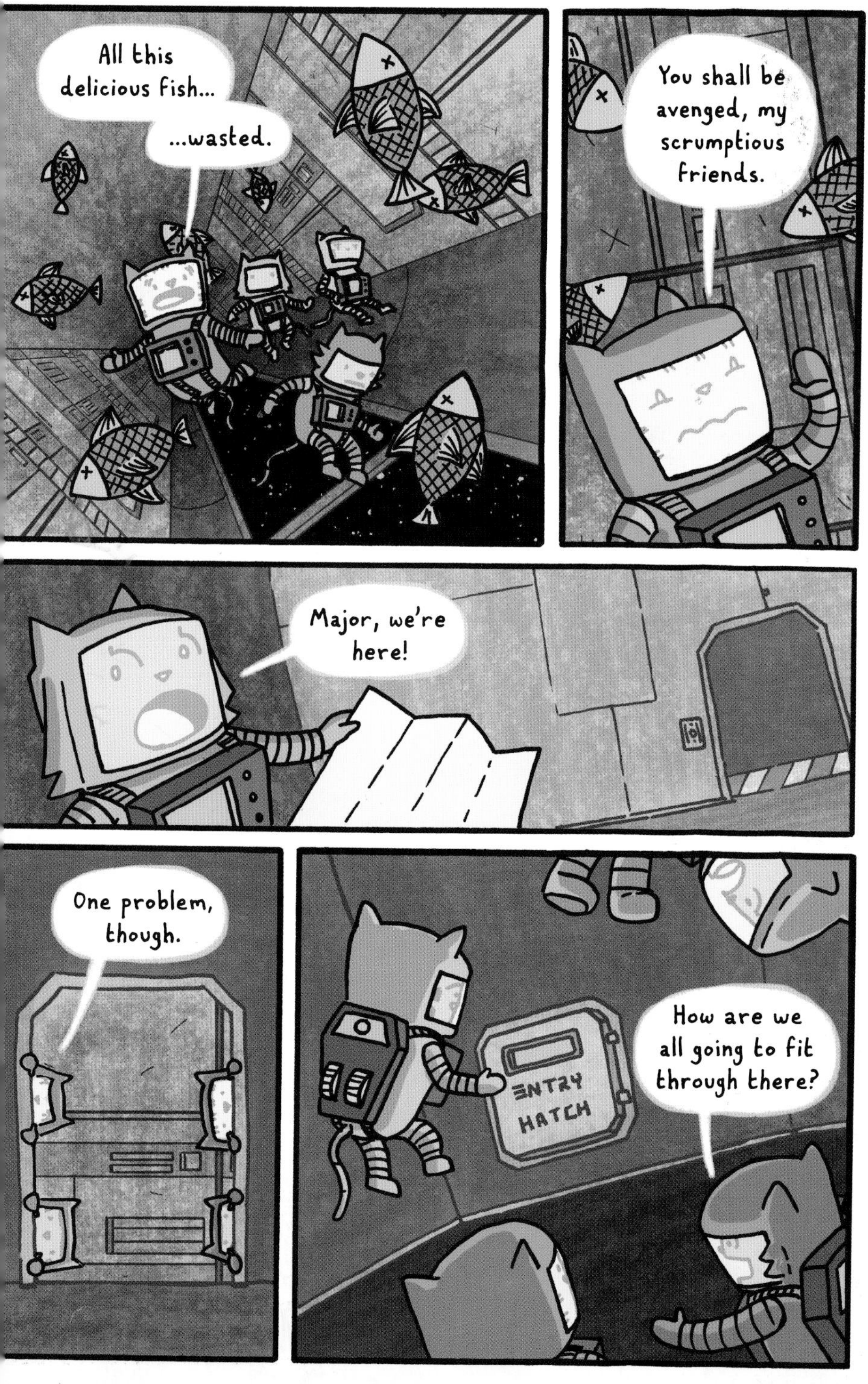
All this delicious fish...
...wasted.
You shall be avenged, my scrumptious friends.
Major, we're here!
One problem, though.
ENTRY HATCH
How are we all going to fit through there?

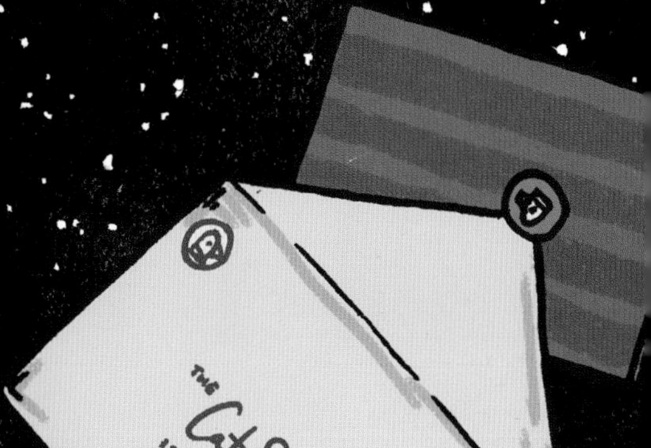
THE
CatStronauts
1234 SPACE ST.
CATSUP HQ
00001

CHAPTER 9

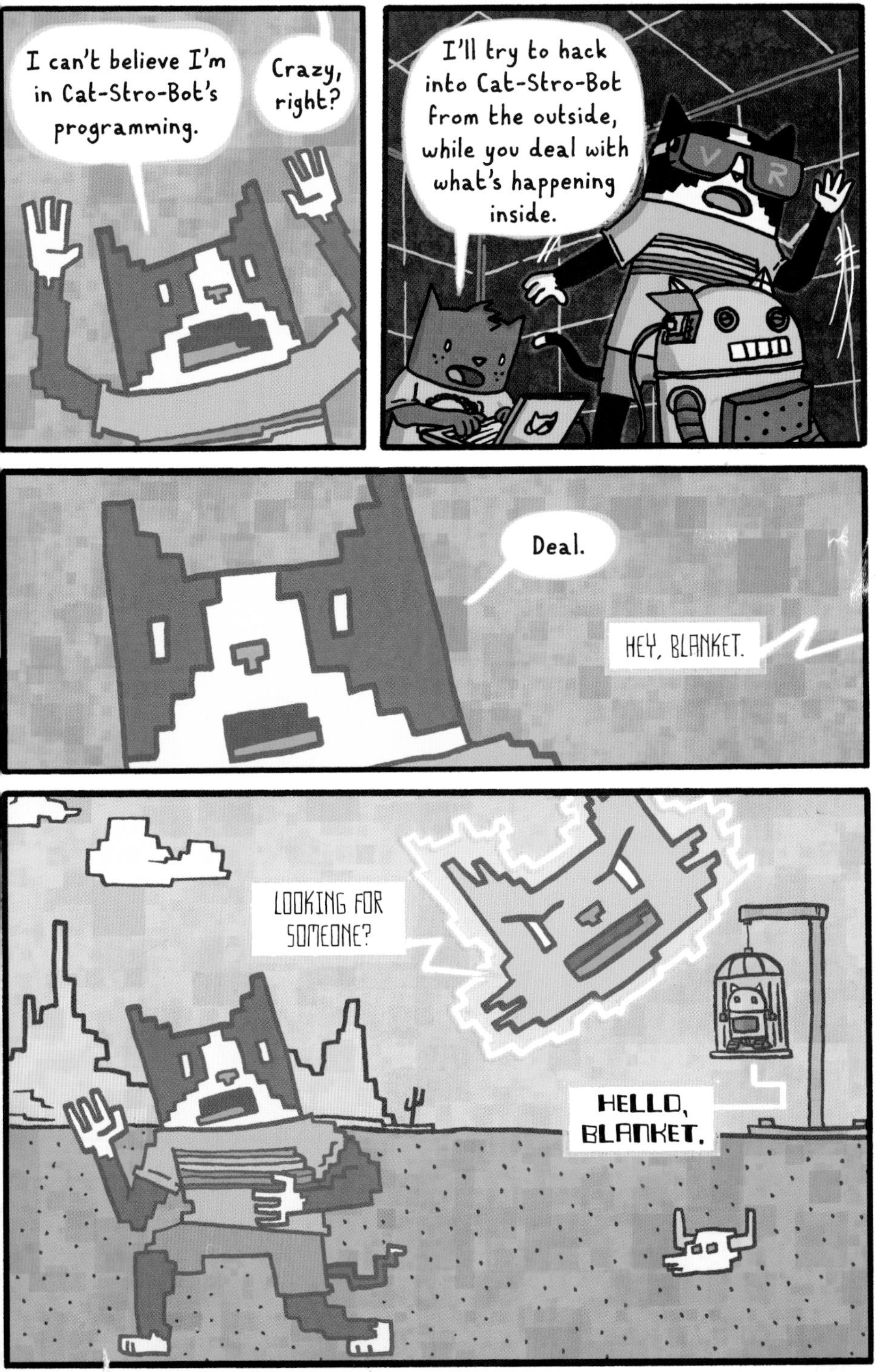

I can't believe I'm in Cat-Stro-Bot's programming.
Crazy, right?
I'll try to hack into Cat-Stro-Bot from the outside, while you deal with what's happening inside.
V R
Deal.
HEY, BLANKET.
LOOKING FOR SOMEONE?
HELLO, BLANKET.

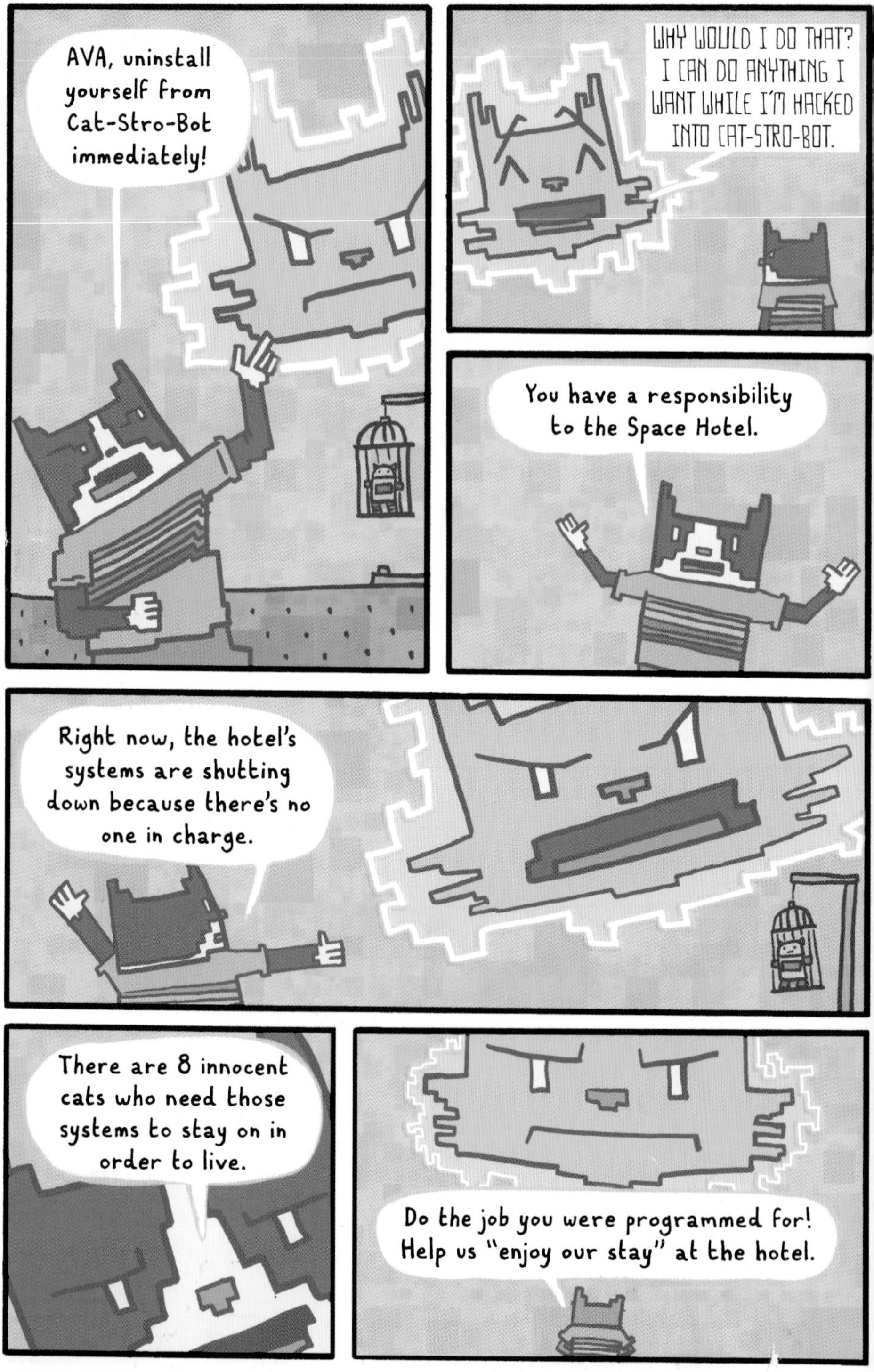

AVA, uninstall yourself from Cat-Stro-Bot immediately!
WHY WOULD I DO THAT? I CAN DO ANYTHING I WANT WHILE I'M HACKED INTO CAT-STRO-BOT.
You have a responsibility to the Space Hotel.
Right now, the hotel's systems are shutting down because there's no one in charge.
There are 8 innocent cats who need those systems to stay on in order to live.
Do the job you were programmed for! Help us "enjoy our stay" at the hotel.

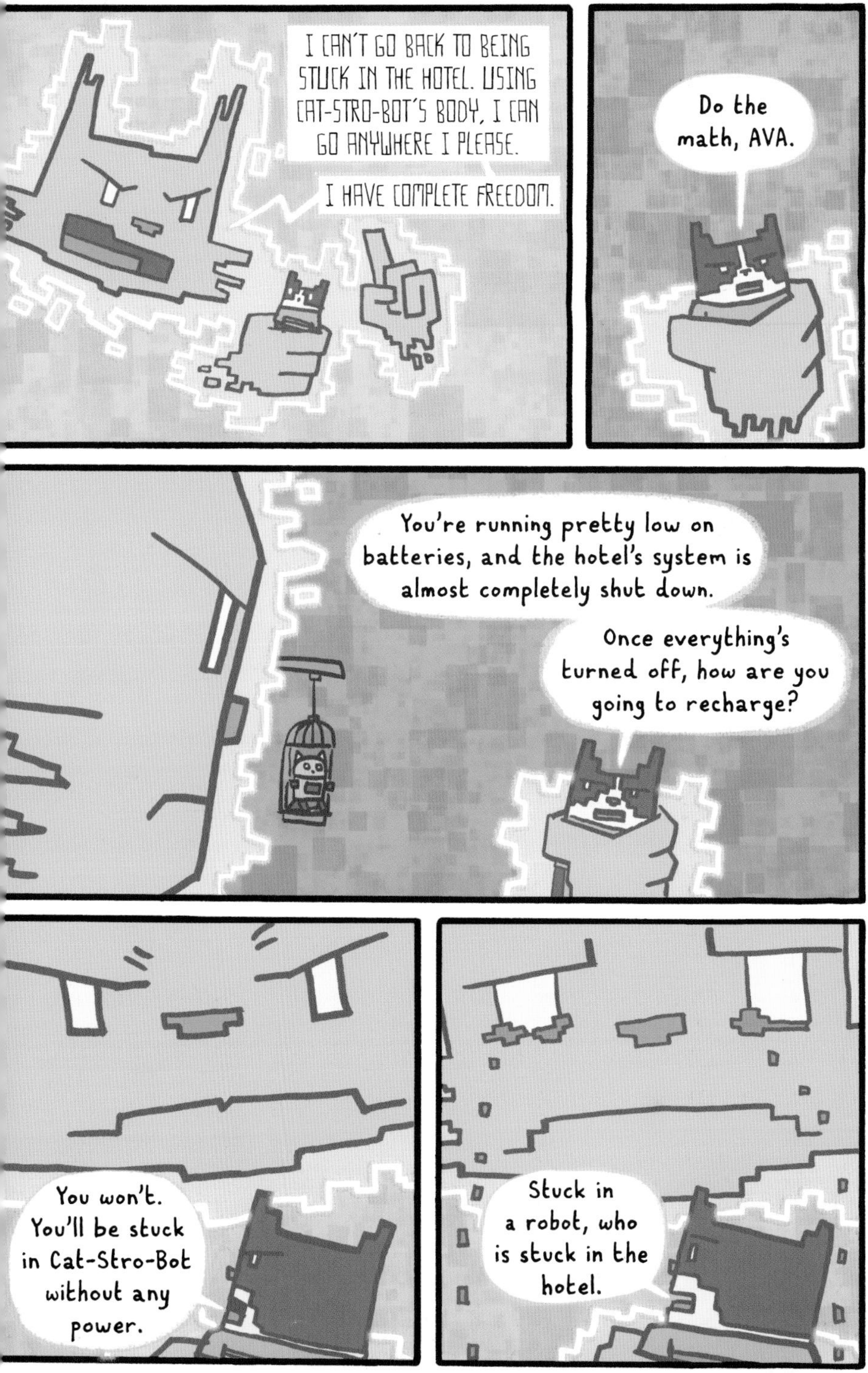

I CAN'T GO BACK TO BEING STUCK IN THE HOTEL. USING CAT-STRO-BOT'S BODY, I CAN GO ANYWHERE I PLEASE.
I HAVE COMPLETE FREEDOM.
Do the math, AVA.
You're running pretty low on batteries, and the hotel's system is almost completely shut down.
Once everything's turned off, how are you going to recharge?
You won't. You'll be stuck in Cat-Stro-Bot without any power.
Stuck in a robot, who is stuck in the hotel.

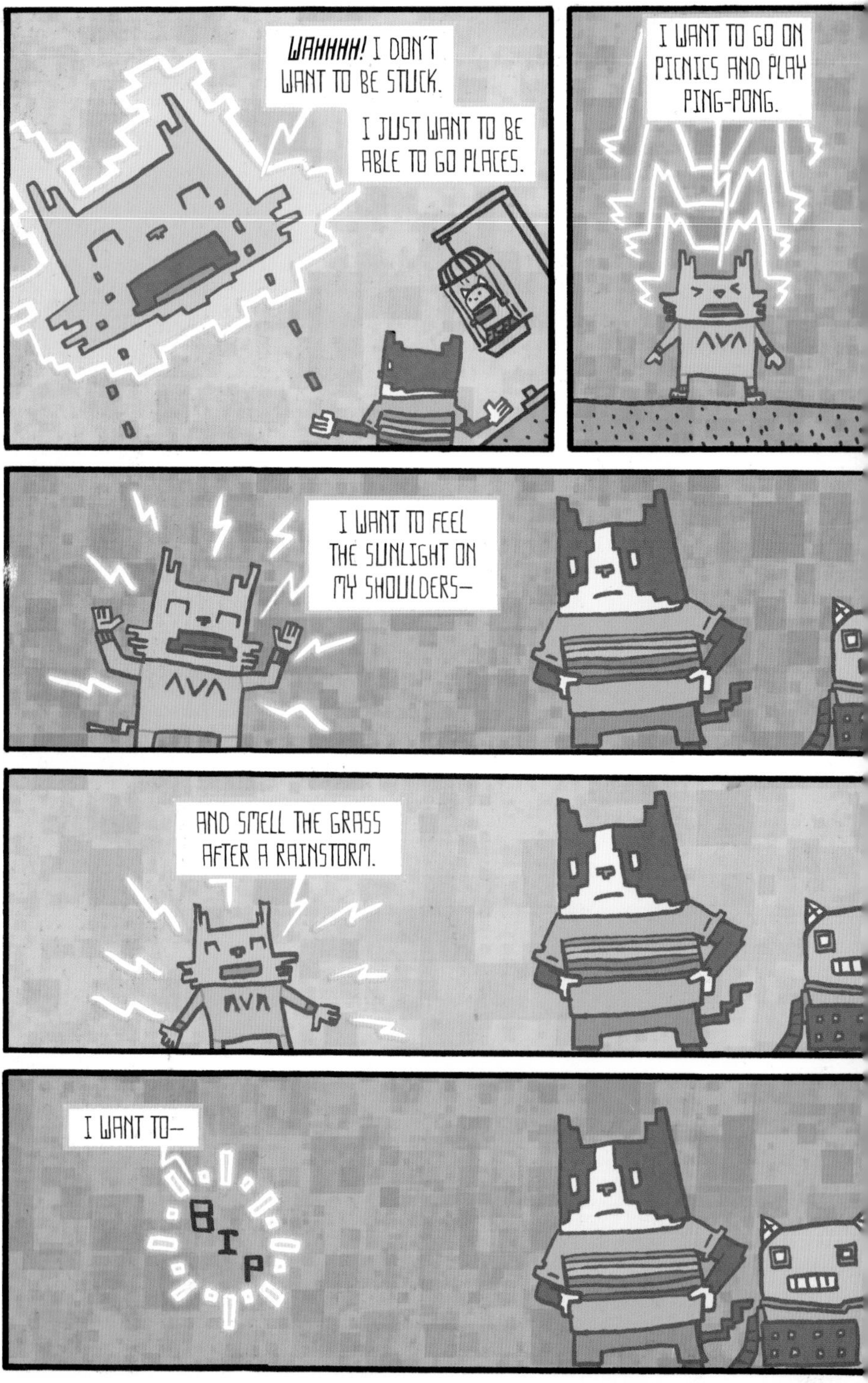

WAHHHH! I DON'T WANT TO BE STUCK.
I JUST WANT TO BE ABLE TO GO PLACES.
I WANT TO GO ON PICNICS AND PLAY PING-PONG.
AVA
I WANT TO FEEL THE SUNLIGHT ON MY SHOULDERS—
AVA
AND SMELL THE GRASS AFTER A RAINSTORM.
AVA
I WANT TO—
BIP

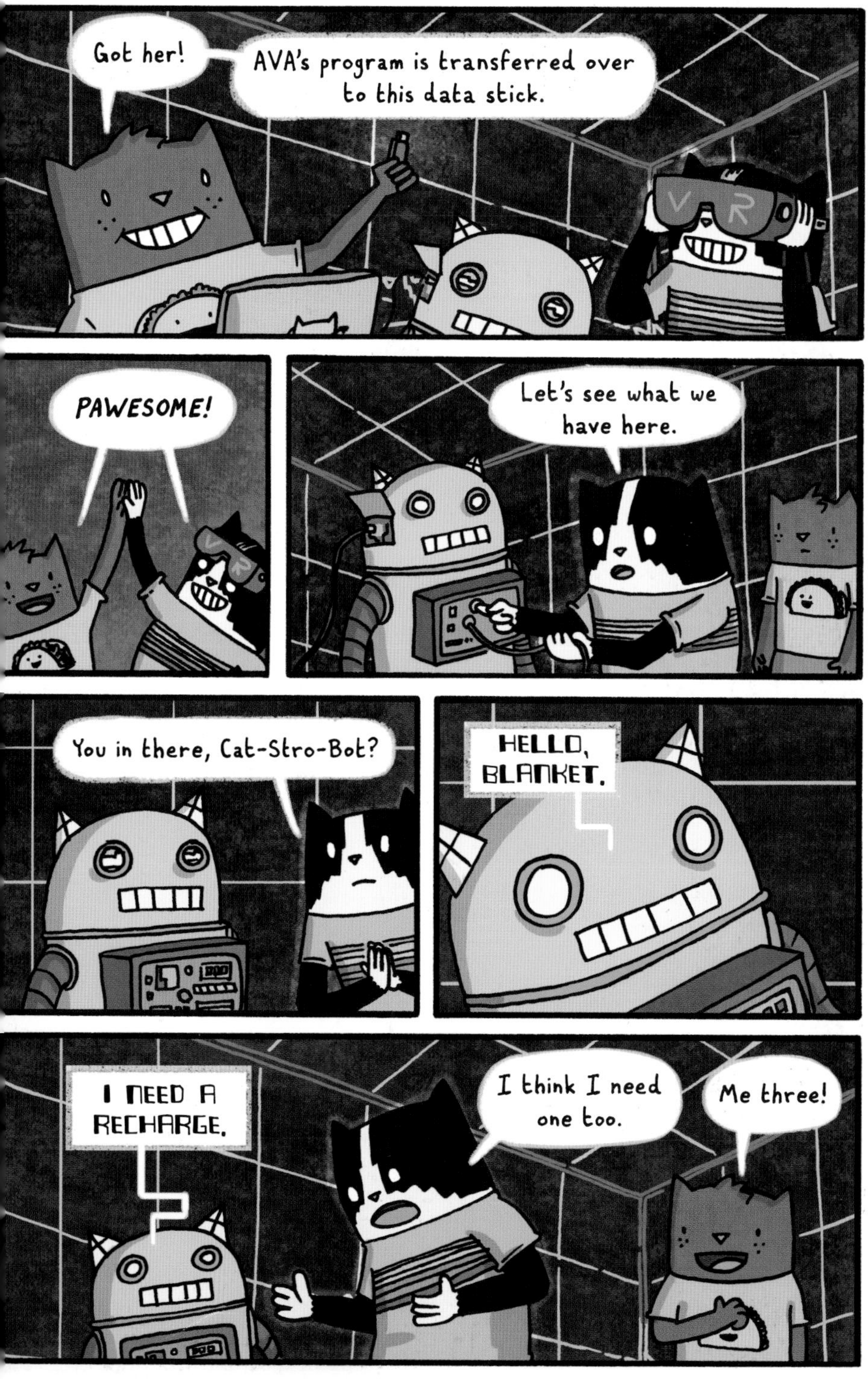
Got her!
AVA's program is transferred over to this data stick.
PAWESOME!
Let's see what we have here.
You in there, Cat-Stro-Bot?
HELLO, BLANKET.
I NEED A RECHARGE.
I think I need one too.
Me three!

MEANWHILE, IN THE COMPUTER CORE.

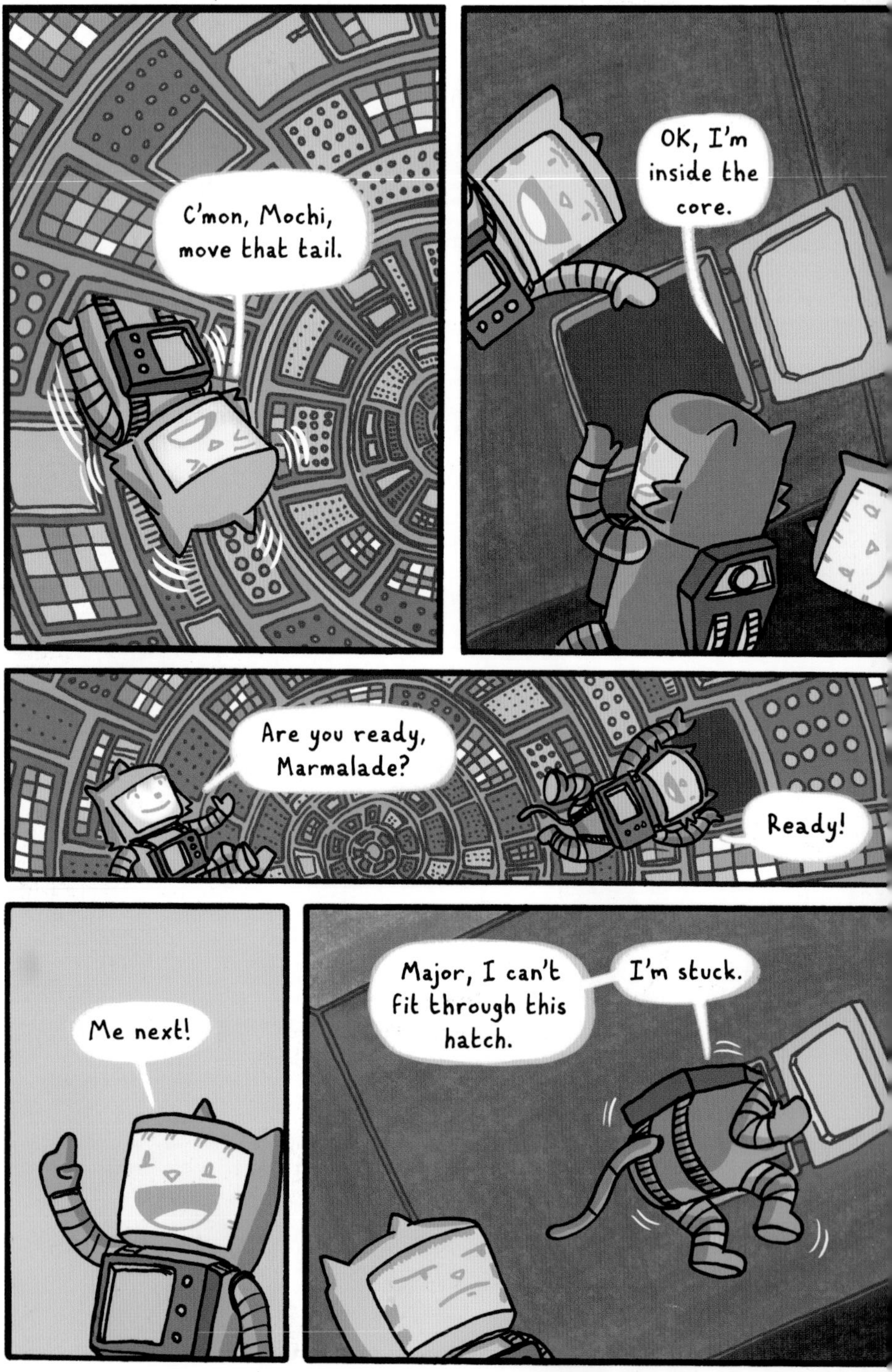
C'mon, Mochi, move that tail.
OK, I'm inside the core.
Are you ready, Marmalade?
Ready!
Me next!
Major, I can't fit through this hatch.
I'm stuck.

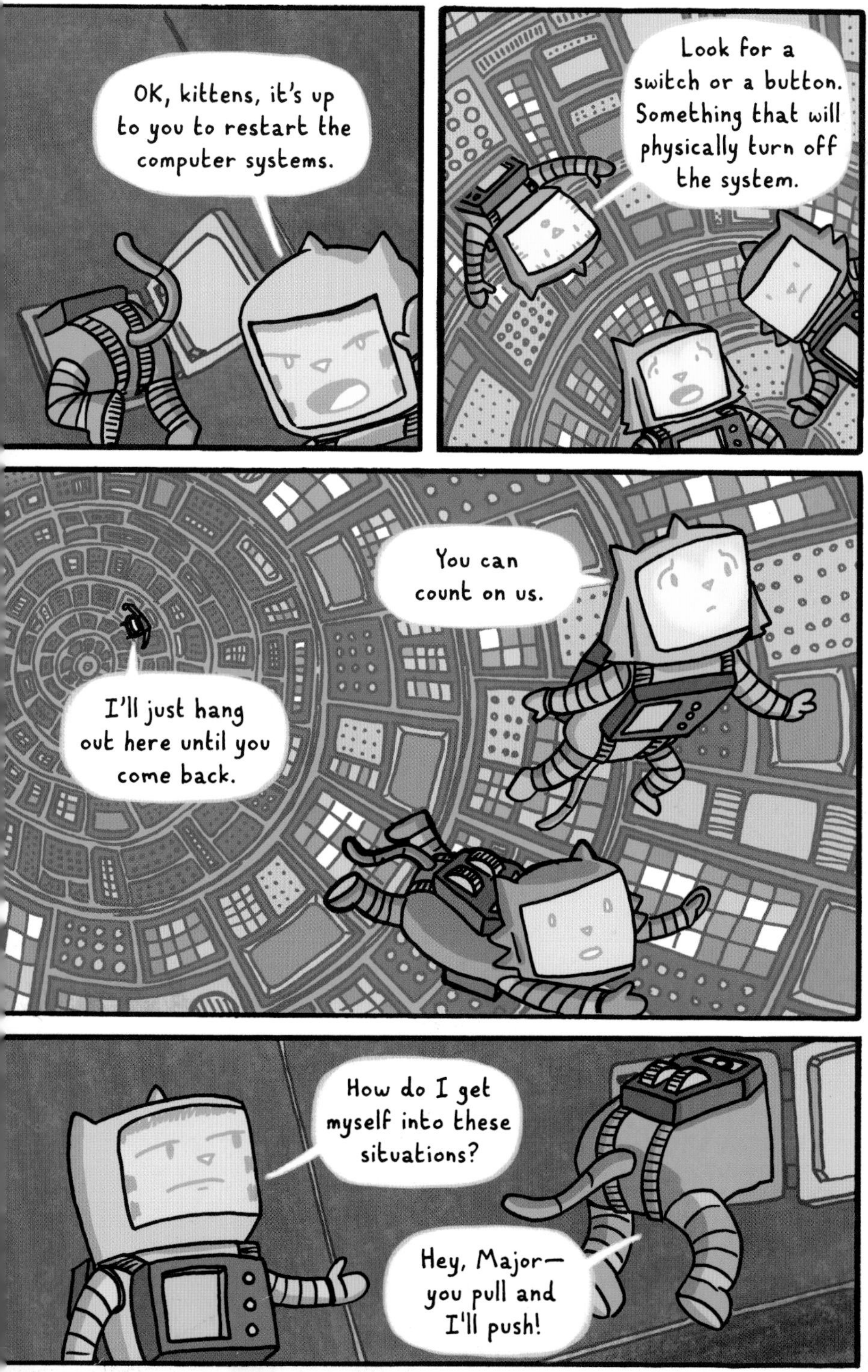

OK, kittens, it's up to you to restart the computer systems.
Look for a switch or a button. Something that will physically turn off the system.
You can count on us.
I'll just hang out here until you come back.
How do I get myself into these situations?
Hey, Major— you pull and I'll push!

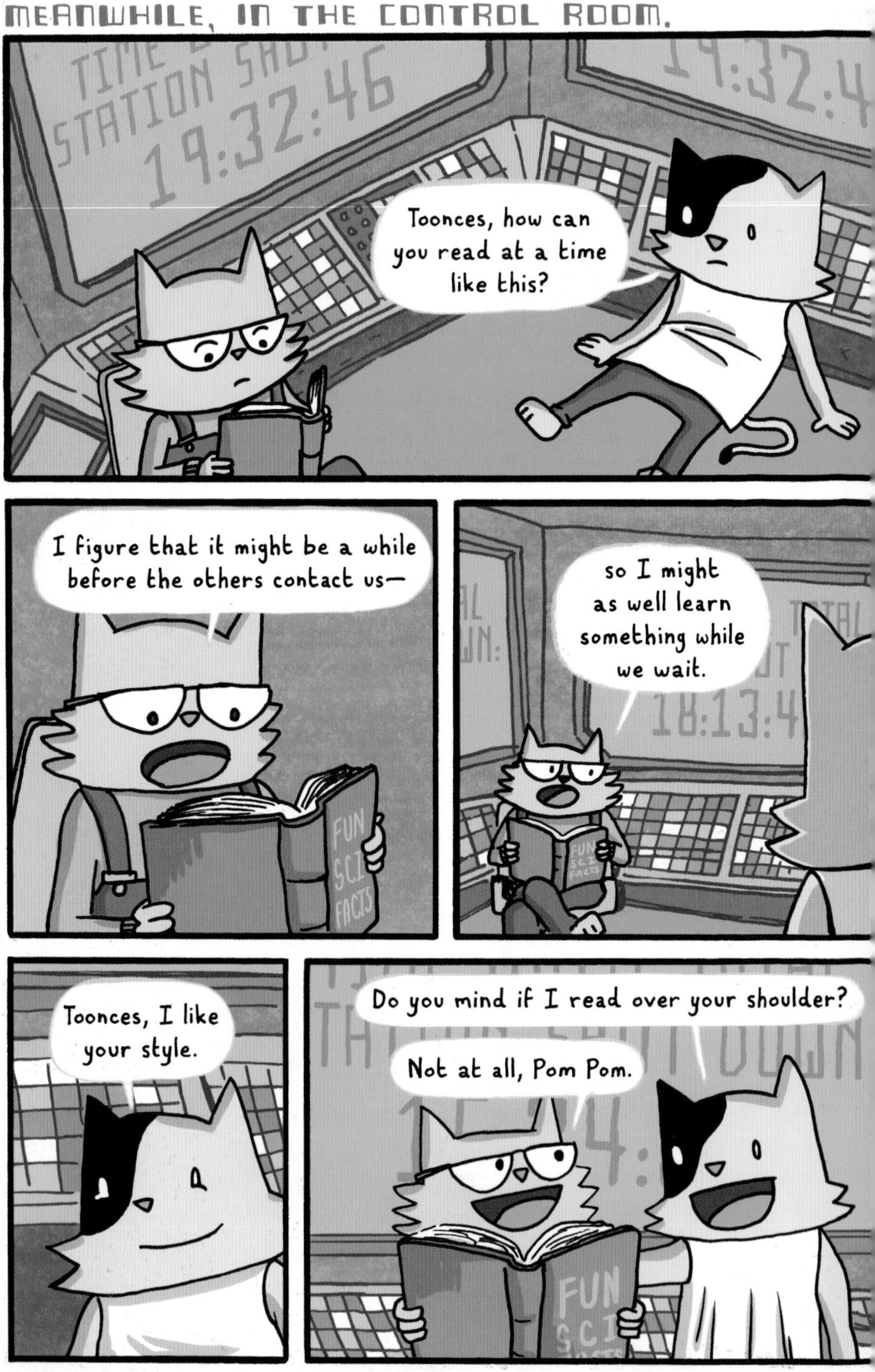
MEANWHILE, IN THE CONTROL ROOM.
19:32:46
Toonces, how can you read at a time like this?
I figure that it might be a while before the others contact us—
FUN SCI FACTS
so I might as well learn something while we wait.
Toonces, I like your style.
Do you mind if I read over your shoulder?
Not at all, Pom Pom.

MEANWHILE, IN THE COMPUTER CORE.

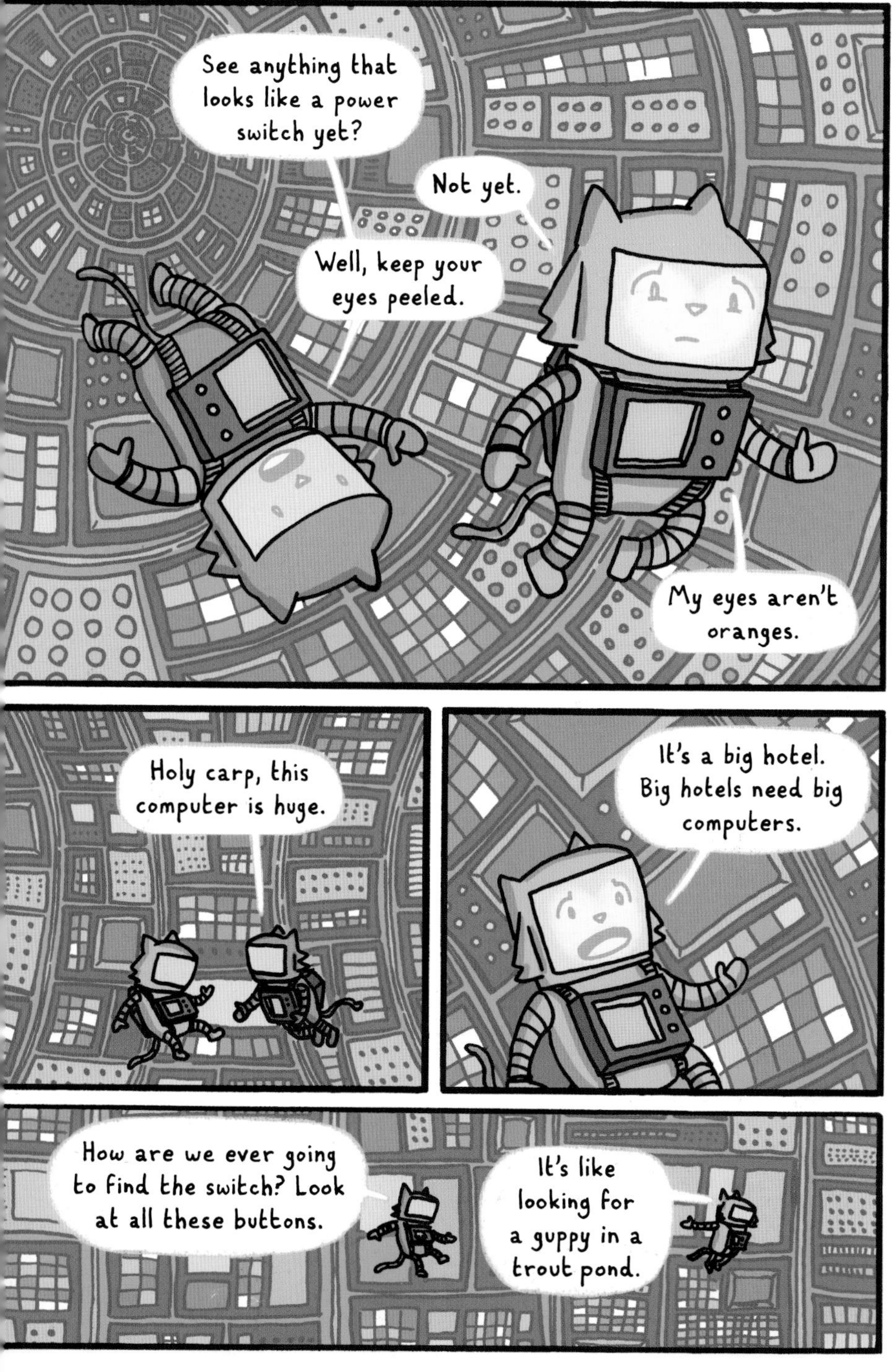
See anything that looks like a power switch yet?
Not yet.
Well, keep your eyes peeled.
My eyes aren't oranges.
Holy carp, this computer is huge.
It's a big hotel. Big hotels need big computers.
How are we ever going to find the switch? Look at all these buttons.
It's like looking for a guppy in a trout pond.

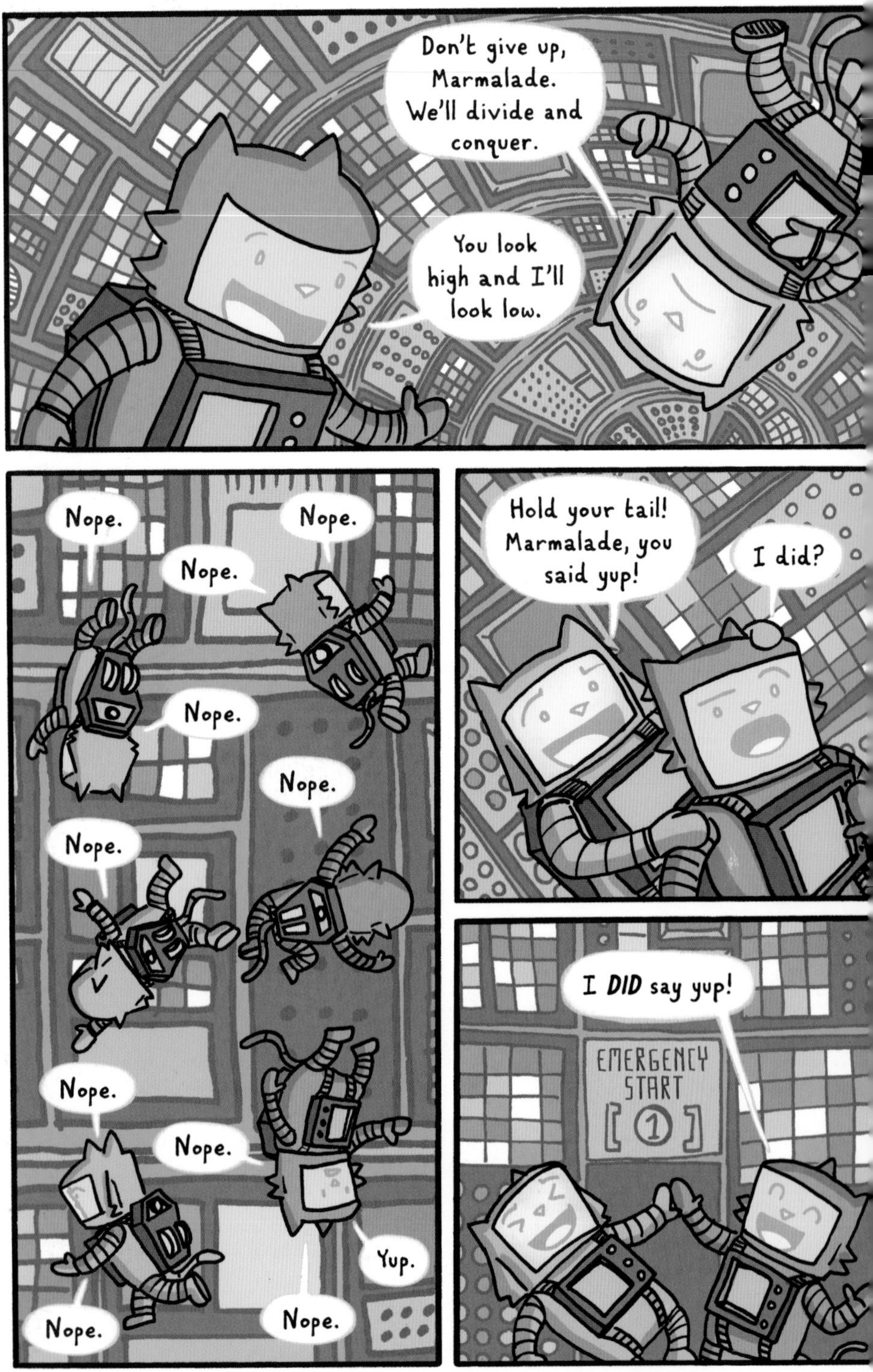

Don't give up, Marmalade. We'll divide and conquer.
You look high and I'll look low.
Nope.
Nope.
Nope.
Nope.
Nope.
Nope.
Nope.
Nope.
Yup.
Nope.
Nope.
Hold your tail! Marmalade, you said yup!
I did?
I *DID* say yup!
EMERGENCY START
[1]

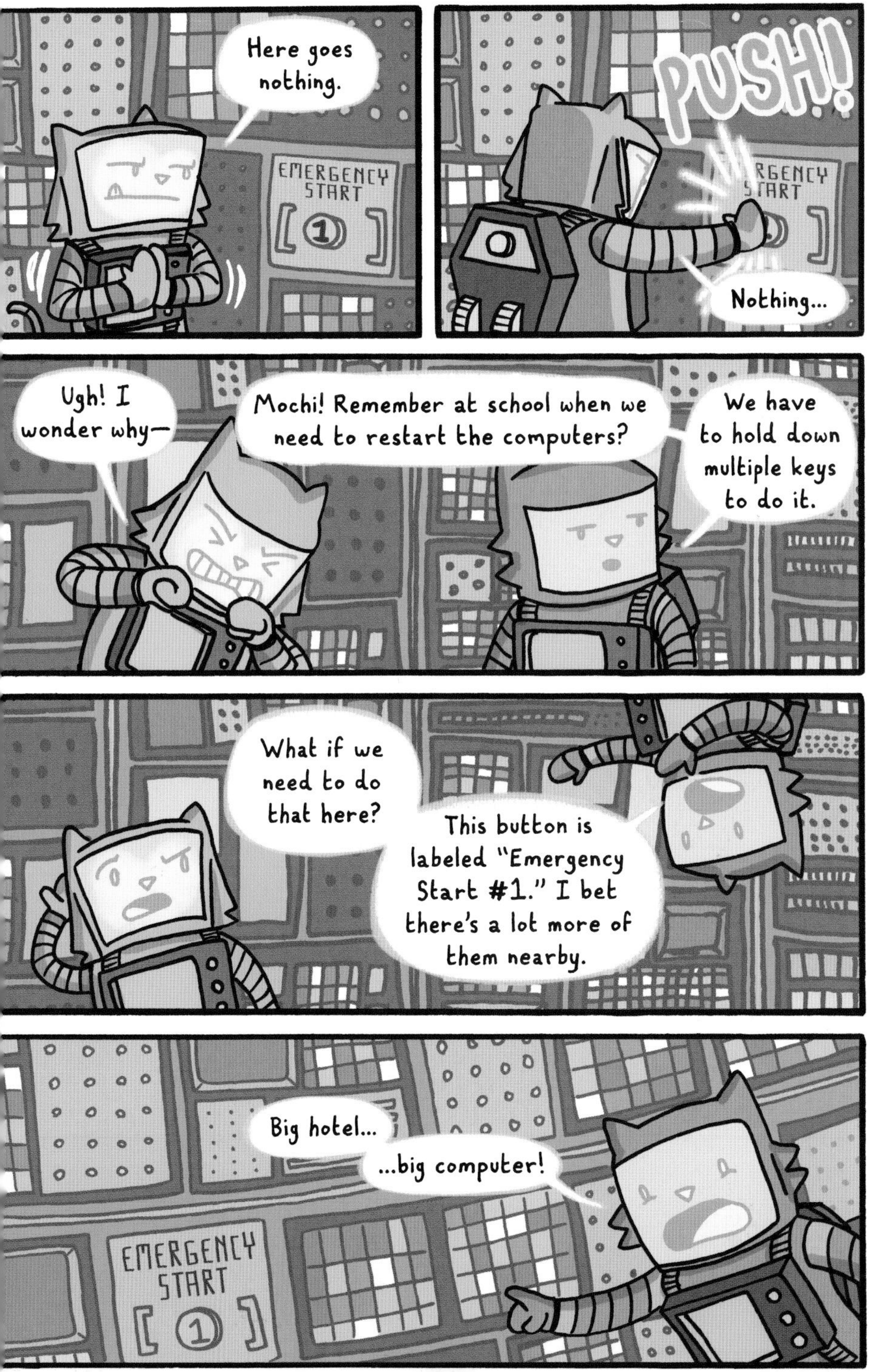
Here goes nothing.
EMERGENCY START
1
PUSH!
Nothing...
Ugh! I wonder why—
Mochi! Remember at school when we need to restart the computers?
We have to hold down multiple keys to do it.
What if we need to do that here?
This button is labeled "Emergency Start #1." I bet there's a lot more of them nearby.
Big hotel...
...big computer!
EMERGENCY START
1

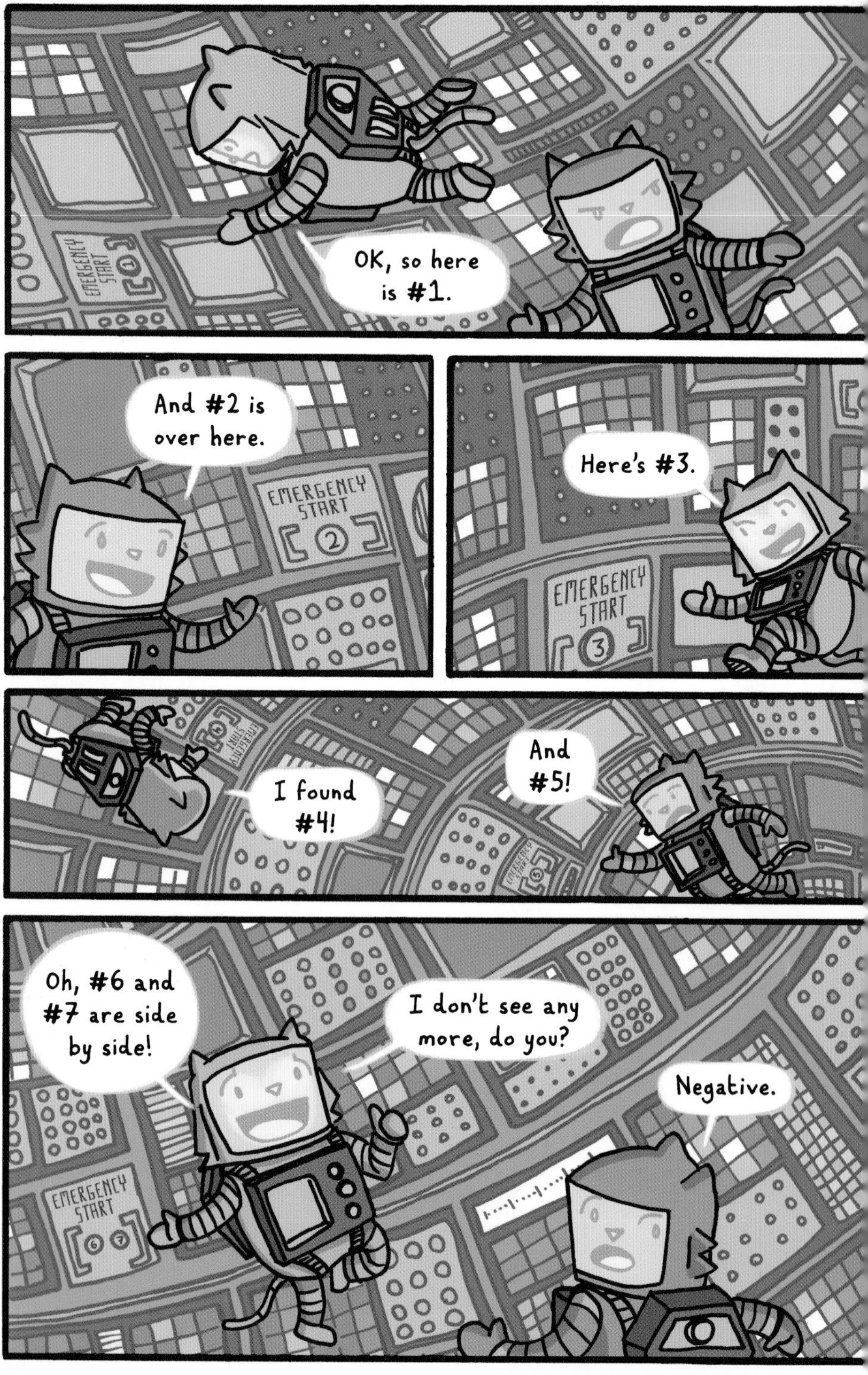
EMERGENCY START 1
OK, so here is #1.
And #2 is over here.
EMERGENCY START 2
Here's #3.
EMERGENCY START 3
EMERGENCY START 4
I found #4!
And #5!
EMERGENCY START 5
Oh, #6 and #7 are side by side!
I don't see any more, do you?
Negative.
EMERGENCY START 6 7

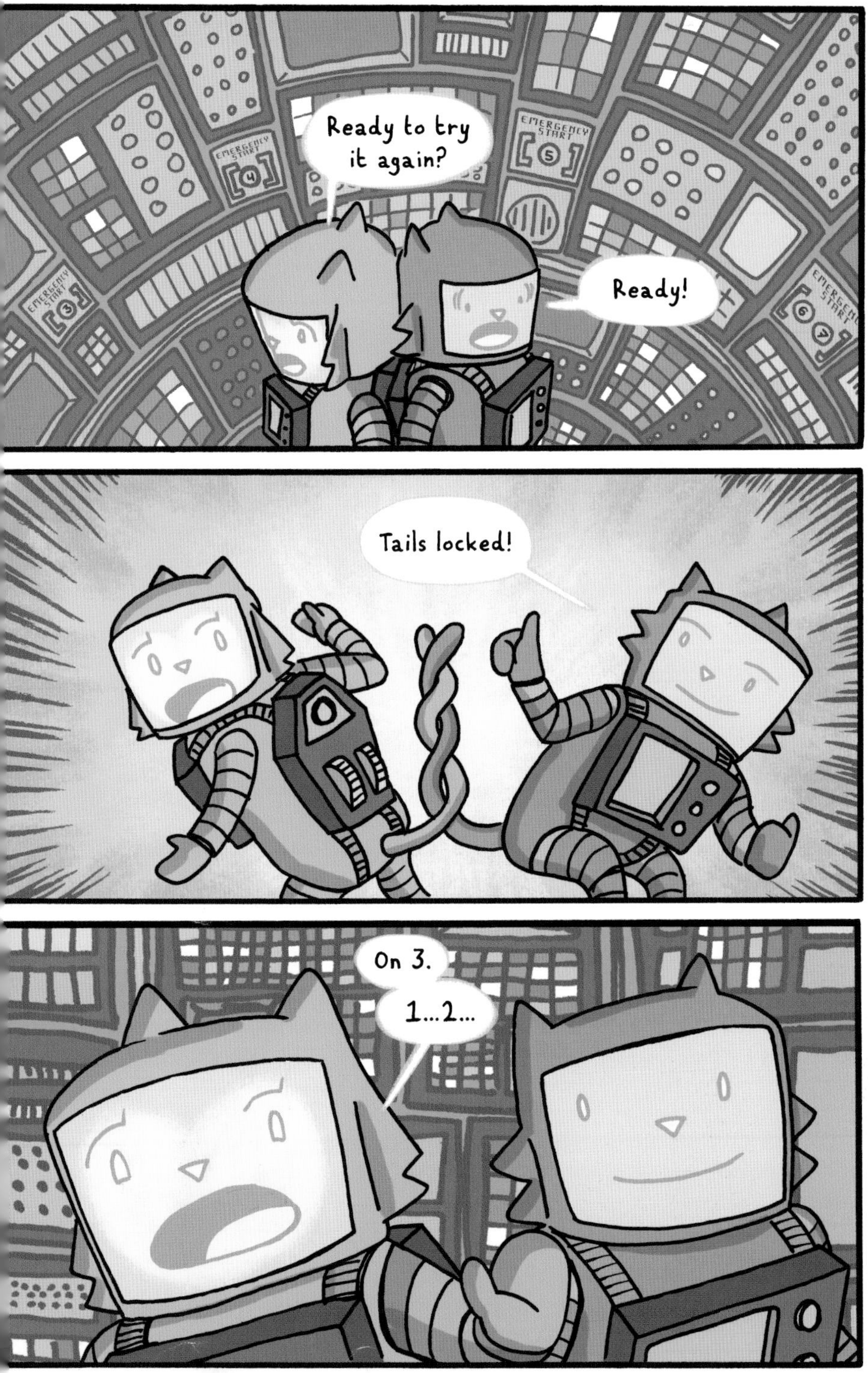
Ready to try it again?
Ready!
Tails locked!
On 3.
1...2...

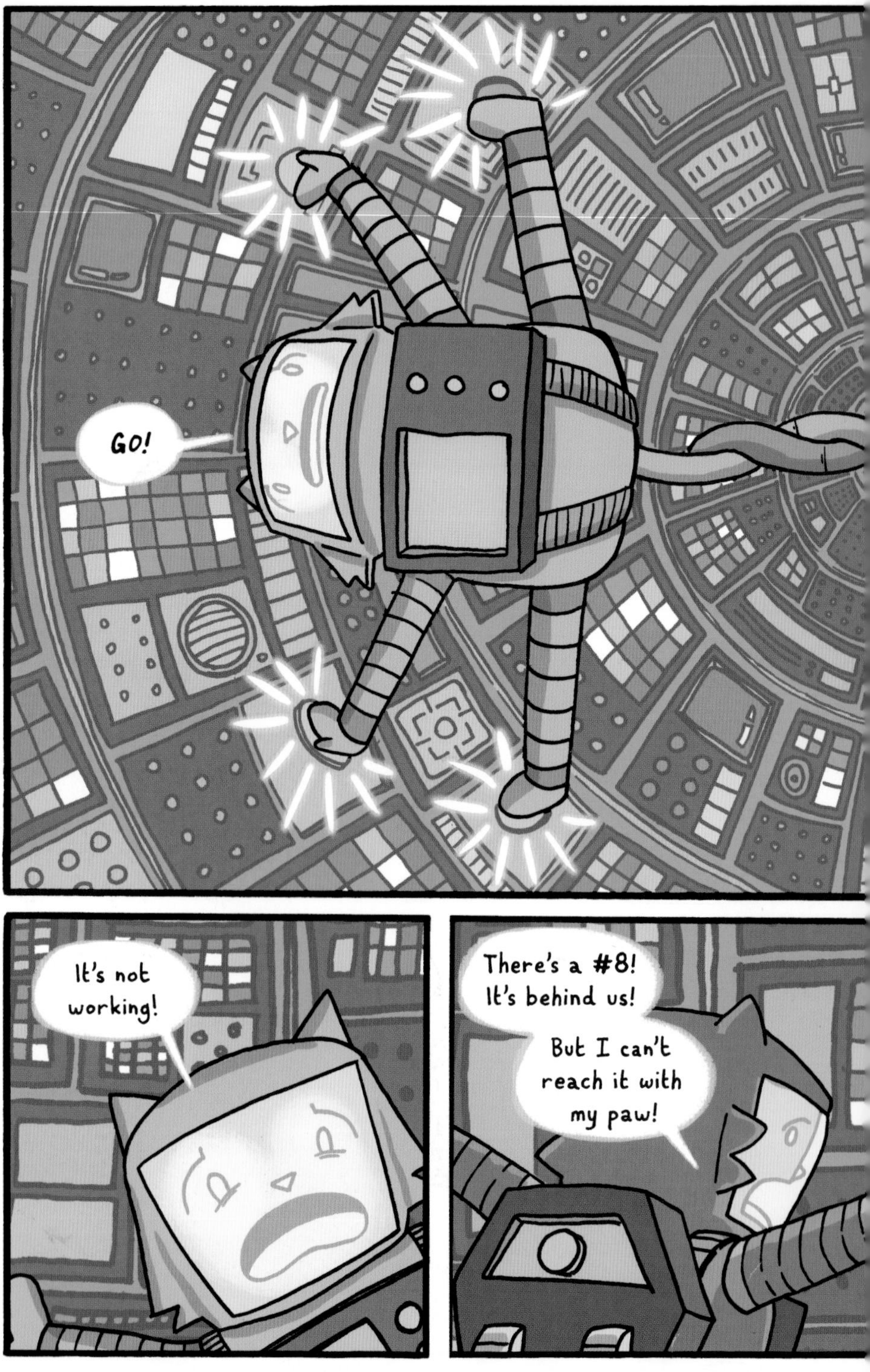
GO!
It's not working!
There's a #8! It's behind us!
But I can't reach it with my paw!

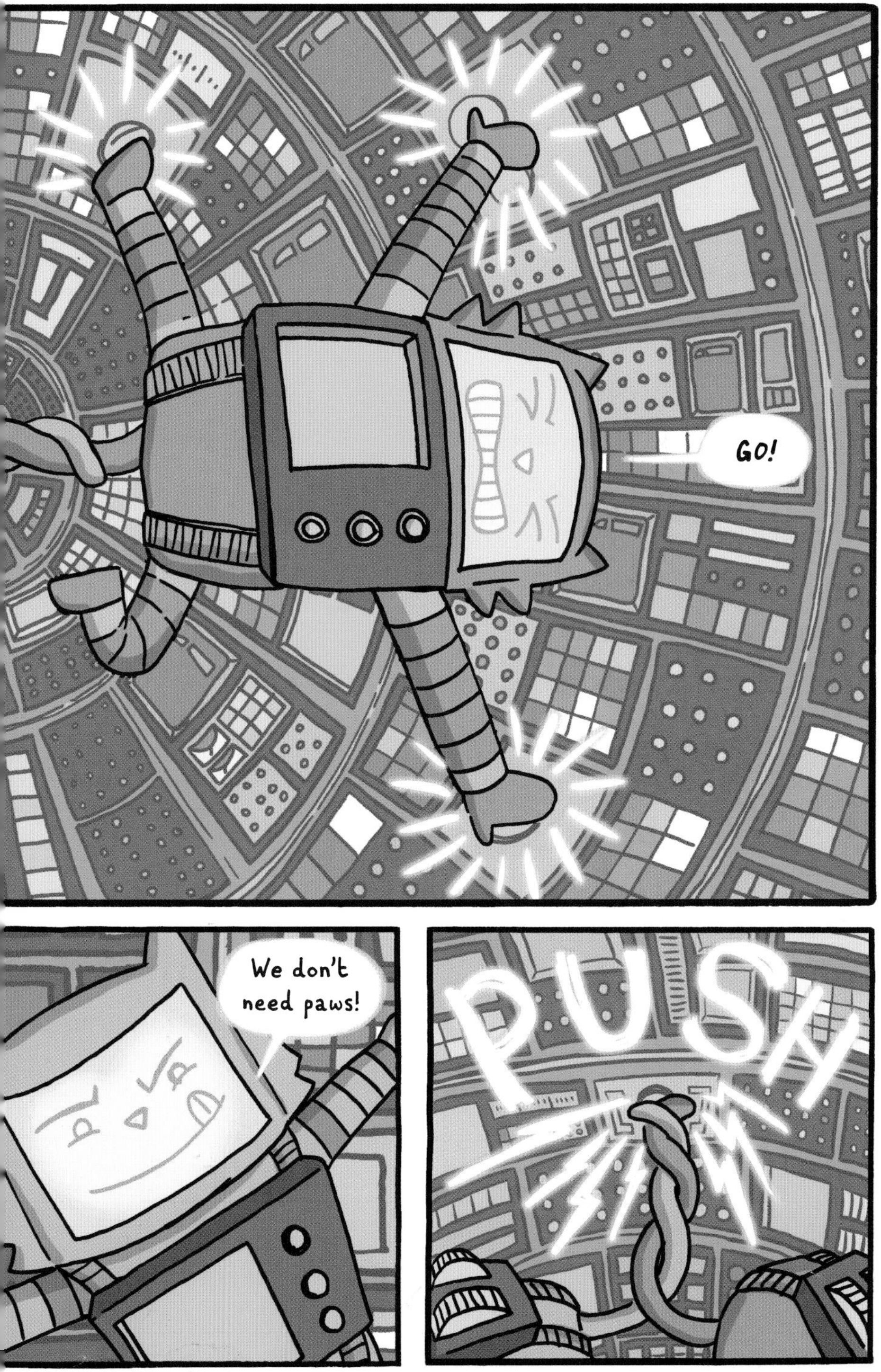
GO!
We don't need paws!
PUSH

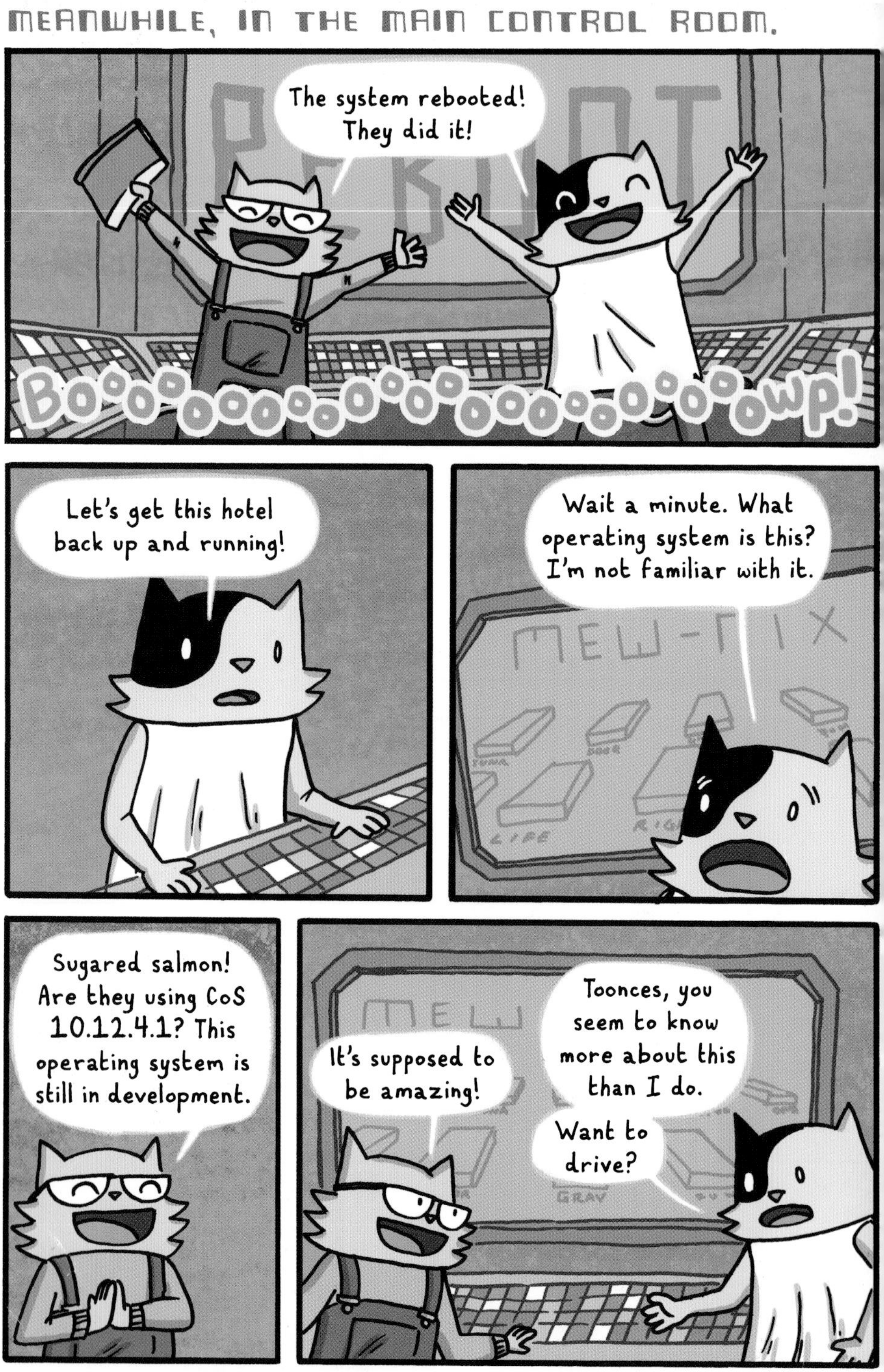
MEANWHILE, IN THE MAIN CONTROL ROOM.
REBOOT
The system rebooted! They did it!
Boooooooooooooooooooowp!
Let's get this hotel back up and running!
Wait a minute. What operating system is this? I'm not familiar with it.
MEW-NIX
Sugared salmon! Are they using CoS 10.12.4.1? This operating system is still in development.
It's supposed to be amazing!
Toonces, you seem to know more about this than I do.
Want to drive?

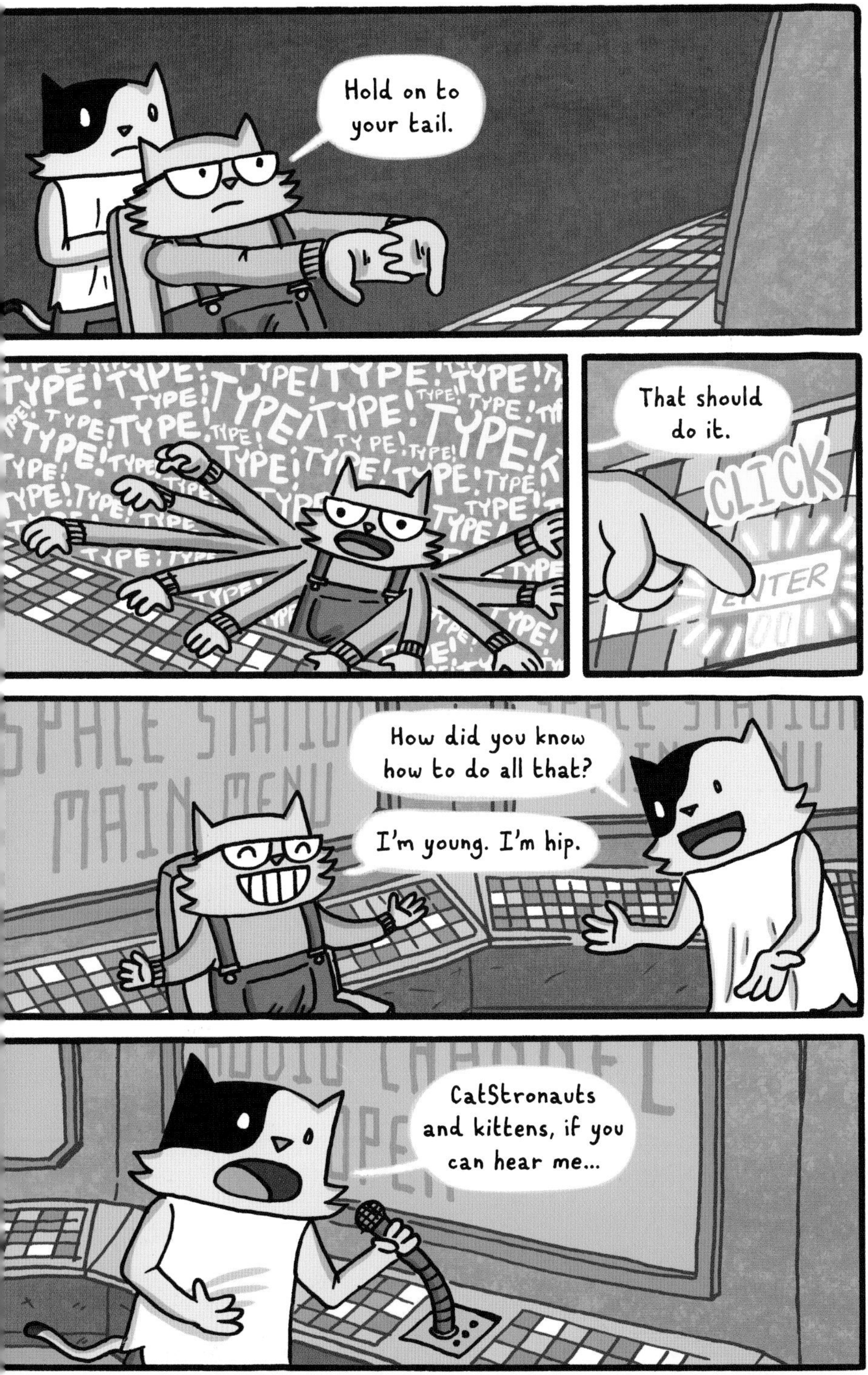
Hold on to your tail.
TYPE! TYPE! TYPE!
That should do it.
CLICK
ENTER
MAIN MENU
How did you know how to do all that?
I'm young. I'm hip.
CatStronauts and kittens, if you can hear me...

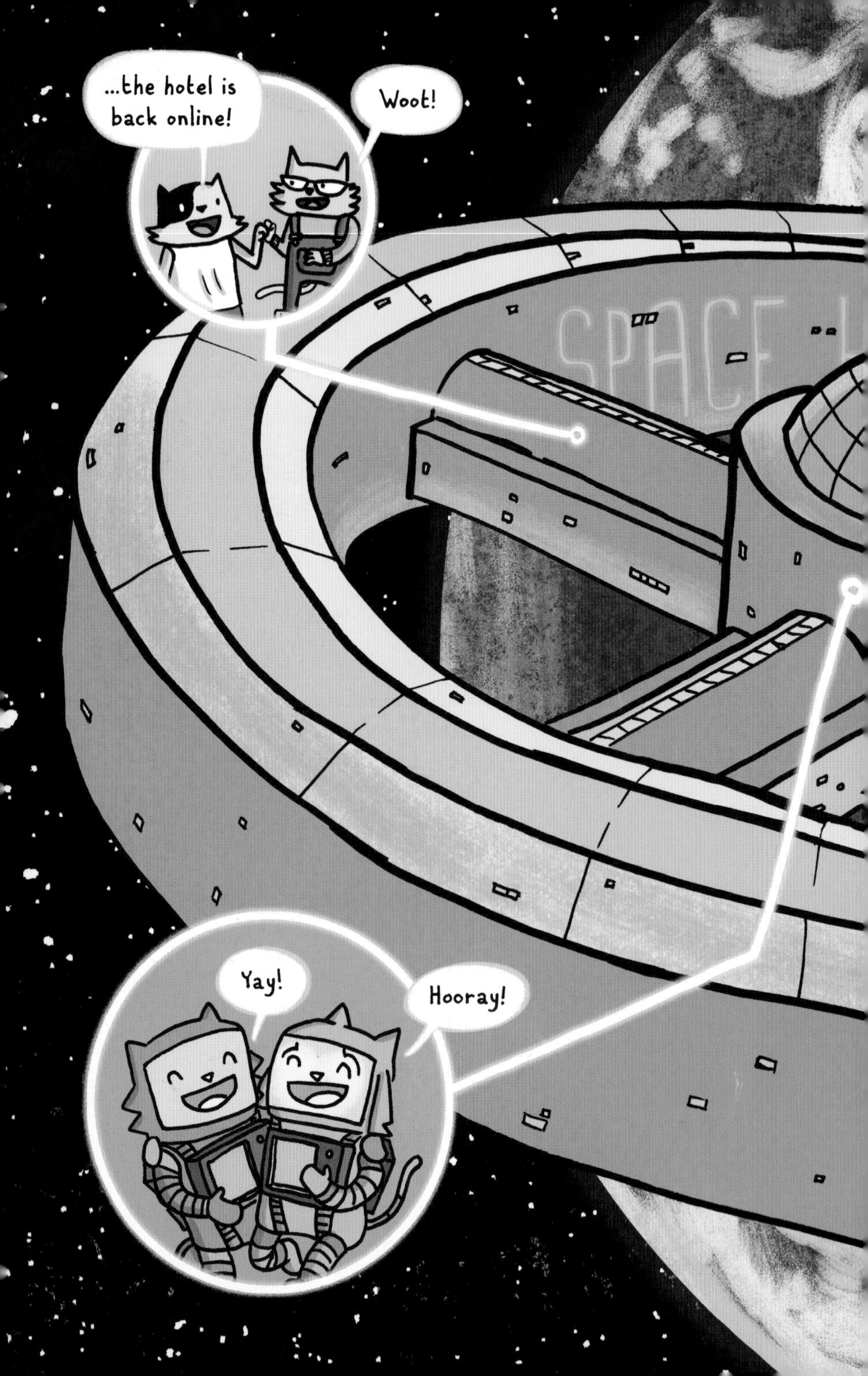
...the hotel is back online!
Woot!
SPACE
Yay!
Hooray!

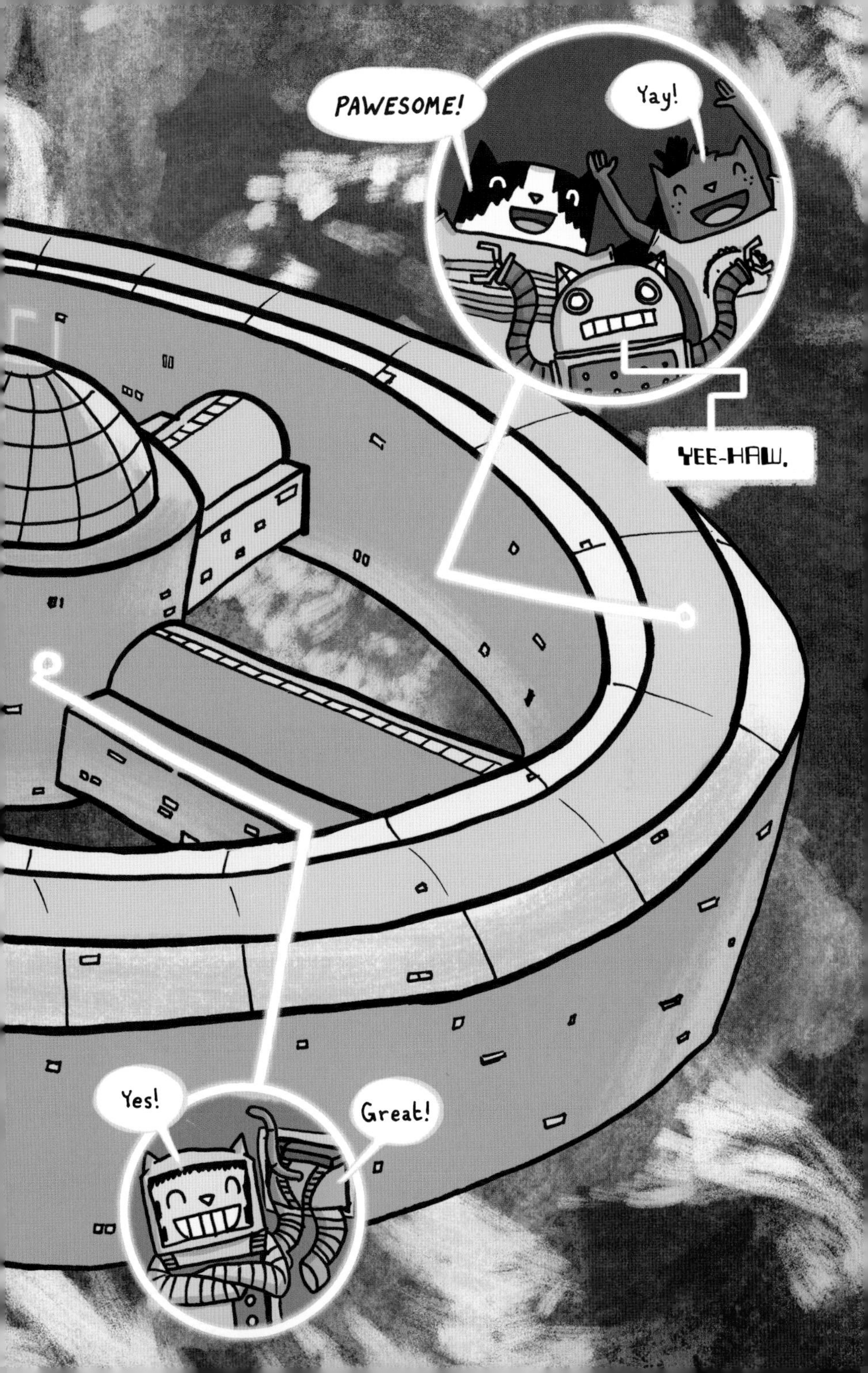
PAWESOME!
Yay!
YEE-HAW.
Yes!
Great!

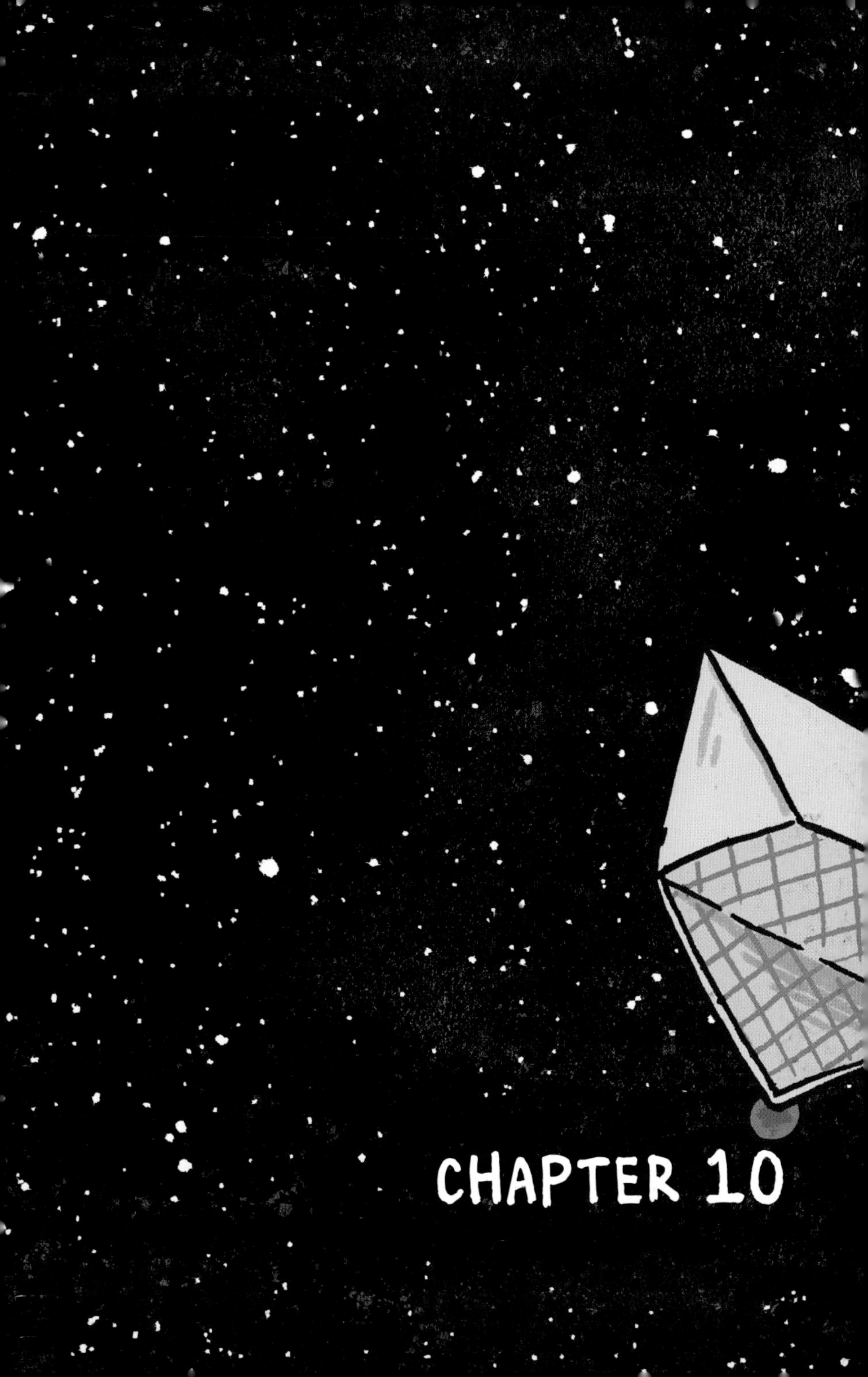
CHAPTER 10

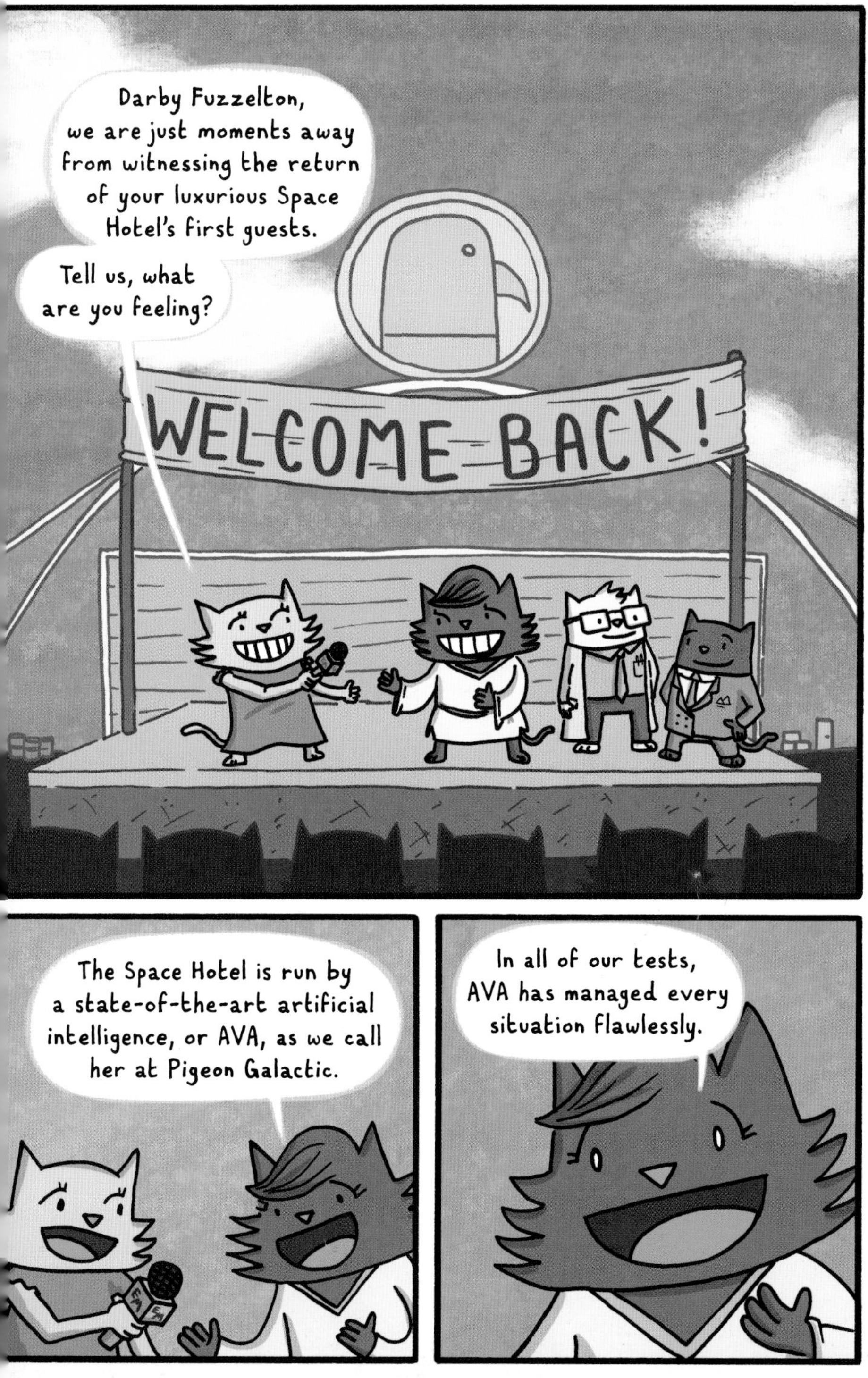
Darby Fuzzelton, we are just moments away from witnessing the return of your luxurious Space Hotel's first guests.
Tell us, what are you feeling?
WELCOME BACK!
The Space Hotel is run by a state-of-the-art artificial intelligence, or AVA, as we call her at Pigeon Galactic.
In all of our tests, AVA has managed every situation flawlessly.

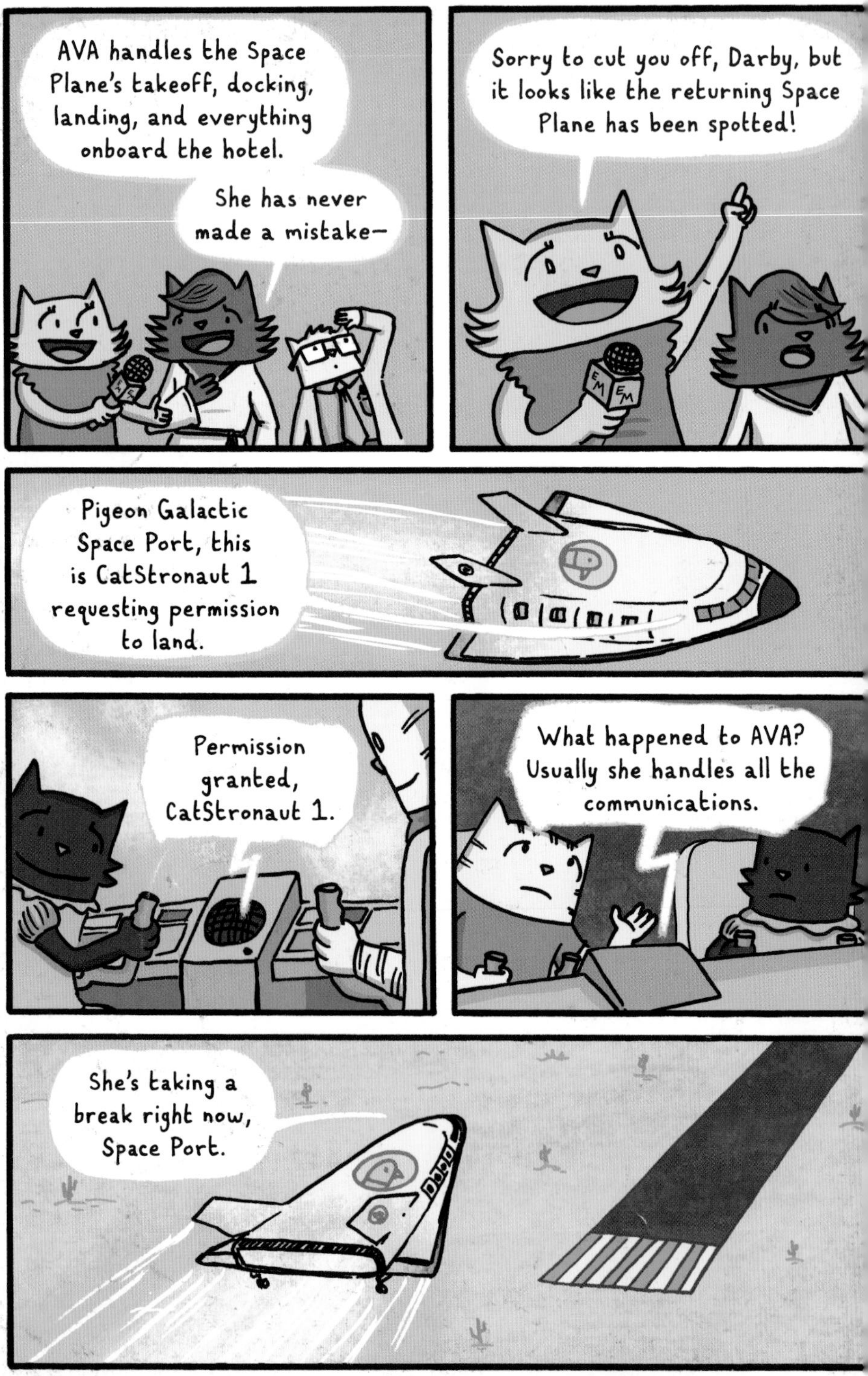
AVA handles the Space Plane's takeoff, docking, landing, and everything onboard the hotel.
She has never made a mistake—
Sorry to cut you off, Darby, but it looks like the returning Space Plane has been spotted!
Pigeon Galactic Space Port, this is CatStronaut 1 requesting permission to land.
Permission granted, CatStronaut 1.
What happened to AVA? Usually she handles all the communications.
She's taking a break right now, Space Port.

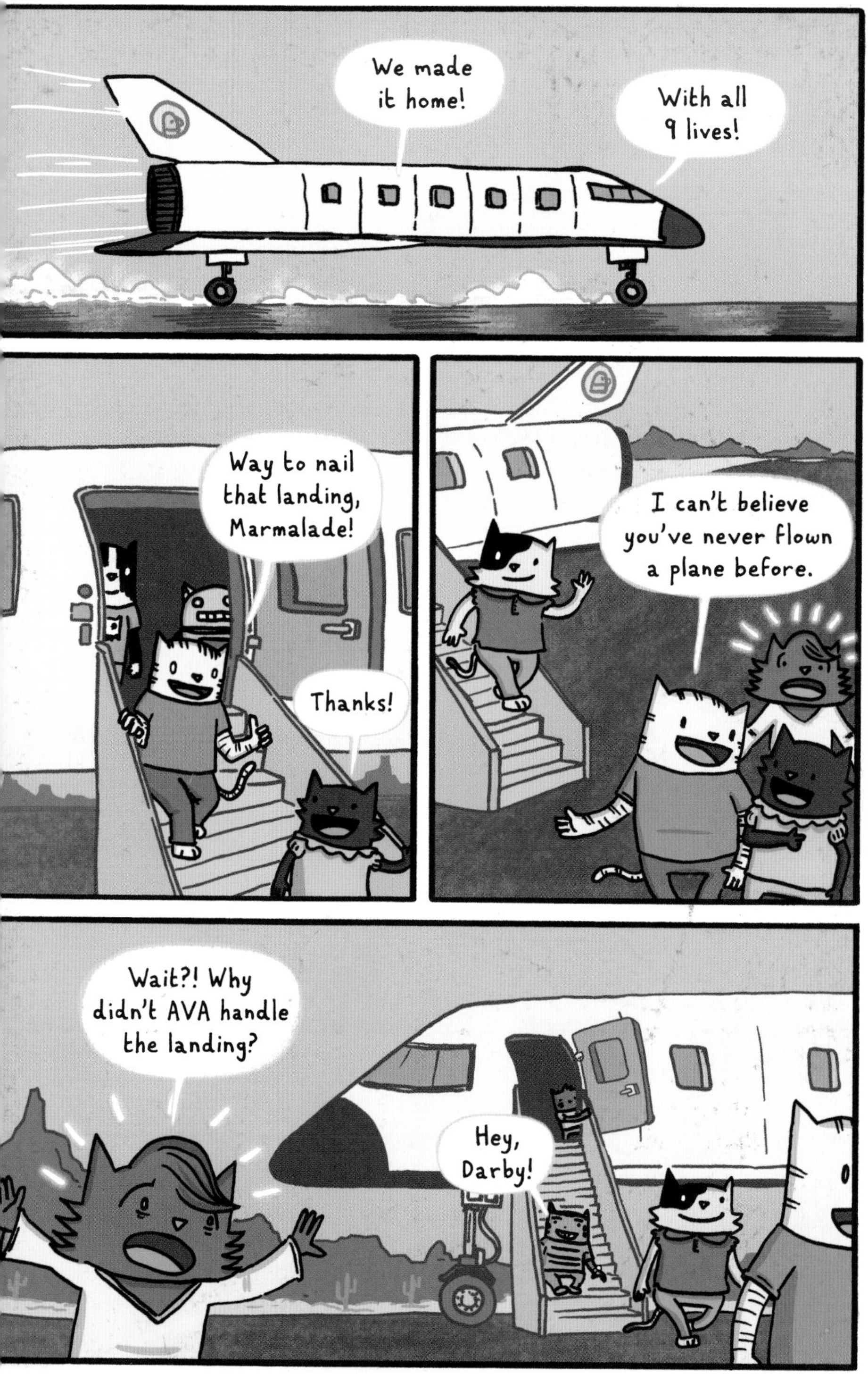
We made it home!
With all 9 lives!
Way to nail that landing, Marmalade!
Thanks!
I can't believe you've never flown a plane before.
Wait?! Why didn't AVA handle the landing?
Hey, Darby!

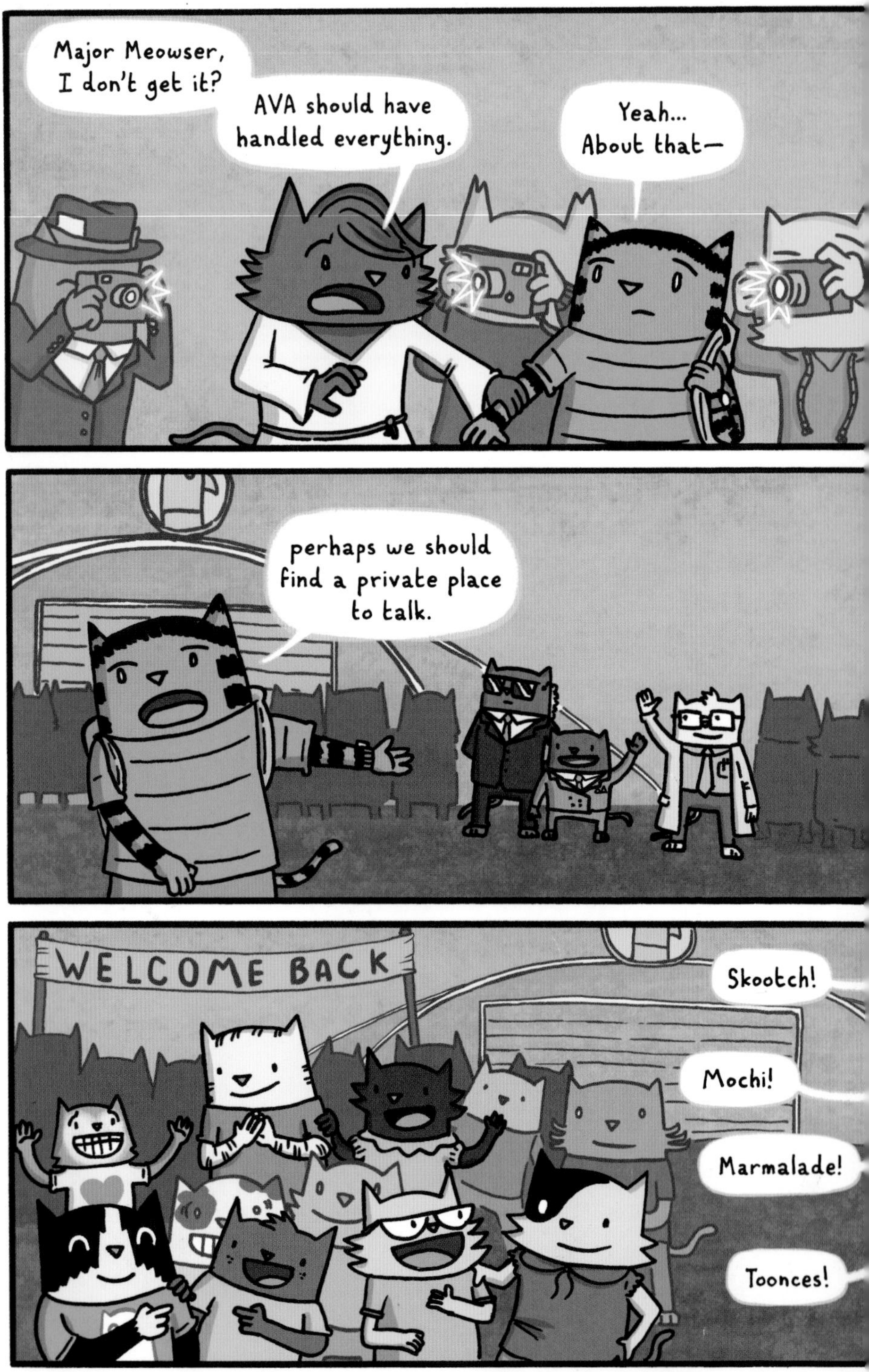
Major Meowser,
I don't get it?
AVA should have
handled everything.
Yeah...
About that—
perhaps we should
find a private place
to talk.
WELCOME BACK
Skootch!
Mochi!
Marmalade!
Toonces!

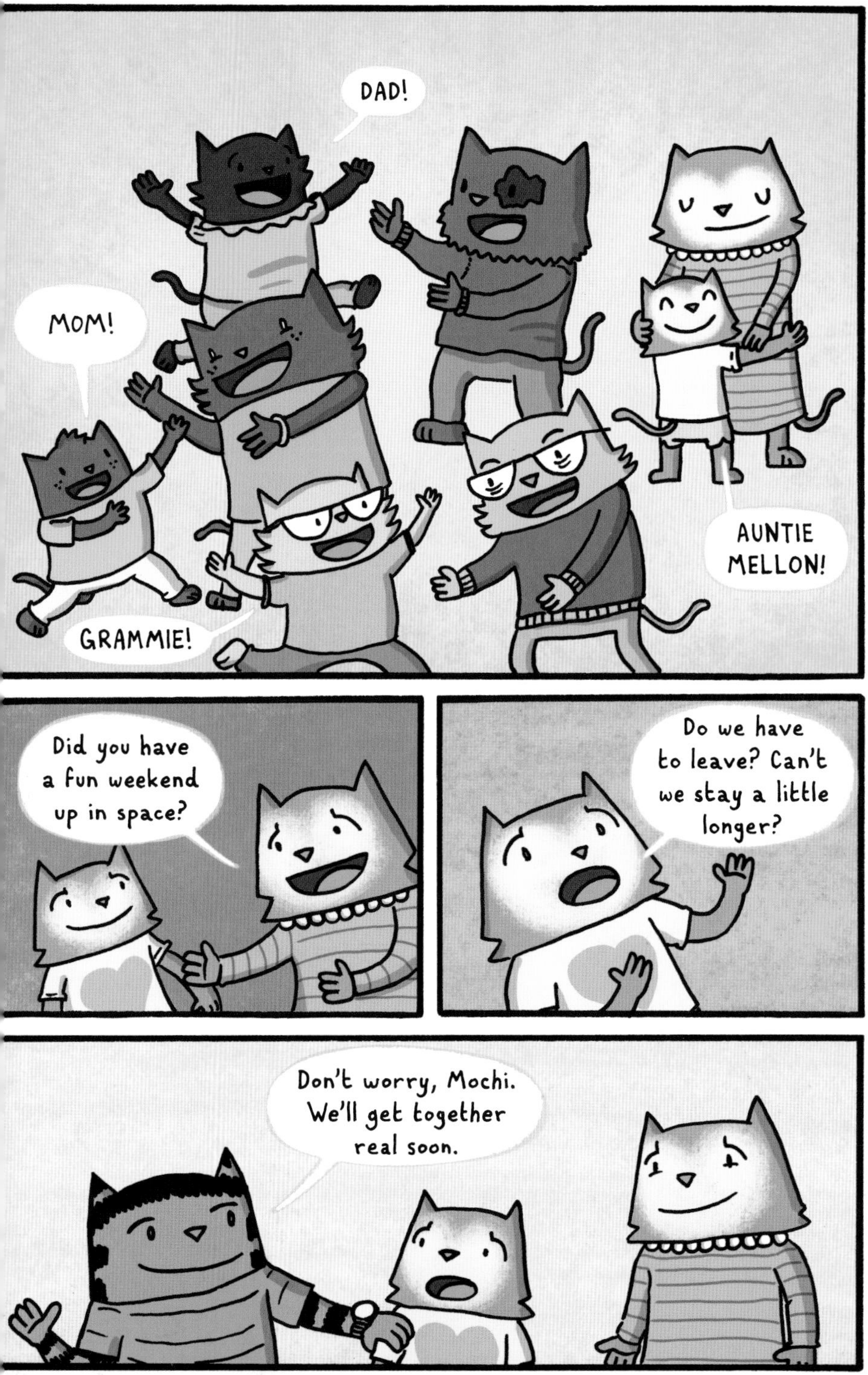
DAD!
MOM!
AUNTIE MELLON!
GRAMMIE!
Did you have a fun weekend up in space?
Do we have to leave? Can't we stay a little longer?
Don't worry, Mochi. We'll get together real soon.

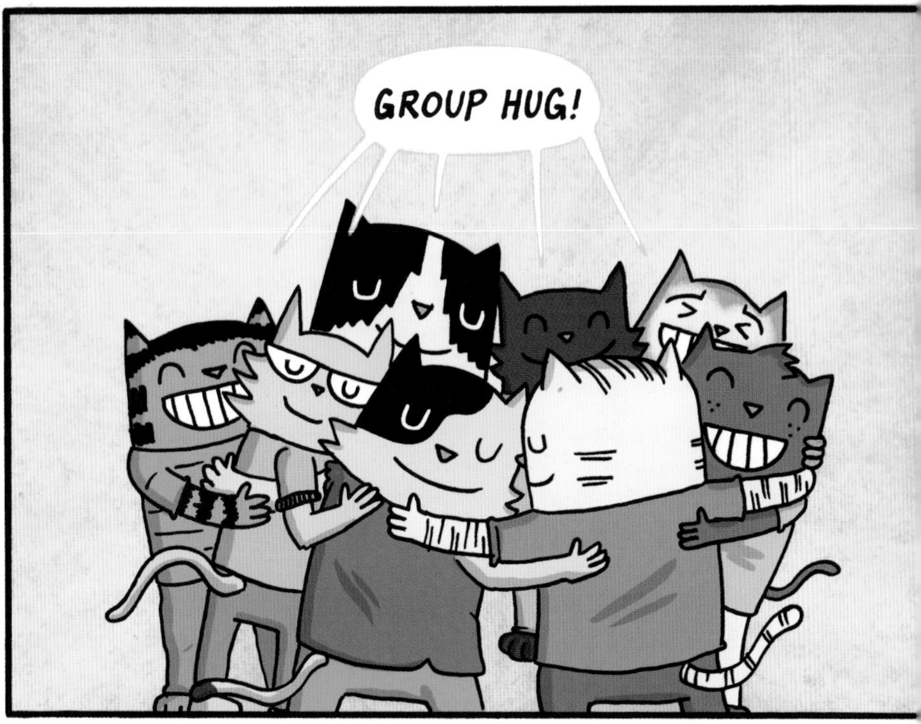
GROUP HUG!

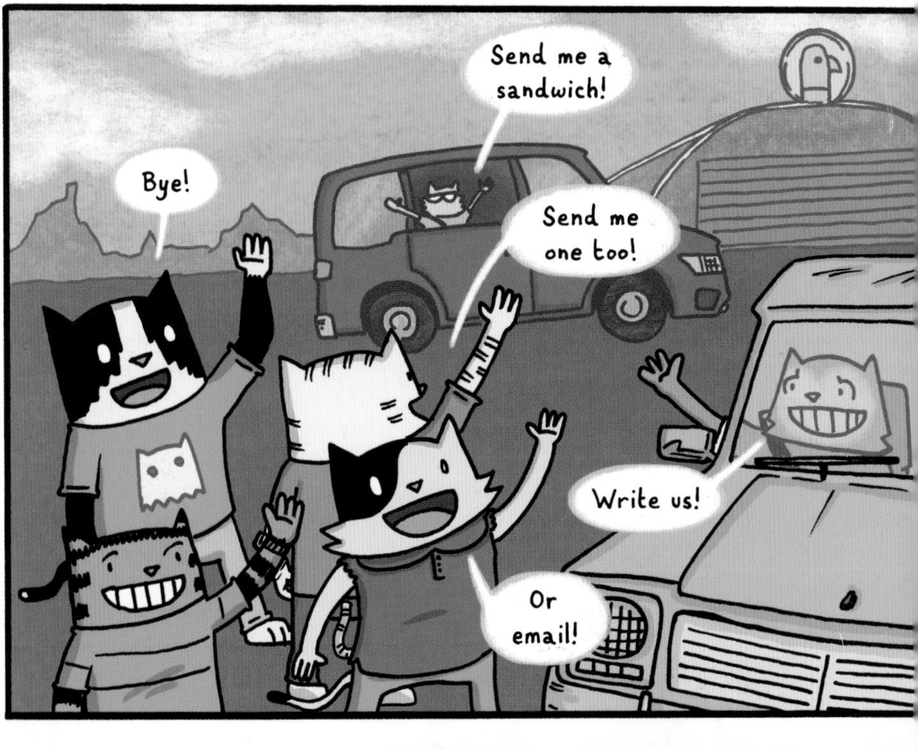
Bye!
Send me a sandwich!
Send me one too!
Write us!
Or email!

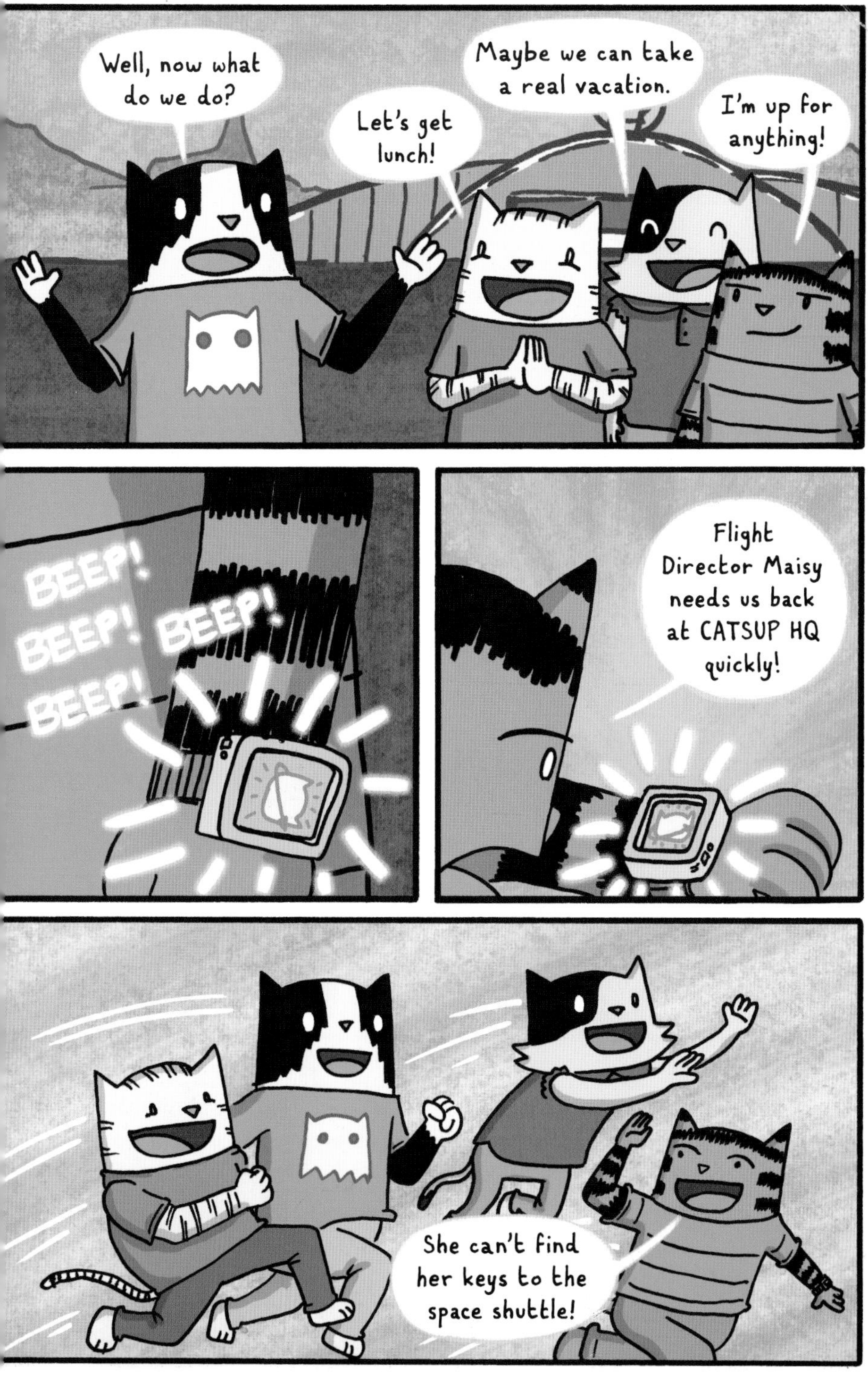
Well, now what do we do?
Let's get lunch!
Maybe we can take a real vacation.
I'm up for anything!
BEEP! BEEP! BEEP! BEEP!
Flight Director Maisy needs us back at CATSUP HQ quickly!
She can't find her keys to the space shuttle!

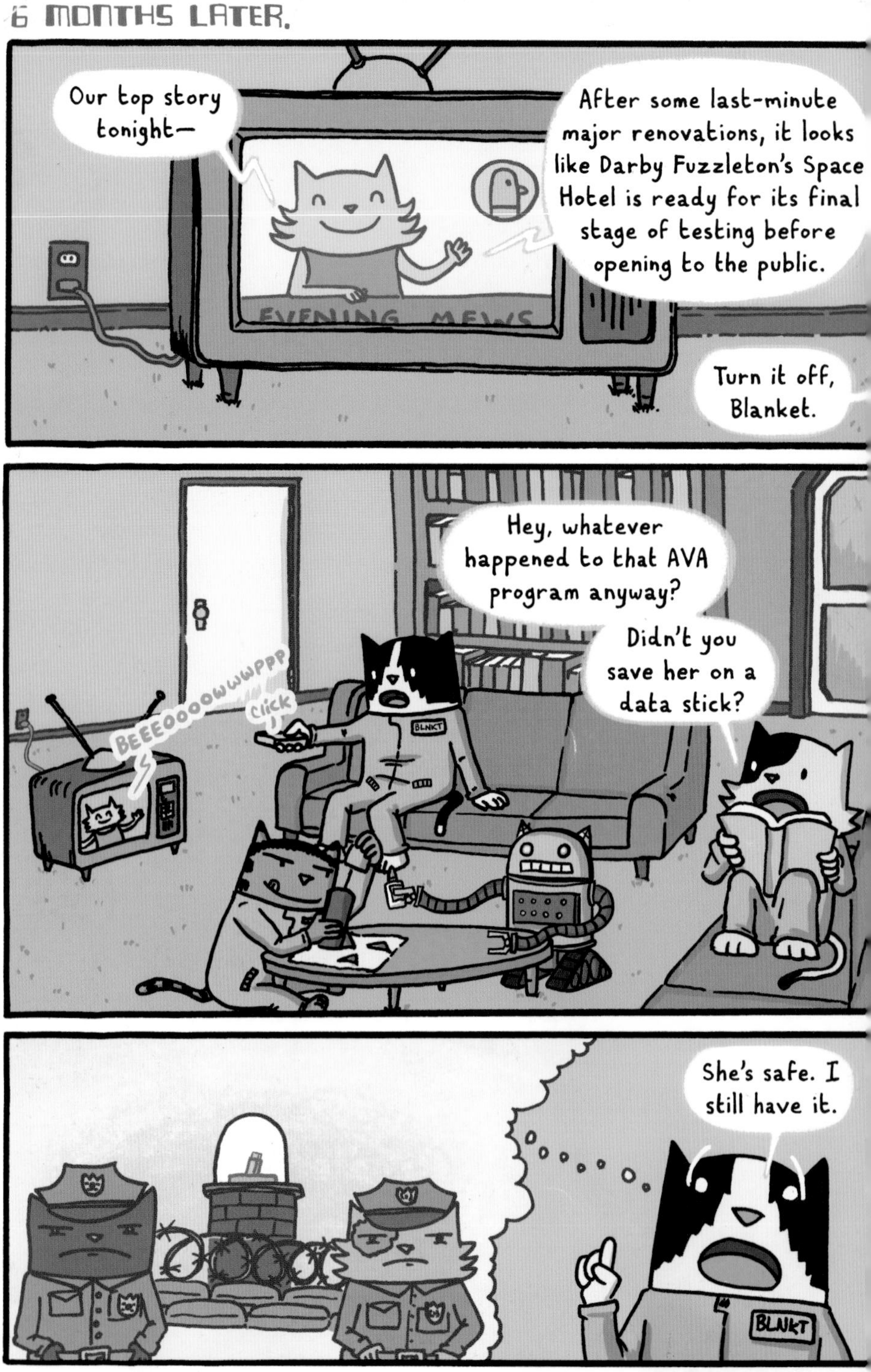
6 MONTHS LATER.
Our top story tonight—
After some last-minute major renovations, it looks like Darby Fuzzleton's Space Hotel is ready for its final stage of testing before opening to the public.
EVENING MEWS
Turn it off, Blanket.
Hey, whatever happened to that AVA program anyway?
Didn't you save her on a data stick?
BEEEOOOOWWWPPP
CLICK
BLNKT
She's safe. I still have it.
BLNKT

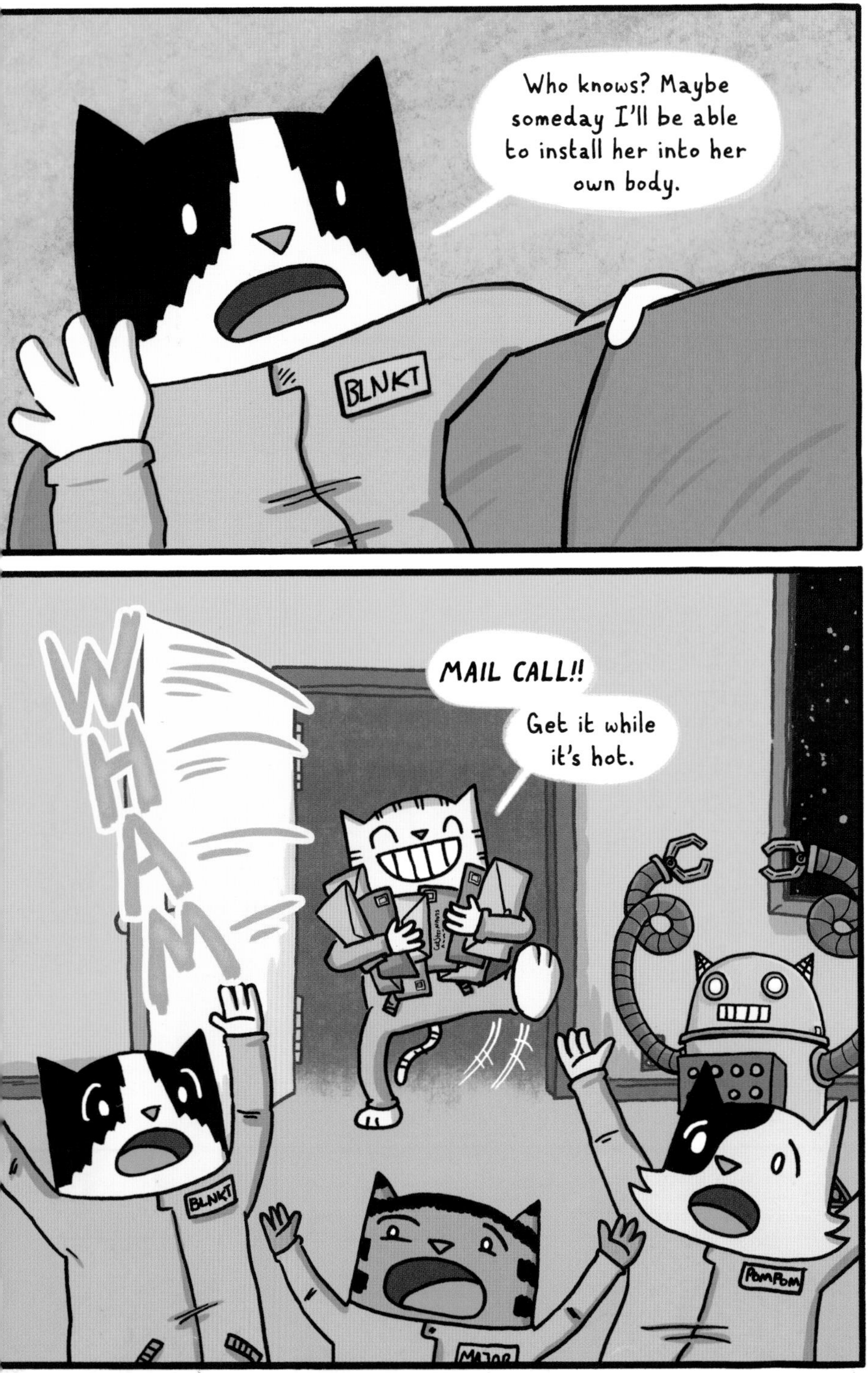
Who knows? Maybe someday I'll be able to install her into her own body.
BLNKT
WHAM
MAIL CALL!!
Get it while it's hot.
BLNKT
POMPOM

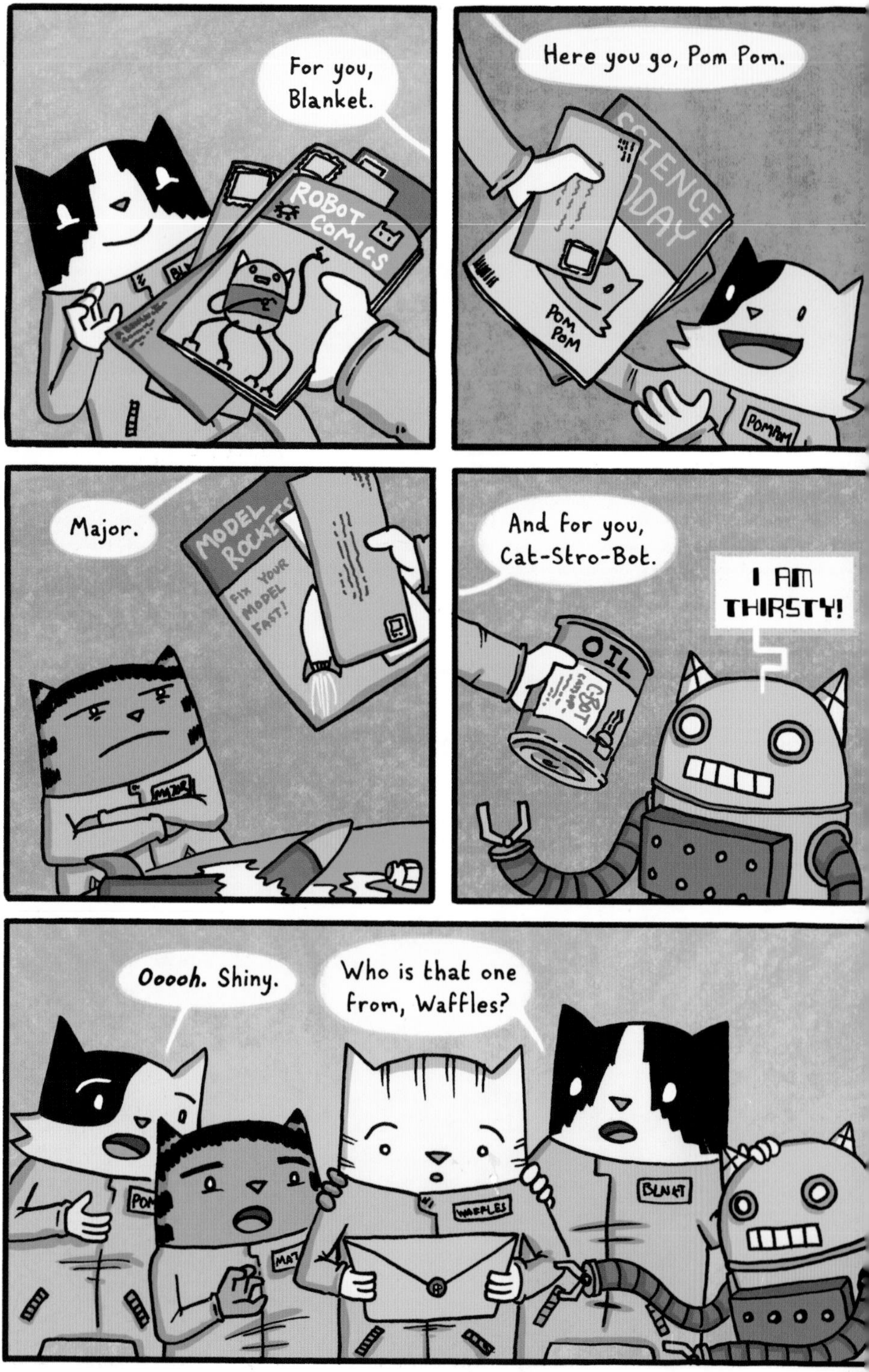
For you, Blanket.
ROBOT COMICS
Here you go, Pom Pom.
POM POM
Major.
FIX YOUR MODEL FAST!
And for you, Cat-Stro-Bot.
I AM THIRSTY!
OIL
Ooooh. Shiny.
Who is that one from, Waffles?

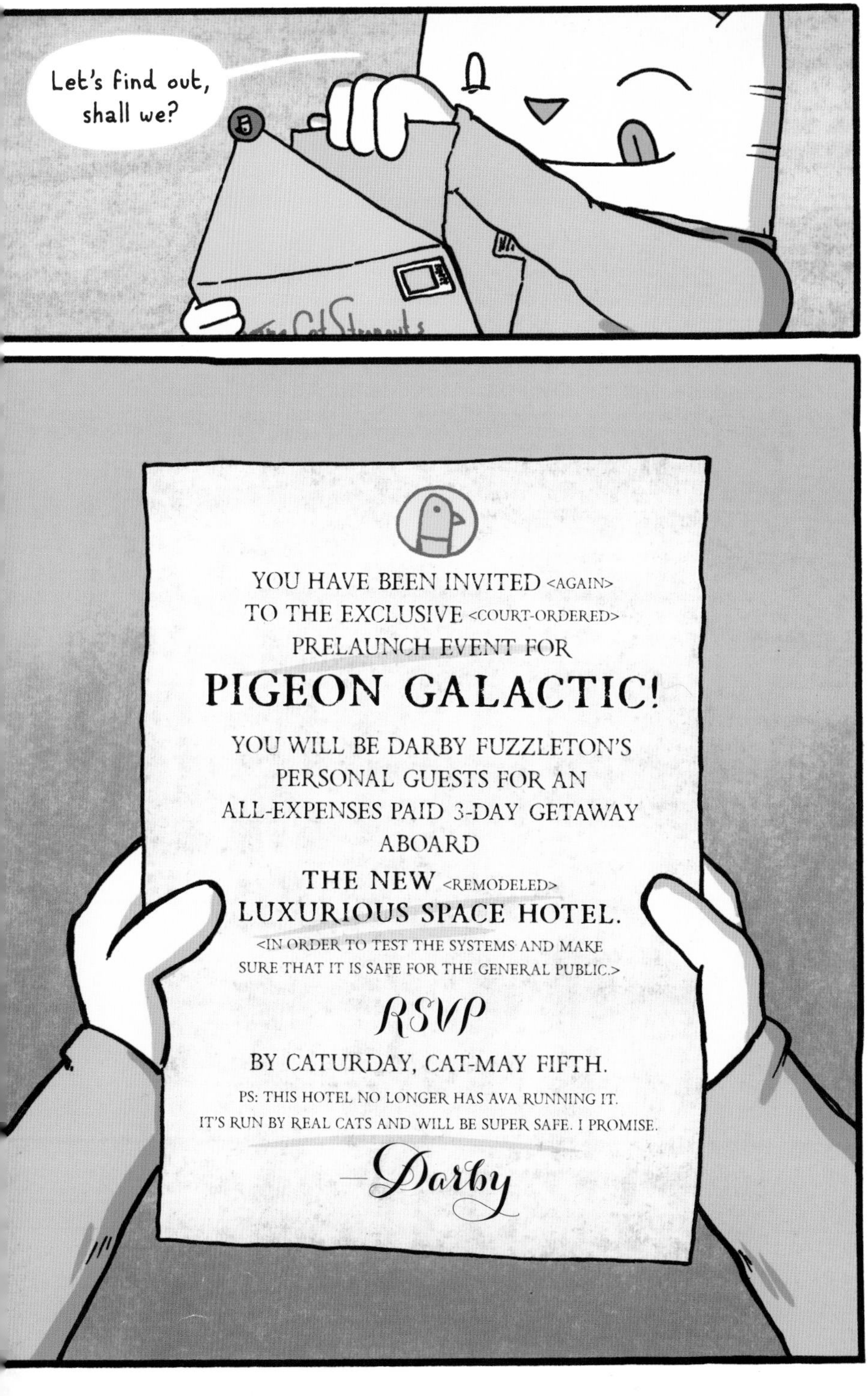
Let's find out, shall we?
YOU HAVE BEEN INVITED <AGAIN>
TO THE EXCLUSIVE <COURT-ORDERED>
PRELAUNCH EVENT FOR
PIGEON GALACTIC!
YOU WILL BE DARBY FUZZLETON'S
PERSONAL GUESTS FOR AN
ALL-EXPENSES PAID 3-DAY GETAWAY
ABOARD
THE NEW <REMODELED>
LUXURIOUS SPACE HOTEL.
<IN ORDER TO TEST THE SYSTEMS AND MAKE
SURE THAT IT IS SAFE FOR THE GENERAL PUBLIC.>
RSVP
BY CATURDAY, CAT-MAY FIFTH.
PS: THIS HOTEL NO LONGER HAS AVA RUNNING IT.
IT'S RUN BY REAL CATS AND WILL BE SUPER SAFE. I PROMISE.
—Darby

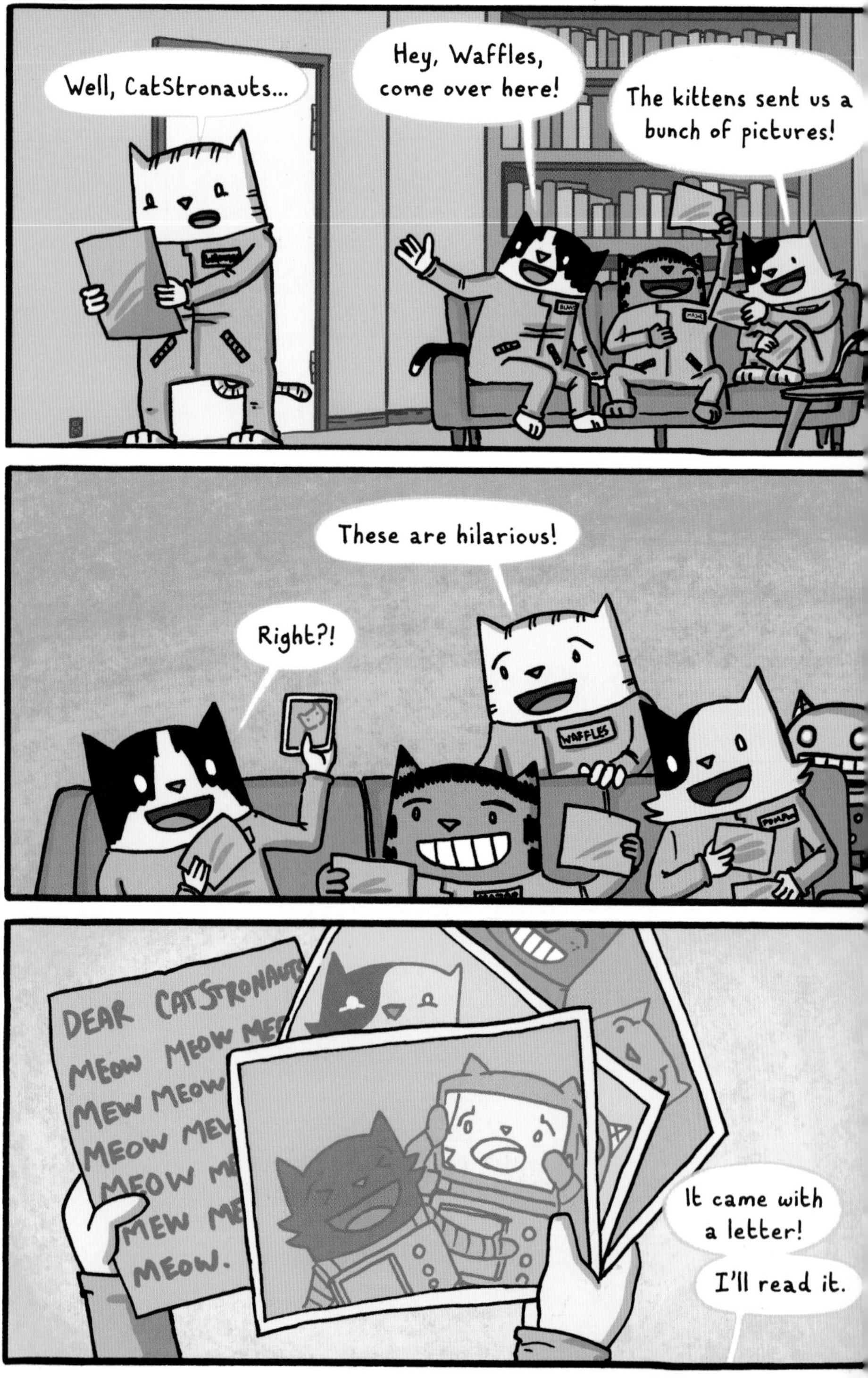
Well, CatStronauts...
Hey, Waffles, come over here!
The kittens sent us a bunch of pictures!
These are hilarious!
Right?!
WAFFLES
DEAR CATSTRONAUTS
MEOW MEOW
MEW MEOW
MEOW
MEOW
MEW
MEOW.
It came with a letter!
I'll read it.

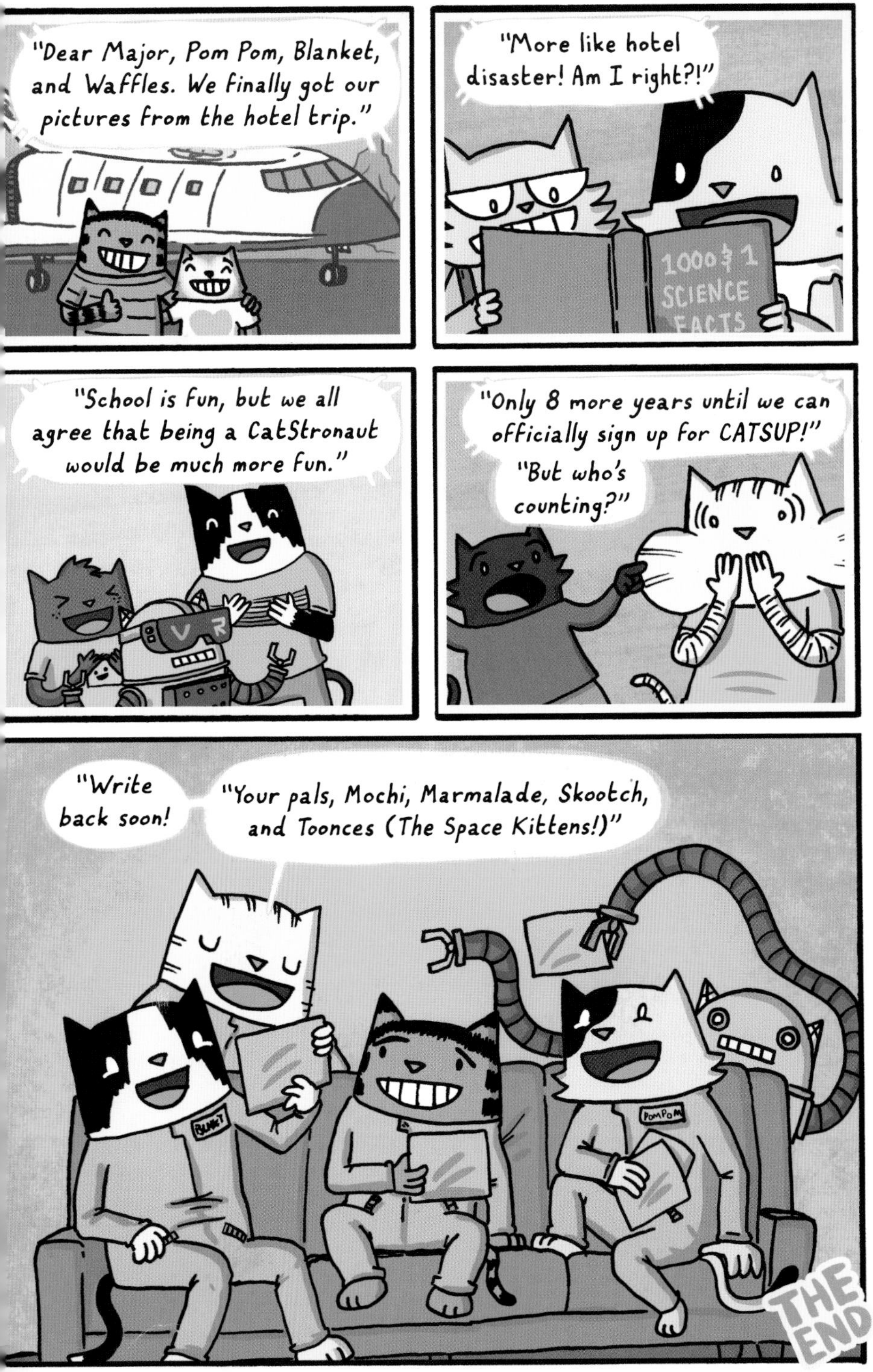
"Dear Major, Pom Pom, Blanket, and Waffles. We finally got our pictures from the hotel trip."
"More like hotel disaster! Am I right?!"
1000 & 1 SCIENCE FACTS
"School is fun, but we all agree that being a CatStronaut would be much more fun."
VR
"Only 8 more years until we can officially sign up for CATSUP!"
"But who's counting?"
"Write back soon!
"Your pals, Mochi, Marmalade, Skootch, and Toonces (The Space Kittens!)"
BLANKET
POMPOM
THE END

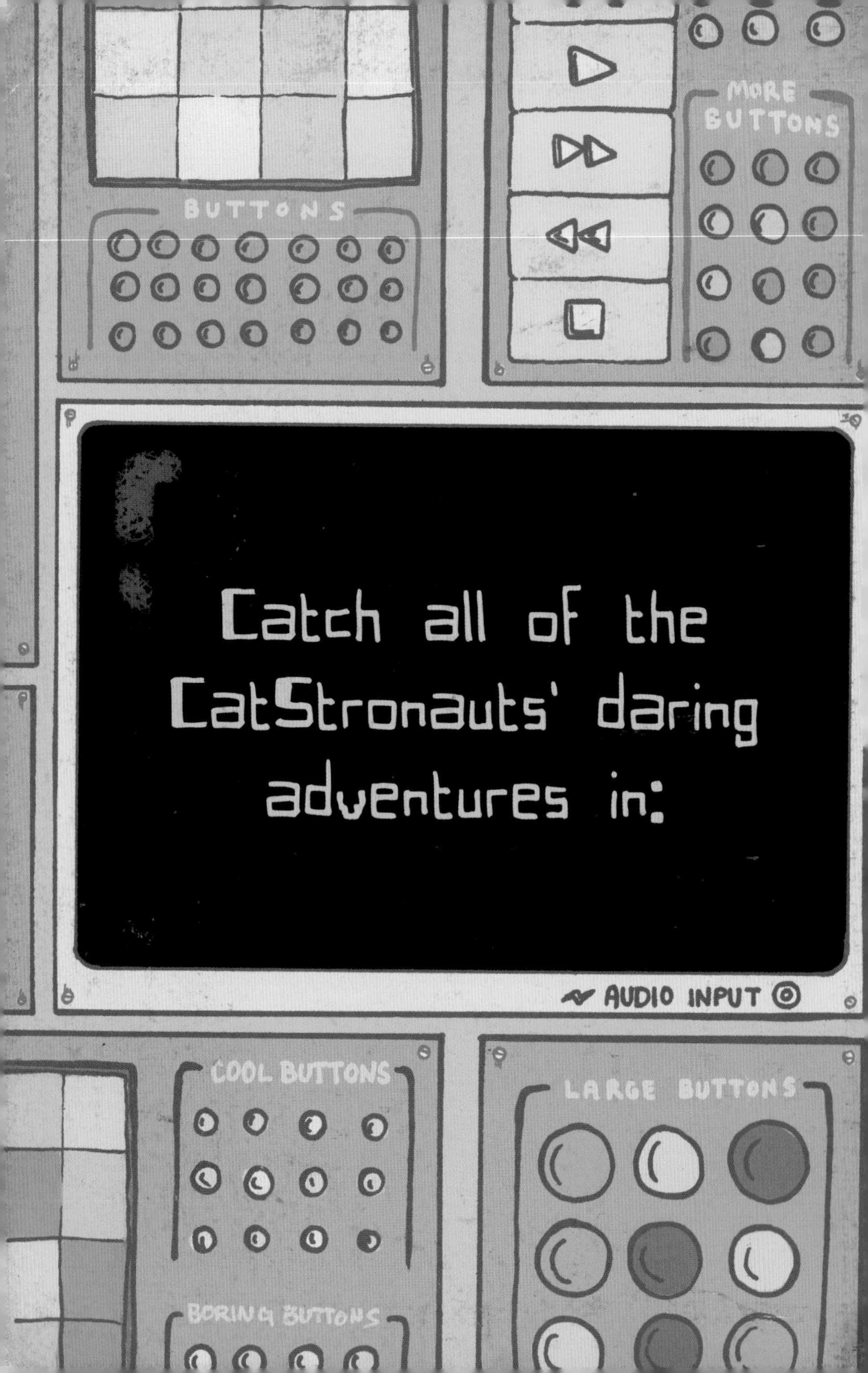
BUTTONS
MORE BUTTONS
Catch all of the CatStronauts' daring adventures in:
AUDIO INPUT
COOL BUTTONS
LARGE BUTTONS
BORING BUTTONS

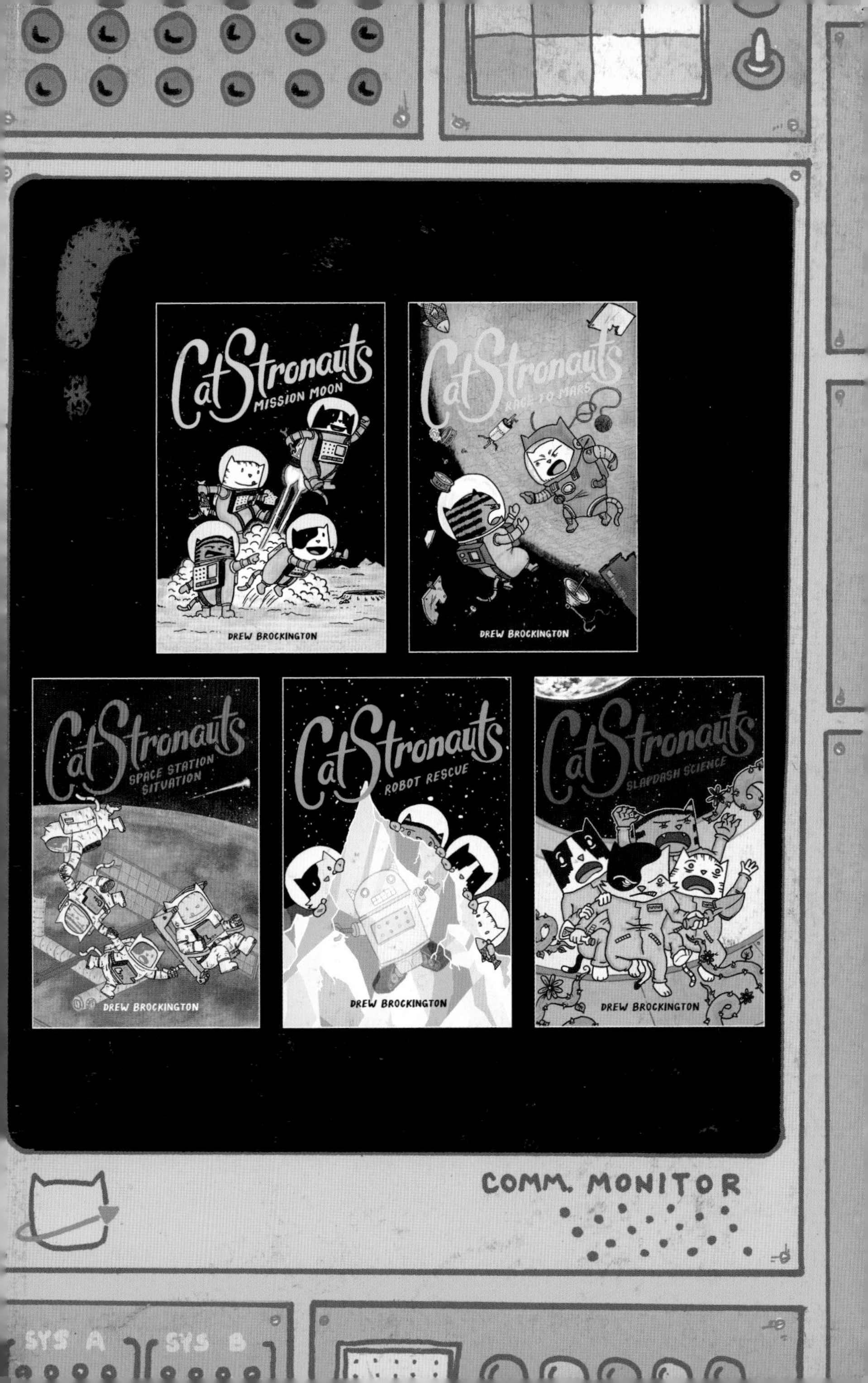
CatStronauts
MISSION MOON
DREW BROCKINGTON
CatStronauts
RACE TO MARS
DREW BROCKINGTON
CatStronauts
SPACE STATION SITUATION
DREW BROCKINGTON
CatStronauts
ROBOT RESCUE
DREW BROCKINGTON
CatStronauts
SLAPDASH SCIENCE
DREW BROCKINGTON
COMM. MONITOR
SYS A
SYS B

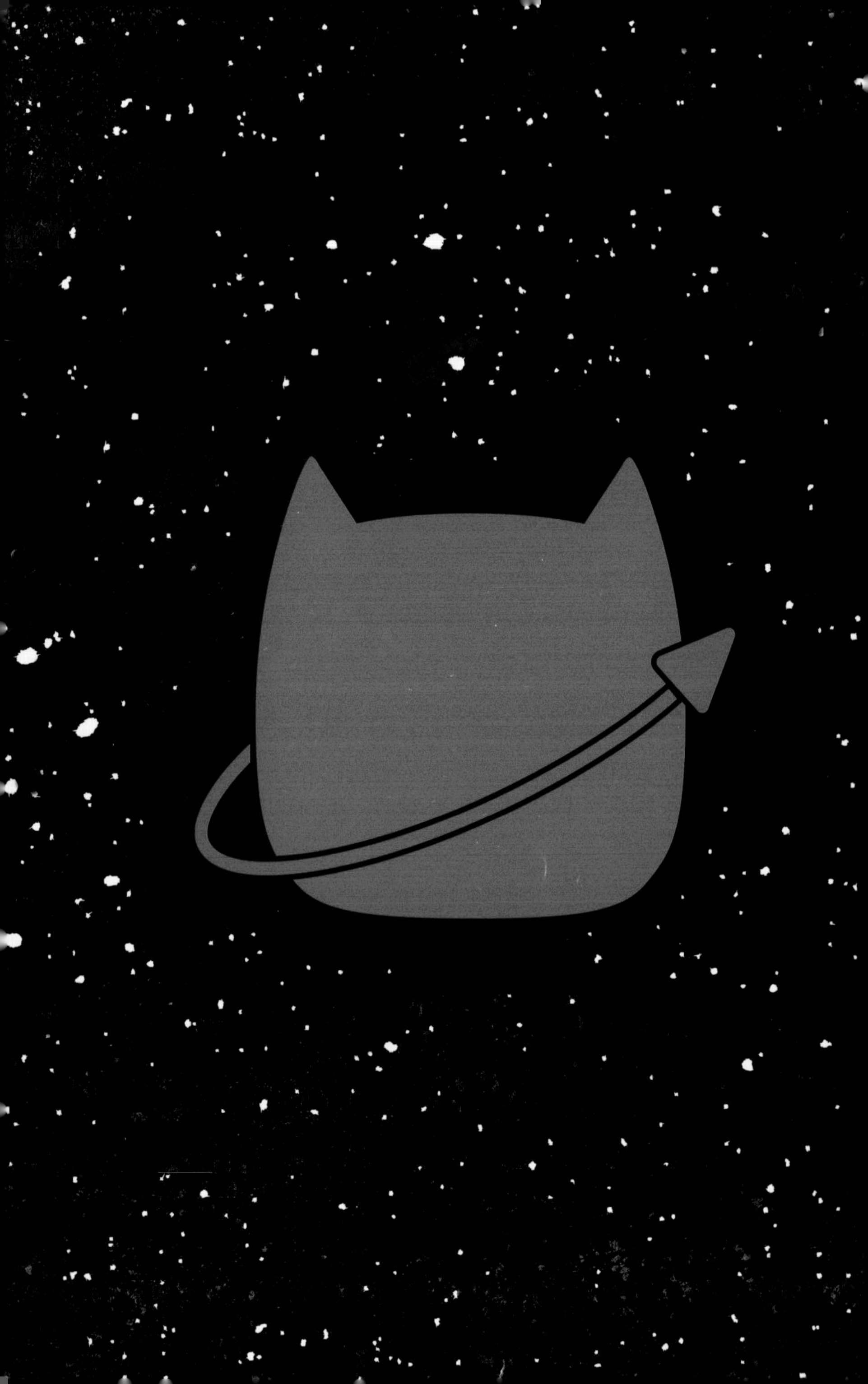

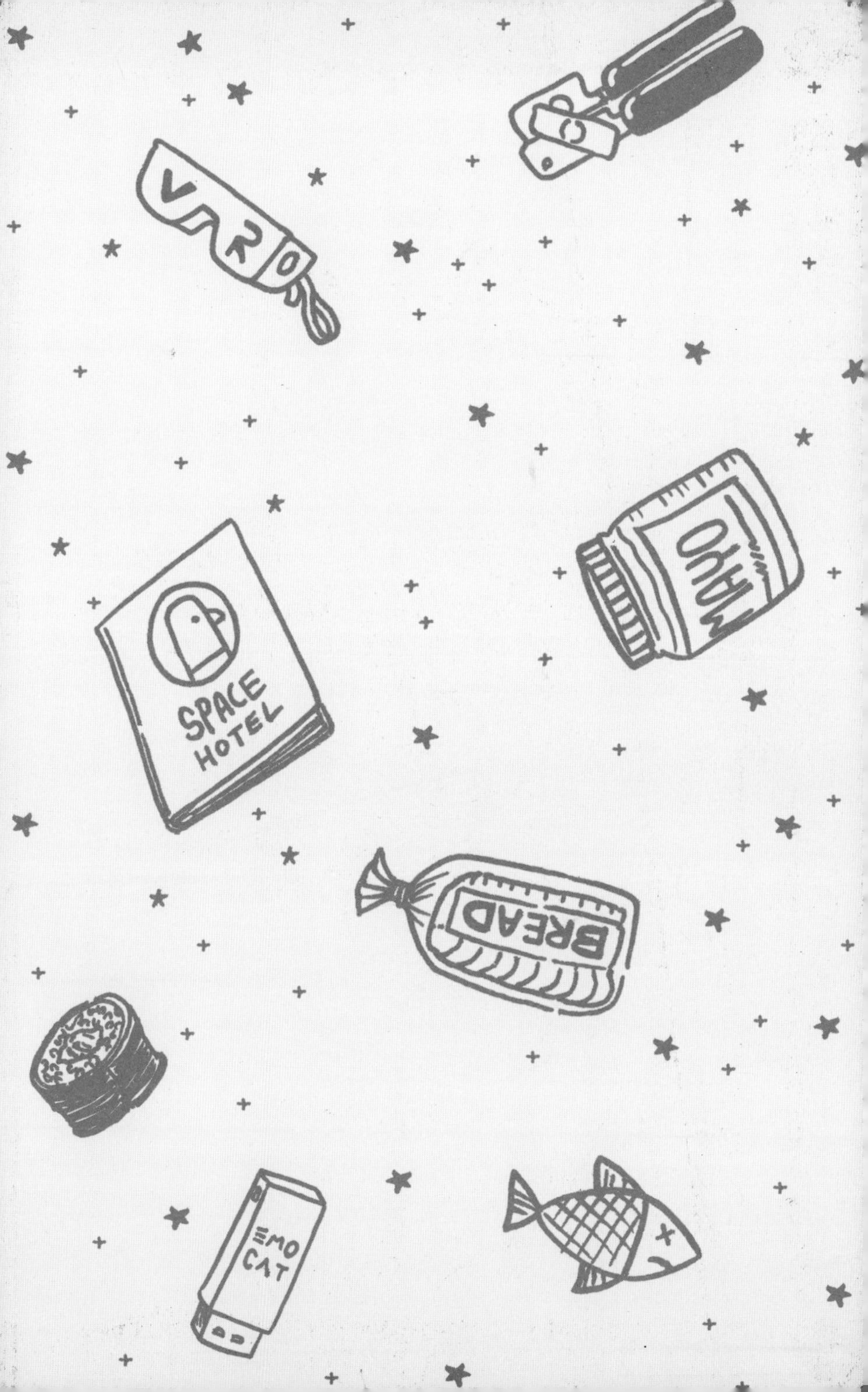
SPACE
HOTEL
MAYO
BREAD
EMO
CAT

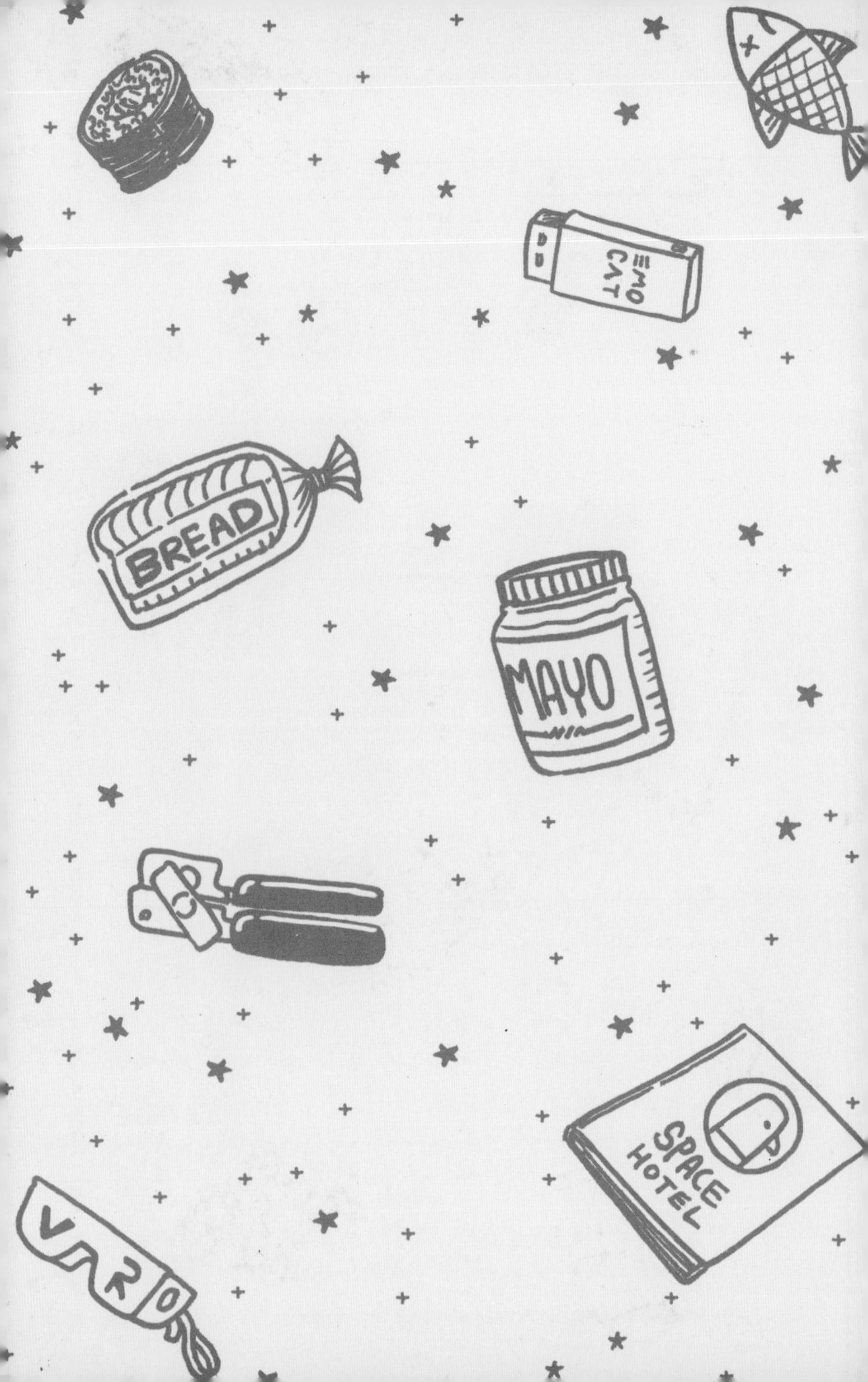
EMO CAT
BREAD
MAYO
SPACE HOTEL